Laws
Of
Contrition

Valerie Thompson

Calmrise Publishing

Published by Calmrise Publishing, 2012

First Edition

ISBN 978-0-9565859-3-6

A catalogue record for this book is available from the British Library

Calmrise Publishing
P O Box 181, BN24 9EU
East Sussex, England
www.calmrise.com

Printed and bound by Lightning Source Inc.

About the Author

This is Valerie Thompson's first novel. Previous works include *Mastering the Euromarkets,* (Irwin, 1996), and *The Logical Magic of Change*, (Calmrise, 2010). Born in Dagenham in 1956, she is a mother and grandmother, and twice divorced. For more information please see the author's web site: www.valerieelizabeththompson.com.

Acknowledgements

I would like to thank John Connor for his invaluable and painstaking critique of the first draft of this novel. John gave generously of his time and expertise, and provided me with much needed encouragement and support. I would also like to thank Tony M., for his market related insights, and Darryl and Lesley Baldwin, each of whom took time out of their busy lives to read and comment on the final draft. Special thanks as well to those who wish to remain anonymous, they know who they are, for their help in relation to police procedures and penalties for certain crimes. And heartfelt thanks to all my friends, including those already mentioned, for their unwavering support. It's taken me years to write this novel, and I couldn't have done it without the deeply kind souls I am lucky to count as friends. Your emails, quick phone calls, cyber hugs, and occasional real hugs face to face, all made a massive difference. Many a time I was kept going by a few comforting, uplifting, and reassuring words. So, to each one of my friends: I feel blessed to have you in my life. Your encouragement and understanding has been both precious and priceless.

In Memory of my Great-Grandmothers and Grandmothers
Annie Elizabeth Lewis & Ivy Dorothy Dodge
Emily Matilda Field & Elizabeth Emily Wood

CHAPTER ONE
March, 2008

Fuck being in a restaurant with him, Tanya Pryce, thought, as she listened to the tubby American, his loud nasally voice jarring her insides. *He needs to get his ears syringed and his sinuses sorted out.*

But she was interested in what he was saying, and glad to be focusing on something other than what to say to her boss, or how her mum was, or not being at home to see her youngest witness snow for the first time.

'Olli, we need to leave,' her colleague, Mark, said to him.

He said 'OK' to Mark and looked at her. 'It's been a real pleasure meeting you, Tanya, but Mark and I have a plane to catch.'

She smiled. 'No problem. It was nice to meet you, too, Mr Vermallen, and if I can be of any help, give me a call.' He was planning to expand into the European fixed income markets, her area of specialisation.

'Hey, call me Olli, and thank you. I shall be in touch. May I have your card?'

She glanced across the trading room at the chair on which she had hastily dumped her bag, briefcase, and coat, and he promptly produced one of his, from his jacket pocket, and gave it to her. 'Email me.'

She said she would and offered her hand, which he shook for too long in her view, while his eyes searched hers in a way that made her feel uncomfortable.

Ugh, she thought, for if she fancied a fling she certainly didn't want one with him, because his surplus pounds and whine of a voice aside, he was a couple of

1

inches shorter than her. And short men reminded her of her dad. If she was forced to say something nice about his appearance it would be that he had a good head of hair, thick, red-blonde, and just shy of his collar. In fact, had she seen him on the street, in his glossy navy cords, crimson cashmere blazer and polo-neck, she would have thought music mogul rather than money magnate. But, as she had just learned, he was a rich-as-Croesus financier, founder of Sky-Rise, a mega successful hedge fund cum private equity cum venture capital firm.

Nonetheless, she continued with her smile on a stick impression, and bid him goodbye with grace.

She retrieved her things and strode up the central gangway, her stomach churning at the sight of so much red on giant screens affixed to supporting pillars about the room. While the right hand side of this vast rectangle boasted views of the River Thames and London Bridge, these electronic displays of real-time trade activity were the main attraction. And red indicated a sale.

The first thing she did after hanging up her coat was check the fishbowls, a bank of glass-fronted offices at rear of the floor, for signs of Nate, as her colleague, Nathan Walthak, liked to be called, but he was nowhere to be seen.

Spineless.

She sat at her desk and brought her four computer screens to life and sped-read each one, while either biting the knuckle of her index finger or pulling at her bottom lip. The prices, charts, graphs and business news made grim reading. So much colour, yet so much misery.

Her dealer board was already alive with callers,

many of the square push buttons flashing red, but she left both her handsets idle. And when Spencer Rivington's voice burst through the speakers, built into a narrow shelf connecting her row of desks with those opposite, she lowered the volume. As chief economist he frequently used the public address system, also known as the hoot 'n holler or squawk box, to inform about economic statistics and share his views.

But of late she found his voice distracting, capable of evoking a sensation of weakness, the last thing she needed right now, because their last after-work drink had ended with him trying to steal a proper goodbye kiss, and succeeding enough to whet her appetite. Since then Tanya had also met his stare in the lift, lust writ large in his racing-green eyes, eyes framed with dark lashes so tight knit it looked as though he wore eyeliner.

This was American investment bank, Kohen Stanzinger's, international hub, its most critical artery outside of the United States, home to hundreds of snappy-suits who spoke in terms of derivatives, futures, options, straddles, swaps, volatility, etc. That one desk's jargon and strategies were rarely understood by any other is not something a lay person would know, which is why those who did seemingly ordinary jobs elsewhere in the building avoided the floor like the plague.

To Tanya, however, an East-Ender who had worked in street markets as a kid, finance was basic. A trading floor was simply a factory floor, a place where money, like meat, could be diced, sliced, and inflated, and made to appear nutritional regardless of nutritional content.

Three members of her team were in: Steve Cranthorp, who traded dollar bonds, Charlie Pedroy, who traded the euro book, and Freddie Truby, the junior. Charlie and Steve stood chatting by the water cooler. She went over to them.

'Have you seen Nate?' she said.

Charlie looked up at lofty Steve, as if for approval, and then peeked inside his jacket. 'He's not in here.' He put a thumb inside the waist of his trousers and looked down. 'Nope, not in there, either.'

Steve laughed. 'Like you could get a grain of sand down there, you tosser.'

'You can talk, pimples for balls,' Charlie said.

Steve glanced at Tanya. 'Look up Bruce's arse,' he said, referring to their boss, Bruce Ghoff, who ran the London office, before continuing his banter with Charlie. 'If your member was as big as mine, your balls would look like pimples.'

She shook her head and walked away.

Back in her seat, she took off her boots, and shoved them under her desk. Opening the lower drawer of a small filing cabinet on her right, which had become her shoe store, she removed a pair of black kitten heels, and put them on.

'Morning, Darlin.'

She looked up to see Andy Struchini, who was head of marketing for money market products, and sat across the aisle from her. The only genuine friend she felt she had in the whole firm, Andy always lent a sympathetic ear. Bar him once suggesting they rent a room for an hour after lunch, an offer from which he back peddled fast and for which he apologized, their friendship was unblemished. Tanya had laughed since she knew he didn't have the bottle to commit adultery, and nor was he her type. While he passed the height test and was taller than her 5'9 inches, he was too plump for her

4

liking, but what discounted him altogether was his cautious nature. If she was ever to have an affair it would not be with a wimp.

'Morning, Andy, can't talk, tell you why, later.'

'No problem,' he said, and returned to work, as did she, calling one of her brokers, Todd, who had posted a price for NCA of 45-47, indicating he was in touch with a buyer of bonds at $45 (per $100 face value) and a seller at $47.

'Todd, how real is your NCA quote, and what size is it good for?'

'It was a firm price as of about ten minutes ago, with both the bid and offer good for one million bonds. Do you want me to freshen it up?'

'Yes, and try and get me a firm, two way price, in size.'

'Can you leave me something to work on?'

Don't be an idiot, she thought, since in asking for both a bid and offer, it was obvious she wasn't willing to divulge whether she was a buyer or a seller.

'No,' she said.

Todd said he'd be back as soon as he had a firm price, and rang off.

Nate had bought fifteen million NCA bonds at 58, which meant a loss, assuming a sale price of 45, of $1,950,000 dollars, although she doubted they could all be sold at 45, and felt $ 2.5 million was more realistic.

KS losing over a billion dollars on CDO's (bonds backed with now rubbish mortgages aptly described as 'toxic') was one thing. That was a years-in-the-making widespread problem, with blame hard to apportion due to the time lapse, product complexity, and various departments involved. But, simple trades that blew a hole in the P & L (Profit and Loss) in hours or days were transparent.

'Freddie, listen up,' she said, looking across her desk at him through a gap between her computers.

He stood, his densely freckly face haunted with apprehension.

'I want a complete rundown of international Algerian bonds with prices and yields in dollars, a list of firms that participated in each deal, and a hard copy of the prospectus for the NCA-Algeria eurodollar bond. Have you got all that?'

'Yes, Tanya, I'll take care of it.'

'Good, you've got till eight fifteen, and I don't mean eight fifteen tonight.'

Freddie blinked repeatedly on hearing this last detail, a reaction Tanya chose to ignore.

Nate still wasn't in. She called his mobile, no answer, and then his landline, no answer, and then his mobile again, and got the engaged tone.

You friggin coward.

She snatched her calculator off her desk, and went to see Bruce Ghoff.

After knocking on the open door to his office, she entered.

He looked up from his *Wall Street Journal* and gave her a weary smile. 'Hey, Kiddo, how's it going?'

'Not good, Bruce, I'm afraid,' she said, wringing her hands. 'We're going to take a hit of about two and half million dollars.'

His smile vanished, and he punched his desk. 'How the fuck did that happen?'

Her eyes were drawn to his pen which jumped before rolling into the puckered join of his newspaper.

Stay calm. Nobody's died.

She took a deep breath. 'Nate bought fifteen million NCA-Algeria bonds from Krevamar, just before the close of business yesterday.' She scratched at her wrist, as his pockmarked face drained of colour. 'I know what you're going to say,' she added, 'and I accept the buck stops with me, but Fiona's been rushed off her feet. I will make sure the backlog is cleared this week.'

She was referring to the off-limits database, a list of securities KS deemed too risky to own, which ought to have included NCA, and which Fiona Ledbern, her p.a., was responsible for updating.

Bruce leapt to his feet, thrusting his chair behind him, and she winced as it hit the wall and sent a framed portrait of Isaac Kohen off centre. He and Archibald Stanzinger had founded KS in 1912. She glanced at the great Isaac and shuddered, for he seemed to be giving her daggers.

'Holy fucking Christ,' Bruce shouted, his six foot, two inch, bulging body seeming twice its size for the anger raging through it. 'Where were you?'

'In Belgium, with Pierre Dubois, pitching to Banque Fouverie. They need to raise a billion euros in the next few months.'

He kicked his waste bin. 'Goddamn it, Tanya!'

Her mouth became parched and her face a grimace, as she watched the bin eject what was left of Bruce's breakfast: A lettuce leaf, sandwich carton, napkin, and coke can, onto the ivory carpet. But she knew another loss, and moreover, one due to lax risk controls, was the last thing he needed after Northern Rock. With his blessing, equity traders had bought millions of shares betting the bank would get bought at a good price, and had lost multiple millions when it was nationalised. That was less than a month ago.

'Have you any idea of the economic and political situation in Algeria?' he said, gesticulating wildly, 'how many coup attempts and political assassinations that country's seen? That its system is corrupt? That a Judge or a Police Officer could be a terrorist? Have you seen the goddamn security around the U.S. embassy in Algiers lately?'

Don't take it personally. He's under pressure.

'Is the loss a conservative estimate?'

Sweating under a long sleeved woollen dress, she pulled at the belt. 'Yes. Nate paid 58, and the bond is currently bid at 45. At that level it's dirt cheap. Krevamar really stitched us up on this one. They knew Nate's price was too high for the amount of bonds they had to sell.'

'They're a hedge fund, for Christ's sake, what do you expect?'

And Nate is supposed to be a friggin trader. The idiot still thinks he's trading US treasuries.

'But I do feel that Nate,' she paused, 'I do think his due diligence was scant. I mean, all he did was—'

'I don't want a post-mortem, Tanya.'

She shut up, but bristled inside.

So much for a free hand.

That's what Bruce had promised when making her head of her desk, after culling her boss in a round of cost-cutting. Weeks later, however, Nate Walthak turned up, an import from New York HQ, and Bruce blithely told her he would be joining her division.

'Phone Krevamar, and find out what they'll pay for the bonds. Maybe Fenshill will throw us a bone.'

She swallowed hard. 'I've already spoken with Denton Fenshill, and he has no interest in buying the bonds back. He said he's got no room in his portfolio.'

Tanya had actually gone as far as asking Denton Fenshill to name his price, but he wouldn't. That meant in effect that there was no price at which he was willing to own the bonds, which frightened her. It brought to mind her purchase of a music system as a teenager, from Romford market, which seemed a great deal, until she found it was a small radio inside oversized casing.

Bruce tilted his head toward her and pointed. 'Make sure we're out of the bonds by the time New York opens, and report back with the precise loss.'

No chance.

She picked at the leather strap of her wrist watch. 'I'll do what I can.'

He stared at her and slowly repeated his demand. 'I said make sure we're out by New York's opening.'

Her legs wobbled. 'Bruce, please. I need two days.' She opened her arms. 'Give me two days and they'll be gone, I promise. One day even. But, don't force me to be an utterly desperate seller, not with the market the way it is.'

Prices were in freefall after Bear Stearns' chief executive, despite denials to the contrary days earlier, had announced the firm might not survive. Bear Stearns was an American investment bank.

'I said get rid of the bonds by the time New York gets in. Forget price, forget tactics, and just sell the whole goddamn position. Is that clear? Or do you want me to come out there and sell the shit myself?'

Her heart pounding, she glanced at her watch. 'OK. I'll make sure we're flat by lunchtime.'

'You'd better, Kiddo. You damn well better.'

He sunk back in his chair, legs splayed, and without looking at her pointed to the door.

'I'll speak to you later,' she said, and left.

CHAPTER TWO

'God, you look like you need hosing down,' Andy said, as she collapsed into her seat.

'Don't ask...' She yanked up her sleeves to nearer her elbows than wrists, as though readying for a fight. 'Have you seen Nate?'

Andy's eyes veered to the left of the room. 'Intermittently, yes.'

She rose from her chair to see him in the walkway by the window, performing a mini-workout, touching his toes, while Fiona, lithe, blonde, and twenty three years old, stood alongside counting his moves.

'Nate!' she thundered.

She saw Charlie nudge Steve, and her Sterling trader, Joe Matanzo, look at her briefly.

Nate straightened his six foot athletic frame, felt his pecs, ran his fingers through his hair, and began a saunter in her direction.

Freddie had left a note stuck to her computer to say there wasn't a copy of the NCA prospectus in KS' library, but that he had sourced one from a bank in the West End, and had gone to pick it up. She screwed the note up, threw it in the bin, and turned to Steve. 'What's your market doing?'

'Yields up, prices down, more sellers than buyers.'

Steve still hadn't come to terms with Tanya's promotion, hence his sarcasm, but she tended to overlook it, wanting to earn rather than demand his respect, as well as restore their friendship.

Being close in age, Steve was thirty eight, Tanya thirty seven, and both married with young children, and

the main breadwinners, they had lots in common. And she missed their chats and jokes, even though he could be, as Tanya's husband Pete had said, 'a cocky bastard'. Pete also thought him ugly, nicknaming him Rock-face because of his high forehead, but Tanya didn't agree on that score, and actually found him quite sexy. She especially liked his mouth and the way an indent above his top lip gave him a permanent pout.

'I want your book down by at least 100 million by the end of the day,' she said to him, before giving the same order to Charlie, and telling Joe to do what he could to lighten up on the Sterling book. Selling sterling bonds in big size wasn't as easy as selling large amounts of bonds denominated in euros or dollars.

Charlie and Joe acknowledged her instructions without fuss, but not Steve. 'What's the problem,' he whined, standing up.

'We own too much stuff,' she said.

'But what's the point in running my book down?' Steve's biggest holdings were in short dated, top quality names. 'What am I supposed to sell?'

'You can get rid of your World Bank and EIB positions, for a start.'

'But both those mature next week,' he said, exaggerating to make his point.

'Just do it, Steve.'

He rubbed his chin. 'I don't know what you're on sometimes.'

'Do yourself a favour, Steve, and zip it.'

He glanced over her shoulder, and she turned around to catch Nate standing in the aisle rolling his eyes, clearly at Steve for he shut up and sat down.

Nate settled at his desk, which was next to Tanya's,

and pulled his chair closer to hers. 'Morning,' he said solemnly. 'I'm real sorry I was late, Tanya, but the traffic was terrible.' He cleared his throat. 'How did Bruce take it?'

As if it's not obvious from my fucking face, she thought, which felt boiling hot.

'Badly. We've got to get rid of the bonds by the time New York gets in. Todd was going to get me a price. Has he called?'

Nate grabbed his phone and pressed Todd's line.

'Leave it,' she said, 'I'll call him in a minute.'

When I'm done with you.

With piercing blue eyes, chiselled cheekbones and narrow jaw, Nate had film star looks, but that was all in Tanya's opinion. She'd heard that his father and Dale Stanzinger II, KS' President, had been at school together, which is why she felt he'd been sent to London and not sacked.

She touched his arm. 'I still don't understand why, since you couldn't reach me, you didn't wait for Steve to get back to the desk?'

He said he had tried to phone her, but couldn't get a connection as she was in transit, and that Steve wasn't around.

'As I said, Krevamar needed an answer.'

'Take me through what happened again,' she said.

He stiffened. 'Is this really the best time to have a post-mortem?'

The echo of Bruce jarred. 'Just take me quickly through the sequence of events.'

He looked into the middle distance for some seconds. 'Krevamar told me they were a seller and of how many bonds. I asked if they had spoken with any

other dealers. They hadn't. I tried to phone you.' His slow punctuated delivery was really pissing Tanya off, but she didn't bite because that would have given him an excuse not to finish. 'I checked a couple of brokers,' he continued. 'One quoted 60-62, another 60-64, both good for two million on the bid. I checked the database. No mention of NCA.' He cast his eyes about the room. 'I looked for Steve. No sign of him. I thought of asking Joe, Charlie or Freddie to go find him, but they were busy as hell. Krevamar gave me a fill-or-kill (trade or lose the business). I lowered my bid by two points to reflect the size. I did the trade.'

He sounds almost righteous.

'Didn't you wonder why they didn't haggle?

Or did you think they'd turned into the Red Cross, you pillock?

He moved his chair away, back in line with his desk. 'Krevamar is a huge account, Tanya, and while I hate to point it out, the bond was on the system, if not the off-limits database.'

He can certainly think on his feet when it comes to himself.

She had been monitoring NCA, as she did hundreds of bonds, for comparison purposes, to help assess value, and didn't appreciate the swipe at her competence.

'Huge account is not the same as major client, and Fenshill is a liar. The price would not be this low unless the street knew there was a big seller. I spoke to the creep earlier. He hates the bonds so much he won't even put a bid on the fucking things.'

Nate scratched the back of his neck. 'What do you want me to say? Why don't we just get on with selling them?'

She sighed. 'I'll deal with NCA. You help Steve.'

'OK, your call, whatever you think is best.'

She went to see Richard Hillbrand, head of bond sales, and as they stood chatting she noticed Nate surreptitiously watching her. Rich subsequently summoned his two best salesmen, and as the four of them talked, she clocked that Nate was still keeping an eye on her. Then, when the group dispersed, he picked up his phone and in her view was feigning interest in talking to the dial tone, as he waited for her to return. But she sat in the spare desk next to Rich for a little while, and made a series of phone calls, her last one to home.

'Hi, Alison, how are my little chaps?'

Alison, a former NHS midwife in her forties, looked after Tanya's children.

'They're fine,' she said breezily, 'except Jamie got into another scrape in the playground with Daniel yesterday. I've told him that's a star off his chart for this week, not that it seems to bother him. Better he can stand up for himself, I suppose.'

'Absolutely,' Tanya said. 'How's Harry? Has he seen the snow?'

Alison chuckled. 'The little mite's out in it right now, in the garden with Leila — Tanya's au pair — trying to make a snowman, and he can't fathom why his efforts keep disappearing. I've taken some photos, and I videoed him for a bit as well.'

'Bless you, Alison, thanks. Is Pete with them?'

Alison hesitated.

'He's still in bed, isn't he?'

'I took him up a cup of tea about twenty minutes ago,' she said awkwardly, 'and he said he was getting up. If you'd like a word, I'll go and bang on the door.'

'No, I've got better things to do. Just tell him I'm going to be late home,' she said, and rang off.

A short while later Tanya was in the bathroom, her slender frame bent over a hand basin, splashing her face with cold water, when Fiona came in. 'Rich is looking for you.'

'Tell him I'll be out in a second,' she said.

'OK.' Fiona let go of the steel door, and as it slammed shut Tanya jumped.

'They should fix that *fucking* thing.' She knew her jumpiness, a childhood habit much mocked by her parents, was due to fear, and hated not being able to stop it.

She dabbed her face with a paper towel, retied the loose pony tail keeping her mound of chestnut curls looking respectable, and glanced in the overhead mirror. 'Don't panic. Nobody's died.'

An agitated Rich Hillbrand, a tall, wiry bespectacled man, stood in the corridor, about a yard from the toilets, his face red and blotchy. 'Vasseur de Credit, Paris, will bid you 41 for five million NCA,' he said breathlessly.

It took seconds for her to work out the loss, seventeen points and a hit of $850,000. If she sold them all at that price she would exceed her worst case estimate of $2.5 million. She proceeded briskly to the trading floor, Rich struggling to keep pace, sat at her desk, and quickly checked various broker screens, and the time. Eight thirty. Less than four hours to Bruce's New York opening deadline. Even after doing this trade, she would still have ten million bonds to sell.

'Do it,' she said flatly.

Rich gave her a sympathetic look, but she saw him

punch down his right fist, which came as no surprise for she had assigned double sales credits as an incentive.

With only six weeks until April 30th, KS' financial year end, and bonus decisions, every cent counted. As the sales-credit for a trade in a junk bond was already double that for one of investment grade, Rich was ecstatic, his glee evident from the way he scooted off down the central gangway to his desk.

He looked back over his shoulder. 'Shinewater's also on the case, Tanya,' he hollered. 'If anyone can root out takers of this stuff, it's him.'

She forced a grin. 'Great,' she shouted.

In truth, she despised Johnny Shinewater, who was renowned for exploiting his client status by crossing bonds between dealers, getting one dealer to offer a bond lower and another to pay a little more for it. What he did would be OK if he was a broker, such as Todd, but it was a dubious, if not illegal, practice when privy to a firm's research, ideas, and best prices. What Tanya found galling was that his methods paid well. Rich had been to his home, a four bedroom detached house in a private road in Surrey.

There's more integrity in prostitution, she thought, unconsciously tidying her desk to vent her frustration. She glanced at her photos of her boys, Jamie blowing out five candles at his last birthday party, Harry in tiny blue swimming trunks, splodges of ice cream on his tummy, to remind herself why she did the job she did.

Noise levels had risen appreciably, and even Nate was busy, his phone nestling in the crook of his shoulder, as he took notes.

He looked up at her briefly, and motioned with his eyes to her coffee mug, underneath which were some phone messages. She read them. Peter had called, as had her mum—twice, and Todd had called and left a 'non-urgent' message for her to call back, his way of saying his bid had disappeared. Her email inbox showed forty seven unread messages, but a scroll through the senders told her none were of consequence. Freddie still wasn't back. She phoned his mobile.

'Freddie, where the fuck are you?'

'On a bus, Tanya. The tube's down because of the weather, but I've got the prospectus, and I'm on my way back,' he took a few breaths, 'and I've prepared the spread sheet, I just need to print it off. I should be with you in about fifteen minutes.'

'For crying out loud, get a cab.' She slammed down the phone.

'Sorry to trouble you, Tanya,' Fiona said, 'but could you sign off on these?' She handed Tanya a pile of expense claims.

Fiona rarely wore make up and with hiccoughs for breasts looked to Tanya more like thirteen than twenty three, which brought out the mother in Tanya. 'I'm sorry, Fi, they'll have to wait,' she said, and put the forms to one side.

'Gotta go, call you back,' Nate said with a sense of urgency, but for no other reason than Fiona's proximity, which always made him skittish.

'OK,' Fi said, 'I'll leave them with you.'

As if Tanya wasn't going to notice, Fi then chose the least efficient route back to her desk, past where Nate was sitting, and he promptly swivelled his chair around and stuck his leg out, in between hers.

Flirty chit chat ensued, which Tanya tolerated for about five seconds, before looking stony faced at the pair of them. 'You've both got work to do,' she said.

Fiona hurried off, Nate's eyes trailing after her, much to Tanya's fury.

Maybe this'll get his attention.

'You won't be talking to Krevamar any more, Nate,' she said casually.

Sure enough, he swung around to face her in a flash. 'What the hell do you mean?'

'Traders are not supposed to talk to clients, and since Fenshill took advantage of you, I've decided he can deal via the sales force in future. As far as I'm concerned, he's abused his privilege. Rich will cover him from now on.'

'Fenshill hates dealing with salespeople.'

'He seemed OK about it.'

Nate's eyes were suddenly ablaze with rage. 'You had no right to change coverage of the account, without consulting me!'

She chewed on her lips for a few seconds. 'I have every right to do whatever I consider necessary to protect this firm's capital.'

You may not have realised it yet, Sunshine, but on this desk ego takes second place.

'What exactly did you say?'

'That the trading desk was too busy to be able to handle client calls.'

Glaring at her, he stood, yanked his jacket off the back of his chair, and headed for the door.

Go on, fuck off, and don't come back.

Tanya just knew Nate was going to be trouble the day he arrived. It was soon obvious she was by far the better trader, no surprise to her for she worked like a dog to compete and always looked for the learning in any situation. And it had nothing to do with Nate only being twenty eight. No matter how long he spent in the business he was always going to be average in her view because he didn't care enough. Life had been too easy for him. He hadn't flourished because he hadn't fought, at least not fairly, which she considered crucial. Unless she won intelligently she felt she had failed, regarding cheating as death to the soul, and she had a lot of time for her soul. No one could mess with that. Her soul was hers and hers alone.

Minutes later, Nate was staring at the iridescent granite floor of the entrance lobby, while on his mobile. 'You reversed your stance, right?' he said.

'Affirmative,' said the voice. 'Go get yourself a tin hat.'

Nate laughed. 'I'll catch you later.'

He returned as Tanya answered Todd's flashing line.

'Yes, Todd?'

'My NCA bidder died on me, but I've got a seller who's offering five million bonds at 44. Any interest?'

Although her guts registered the bad news with a thud, she didn't turn a hair. 'You're too late,' she said, to give the impression she had dealt without actually lying. 'What else are you seeing?'

'There's a run on GMAC, short sellers cleaning up after the downgrade.'

'I know what's going on in autos, Todd. Even my friggin dog knows what's going on in autos.' Not that Tanya had a dog. 'What are you seeing that's original?'

'Not much, to be honest. People are bricking themselves, too scared to give me prices.'

She ended the call and turned her attention to Steve.

'How are you doing, Steve?'

'I've off loaded seventy million so far, mostly to clients, and at good prices.'

His tone was conciliatory, which told her Nate must have told him about NCA. She unconsciously flashed him an affectionate wink. 'Good work. Keep going.'

She called KS' Tokyo office. 'Hi, Scott, any luck?'

Scott was Scott Ingram, head of sales.

'I'm afraid not,' he said, and gave her a miserable update.

'...prices are gapping down on virtually no turnover. I've had Yoshi and Saito dedicated to the cause, and we've all given it our best shot, but at this late hour—'

'Tanya, your mum's on line seven,' Joe yelled.

'Hang on, Scott.'

'Tell her I'll call her back, Joe.'

'Sorry about that. So, you've no hope of finding a buyer, right?'

Scott confirmed that to be the case, and she thanked him and finished the call.

Where the fuck is Freddie? She phoned him again, her frustration rising at no pick up, when he burst through the double doors and rushed toward her.

His copper locks were dripping, and his shoes made a squelching sound, as he held out a cold, damp brown envelope. 'I'm,' he took some breaths, 'I'm sorry it took so long, Tanya.'

She took the envelope from his icy hands, and got up. 'Use your loaf in future, Freddie. I told you I needed that information urgently. I'll be in my office.'

He apologised and promised her the rest of it within minutes.

Tanya actually had a lot of time for Freddie, who had won a scholarship and got a Double First in Mathematics and Physics. After just seven months at KS he was already earning his keep, and she had no doubt he was destined for success, because he had brains, courage, humility, and a second to none work ethic. That he was only about five feet five inches tall, Tanya barely noticed, because she saw him as a boy rather than a man—as her little boy.

A short while later a shoeless Freddie, his polyester trousers clinging to his calves, stood outside her office. She was on the phone, but waved him in, and he carefully laid the papers on her desk and turned to leave, but she clicked her fingers. He waited.

'I look forward to speaking with you again shortly, Mr Hasseen. Thank you very much indeed for your time.' She tenderly replaced the receiver.

'I could do with a coffee, if you wouldn't mind, Freddie. My mug's on my desk.'

'I'm on my way,' he said, and left.

She studied the spreadsheet he had prepared, and as she suspected it confirmed NCA was ridiculously cheap.

Mr Hasseen, Treasurer at NCA, agreed, but whether he would buy her last ten million bonds remained to be seen. If he did, she would need a middle man, because KS, consistent with not wanting to own the bond, did not have an account with NCA. She felt Theodore Jemayer (TJ), who worked for competitor Farraday Levy Inc., would undertake that role if need be, and was dialling his number when Joe Matanzo popped his raven head inside her office.

'Your mum's on line five,' he said, holding the door, 'yea or nay?'

She closed her eyes, pinched the bridge of her nose, and heaved a sigh. 'OK. I'll take the call.'

'Mum, what is it? I'm really busy.'

'I need you to come over right away. I've got a mouse in the flat. It's been scratching all night.' She sounded very het up.

'I can't just drop everything, and leave work.'

'Well what time can you get here, because I need my pills and they're in the kitchen?'

'Isn't Julie around?' Tanya said. Julie lived in the flat below.

'I'm not asking her for help. I'll be the talk of the street.'

'Look, I'll call Pete, and get him to pop round.'

'What time will he get here?'

'I don't know. I won't 'til I talk to him, will I? It'll depend on where he's working. But don't worry, if he can't get to you soon, I'll find someone who can.'

'Who? You know I don't like strangers in my place.'

'Mum, this is really a bad time. Look, if Pete's busy, I'll get Alison to drop in.'

'I don't want *her* in my flat.'

Her mum didn't like Alison.

'In that case, you'll have to wait for Pete. I'll call you back in a bit,' she said, and hung up.

For a few seconds, Tanya was sure she could smell the odour from the small tin the man from the council used to bring to the house, when she was little. No one could go near it and all doors and windows had to be sealed before the lid was removed. Then it did its work to rid the place of bugs. An image surfaced of her mum, Barbara, tearfully clawing at her hair, while waiting for the official to arrive. He came a few times, yet Tanya never saw any of the devil bugs she insisted haunted the place. They were, apparently, black and extremely small and whatever Tanya thought, Barbara knew for certain there were thousands of them—everywhere.

She can't help it.

She called TJ.

'Hello, Gorgeous. What can I do you for?' he joked.

'I may end up doing a trade with Mr Hasseen at NCA, but we don't have an account with him. Will you act as middleman, for an eighth?'

She meant an eighth of a point, and thus $1,250 per million bonds.

'Dealing with the old rogue, are you?' he said, laughing. 'How many bonds are we talking about?'

'Up to ten million.'

'I'll do it on one condition, that you'll let me whisk you away for a romantic weekend, allow me to delight all of your senses, and pander to your every whim.'

In another lifetime, maybe, she thought, considering TJ the bling of the square mile, with his come-to-bed eyes and pony tail, and flawless enunciation. His talent didn't stop at finance either. He sailed, skied, and surfed, and was lead vocalist in a rock group he had formed with a couple of school chums. What Tanya most liked about him though, was that he wasn't one to boast, and nor was he spiteful, both rare traits within investment banking.

She laughed. 'Tryst with a toy boy, eh? Tempting, my Darling, but I'm a married lady, although lunch would be nice if we get something done.'

'Lunch would be nice regardless.'

'It would indeed. Once I've dealt with NCA, I'll

give you a call to fix a date, OK? Speak soon. Bye.'

Freddie was waiting outside her office, with her coffee. She ushered him in.

'Thanks,' she said, taking it from him. 'Now go and dry your hair or you'll catch pneumonia. One of the secretaries must have a hair dryer. If not, the cafeteria must have some towels. Ask if you can borrow one.'

He smiled, said he would fine, and left.

She stood, both hands around her mug, looking out of the window, at sleet swirling around in ferocious cross winds.

'Pete's on line three, Tanya. Do you want to pick him up?'

She turned around to see Steve, his broad shoulders filling most of the doorway, looking at her with sympathy.

'Not especially, but I will.'

He hovered. 'Sorry about this morning. I had no fucking idea about NCA.'

'Don't worry about it.'

He smiled appreciation. 'If you want any help, just shout,' he said, and left.

A silver lining.

After a brief and sugary chat with Peter, which felt like another prostitution exercise so as to get him to go to Barbara's immediately, which he agreed to do, Tanya returned to the trading floor, and a host of messages from Rich Hillbrand; a chronicle of his clients' reactions to offers of NCA.

'...expects the bond to be cheaper next week.'

'...thought it was an early April fool joke.'

'...considers it a submerging rather than emerging credit.'

'…nearly pulled my line.'

'…is buying me lunch for the laugh.'

'…rhymes with pray, which is what he thinks we ought to do.'

Prick.

While alternating between biting the top of her biro and pressing its point hard into the pad of her thumb, she studied broker screens and electronic trading platforms, absorbing information about prices and activity. It was a random process she undertook when she felt stumped, which often led to insights and new trade ideas.

Freddie returned from another cafeteria visit, this time with an order for Nate, which included a bag of bananas.

'I think we all need a bit of brain food today,' Nate said, offering one to Tanya.

She declined, too fretful to eat, and resumed her computer trawl, until raised voices drew her attention.

Charlie and Joe were locked in a spat involving a client covered by Max Jackson, who stood between the two of them.

'What's the problem?' she said, standing up.

Charlie acted as spokesman. 'Max's client wants to sell some Lloyds TSB in sterling, to help fund a purchase of some Bank of America bonds in euros, and he wants a slight mark up in the price at which he sells Lloyds, with a commensurate adjustment in the price at which he buys B of A. But Joe won't do the trade.'

Tanya heard Joe's version of events next. 'What Charlie means by a slight mark up is two points, which is well outside the bond's trading range, which he knows full well is illegal.'

A trade at a non-market price would constitute market abuse under FSA rules.

'Joe's exaggerating,' Charlie said, angrily. 'We're talking an odd amount of Lloyds, so a price adjustment would be normal.'

'I wouldn't suggest anything illegal,' Max said, looking at Tanya.

Not half you wouldn't.

She wasn't a fan of Max's. He had shifty eyes, the type that flit around and don't look at you, and his trades were always complicated.

'Your problem,' Joe said to Charlie, 'is that you're too wrapped up in your own P & L instead of the good of the firm. Your adjustment's fuck all compared to mine, so it would be my head that would roll, not yours.'

'Fuck off,' Charlie said. 'That's fucking bullshit.'

'Steve, come and sort this out for me,' she said, waving at the fracas. He was on the phone but raised a hand to indicate he would be right there.

She glared at Max. 'This trade had better be worth five people's time.'

There were stretchable facts in her view. The sterling market was volatile, and it was probably a borderline trade in terms of being legally compliant, but she had worse things to worry about. She felt good being able to call upon Steve.

Seconds later, she saw Rich's gangly body making haste in her direction.

'Tanya, Tanya, we're in business,' he shouted.

She stood, waiting with bated breath.

'Shinewater will bid us 35 for the other ten million,' he announced, as if he had found the Holy Grail.

'You are joking?' She shook her head slowly. 'Jesus, Rich, at least Dick Turpin wore a fucking mask.'

'I know it's a low bid, Tanya, but it is a firm bid, an outright bid, and a bid for the whole amount.'

She thought for a bit, while chewing the inside of her mouth. 'Can you get him to split the difference and pay 39?' She had offered the bonds at 43.

He pulled a face. 'I can try but Shinewater's taking a punt on this one. I'll give it a go if you want, but you need to consider the time constraint we're under.'

She rubbed her pinched brow as she considered her options. If she countered Shinewater at 39 he could lower his 35 bid, even pull it. She doubted he would do that, but felt certain he would lower it and knowing the slime ball character, his next bid would probably be 30.

You'd better Kiddo. You damn well better.

She recalled Bruce's warning with trepidation, but lining Johnny Shinewater's grubby pockets felt akin to Oliver Twist giving his last crumb to the big fat bloke.

'Tanya,' Freddie said. 'Mr Hasseen is on line four for you.'

Her heart skipped several beats. 'Tell him I'll be right there,' she said, and ignoring Rich ran the few yards to her private office, but Rich followed so closely he almost tripped on the back of her heels.

'What do you want to do about Shinewater's bid?' he said.

'Keep him on hold for another minute or so and I'll let you know.'

'I can't. He's been hanging on for ages already. I've got to give him an answer.'

Won't more like, all you're thinking of is your friggin bonus.

28

She asked Mr Hasseen to hold for a moment, covered the receiver with her hand, and looked at Rich anxiously, her eyes begging his understanding, but his body was edgy, his face full of panicked self interest.

'I need a decision,' he said.

'In that case tell Shinewater my 40 offer is out.'

'OK, OK, have it your way. I'll see if I can get him to pay 39.' He turned to leave.

'Too late, Rich. My offer is out, completely and totally one hundred percent out.'

He flapped his arms. 'You can't do that.'

'Oh yes I can, and I just have.'

'But—'

'I need to take this call,' she said.

Now fuck off.

He stormed out, shaking his head.

'Mr Hasseen, I am so terribly sorry to have kept you waiting.'

CHAPTER THREE

Tanya returned to her trading desk and sent three brief emails.

Bruce, we're out, down $2,950,000. Best I could do.

Rich, FYI Shinewater did have a buyer lined up – the issuer – and he was trying to take two points out of the trade. Don't you have any real clients?

TJ, we're done in ten million NCA. I sell to you at 36 7/8^{ths}. You sell to Hasseen at 37. Cheers. I'll phone you later.

She mournfully entered the transaction on the system, and then stood over Nate, forcing him to wrap up his telephone conversation.

He looked up at her.

'Three million dollars down the drain,' she said, scratching her wrist.

He blinked amazement as he gave his sandy tufts a hand groom. 'Who bought them?'

'What's it to you? Just be relieved we're out.'

'I am, but who bought them?'

'Farraday Levy.'

'Farraday —'

'Yes. Farraday Levy.'

Addressing the rest of her team, she motioned to her office. 'I need your attention guys for two minutes.' She looked down at Nate. 'You too.'

Biting her pen, she stood in front of her desk, as Steve, Charlie, Joe, Freddie and Nate filed in.

Nate closed the door.

'OK, I'll be brief,' she said. 'This complete balls up

with NCA has just cost us nearly three million dollars.'

'Jesus,' Steve gasped.

'Fu—king hell,' Joe said.

'Quite,' she said, acknowledging the looks of astonishment. 'It's a scalding reminder of the risks and vigilance required. In the same way salespeople have to know their clients, as traders we have to know our bonds, know the details and history of every security we trade, as though it's a foster kid. If we haven't traded a bond before, that should tell us something. If it's a junk bond, that should frighten the fuck out of us. And if the client's a hedge fund we need to be absolutely certain we know what we're doing. If we don't we'll get stiffed, as we did yesterday.' She looked at Nate, but he was leaning against the door, head bowed, arms folded.

'Now, for any of us to get a meaningful bonus,' she added, 'we have to make that money back, so we're all going to have to start thinking out of the box.'

A doubtful silence ensued. Charlie chewed the side of his thumb, Joe dribbled a make believe ball around the carpet, Nate stared at his shoes, and Freddie blinked nonstop. Steve was the only one looking vaguely in Tanya's direction, but even he was bouncing nervously back and forth on his heels, with his hands in his pockets.

She took a calculator from her desk and prodded it a few times. 'We've got six weeks, so if each one of us can pull in ninety thousand dollars a week, we'll do it. I reckon that's achievable. What do you think, Nate?'

Startled out of his shoe inspection, he showed off his Adam's apple and polished his crown on the glass door, before making eye contact with her. 'Um, we...' He cleared his throat. 'We have to give it a go, I guess, but the markets are real jittery, and we could see a lot more volatility in here.'

How can a Harvard graduate be so friggin docile?

She stared at him, scratching her temple. 'Have you ever traded a flat line, Nate?'

Unless a price moves up or down, there's no chance whatsoever of making money, so volatile prices meant opportunities to make a profit.

No one dared laugh, not that anyone was in the mood.

Nate gripped his jaw. 'You know what I meant. There's a lot of goddamn uncertainty and pessimism out there, and we could as easily get caught on the downside as the upside.'

'It would be better if you kept your negative thoughts to yourself,' she said, 'and that goes for everyone. We can't afford to be pessimistic. Right, let's reconvene at five thirty for a brainstorm, and don't come empty headed. I want sensible ideas from each one of you. Think small trades and strategic plays, not ways to bet the friggin bank.'

Nate hung back after the others had left. 'I appreciate the loss is bad news, but there's no need to be sarcastic.'

'Three million dollars is a lot of oh-ones, Nate.' She meant cents, an oh-one being one cent.

He rubbed the back of his neck. 'Don't you think I know that?'

'I'm sure you do, but what you don't know is Credit, which is what you're now trading. And this is a not a dig, because I know you're still learning, but you know even less about Europe and Europeans than you do Credit. Denton Fenshill runs a fucking bucket shop.'

'And if you ask me,' she added, 'he saw you coming.'

'What do you mean?'

Hello?

'Put it this way. He wouldn't have phoned me, because he knows I would have told him to get stuffed.'

Nate's chiselled features froze.

She walked out and stopped by her desk to collect her bag. 'Steve, keep an eye on things for me. I'm going out for a bit, but I'll have my mobile with me.'

In Fabio's café five minutes later, Fabio, a short dumpling of a man with a moustache, greeted Tanya with a serenade. 'You are my sunshine, my only sunshine…' he sang, gesturing to the gloom outside.

She felt like bursting into tears, but her smile was wider as a result, the effort Fabio put into to selling one cappuccino enough to put anyone to shame. She felt a bleak kinship with him as he danced around her, sensing both tiredness and sadness beneath his jollity.

Perched on a stool facing the street, she sipped her coffee and stared at the mayhem outside. The wind remained fierce, sleet had turned to rain, and a torrent gushed from the faulty awning of a sandwich shop across the road. Two people bumped into each other as they stopped sharp to avoid the water fall. The kerbside was no better as buses hurtled by, spraying up gallons of murky slush. The punch of defeat heavy in her stomach, she wondered if sixteen years of hard graft and sacrifice had just been destroyed. That the thought had even crossed her mind, made her feel sick.

'Boo!'

She looked up to see Spencer, his eyes dancing with devilish gaiety.

'It's not been a great morning, Spence,' she said

gravely. 'I'm not up to being good company.'

His expression changed to one of concern, and he put an arm around her shoulder.

She looked at him, her big brown eyes misting over, and swallowed hard.

'Come,' he said. 'Let me take you to Champers.' This was KS' local wine bar, a minute's walk away. 'You need a proper drink.'

She sniffed. 'OK.'

Spencer found a table by the window, helped her off with her coat, and went to the bar, while she sat staring through rain beaten glass at blurred figures jostling for brolly space, reflecting on her trip to Belgium.

I could have sent Steve. Even Rich could have taken my place. But...

She bit her lip, as she acknowledged she had wanted to go, had wanted a rest, and to get away from her mum's whinging, which made her feel guilty. But she also felt it was a strange coincidence the trade occurred while she wasn't there. Something didn't feel right.

Spencer returned with a bottle of Chablis and a plate of cream cheese and smoked salmon sandwiches. Tanya welcomed the wine but only ate one triangle of food, as she told him what had happened.

'...I knew Nate was going to be trouble the second I clapped eyes on him. In fact, when I first saw him he gave me the creeps. It was like I knew him, but didn't know him, if you know what I mean, like there was something hauntingly familiar about him, about his type at least.'

'A trader's hunch?'

She nodded. 'I've got another one, too. I'm not convinced what happened was a mistake.'

'Gosh, what do you mean?'

'I'm not entirely sure, but it just seems very odd the trade just so happened to have occurred while I was away. I mean, I hardly ever go away, and I was only away for a day. And while I realise the markets would not have fallen so badly had it not been for the news about Bear Stearns, it still strikes me as very odd that the trade was done on the one day I'm not there.'

'Yes, but Krevamar could easily have anticipated the Bear Stearns announcement and acted to protect themselves. I imagine there are a lot of traders nursing losses today.' He squeezed her forearm affectionately. 'There's no point going down the conspiracy route.'

She shrugged and sighed. 'You're right. I'm probably in what they call the denial phase.'

He looked perplexed.

Holding up a finger for each word, she elaborated. 'Denial. Anger. Bargaining. Depression. Acceptance. They're the five stages of grief, but they also apply to life in general.'

He smiled. 'Thank you for elucidating. One learns something every day.'

'On a serious note,' she said, 'if I don't make back the loss before year end my desk's profit will be less than last year, which is going to hurt bonuses. And this is my first year as the boss. To top it all, because NCA is a junk bond and I trade the junk book, my track record's kaput. I'd increased the profit on that book five years running.' She heaved a sigh. 'Anyway, enough about me. How was your morning?'

'Trifling by comparison, boring in fact, although it's good to be home, and in the warm, relatively speaking of course.' He had been to Moscow.

'I don't know how you cope with all that travelling. I would hate it.'

'One gets used to it.' He paused. 'How is your mother?'

Tanya fidgeted and looked around her. Whilst the few pills Barbara had taken wouldn't have killed a cockle, it still ranked as a suicide attempt, which made her feel angry, ashamed and guilty. 'She's OK,' she said, quietly, 'but what I told you is highly confidential. I've not even told Andy, and the last thing I need now is for Bruce to find out. It would sound like an excuse for why we've lost three million bucks.'

'He couldn't possibly see it like that, Tanya. It's not as if you were tending to your mother when Nate did the trade.'

'Trust me, Spence. Links get made when money gets lost. Now promise me that you won't say anything about my mum to anyone.'

'My lips are sealed.'

'Thank you.'

'How is life at home otherwise?'

She heaved another sigh. 'My boys are doing great, but I missed out on seeing Harry see snow for the first time today.'

'Gosh, you really are having one miserable day.' He rubbed her shoulder.

'Don't feel sorry for me. You'll make me feel worse. Anyway, in the scheme of things, I count myself lucky. Life's all about trade-offs, and I've got a good job, two healthy kids, and a live-in nanny.'

'But not such a good husband.'

'Even Pete's alright, and in some ways I feel sorry for him.'

Spencer raised his eyebrows. 'Sorry for him?'

'Well, yes, because when it comes to eking out what little time I've got, it's my boys, my mum and then him, and to give credit where it's due, he's been really good about my mum, even went to check on her for me today.'

'He has the time of course.'

'You're talking your own book, Spence. Call Verity. I'm sure she'd love to hear from you.' This was his ex long term girlfriend, from whom he'd recently split.

Tanya wasn't putting herself down. She felt this way because she was the total opposite of hat designer, Verity, who wasn't much bigger than one of her hat pins, and in direct contrast to Tanya had short blonde hair, and came from privileged stock. Although part of her wanted to believe otherwise, she understood her appeal in the circumstances. She merely represented an exciting alternative, a dynamic contrast, and a passing one.

'I can assure you if I never saw Verity again, I would live, and quite happily.'

'Maybe so but it's obvious you're at a loose end, and since we're on the subject you need to learn some restraint. Controlling our impulses is life's major challenge, the way we grow.'

Tanya's opinion was borne of experience, both her parents having been out of control. As a consequence she became the responsible one, and in effect played mum from a tiny age, keeping her natural urges in check so as to keep the peace and survive.

'Giving in to one's impulses also has its merits.'

'Not if you're married with kids.'

She suddenly started, noticing the time. 'Jesus, I need to get back.' She got up, pulled on her coat, and felt in her bag for her wallet. 'Let me give you something toward lunch.'

'I wouldn't hear of it.'

Briefly meeting his gaze, she felt the pain of longing. 'Thanks.'

'Good luck with everything, and call me if you need to talk.'

She nodded, and pushed her way through the now crowded bar to the exit, feeling another wretched dose of anger, guilt and shame, this time about her marital lot. Unlike Spencer, Peter wasn't much interested in hearing about her woes, and nor was he capable of a deep and meaningful conversation.

*

The disgusting taste of mango chutney with natural yoghurt, and Jamie at her bedroom door in the small hours, rubbing his eyes with both fists, asking for a cuddle, defined the next month of Tanya's existence.

Sleeping inches from her phones and laptop, trading during the night became the norm as she pushed herself and her team to the limits, in an effort to recoup the NCA loss before year end.

Her sex life remained intact, an orgasm as much of a release for her as Peter, but he invariably took to the spare bedroom afterwards. She didn't mind. In fact, she felt guilty, although not as guilty as she felt about short changing her boys.

She never refused Jamie's requests, and he'd cuddle into her back and drape an arm around her, always careful not to move around. Once, while holding his hand, she'd cried quietly, feeling great bitterness toward Nate. That would remain an abiding memory. As would her having mistaken the easy squeeze bottle of mango chutney for honey, in her rush to sweeten her yoghurt and down some protein before heading out the door.

At work her team had no choice but to get used to her ruthlessly dissecting their ideas and overriding their decisions. To find their trading books re-landscaped, due to her overnight trading with the US and the Far East, was par for the course, as were her blistering dressing downs.

'We made one thousand dollars on the trade,' Charlie said, by way of defence, after selling five hundred and seventeen Wal-Mart bonds to a competitor via the brokers market.

'But you've left us with an odd lot. Where the fuck are we going to sell four hundred and eighty three bonds? We'll be looking for those seventeen forever.' She looked at him despairingly. 'Use your friggin loaf, Charlie. You've made KS look like a laughing stock.'

Lunch breaks were banned, as was time off and leaving early. Leaving at all was hard, and it got to her team, especially Steve, who yelled at her one day. 'Back off. For fuck's sake, Tanya, back the fuck off and leave me the fuck alone.' She did, for about an hour, but thereafter it was business as usual with her quizzing and second guessing him, and the more she did this the more he began to act as if he wanted to screw her. Literally. He didn't say anything, but a few times when they chatted she found herself stepping back to create more distance between them. Not that she pulled him up about it because he was making money. But she knew that had it been Charlie, or some other toe curler of a guy, she would have spoken up, which made her feel shallow.

*

'Nate,' Tanya said, scratching her top lip, 'remind me why you didn't check with me before you did the NCA trade?'

It was late in the day, and in a rare idle moment she had brought the trade up on her computer screen and scrutinized the details.

Nate stretched his arms wing-like and made a buzzing sound. 'You were on a plane, remember?'

'Mm, that's what you told me, and that's therefore what I thought, but it says here that the time of the trade was sixteen twenty-one. I hadn't even boarded by then.'

He broke eye contact and rubbed the back of his neck. 'What difference does that make? I tried your phone, and got the busy signal.'

She eyed him suspiciously, clearly recalling him saying he couldn't get a connection, and it suddenly dawned on her that her itinerary put her on the four o'clock flight, London time, whereas she had taken the five o'clock. That her meeting had overrun, was something Nate would not have known.

'If my line was busy, why didn't you try Pierre's mobile? You had a copy of my itinerary, and both our phone numbers were on it.'

'I couldn't remember where I'd put your itinerary. Anyhow, there was no time to call Pierre.'

If he didn't have my itinerary to hand, how on earth could he have known I was in the air?

'You didn't try to reach me, did you, because you thought I was on the four o'clock flight?'

'Hey, don't try to cast aspersions on me to save your own butt.' He ran his tongue around his gums. 'Don't forget that if you'd made sure the off-limits database was up to date, I wouldn't have had any need to ring you.'

She looked at his keyboard. 'Can you log in to the database so that I can see the last time you accessed it?'

He did a double take. 'I don't like where this conversation is heading. If you have concerns about my integrity, we have a real problem.'

Ah, I get it. Fifteen million, no problem, shoot em in. He didn't check the database or try to call me, because he was playing big swinging dick.

An idea sprang to mind. 'I'm sorry for the way I put that, Nate. It's just that I want to review the transaction so that I can file a loss report.'

He smirked. 'Nice try.'

'I'm serious. Plenty of banks file loss reports for big hits, and I want to introduce the discipline here.'

'Really? Well, why don't I take care of that?'

'Thanks, but as head of the desk it's my job. Besides, it needs to be done by someone who wasn't involved in the transaction.'

'But you were involved. The trade occurred because you didn't update the database, remember?'

'I fully accept that may have contributed to the cock-up, and I shan't shy away from mentioning it, but I also need to examine desk procedures. I'm sure we can all learn lessons from what happened.'

He turned away, and picked up his phone, but being ignored was the least of her concerns, for she knew that if what she surmised was true, Nate was dangerous. Flash traders always blew up eventually, and he was playing with her livelihood.

'Hey, Pop, how you doing,' he said loudly, moments later.

That's it, run to daddy, she thought, for this was a familiar line she often heard when things weren't going Nate's way.

She went to her office and summoned Charlie and Joe in turn and quizzed them for their recollections of events, and when Joe left Nate appeared at her door.

He placed a hand either side of the frame and leaned forward. 'Tanya, I sure as hell hope this isn't a witch hunt, as that would constitute harassment.'

Fuck off.

'I told you, Nate. I need to file a loss report and to do that I need to understand all of the elements that contributed to the trade. I assure you it's not personal.'

'It had better not be.'

Don't threaten me.

'I'll do you a favour and ignore that remark. Now, what I need from you is a written recap detailing how the trade came about.'

His face took on a constipated look. 'Why can't you just accept your own incompetence? The trade resulted from *your* failure to update the goddamn database. An elaborate time-consuming post-mortem is not going to alter that fact.'

'In my experience, Nate, these things are never that clear cut.'

'Good luck with your witch hunt,' he said, and walked off.

After three further polite requests for his version of

events fell on deaf ears, she decided to let the matter drop, purely because she felt she had accomplished her mission. In her view Nate hadn't cooperated because he knew she knew he had lied, and that she could nail him if she so chose, which she felt was enough to ensure he took more care with the firm's money in future.

*

'Ah, Mr Hillbrand,' the maitre de said, clasping Rich's hand. 'It's such a pleasure to see you again. Come this way. Your table is ready.'

Centriko's restaurant, the antithesis of such places as the Wolseley, with less than fifty covers, was aglow in buttery peach, its tables classically dressed in white linen, each bearing a posy of fresh roses.

Over an aperitif of vintage Bollinger, Rich made the introductions. 'Francis, you know everyone of course, but Sally, let me introduce my colleagues. This is Spencer Rivington, our chief economist. Tanya Pryce, head of credit trading. Steve Cranthorp, our senior dollar trader. Joe Matanzo, our sterling specialist.'

Francis Greenfield was head of investments at Astrar Hoffman Asset Management, and Sally Lever was his deputy, and they were planning to invest heavily in the bond markets.

Tanya laid her napkin on her lap and looked across the table at Sally, who was talking to Joe, and couldn't help but compare auras and styles. There she was all glammed up in a figure hugging chic pastel knit suit, while Sally had not a stitch of make up on, and was in a drab tweed effort with a flared skirt, teamed with a white shirt secured at the neck with a brooch.

Must be a lesbian.

A quiet drama caught her attention next. The head waiter appeared to be reprimanding a newbie who hastily removed a pen from behind his ear and attached it to his belt. Tanya looked at the other waiters. No pens behind their ears.

Poor bugger.

Spencer's performance during dinner was electric. Facts and statistics flowed effortlessly as he gave his views on the state of the global economy. Economists love detail. Their job is to try and predict the direction of interest rates in major economies, and their forecasts can be both right and wrong given enough time, which wasn't much use to Tanya. All she cared about was whether to buy or sell and, crucially, when. But watching Spencer stirred all her juices, despite his gloomy forecasts. He had a tendency toward pessimism, but tonight he was particularly down beat: JP Morgan-Chase's purchase of Bear Stearns was the tip of the iceberg, we hadn't seen the last of sub-prime write-downs, the UK Chancellor's prowess with a wand hid dangerous shortfalls, Iceland was effectively bankrupt, and the West was going to end up in hock to China and Russia.

But none of that bothered Tanya tonight. The wine, a red called Merryvale, which she had never heard of but which Francis waxed lyrical over, was going down a treat. And it went down a lot better after she had taken centre stage and given her spiel on opportunities in the credit markets. Even by her own standards she had done well. She liked male attention and this was about as good as it got. Smart minds in smart suits, in a smart restaurant, all hanging on her every word.

Once the waiter had taken dessert and coffee orders, Spencer went to use the men's room. A minute later, she excused herself to go to the ladies and, as she had hoped, she saw Spencer, coming down the stair case as she was going up. For a split second her head was level with his zip, and she deliberately licked her lips.

'Firing on all cylinders tonight, aren't we?' she said, as they passed.

'Not quite, but I would certainly like to,' he quipped, giving her the once over. 'Mm,' he leaned toward her, 'you smell divine.'

She winked at him, and went on her way.

Upon departure, there was much handshaking, smiles and gracious exchanges of appreciation, before Rich saw Francis and Sally into waiting taxis, on the firm's account.

Tanya was offered the next cab, and felt obliged as the woman to accept it. Spencer held the door for her.

'Well done, Rich, you too, Spence,' she said. She turned to Steve and Joe. 'And you guys were brilliant. You did me proud.'

'You were the star, Tanya,' Spencer said, as she climbed into the cab. The others concurred.

'Now get home safely,' Rich called out. 'My mortgage depends on it.'

She laughed. 'Which one?'

Spencer stared at her for a few moments before he shut the cab door, his eyes saturated with longing. Allowing herself to be drawn into them, she slightly opened her mouth and parted her knees just enough to convey eager want.

As it was still early and ahead of the exodus of theatre goers, her taxi hurtled around the neon-lit billboards of Piccadilly, down on to the embankment, and around the City's waterside in no time at all. Tower Bridge was in sight when her mobile beeped with a text message, from Spencer: *I am in the bar at the Meridien Hotel. Please join me for a nightcap.*

They sat across from each other in squidgy leather seats, the atmosphere between them thick with lust, and after exchanging a few dutiful words about Astrar Hoffman's investment strategy, the conversation died —by mutual consent. Spencer had bought a bottle of Bollinger, albeit a less expensive one than Rich had bought earlier that evening, and they drank it in silence, while staring at each other. It started out as a joke, a game of bluff as to who would speak first, but deepened into what Tanya imagined to be tantric sex. Spencer's waistcoat was undone, his grey silk tie loose, and when she wasn't looking into his commanding, dangerously sexy eyes, she was staring at the caveman coating beneath his pale pink shirt, which started at the neck and travelled all the way down.

She put down her empty glass. 'I need to get going.'

He ran his thumb and forefinger up and down the stem of his champagne flute. 'Come home with me.'

She shook her head. 'Don't be ridiculous, Spence. You know my situation.'

'Meaning, if your situation was different you would say yes?'

'I didn't say that,' she said. Nonetheless, the gap between her knees increased.

Spencer smiled.

Just then she spotted a cushion on a sofa nearby that was identical in colour to her toddler son's, Harry's, anorak, and it cut her to the quick. Flustered, she grabbed her bag and got up. 'Forget it, Spence, forget everything, forget this bit of tonight ever happened, OK?'

'I'll get you a taxi.' He hurriedly called for the bill.

The moment they were outside the hotel, Tanya lit a cigarette.

Calm down. Nobody's died. You've not done anything wrong.

Spencer was a few yards away, standing in the road, his arm ready to launch itself high at the sight of a vacant cab. Her eyes were glued to his rear, and the contours of his toned thighs. How she'd love to dig her fingernails into the flesh of that backside, and feel those thighs inside hers.

Why is life so complicated?

After ten minutes and no sign of an orange light, he suggested going to Hyde Park corner. 'It will be easier there to find a cab.'

They walked in silence but close enough to transmit their desire, brushing hands every few seconds.

A stretch limo rode past, music blaring, and a young woman stood in the roof section, her long hair billowing in the wind, waving at passersby and shouting merriments in what sounded like Swedish.

In another life time, maybe.

They came to a small queue for cabs, and joined it. A middle aged couple, he in black tie, her in a purple evening dress and white cape, were at the front, behind them a man with a bulging briefcase who was talking quietly into his mobile. Glad of the wait Tanya lit another cigarette, and she and Spencer stood silently, awkwardly, as though lovers who had quarrelled.

After dropping her cigarette end into a drain, she

took a packet of polo mints from her bag, and offered him one. He accepted but slipped it into her mouth, and she instinctively closed her lips around his finger, which he withdrew slowly, as they looked into each other's eyes.

Shuddering, she averted her gaze, and looked at the oncoming traffic. They were now the only ones in need of transport, and a taxi soon came.

Spencer opened the door, and she put her bag under her arm, clasped her hands to her waist, and looked at him. 'Thanks for the champagne.'

He pressed a finger to his lips and then placed it on hers. 'If only you weren't married, Tanya.' He saw her into the cab, and gave the driver a paper tip to *see this precious cargo home safely.*

She swallowed hard as her driver pulled away.

If only you weren't married. The words were laden with untold promises. And no one had ever referred to her as precious cargo. *You smell divine. You were the star, Tanya. If only you weren't married—what a wonderful opening to a story that would make.*

All the way home she imagined the middle, at times tearfully, the two them always seized with breathless passion. There was no end.

Once outside her house, however, her heart began to race but she again reminded herself that, technically at least, she hadn't done anything wrong.

Turning her key quietly in the lock, she crept inside and gently closed the door. All was peaceful, and dark, save for the low light of a lamp on the hallway table.

Phew! I need a cup of coffee, and a cigarette, she thought, and tip-toed to the kitchen. Where, to her great shock, she found a sullen-faced Peter sat hunched over the breakfast bar, his face stubble and blackened fingernails signs he'd been working, and not out with his mates as she had expected.

Her heart started to pound and so loudly to her she thought he might to able to hear it.

Calm down. Calm down. CALM DOWN! You've not done anything wrong. You've had a drink with a colleague, that's all. Nothing happened.

CHAPTER FOUR

'What time do you call this?'

She glanced at her watch, half past midnight. 'I'm not fucking Cinderella, Pete.'

He picked up the open carton of milk in front of him and added some to his cup. 'Why has your mobile been switched to answer phone all night?' he said, stirring his drink as though it was treacle, his spoon some kind of weapon.

'I would have called, but I thought it was quiz night at the pub.'

And that you'd be in bed by now in a drunken sleep.

'It was a major client. I had to divert my phone.' She filled the kettle. 'So why no quiz night?'

'Jack's car broke down on the M25. Me and Mickey had to go and lend a hand. We had to tow him back in the end. Head gasket had gone.'

'Oh,' she said, 'shame.'

His eyes narrowed as he observed her face. 'What's happened? Have you been crying?' he asked, about to get up.

'Me, cry? Don't be ridiculous,' she said, raising her pitch. 'I've just been doing this, that's all.' She rubbed her eyes. 'My mascara's new. I must be allergic to it.'

He settled back on his stool.

She looked around, at her cream Aga, white maple units, limestone surfaces and floor, no change out of £45,000, and back at Peter. 'Tell you what, though, Pete, I am fed up enough to cry. Fed up with getting up at five thirty every fucking day, fed up with arguing with Nate, fed up with having to go to client dinners that drag on for hours.'

He looked into his cup.

Sighing wearily and careful not to arouse suspicion, she snail paced her way out to the hallway and the downstairs loo. Once there she took some deep breaths and again reminded herself that she had not done anything wrong.

A few minutes later, she popped her head inside the kitchen door. 'I'm sorry for snapping, Pete. I'm just dog tired.' She smoothed her hand across her forehead. 'Would you make me a coffee, while I take a shower? Then maybe we can have a cuddle, eh?'

His tattooed arms relaxed, because cuddle was code for sex. 'Go on, you go up. I'll see to things down here,' he said, as though doing her a big favour.

'Thanks.'

The Pryce family, as Tanya had depressingly come to realise, were a dysfunctional lot. Peter's mum, Kay, lived like a robotic skivvy with the control button jammed on fast forward, doing a host of menial jobs to make ends meet, while his dad, Jim, a car salesman by trade, hadn't worked in four years. When his employer of twenty years had folded with huge debt, wiping out his pension, he seemed to give up, and since then he'd had a minor heart attack, not that his motivation to work had ever been high.

And Peter had his dad's work ethic and his mum's disposition, for which Tanya blamed Jim. Of Peter's childhood recollections an incident that occurred when he was in junior school, particularly turned Tanya's stomach. His mum was feeling poorly, so poorly she had dozed at the kitchen table, resting her head on her

51

arms, and when Jim saw her in this sorry state, he punched the table, breaking crockery in the process, to liven her up. It turned out Kay had a serious throat infection. Jim still had a temper on him, Tanya could see that, but age, ill health and too many mince pies had clipped his abusive wings. That said, when he got angry, she noticed Peter would clench and unclench hands repeatedly, while Kay would get in a flap.

For once Tanya was grateful her and Pete's romping routine was both quick and, bar the grunts, conducted in silence. She turned onto her side afterwards, facing out, not unusual, and Peter cuddled her.

'I know it's hard, Darlin,' he said, kissing the back of her neck, 'but even if you left KS you'd still have to work, and you wouldn't earn anything like you do now.'

She patted his hand. 'I know, Pete. I'll be alright in the morning.'

'Don't forget Jack and Lizzy are coming over on Saturday.'

'I haven't forgotten,' she mumbled.

He gave her stomach a friendly squeeze, turned over, and flaked out within minutes.

Phew!

Spencer's aftershave remained fresh to her senses, and in her mind's eye she could still see his hirsute hand pressed against his thigh, his thumb tantalising close to his cock, as his eyes undressed her. Excited and frightened, she swung from fantasising about outcomes if she hadn't lost her nerve, imagining them sampling each other's most intimate secretions in some deep doorway in Shepherd Market, to rationally considering the impact of embarking on an affair.

NCA and her Belgium trip kept coming to mind,

and felt like a warning, symbolising the consequences of weakness. And she certainly felt weak, yet she also knew she had to be the one to take control, because Spencer was footloose, and desperate for sex.

He's got no downside.

Hours later, she sat nervously in her driver, Ted's, car, and sent him a text message: *No more drinks. I want to stay married. Sorry.*

He texted back: *That saddens me, greatly.*

Me too, but life is full of tough choices.

She didn't look at him once during the morning meeting, but as they left the auditorium he sidled up to her. 'I care about you,' he whispered, and walked quickly on.

I've got to think of my boys.

Back at her desk she threw herself into work with enthusiasm bordering on manic. After quizzing her team every which way imaginable about their trades, strategies and market views, she moved onto the sales force, grilling whoever was available about what their clients were doing and thinking and why. Thereafter, she rang a few brokers for a general market related chat.

Come lunchtime she felt very on edge, but couldn't slow down, aware on some level that if she did thoughts might emanate from her heart to overpower those in her head. So she dealt with expense claims, and as she read one submitted by Charlie she started giggling.

It was for accompanying one of KS' best clients to Old Trafford and back in a limo, to watch a Manchester United game. Great one might think except the client was Jacob Robensteyn, an orthodox Jew who went home at sundown on a Friday, and was monosyllabic except when talking about finance. And teetotal.

After the salesperson Rich had assigned to the task fell ill the day before the game, and no other member of his team was willing to step in and sacrifice an entire Saturday, Tanya had volunteered Charlie, and then enlisted Joe and Steve's help to psyche Charlie up, to get him to think he was in for one of the best days of his life. Her contribution was to refer to Jacob as Jay, and casually add that he had a bit of a problem with drink. In the event, Charlie spent eleven hours, five and half each way, in the limo, drinking sparkling water and chatting about finance.

She stood and looked across her desk at him with unashamed amusement. 'How is your mate, Jacob, these days?'

Joe and Steve started laughing.

'You fucking wankers,' Charlie said to them, his chubby face reddening.

'Don't be like that, Charlie,' Tanya said. 'Some people would give their right arm to go in a limo, to see a Man U game.'

'Shame that karaoke system didn't get an airing,' Joe said, for Charlie had spoken of his hopes for a sing-song while knocking back the beers.

'Or that porno,' Steve said, which was a blank DVD Steve had pretended to borrow from a mate expressly for Charlie, nipping out of the office to collect it.

Tanya erupted into giggles again, this time to the point where she was holding her stomach. That Charlie wasn't laughing didn't register with her until she had calmed down, whereupon she apologised.

'Sorry, Charlie, I wasn't laughing at you, really I wasn't, I just needed to laugh.'

He shrugged and gave her a half-smile.

What's up with him?

'Are you OK, Charlie?'

He nodded unconvincingly and she ushered him into the aisle, where they could have a relatively discreet chat.

'I didn't mean to offend you, Charlie, really—'

'It's not that, Tanya.' He went on to explain that the previous night during a fierce argument with his wife Katherine, who was Scottish, Katherine had threatened to leave both him and London, to return to the Highlands to be near her parents. They had three sons, aged fifteen, twelve, and ten.

He ran a hand over his face. 'It's not the first time she's said it either, and what could I do if she did? Fuck all. She's got me over a barrel.'

'Look, why don't you get your parents to look after the kids for a few days, and take her away somewhere?'

'Thanks but I think we're a bit beyond that.'

'Come on, Charlie, think positive. There's got to be something you can do to turn the relationship around.'

'Like what?'

'When was the last time you two had sex?'

He looked swept with embarrassment by the question.

'Sorry, I didn't mean to pry. It's just that sex can bridge gaps in conversation and stuff, and if you're not conjugally joining up, it's no wonder you're arguing and drifting apart. What you need to do is woo Katherine, buy her flowers, chocolates and stuff. Make her feel special.'

He folded his arms. 'I know you're trying to be helpful, Tanya, but there's more chance of me buying her a fucking noose.' He paused. 'She knows the kids are my world, and now she's using them as a weapon.'

'It could also be a cry for attention.'

'Could be, but it's not. My eldest told me she's already run the idea by the three of them. So now they know she's a whore.' He grinned with misguided pride.

Jesus.

He'd clearly told them about a brief affair Katherine had had about eight years earlier. But Tanya's view at the time hadn't changed. Charlie was as much to blame for what happened. When their youngest was a few weeks old Charlie had pissed off on a three day break to Spain with his mates, leaving Katherine to cope on her own, and boasted about it, saying it was his way of celebrating.

'It's not fair to involve your children, Charlie. You'll curdle their brains.'

'Not my three, they're bright kids.'

'They're still kids, Charlie, and...' Her train of thought suddenly vanished because Joe yelled to Steve that Spencer was on the phone for him.

I care about you. If only you weren't married.

She shook her head. 'Sorry, Charlie, I didn't get a lot of sleep last night. As I was saying, they're still kids, and if you start rubbishing Katherine to them, you'll be playing into her hands.'

Maybe I should take a leaf out of Katherine's book.

Then, in her mind's eye she saw that cushion on the sofa in the Meridien Hotel.

*

Standing behind his chair, Tanya massaged Steve's shoulders as they talked about bonuses and, given that they had not managed to recoup the money lost on NCA, how bad they were likely to be.

He groaned appreciatively. 'Look on the bright side. You can always become a masseuse.'

She let out a brief laugh. 'What, fifty quid a throw, four clients a day, a grand a week? After tax, that wouldn't even pay the costs of Alison, let alone the mortgage, the overdraft, and school fees.'

Pre the NCA debacle she had hoped to be able to pay off a chunk of her mortgage with her bonus, although Peter also wanted a holiday apartment abroad. Both seemed pipe dreams now.

'I know the feeling,' Steve said, 'and you can tell Bruce from me that if he legs me over, I'm off.'

'Don't worry. You're my number one priority.'

He looked up at her and smiled. 'Good.'

'Hey, Tanya,' Nate said. 'Over here, my shoulders are full of knots.'

So is your friggin brain.

She gave Steve's shoulders a squeeze. 'That's your lot, I'm afraid. I'm popping out for a fag.'

'Aw, I was enjoying that.'

She looked at Nate. 'Sorry, but I'm going out for a cigarette.'

'You need to quit the habit. It's real bad for your health.'

'I can think of worse things.'

You for example.

Steve stifled a chuckle, having understood what she meant. 'You go and enjoy your fag, and I'll hold the fort.'

'Thanks,' she said, and left.

A few minutes later Fiona came to the desk with her

new mobile phone, looking for help on how to use it, and Freddie rushed to assist.

Ten, nine, eight, Steve thought, seeing Nate cast them a tetchy glance, and as he suspected it didn't take Nate long to think of an excuse to interrupt them.

'Hey, Freddie. Since you've nothing better to do, go get me a sandwich.'

'OK. What would you like in it?'

Nate waved him away. 'You choose. I'm busy.'

'I'll come, and keep you company,' Fi said.

'Er, I don't think so, Fiona,' Nate said. 'You need to man the phones.'

A rankled Fiona snubbed Nate and with her nose in the air returned to her desk, where she could undertake that task just as easily.

Well done, Fi.

Nate shook his head, his face a grump, and looked at Steve. 'She needs a good smack on that tight little ass of hers.' He gestured his fantasy, giving the air a short sharp whack.

Steve laughed. 'If that's what you're after, Nate, I think you need a few lessons, because you've just pissed her right off.'

Nate winked. 'It's part of my strategy. Chicks like that need a firm hand. They pretend they don't, but they love it.' He sighed wistfully. 'Wouldn't you love to squeeze those tiny little butt cheeks of hers?'

'Not particularly. I like a good arse, but I need a good pair of knockers as well, a major pair of bristols to bury my face in. Anyway, I prefer brunettes, and a woman with experience.'

While this described many women it also described Tanya, which Nate realised. 'Don't tell me you've—'

'Of course not,' Steve said. 'Tess would kill me.'
Tessa was his wife.

Not that I'd say no, if I got the chance.

'No, tits don't do it for me. A tiny tight little ass is what I like.'

'That's because you weren't breast fed.'

All of a sudden Nate's face became a snarl. 'What the fuck are you talking about? Ugh. That's gross, the grossest thing I ever fucking heard.'

'What are *you* talking about? What's gross? I don't follow.'

Grimacing, Nate shook his head but offered no verbal clarification, and Steve let the conversation die.

The guy has some serious fucking issues.

Freddie returned, and gave Nate a greaseproof package.

Nate opened it, and cackled. 'Don't give up the day job, low boy. I need a goddamn ladle to eat this.'

'But I thought you liked prawn and avocado.'

'Not with a gallon of mayo, you dipstick.' He threw the sandwich in the bin. 'Go and get me another one.'

Freddie laughed nervously. 'OK, but tell me what you want in it.'

'I got a better idea,' Nate said. 'You choose, and if you goof up again, you buy me lunch for the rest of the week. Do you think you can *rise* to that challenge?'

'Ease up, Nate,' Steve said.

'Why? We need to make a man of the boy.'

Nate made to take Freddie's hand. 'Deal or no deal, chicken-shit?'

Just then Tanya returned. 'What was that?' She cast a reproachful eye at Nate as she put her bag on her desk.

'Don't worry, Tanya,' Nate said. 'He's still in one

piece, which is more than I can say for the sandwich he brought back.' He looked in his bin and laughed.

Freddie was blinking nonstop while running his hands up and down his shirt front. 'It's OK, Tanya. I can take a joke.'

She stared at Nate. 'Why don't you do us all a favour, and fuck off back home?' To deny him a retort, she answered a call from a broker, and Steve and Freddie followed suit, each picking up a phone, so that Nate was left out.

A minute or so later, Nate said, loudly, 'Hey, Pop, How you doing?'

He's not worried about bonuses, is he? No, because he doesn't have to worry. Spoilt git. Not that it's done him any good, since he can't stand on his own two feet. If he didn't have his daddy to phone for strokes and reassurance, he'd be on the floor. He should have had my life. She sighed heavily. *Come on, cheer up. He may have money, but he's got fuck all else.* She pondered her last thought. *That's not true. He's got looks, a job for life, and the time and money to piss off to Europe sightseeing every weekend.* She glanced at her pics of her boys, and reflected on how hard life had been since he arrived. *I wish he'd drop dead. You don't mean that. I do. I hope he dies. That's not very nice, is it? So what? What good has being nice done me? I hate this fucking place. It's bollocks that hard work pays.*

At the back of her mind, behind all these thoughts, was Spencer, with whom she had not socialised for weeks, turning down his many invites to buy her lunch, dinner or simply a drink after work. And each time she said no, her craving for him increased.

Whoever said 'what doesn't kill us makes us strong'

is a fucking idiot. It's all bollocks. All that stuff about be nice, work hard, and things will come right is just a lie to get people to be friggin fucking idiots. She looked at the flashing lights on her dealer board. *Fuck off, the lot of you.* Then she glanced at Nate. *Like they say, it's who you know, not what you know.* With a heavy sigh, she picked up a call.

A hectic afternoon followed for which she was thankful, glad to be doing something worthwhile instead of dwelling on all that was wrong in her life. That is, until Joe interrupted her.

'I've got Suzy on the phone, Tanya,' he said. 'Her car still keeps cutting out. Can you give me Pete's mobile number again? I'm sure I could fix it but I've a client dinner tonight, and she needs it for the school run in the morning.'

Tanya felt her face going red. As a mechanic Peter knew everything there was to know about cars, and she suspected, given that she felt he was jealous of Joe, that he had rushed the work on Suzy's car.

'I'll call him, Joe, and tell him to call Suzy.'

'It could be Suzy's fault,' Joe added. 'She can be a dizzy bint, can Suzy.'

Bless him, she thought, for she sensed he was trying to help her save face. To her Joe was one of life's nicest guys, as well as a kindred spirit, having like her crafted his own silver spoon. He was also handsome, with jet black hair and olive skin, although she didn't find him attractive in a sexual sense. Even so, she found him a pleasing sight.

She was relieved Peter answered his phone.

'Did you bodge the job on Suzy's car, because it's on the blink again?'

'No I didn't. The woman's a hypochondriac.'

'It's her car that's playing up, you idiot, not her body.' She felt ashamed, even though no one else could hear. 'Call her and get it sorted, and quick, because I don't want people thinking you can't even fix a car.'

Fuck.

'I didn't mean it like that, Pete. What I meant was that I want Joe's wife to respect you for what you do, as much as Joe respects me.'

'Your mum's dead right. You do have a vile tongue.'

'I'm sorry. I didn't mean it to come out like that.'

'Forget it.'

'Be reasonable, Pete. I've said I'm sorry. I'll make it up to you.'

'How?'

'However you want.'

He was quiet.

'I promise I'll come up with a treat to show you I am really, genuinely, sorry.'

He thought for a bit. 'OK, but watch that tongue of yours in future. I'm not one of your work lackeys.'

How could you be? You hardly ever go to work.

'You will call Suzy, won't you?' she coaxed.

'Yeah, I'll ring her, but it won't just be a phone call, will it? I'll have to go to her place to fix the fucking thing.' He huffed. 'I was supposed to see Jack tonight.'

'I'll have a large gin and tonic waiting for you when you get home,' she said through gritted teeth.

'I'll need it,' he said, and cut off.

Two peas from the same fucking pod, him and Barbara. At least he won't be there when I get home from work.

'Jamie, Harry, listen to Mummy.' Tanya focused her camera on them. 'On the count of three, I want you to say wellingtons, OK? Right, here we go. One. Two. Three!' Click.

Harry was on Peter's shoulders, Jamie in the A of his legs, a trio of bliss amid the sunny backdrop of a boating lake, manicured lawns, and lush trees.

They were in the Staffordshire countryside, at Alton Towers, on a hastily arranged weekend break organised by Tanya as a peace offering, because the problem with Suzy's car turned out to be Suzy's fault.

Harry and Jamie swapped positions for the next snap. Peter then got a passer-by, a young Chinese man, to take a shot of them all, and he and Tanya stood, an arm around each other's waist, with their boys in front.

So there they were, looking like all the other families milling around with cameras, drinks and ice creams. Peter stroked her arm as they queued for the carousel, while she laid her head on his shoulder and lazily twirled a strand of her hair around her finger.

But Spencer was on her mind, and she was secretly wondering how happy the families in her midst really were, how many couples were on their second marriage, and how many offspring were step children. And as she watched Jamie and Harry squabble over who was going to ride with Peter she felt she'd sunk to a new low.

*

Bruce lingered over Tanya's bonus figures for about a minute. 'I said slash not shave, Kiddo. These numbers are still way too high, and I see you've still not put anything down for Nate.'

She shrugged. 'He's only been here a matter of months.'

'We'll come back to Nate later. Take me through your logic for each of these guys first.' He looked back at her notes.

She painstakingly went through the merits of Steve, Joe and Charlie, giving examples of pay deals achieved by their peers, and emphasising the demand for good traders to justify her allocations. '...and now we get to Freddie,' she said, 'who's done an amazing—'

'I'm not interested in the small amounts, Tanya. Let's get back to Nate.'

She noted the switch from Kiddo to Tanya, Bruce's way of showing his annoyance that she hadn't assigned Nate even a token amount, and it irritated her.

She swung a shapely left leg over her right one, folded her arms, and took a deep breath. 'What do you want me to say?'

He rolled his eyes. 'This feud between you two has to stop. It's time to put the NCA trade behind you. Whatever you may think, Nate is a senior level guy. He knows a hell of a lot about how things work stateside, and personally I think you need to give the guy a break.'

Stay calm.

'He's self-serving, Bruce, which in my book makes him dangerous and senior level or not, he was still responsible for losing the desk three million dollars. As for giving him a bonus,' she paused and shrugged, 'well let's just say, unlike the rest of my group, he is not going to suffer if he doesn't get one. I imagine he blows ten grand every weekend.'

Nate made no secret of his lavish excursions, and had already notched up trips to Amsterdam, Budapest,

Helsinki, Prague, and Rome, always leaving early on a Friday and coming in late on a Monday, to maximise his fun. Not that Tanya minded that bit, for she considered his absences sound liability management, although it did rile her shareholders money was being frittered away.

Bruce yawned, slung himself back in his chair and clasped his hands behind his head. 'It's not wise to get emotional about these things.'

Fuck you.

'I'd say I'm being honest, and practical, rather than emotional, Bruce.'

'C'mon Kiddo, you know what I mean,' he said with a wave of his heavy forearm. 'I'm simply asking you to take a broader perspective. I want to see you grow as a manager, so that in a few years time you're sitting my side of the desk.'

He gave her a cheesy condescending smile which she had no inclination to return, the hollows of her cheekbones defiantly frozen. 'Thanks, but I don't feel I'd be growing as a manager if I took money away from people who had given their all, and gave it to Nate. It would send out all the wrong messages.'

He slurped from a can of coke. 'I understand where you're coming from, not that I necessarily agree, but you need to start thinking longer term now.'

'I am,' she said, and gave him a spiral bound document, brazenly entitled A European Bonanza.

This was her first report as head of her division, and it detailed her ambitions for KS in the European debt markets. She had been working on it for months, and wanted Bruce to read it before deciding her bonus.

He leafed through it briefly. 'Well done, Kiddo, this looks interesting.' Then he placed it to one side.

'I would love to know what you think of it, once you've read it properly. I've been working on it ever since I took over the desk.'

He smiled. 'It will receive my full attention, don't worry.'

Patronising git.

She got up and retrieved her papers from his desk. 'I'll leave you in peace.'

He nodded, and again perused the sheet of paper detailing her bonus proposals.

'It took me ages to come up with those numbers Bruce, and based on what each of my guys can earn elsewhere, and what we'd have to pay for replacements, they are more than sensible. If anything, they're too modest.'

'I don't doubt what you're saying, but the bonus pot is finite.'

'Maybe so, but cut them much more, and my desk will be like a graveyard.'

'I hear you, Tanya, but management is all about retaining people cost-efficiently,' he said, his tone firm. 'This is a risk-based business. Your job is to manage that risk, human and otherwise.'

With a forlorn nod, she left, and without giving it a second thought rang Spencer. 'I've just had a really crap meeting with Bruce, and,' she paused, 'fancy a drink?'

'I'm reaching for my jacket. The Ship Inn?'

This was a worn out drinking hole with soiled carpet and a sticky bar, but it was in a backstreet and had partitioned areas that afforded extra privacy.

Spencer was already there when she arrived, his fit suited shoulders and dark hair unmistakable through the engraved glass divider.

She heaved big sighs as she sat down. 'Thanks for coming, Spence. I don't want you to get the wrong impression. I just need someone to talk to.'

He smiled and filled her glass high. 'I understand.'

She told him about her and Nate's latest exchange, and briefed him on her meeting, but didn't divulge numbers. '...I know I'm alienating myself, and that Bruce thinks I'm jealous of Nate, but it's not like that. If it had been Steve who had fucked up, I'd be just as hard on him. I'm fed up with Bruce calling me Kiddo as well. It was OK ten years ago, but not now.'

'But that's simply a term of endearment.'

'I know, but it also means he still sees me as a kid.'

'If that was the case, he wouldn't have put you in charge.'

'I'm in charge because I'm cheap. If the firm tried to hire someone with my experience and skills they'd have to pay multiples of what I earn.'

'Have you ever considered leaving?'

'Of course, and over the years I've had plenty of offers, but,' she shrugged, 'I made a lifestyle choice, I suppose. The best time for me to have moved on was when I was thirty, but then I'd just got married, and I wanted children, and I knew Pete was never going to make bundles. So, I opted for security.'

'You must have been madly in love with him.'

'I'm not sure I'd say that but I definitely fancied him.'

'Do you still fancy him?'

'Let's not go down that road, Spence,' she said, and returned to talking about Nate.

'...If he's such a 'senior level' – she made quotation marks – guy, how come New York sent him over here? If KS' shareholders knew how much money he'd cost them, they'd be outraged.'

Spencer stroked the bridge of his nose.

'What's up?'

He shook his head. 'Nothing.'

'Don't *nothing* me, Spence. I know you better than that.'

He thought for a moment, before responding. 'Nate couldn't possibly have known the loss would escalate to three million dollars.'

She threw out her hands. 'That's *not* the point! The point is that he didn't care whether the firm lost money or not, only about the kudos he got from Krevamar. His ego and reputation is far more important to him than the P & L.'

He topped up her glass. 'Bruce has to work that out. He's not an idiot.'

'I'm not sure he wants to work it out, and even if he does, what's it going to take? Another great loss, if you ask me.'

'Don't say that.' He paused. 'Maybe Nate will tire of London, and go back to the states.'

'And pigs might fly. He loves it here.'

She heaved a sigh.

He slipped his fingers in between hers.

'Don't, Spence,' she said, but she didn't pull away.

'I hate to see you this down in the dumps. I wish there was something I could do to help.'

'You are helping just by listening.'

He smiled. 'I am more than happy to do that Princess, whenever, wherever and however you want.'

Princess? How lovely.

In an instant her spirits rose.

'I've been called a lot of things, but never Princess, not that I'm complaining. It's a darn sight better than Kiddo. What made you call me that?'

'In The Princess and the Pea by Hans Christian Anderson the maiden is very beautiful, very clever, and very sensitive. Just like you.'

She smiled, her heart melting. 'I bet you had a really good childhood, didn't you?'

Fairy tales at bedtime and all that money can buy.

'Yes. I was very fortunate.'

That's why he's so confident, and gorgeous and wonderful. He knows he's loved. And that's why he's lovable.

'I thought so. That's why you're so...' She sighed wistfully. 'I won't finish, or I'll get myself into trouble.'

He laughed. 'What was your childhood like?'

'In a word lousy, because my mum was ill.'

A memory surfaced of a perishing cold Saturday when she was working on a market stall, and her mum, who suffered from agoraphobia at the time, had walked the quarter mile from their house with a mug of warm tea for her. It was one of three acts of kindness Tanya would never forget.

She did care about me.

'Where was your father?'

She glanced at her watch and withdrew her hand. 'Jesus, is that the time. Sorry, Spence, but I've got to go.'

Tanya could see he was disappointed.

'I don't want to go,' she added, 'but Ted's waiting, and I want to see my boys before they go to bed.'

'I understand, but can we please do this again soon? I've missed you horribly.'

I know the feeling.

'I'd like to, but I can't promise anything.'

'I know you can't. I'll just wait for you to call and hope that's it's very, very soon.' He looked at his watch. 'I'll be back from my run about nine o'clock.'

She laughed, as did he, and they both stood, and looked at each other.

He sniffed the air. 'Mm, what is the name of that fragrance you wear? I've been meaning to ask you for ages.'

'You'll laugh when I tell you. It's called Chance, by Chanel.'

He did laugh. 'Perhaps that's a sign you're one step closer to taking one.' He paused. 'I shall buy some, to spray on my pillow.'

'You're not serious.'

'Do I look as though I'm joking?'

He didn't, and she was suddenly overwhelmed with sadness and guilt.

'Spence, please don't torment yourself. You know my situation, and I'm stuck, OK? We can have a drink, but that's about—'

'To borrow from Shakespeare, Princess: *It is not in the stars to hold our destiny, but in ourselves.*'

They looked into each other's eyes and she let her face tend toward his until their lips brushed, whereupon she bolted.

CHAPTER FIVE

Tanya wiped her mouth with her napkin. 'What do you think of Denton Fenshill?' she asked TJ, having told him how she had come to own the NCA bonds on which he'd acted as go between.

'To be totally honest, not very much. Fenshill might wear a bow tie and peer over his narrow gold frames as though a learned professor, but he's a numpty, and there's something conspiratorial about his quiet manner.'

She smiled, TJ's posh accent adding to her pleasure.

'I couldn't agree more. Personally, I think he's a closet homosexual. Has he ever made a pass at you?'

TJ held a hand to his stomach. 'Please. I'm still digesting lunch.'

She laughed. 'OK, onto to more serious matters.' She paused. 'I've got a potential proposition for you.'

TJ immediately ordered another bottle of wine.

'I got a call last week from Olli Vermallen at Sky-Rise.' TJ's eyebrows shot up. 'He wants to chat about my running what he calls a slush fund, and he proffered a figure of fifty million dollars for starters, plus leverage of course. I've told him I can't do it on my own, that I'd need derivatives expertise, and that I had someone in mind.'

He leaned forward. 'Where do I sign?'

She pushed her curls behind her ears. 'Are you serious?'

'Deadly. I feel the same way as you about this business. Hedge funds are where it's at, and we would

71

make the perfect team. And Olli Vermallen... The fellow's rumoured to be worth in excess of one billion dollars.'

'I know. Do you know how he made his money? I heard it was from dotcom.'

'That's how he made his first pile, with an on-line card payment system and some kind of careers site, but he was also the seed backer of Rider Records and Zeb Health Clinics.'

Tanya gasped, both companies now being major concerns. 'Wow. I didn't know that.'

'Not many people do. He's a very private fellow, is Mr Vermallen, not one for interviews.'

She let out a giggle. 'I think that's in the public interest. Have you heard him speak?' She followed with an impersonation. 'He's got this really funny voice.'

TJ laughed. 'I know, but I'm sure we will get used to it. When does he want to meet?'

'He's waiting for me to proffer some dates. I'll suggest mid June onwards, as by then I'll know what my bonus is going to be.'

'I'm around.'

'Great. I just hope KS don't shaft me too badly, as it will be the benchmark on which Olli Vermallen judges my worth.'

'I wouldn't worry about that. Your tenure with KS gives you a lot of leverage.'

She pulled at her lip. 'I hope so, because my loyalty has been a complete and utter waste. If I'd job-hopped, I'd be earning a fortune.'

'Loyalty is never wasted, and if you had hopped and skipped around the City, you wouldn't be you, and we would all be the poorer.'

'Flattery will get you everywhere. Now, since we need to keep this under wraps, let's refer to Olli as Rusty. My first thought was to call him the Russian, because he seems a no-nonsense kind of person who'll give it to you straight, but then I had visions of being trailed by MI5, so I toned it down.'

He laughed. 'To Rusty,' he said, raising his glass.

Tanya raised hers, and they toasted their secret.

*

'Tanya, your Aunt Jackie's on line six,' Freddie shouted.

'What? Who? Speak up, Freddie. I can't hear a friggin word you're saying.'

The oil price had surged more than $10 in New York, its biggest one day rise, to $139 a barrel, and US unemployment had suffered its biggest rise in twenty years. The dollar was getting hammered, and talk was of America suffering a significant economic slowdown, possibly a recession. All this had sent the markets crazy, the floor a fusion of bingo hall screams and school playground motion, with phones ringing off the hook.

Freddie now stood beside Tanya. 'It's your Aunt Jackie. She's on line six.'

Tanya held her hands to her face. 'For crying out loud.' She dashed into her office, shouting she would take the call there.

'Hi, Jackie, what's up?'

'What's up? As if you don't know what's up,' Jackie roared. 'Your poor mother is what's up, my girl. She's sitting here crying her eyes out because of you. What sort of daughter ignores her own mother for weeks, after she's taken an overdose? You should be ashamed of yourself.'

Jackie had what you might call an old mucker's voice which as a child Tanya had found very intimidating, but not now.

'What's she been telling you?' Tanya said, as she imagined Barbara shrinking into Jackie's tapestry settee, wearing her best *Oh woe is me* face. She had, in fact, spoken to her mum three days earlier, although it was true that she hadn't seen her for two weeks.

'It's not just what she's been telling me, it's also what I know. Don't forget I've watched you grow up. You've always been a madam.'

Fuck off, you old bag.

'Tell me what mum's been saying.'

'That you ignore her and let that cow Alison laugh at her. And by the sounds of it you seem to think more of Kay and Jim than you do her. If you saw your own mother as much as those greedy buggers, she wouldn't be so ill. There's a word for people like you. Selfish. That's what it is—selfish!'

Tanya could picture Jackie in her hallway delivering her missive, the glazed door of her sitting room open so that Barbara could watch her in action. No doubt she was looking alternately in the mirror above her phone and at Barbara, bingo wings flapping and her big fat arse swaying. Tanya reckoned she was at least thrice Barbara's impoverished six stone something.

The elder sister by two years, although Barbara didn't especially like Jackie, she always turned to her when she was angry. The pattern was entrenched from childhood. Jackie always stuck up for her little sister.

'Put her on the phone, Jackie.'

'Hello?' Barbara said timidly.

'What's all this about, Mum?'

'What do you mean, what's it about? It's about what Jackie just said it's about, that's what it's about,' she said indignantly.

Tanya was hugged over her desk, gripping her forehead. 'Mum, Alison is not the sort of person to laugh at anyone.'

'You don't know her. In front of you she's all sugar and spice, but when you're not there, she's full of put downs. Acts as if she runs the place, she does. Cocky cow.'

Barbara was oblivious to the irony, and Tanya saw no point arguing. Barbara invested an impure motive in virtually everything Alison did or said. The offer of a cup of tea was extended purely to assert authority, asking how she was, a ploy to garner secrets.

'OK, I'll have a word with Alison, Mum, but it's not true that we see Kay and Jim more than you. In fact, I reckon we see you twice as much.'

'When did you last see them, then? Whitsun weekend, I suppose.'

'Mum, I saw you that weekend. I came over on the Sunday.'

'Mm, well it was so long ago I can't remember. When did you last see them?'

'No idea. Six, seven weeks ago, but look, they're coming to stay this Saturday. Why don't you come, too? Let's all have a nice time, eh?'

She looked at the harried faces of her team.

'Will *she* be there?' Barbara said.

'No. It's Alison's weekend off.'

Barbara was quiet.

'Mum, I must go, but I'd love you to join us this weekend. I've missed seeing you.'

Barbara telling her as a child to wash her mouth out with soap crossed her mind.

'Can you pick me up?'

'I'll send a cab for you, if that's alright?'

'It'll have to be, I suppose.'

'I can run you home on Sunday, but on Saturday I've got stuff to do.'

Barbara didn't respond.

'I'll send a cab at half five, OK?'

Barbara responded with a muted 'OK.'

'I have to go now, Mum, as work's really busy.'

Tanya rang off and called Peter.

'Hi, Pete. Look, I've had to invite my mum on Saturday. She's playing up again.'

He laughed. 'She can't keep away, can she?'

'Sorry, Pete.'

'It don't bother me. She can do the washing up.'

When it came to Barbara, Peter was remarkably tolerant, for which Tanya was grateful. He'd spent two hours tipping her flat upside down looking for her imaginary mouse-guest. Nonexistent gas leaks were another recurring problem. Tanya had lost count of the times Peter had dashed to Barbara's, to allay her fears of an imminent explosion. Each time he would go through the motions, holding lit matches to every pipe join, including water pipes, whilst Barbara watched, to reassure herself.

'Any news as to when you'll find out about your bonus?'

She bit her lip. 'No. Look, I can't chat now, as the markets are going mad.'

'Do you think you'll get it in your June pay check?'

'Probably, but June or July what does it matter? I'm going to get it anyway. Another month's overdraft charges are hardly going to make much difference. I'm sorry, Pete, but I've got to go.'

'OK, just one last thing, Darlin. Did you book the holiday?'

She took a deep breath. 'Yes. I had Fiona do it this morning. We've got an afternoon flight.'

'Lovely stuff. Well I suppose I'd better let you get on, Darlin. See you later.'

*

As Tanya and Andy stood nattering about bonuses, Nate sprinted up the gangway of the trading room, still wearing his Versace sun shades, whilst talking into a speaker pod by his mouth.

They exchanged mocking glances. 'Is he for real, or what?' she whispered.

Hermes tie whipped over his shoulder, his hair like jumbled straw, he put his briefcase on his desk and with a look of serious surgical intent, snapped it open, took out a magazine, and hurriedly leafed through its pages, whilst shrugging off his jacket, and continuing to talk.

'How much do those convertibles he's got, cost?'

Nate had just taken delivery of a Mercedes SL 65 Roadster.

'About a hundred and fifty grand, I think,' Andy said, 'pounds that is, not dollars.'

She gasped quietly.

'For the record, I think you're worth double,' Andy said, referring to her bonus expectations, while staring

77

at her boobs as she absently pushed her silk blouse further inside the waist of her skirt.

She gave his shoulder a playful push. 'Stop that. You'll make me self-conscious. Now, will you book lunch or shall I?'

'I'll do it,' Andy said.

Tanya returned to her desk. 'Morning Nate,' she said stiffly.

He looked at her and wolf whistled, and she looked behind her, but the whistle was for her.

'You're looking mighty pretty today, boss-woman,' he said, unscrewing a plastic bottle of juice.

She crossed her arms. 'Really,' she said, and sat down.

'Yes, really.'

He's so transparent, all happy friggin clappy, just because he's got a new car.

She read an email from TJ. *Both the day and time are perfect. X.*

Smiling, she deleted it, and got on with her day, her mood much improved by imagining life after KS. But the uplift didn't last long.

'How are you, young lady?'

She looked up to see the abundantly fed and richly groomed figure of Dale Stanzinger II looming stealthily in the aisle, his bulbous baggy eyes giving her quite a shock.

'Dale! How lovely to see you.' She shot from her seat as though it was on fire and shook his porky right hand vigorously. 'How long are you here for?'

'I'm not staying. I'm just passing through, on my way to Paris.'

She tried not to show her disappointment. 'That

sounds nice, Paris is great, but do you have time before you leave for a quick chat, just for ten minutes or so?'

She wanted to show him her strategy report and give him an overview of her plans.

'Nothing would give me more pleasure, young lady, but I've a tight schedule. But Bruce has been telling me what a splendid job you're doing.' The big chief made a regal sweep of his right hand.

She felt reduced to maid status.

Nate swiftly wrapped up his phone call and sprang from his chair, shoving Tanya slightly as he took an exuberant step toward Dale. 'Sorry, Tanya.'

Cunt.

'Hey, Dale! How are you? How was your flight?'

So he knew Dale was coming.

Dale parted his lips to show teeth so bright they could double as street lights, took Nate's shoulder and shook his hand firmly. 'My flight was good, thank you, and I'm doing terrific. It's great to see you. You're looking well.'

'Thanks. I feel it.'

'That's good to hear. Have you got yourself an apartment yet?'

'You bet. I've rented a really neat place, in Onslow Gardens, South Ken.'

'Good choice. That's a great part of town.'

Nate nodded. 'You'll have to come by and check it out.'

'I'd love to.' He paused to examine his left thumb and after feeling the nail and telling Nate to give him a second, he looked at Tanya. 'Would you happen to have a pair of nail clippers I could borrow, young lady?'

She seized a mug on her desk, in which she stored

odds and ends, tipped out the contents, retrieved a pair of nail clippers, and with a smile gave them to him. 'Be prepared, that's my motto.'

'Thank you.' He creased his baggy eyes at her, positioned the clippers over the section of nail he wanted to cut, but looked at her again before doing so.

Acting on instinct, as though tending one of her boys, she offered her mug as a refuse bin, and held it in position. Dale smiled, squeezed the clippers, and into the mug went the first severed bit of his nail, followed by several more as he meticulously finished the job.

He gave Tanya back her clippers. 'Much obliged to you, young lady,' he said, and promptly turned again to Nate. 'Have you been to Lucio yet? I love that place.'

Tanya remained standing, mug in hand and a picture of idiocy, until Nate manoeuvred Dale to the walkway at the back of the aisle, ostensibly to make way for the endless stream of human traffic.

She kept her phone calls brief, and tried to catch what they were talking about, but couldn't hear above the chatter and business of the floor, so she went and had a moan to Andy, who had looked compassionately at her as she stood with her mug, painfully left out of Dale and Nate's conversation.

'My heart went out to you, Darlin,' he whispered. 'Nate is obviously insecure, and I'd hate to have him in my team, but Dale behaved badly too.'

She nodded. 'Did you know he was coming?'

'No.'

'He's not staying. He's on his way to Paris.'

'That figures. I heard he's got a new Parisian bit on the side.'

This was news to Tanya, although it was common

knowledge Dale was a philanderer. 'Dirty old git. I should have guessed.' She paused. 'By the way, that wasn't a car mag Nate took out of his briefcase. It was a copy of *Country Life*, and he's left the page open at an advert for a two million quid mansion.'

Andy's mouth fell open.

'I know,' she said. 'His dad must be extremely bloody rich.'

'Doesn't seem fair, does it?' Andy said.

She shrugged. 'I'm not jealous of people with money, but if there's one thing I can't stand in a person it's arrogance and Nate is very friggin arrogant.'

'He's on his way back,' Andy whispered.

'Thanks. See you later.'

As Tanya stepped across the aisle, she caught Dale's parting comment to Nate. 'Keep up the good work, Son.'

Nate sat down dreamy-eyed, and gave Tanya such a genuinely generous smile, she felt like punching him in the face.

Her day didn't get any better. Charlie came in late, looking awful, in a shirt that was barely ironed. 'What's happened now, Charlie?'

'She's not coming back, and she's filing for divorce.' Katherine was in Scotland, supposedly on holiday. 'I got the letter at home last night.' He tried to be stoical, but then let out a quivering sniff.

'Let's nip into my office,' she said. 'Freddie, field our calls.'

They sat on a leather sofa, Tanya so that she could see the trading floor and Charlie so that he couldn't.

'Why don't you go and stay with your parents?'

'I can't. I've not told them yet. They'd only worry.

I'll tell them once I've sorted myself out.'

Lost for anything meaningful to say beyond that she was sorry, Tanya sat quietly as Charlie chewed his nails and stared in the direction of the window.

'My house echoes,' he said eventually. 'I wouldn't have thought it was that big. It feels really weird. And I can't get my head around the silence. No tussling for the TV remote, no boisterous tackles, no crashing up and down the stairs, no noise at all, just empty silence. Empty—sad—silence.'

Seeing tears in his eyes, she grabbed a box of tissues from her desk and gave them to him.

'Ta,' he said. 'You know what I miss most, the kids playing with my feet, while I watch TV. They always did that to annoy me.'

She placed a hand on his arm, but there was no physical response. 'Look, why don't I get you a flight to Scotland, and book you in a hotel near Katherine, so you can spend the weekend with them? Take Monday off as well. The firm will pay for it.'

If they don't, I will.

He gave his nose a hearty blow. 'Nice idea, Tanya, but they're all off to Spain on Sunday, the bitch's way of easing the boys into their new life. Her parents are going too.'

She heaved a sigh. 'There must be something you can do to get her back, Charlie.'

'I don't want her back. She can fry in the bowels of a fucking volcano for all I care. I just want my boys.'

'In that case, go for custody.'

'No point. Men don't get custody of children.'

'You could always move to Scotland.'

'What, and collect golf balls for a living?'

82

'There are a lot of fund management firms in Scotland. I'm sure you could get a job.'

He folded his arms. 'I'm a trader, Tanya. The best job I could get the other side of the fence would be executing trades for portfolio managers. I'd be a mopper-upper, and earn what? Sixty grand a year tops. What's that going to leave me with after I've paid the bitch her whack? Not even enough for a bed-sit.'

Charlie was exaggerating but she didn't feel it would help to point it out. 'Look, I've Pete's parents and my mum over tomorrow night. Why don't you join us? We've plenty of room for you to stay. You shouldn't be on your own at the weekend.'

'I'll pass, if you don't mind. Anyway, I've got cleaning and shopping to do.'

'I know this is awful for you, Charlie,' she said gently, 'but you will come through it. And I bet as soon as they're old enough your sons will want to move back here, and live with you.'

'Nah. It'll be three years until my eldest is eighteen and then he'll be off to university. Besides, it wouldn't be right to split them up. The reality is that I've lost my kids forever.'

She sat up straight. 'That's not true, Charlie. Your boys love you and they'll make sure they get to see you. It's not as though they're infants. They can come to London for weekends. The trains are so fast these days. I know you're feeling like shit at the moment but this is the worst bit. You're still in shock, and that will pass.'

He let out a beleaguered puff. 'Come on. Let's go back to the desk, and try and make a few quid.'

'OK, but give some thought to tomorrow night, and if you change your mind, just turn up.'

This friggin business is a jinx on marriages.

Andy cancelled lunch at the last minute, and as Tanya was making do with a sandwich at her desk, Spencer came onto the floor.

He stood in the gangway with his back to her, hands in his pockets, chatting with Rich Hillbrand, giving her a direct view of his athletically plump backside and, as the cuffs of his shirt were folded back, all that hair on his forearms.

She shuddered and looked away, at her photos of her boys, and thought of Charlie. Then she retreated to her office.

How am I going to cope when he gets a girlfriend? He's too gorgeous and hungry for sex to be alone for long.

Last thing every night she thought about him, and at weekends he was constantly on her mind.

I've got a choice. If I want to sleep with him, I can. Like he said, sometimes it's a good thing to give in to one's impulses. Maybe it's time I did, for once.

CHAPTER SIX

'Hello, Barbara. How are you?' Jim said. 'I would get up but the old ticker can't take the strain.' He patted his heart.

He was stretched out on the sofa, feet draped over the end, spectacles half way down his nose, and braces unclipped. Whisky in hand and a small plate with a sandwich resting on his beach ball of a stomach, he looked, to Tanya's irritation, most content.

Kay was motionless on the rug by the hearth, playing dead bandit for Harry and Jamie, while Peter sat in an armchair with a tumbler size gin and tonic, box creases still evident on his new shirt.

Kay got up, and smoothed the pleats of her skirt. 'Nice to see you Barbara,' she said, fingering her fringe.

'Alright?' Peter said, staying put.

Tanya was relieved Barbara offered up smiles to all, and glad she had made an effort with her appearance. Her choice of a long sleeved dress did justice to her skeletal frame, and she'd put some lippy and blusher on, and curled her hair.

In T-shirt and jeans, her face bare, Tanya was the scruffiest, but had the looks to get away with it. 'Jamie, Harry, come and kiss Nanny Barbara hello,' she said.

'Ooh, what have you got there?' Barbara asked.

'It's a bow and arrow set,' Jamie said proudly. 'Nanny and Granddad bought it for us.'

'Me have a go now, me have a go,' Harry said, hopping impatiently and trying to wrench the bow from Jamie's slowly elevating hand.

85

'Don't tease him, Jamie,' Jim chided. 'You must share things and take turns.'

Barbara's face immediately became pinched, and she flashed her mink eyes at Tanya.

'He's OK, Jim, leave him be,' Tanya said, responding to Barbara's silent dictate.

'No harm in encouraging good behaviour, Tanya. Manners maketh the man.'

Tanya wrestled the bow from Jamie's hand and passed it to Harry. 'Jamie, come and help mummy make some more sandwiches.'

'I've got a better idea,' Kay said. 'Jamie sweetheart, why don't we read the comic I bought you?'

Jamie's eyes brightened and he climbed on Kay's lap, while Barbara followed Tanya out to the kitchen.

'How long have they been here?' Barbara said, cocking a thumb in the direction of the lounge.

Tanya's heart pounded. 'Not long. They caught an earlier train. I didn't expect them till about now.'

'Hark at that fat lump of lard,' Barbara said. 'Manners maketh the man. Who does he think he is, chastising Jamie?'

'He doesn't mean any harm, Mum,' Tanya said, wringing her hands.

Aside from her kitchen and bar duties, Tanya spent the evening tensely monitoring Barbara's every word and facial nuance for signs of distress and impending trouble, which inevitably came.

Kay, who was sat perched on the edge of the sofa in front of Jim's legs, in doing her best to make polite conversation with Barbara, spoke of a mishap she'd had earlier in the week, wherein she had dropped a pile of clean wet washing on her kitchen floor.

'You can imagine how upset I was?' Kay said.

Barbara turned her nose up. 'Well it depends how dirty your floor was, doesn't it?'

Kay's cheeks turned scarlet.

Tanya interjected swiftly. 'Take no notice of her, Kay. She's had too much to drink.' She glared at her mum, but her lips were curled down in self-satisfaction.

'When are you off to the South of France, Son?' Jim said.

'July the fifth,' Peter said, rubbing his hands together, 'and I can't wait.'

Tanya mumbled about it being stuffy, and went to the far end of the room to raise the sash window further, but in truth she just wanted distance.

'Alright for some,' Barbara said.

'You could have come with us, Mum.'

'You only asked me because you knew I'd say no.'

Tanya spun round. 'That's not true, and you know it!' she said, stung by the accusation.

'We're going to look at some apartments while we're there, too, aren't we Darlin?' Peter said.

Tanya suddenly suffered a painful stomach spasm, and for some seconds couldn't speak with the pain. Not that Peter or anyone else noticed. Why would they? They were all wrapped up in their own little worlds. She knew it was due to tension, as her stomach had a habit of reacting when she felt nervous, and could tell Peter was trying to wind Barbara up. His tone of voice told her that, and he'd exaggerated. They only planned to chat with a few estate agents.

Sneering at Tanya, Barbara took a swig of her rum and coke. 'So that's what you're up to, is it, emigrating without telling me?'

'Don't be stupid, Mum. Of course we're not. We're only going window shopping, anyway.'

'I don't think you should buy a place abroad, Son,' Jim chipped in. 'Foreign places are dodgy. If they want the land back, they just take it. What you need is a nice little cottage somewhere in Kent.'

'Maybe we'll be able to afford both.' Peter flashed a wink at Tanya. 'I'll let you know next week.' He then turned to Barbara. 'I might even buy you a new broomstick.'

Jim and Kay roared with laughter.

'Mum, he's winding you up. He knows we'll be lucky to afford two bleeding tents.'

'He doesn't mean it, Barb,' Kay said. 'He talks to me the same way.'

'On what he earns he couldn't even buy a toothpick,' Barbara said.

'You're only jealous,' Peter goaded, alcoholically unperturbed.

Before Barbara had a chance to respond, a plastic arrow, launched by Jamie, shot across the room, and hit her on the forehead—and stuck there.

Hahahahaha. Justice. Serves you right.

It took all Tanya's willpower not to erupt into a fit of the giggles, the sight hysterically funny. Jim, Peter, and Kay, however, laughed openly, and even Harry was holding his hands against his tummy, and giggling.

Jamie ran straight into Tanya's arms for protection, but also started laughing once it registered with him that she was also shaking inside with amusement.

Barbara yanked the arrow from her forehead, and sat bending it with both hands in an effort to snap it in half, but it was too flexible.

'S-s-say sorry to n-nanny B-b-barbara,' Tanya said, struggling to keep a straight face.

Barbara flung the offending weapon on the floor. 'What a bloody stupid thing to buy a kid,' she shouted. 'That could have taken my eye out.'

'Oh, Mum,' Tanya said, composing herself. 'It was an accident. Jamie's tired and over excited. I'm going to take him upstairs for a bath.'

She lifted Jamie into her arms and carried him out of the room, making eyes at Peter and then the drinks cabinet, to indicate he should administer big refills to disperse the tension.

Later, back downstairs, things were calmer but an undercurrent remained, and to soften the atmosphere Tanya coaxed Jamie to demonstrate his recently acquired piano skills. Nearing the end of London Bridge Is Falling Down, he went off key, and sought solace in Tanya's arms, burrowing his head into her shoulder. She stroked his bristling crew cut. 'Well done, Sweetheart. I can see you've been working very, very hard.'

Just then Jim tapped his watch and looked at Kay. 'Kay, I should have had my tablet ten minutes ago, shouldn't I?'

Kay jumped to her feet with her hand clamped over her mouth. 'Oh! Oh!' She ran from the room and quickly returned with a glass of water and one tablet and stood over Jim, hot, bothered and fussing as he swallowed it.

'I'll have to trade you in,' he chortled, as he handed the glass back to her.

'Sorry,' she simpered.

I'd give him more than one fucking tablet.

Having had enough, Tanya took Jamie and a

sleeping Harry from Kay's arms, upstairs to bed, saying she wouldn't be long, but as soon as they reached the bedroom, Harry, with some encouragement from her, woke up. 'Story, Mummy, story,' he bleated.

She selected *Paddington Bear* from the white painted bookshelf in the alcove, which always made for a very long story. And the three of them snuggled together under the duvet in Jamie's double bed, Harry one side of her sucking his thumb, Jamie the other, with his head on a pillow propped on her arm, so that he could see the pages.

The children were soon asleep, but Tanya felt too shattered to go back downstairs, and lay pondering Barbara's emotional constitution.

As far back as she could remember it had been her duty to do Barbara's bidding, however irrational her requests, but she had always expected her to get well one day. Now she wondered whether she just wanted help to stay sick.

Since Barbara was only 59, that possibility evoked dread, and not for the first time that day Tanya became gripped with panic. Thinking about Peter, and how he enjoyed upsetting Barbara, added to her anxiety. To banish her torment, she focused on Spencer.

I bet his parents are refined and sophisticated, and that he calls his mum, mother, and his dad, father. They probably live in a rambling house in the country, take tea on the lawn, and go to The Last Night of The Proms.

She dozed off imagining a picnic on their lawn, her a picture of femininity in some flouncy squishy floaty number – she could not make up her mind between long or short sleeves, perhaps a shawl – Spencer in rust cords, and a tweed jacket.

Sheer terror forced her awake, in the middle of the night. She had been dreaming about Jim, who had a gun and was searching for her. Sweating, she eased herself out of Jamie's bed, popped Harry into his own, and rushed to the safety of hers, shivering feverishly as she cuddled into Peter's back.

The following morning, with Harry and Jamie in tow, Tanya drove Barbara home, and pushed a wad of notes into her hand as she went to get out of the car.

'I don't want your money.'

'Go on, take it. Buy yourself something.'

Barbara managed a smile. 'It will come in handy, I suppose. I've got the gas bill due.'

Tanya felt a stone lighter as she drove away. Her next port of call was the supermarket, where Harry, angry at being confined to a trolley, repeatedly kicked his heels against it while crying, and where, at the checkout, both boys made endless requests for sweets they weren't allowed. Tanya was furious with Peter for lumbering her with the children, while he took his parents to the train station, and when she got home she deposited Harry in his play pen, and barked to him to 'Get out here and help, for God's sake.'

He helped her carry the groceries into the house and to put them away, and with that chore done Tanya informed him she was going out.

'Out? Out where?' he said.

'None of your business.'

She went to the park and pitched under an oak tree using her jacket as a cushion, and sat facing a small gapped fence and beyond that a quiet side street lined with parked cars. And with her jean-clad legs crossed, her back to the noise of adults and kids enjoying their

Sunday, she lit up a cigarette, grateful she couldn't see anyone. If there had been a tree-house into which she could have retreated, she would have, such was her need to get away.

Detecting both the scent of cut grass and dog shit, the mix struck her as symbolic of life, that nothing was perfect, but it didn't much help her mood.

While she knew she had loads for which to be grateful, she also felt short changed, as though a chunk of her was missing out, which evoked guilt followed by anger, followed by daydreams about Spencer, followed by more guilt. A vicious never ending cycle. She thought of her dad, to whom she had just posted a letter she had written a few years earlier, in which she told him what she thought of him. It wasn't a nice letter. Fear had stopped her sending it sooner, but today she had found the courage, although she had not included her address.

He probably won't even read it. Or, if he does, he'll say I'm doolally like Barbara. She heaved a sigh. *It must be great to live without baggage.* Another sigh. *Don't be stupid. Everyone's got baggage. Look at Charlie, poor sod.*

She put a hand on the grass.

Where there's life there's hope. You were the star, Tanya. If only you weren't married. To borrow from Shakespeare, Princess: It is not in the stars to hold our destiny, but in ourselves.

That she was going to see Spencer the next day lifted her spirits, and she headed back with a spring in her step.

Maybe Pete will have an affair. If only.

Nearing home she saw Mrs Cologne, who lived in

the same street as she did, on the public side of her green wooden gate, tending her roses. In no mood for small talk, but unable to avoid passing her, she quickened her pace, but when the old lady saw her approaching she removed a garden glove, pushed back the headband that cut through her silver flick ups, and waited. 'Hello, Tanya, dear, how are you?'

'I'm good, thank you, Mrs Cologne, although I'm in an awful rush.' She looked pointedly at her watch.

'What a pity. I was hoping to ask a small favour of you.'

Oh, for God's sake!

'I really am running late today, Mrs Cologne.'

'It will only take a minute, Dear.'

'What sort of favour, is it?'

'It's rather private,' she whispered. 'I need you to come inside, if you wouldn't mind.'

Tanya reluctantly followed Mrs Cologne into her house, praying she wasn't going to be asked to do something unsavoury, such as pick up a dead mouse or rat, and was most relieved to be shown into the lounge.

'Take a seat, Dear. I won't be a moment.'

Tanya remained standing—and awestruck. Framed manuscripts and theatre programmes, and photographs of black-tie gatherings adorned the walls, and there was an enormous bookcase – at least five foot wide in Tanya's estimation – crammed with books. And the French doors to the garden resembled a stage, being dressed with purple velvet curtains tied with purple and gold sashes, and overhung with a matching pelmet, and to the left of the doors was an ebony grand piano.

Tanya couldn't resist taking a closer look, a Steinway no less, and feeling the curtains.

Jesus, they must have cost a fortune in their day.

'It's this, you see, Dear,' Mrs Cologne said, reappearing with a bottle of red wine. 'Would you mind opening it for me? I usually ask my gardener but he's away on holiday and my home-help... Well, she's a little forgetful.'

Tanya's stomach experienced the most sickening roller coaster swoop. If there were grades of shame, this was a ten out of ten. She took the bottle and the corkscrew out of Mrs Cologne's veined hands, and immediately accepted her offer to partake of a glass. Nearly two hours later she was still there.

During that time she learned that Mrs Cologne, Daphne now, was a pianist and had spent her life working in the theatre, that her late husband, Hector, a former engineer, had been dead ten years, and that their only son, Humphrey, a bachelor, and now retired architect, had a 'special' friend and lived in Australia.

Tanya's jaw dropped when Daphne revealed she was eighty three years old. *If only Barbara looked that good now*, she thought, for Daphne's eyes glowed with interest, and when she smiled she looked pretty as a cup cake, her delicate features seeming to find their proper home. And big pearl earrings, the size of clip-on ones yet Tanya reckoned they were real pearls, and pink lipstick suggested a playful side. That Daphne's back was straight, her shoulders square, also impressed Tanya, but what she found most riveting about Daphne was that she was not a churchgoer, because she seemed that type.

'The Good Lord is in here, Dear,' Daphne said, holding her hand to her heart. 'On tap, as they say. I don't need to visit a church to have a word. If I did, I would be sleeping on a pew.' She let out an endearing rasping twitter. 'He answers my questions wherever I am, because he's Omniscient, Omnipotent and Omnipresent.'

Hmmm, sounds like a clever bloke, Tanya thought, smiling inside, but she made a mental note to look the words up in the dictionary, and posed a serious question.

'Have you ever asked the Good Lord about guilt? I mean how to deal with it.'

Daphne smiled. 'When we love thy neighbour as thyself, Dear, guilt doesn't exist.'

Tanya didn't follow, although her heart felt like it had been fed something holy.

Upon leaving, they kissed each other on the cheek.

'You have blessed my day no end, Dear. It's been an absolute joy chatting with you.'

'You've blessed my day too, Daphne, and as I said, if you ever need a bottle of wine opened, call me, whatever the time.' She had uncorked a second bottle for her, and put an easy pull stopper in it.

Tanya felt finger high as she walked home, but grateful to have been humbled.

She drifted through the rest of the day in a curious haze, letting Peter's grumbles go right over her head. It was a weird but pleasant state wherein she felt chilled and special. She was also happy to have made a friend, especially one who was as interesting and lovely as she considered Daphne to be.

CHAPTER SEVEN

'You need to look on the stock substitution as a privilege, Kiddo, not a punishment,' Bruce said. 'With the price this low (he was talking about KS' share price which had fallen 25% in the last few months) there's plenty of room for upside. It could easily treble within three years.'

'I appreciate that, Bruce, but to withhold such a large percentage is a restraint on trade in that it ties me to the firm. And however much I love working here, that doesn't seem fair.'

Fucking blackmail is what it is, she thought, having calculated she'd be left with about £75,000 cash after clearing her overdraft. That might sound a lot but her overheads were high and each month she had a shortfall in the thousands. The rest of her bonus, around £250K, would vest over three years, and she would only get it if she was still working for KS.

'You're part of management now, Kiddo, and in austere times management has to band together. You need to think longer term, and more broadly. Everyone is suffering. We're all in the same boat. Every manager in this firm, including Dale Stanzinger, will have forty percent of their compensation held back.'

Huh! Like forty percent of your millions or Dale Stanzinger's tens of millions, is the same.

'What you need to remember, Kiddo,' he added, 'is that we all benefitted in the good years.'

We did? I did? KS Shareholders did? Why can't you be honest? Deep breaths. Save your anger for when you tell him to stick his job. It's still a lot of money. Some parents can't afford the petrol to take their kids swimming, let alone to Alton Towers, or the South of France.

She forced a smile. 'Thanks for sharing your perspective with me. Shall we move on?'

'Sure,' he said. 'Let me take you through my revisions to your figures.'

She winced as he did so. *Steve's history,* she thought. As if the cuts weren't bad enough, in what felt like a tit for tat exercise, he skipped over Nate.

'What's Nate going to get?'

'At this juncture, I'm not entirely sure. It's still being decided by New York. I'll deal with him personally, this afternoon.'

'I'd like to be there when you do,' she blurted.

'Calm down, Kiddo. What you need to understand is that Nate's compensation is not directly comparable to yours, or any of your guys. Ex-pats are dealt with differently. His comp is partly funded by New York.'

She was gob smacked. 'But how can I manage the desk, if I don't know what our overheads are?'

'The element of Nate's comp to be borne by London is going to be peanuts,' he said.

I don't care if it's ten fucking quid. I'm supposed to be the manager.

'Am I allowed to be at the meeting?'

He frowned. 'Time out, Tanya. KS has always been, and remains, a meritocracy.'

She considered the switch to Tanya a veiled threat, which angered her even more.

'I just want to ensure a level playing field for every one of my guys, Bruce.'

97

'Relax. The field is level.'

She bit her lip. *Fuck you.*

'Shall we move on?' she said, deliberately dismissing his reassurance.

'Tanya,' he said, with a sigh of frustration. 'Assessing the contribution of an employee who relocates midyear is complicated. Nate worked for two divisions stateside before coming to London. You get the picture? Try looking ahead to next year.'

Oh I am, and I won't be sitting here.

Tanya felt she deserved an Oscar for her performance when telling Steve, Joe and Freddie their bonuses, emphasising the marvellous job each had done, and how their sacrifices had been noted. Bruce reinforced her words by stressing that unity would be rewarded when the good times returned.

She felt thankful Charlie didn't show for this charade, for she could feel her lips beginning to quiver with the falsity of her smile.

'Well done, Kiddo,' Bruce said. 'You're learning fast.'

She smiled. *Indeed I am.*

Bruce took off his glasses and rubbed an eye. 'Make sure you impress upon your guys, the need for discretion.'

She nodded. 'They know the rule, Bruce.'

The rule was not to discuss bonuses, and only existed in Tanya's view to prevent gross inequalities becoming known. Many flouted it, for that reason.

He smiled. 'Good. Ask Rich Hillbrand to come in. And let me know when you hear from Charlie.'

Her team were understandably subdued when she returned, while Nate looked positively distraught.

'Where's mine?' he said.

'You'll be done this afternoon. I thought Bruce would have told you.'

The creases on his face disappeared. 'I guess a thirty second phone call was too much for him.'

She felt comforted to know Bruce wasn't treating him with any more regard than her.

'Can you give me a ball park figure?' he asked.

'No. I won't be privy to what you make. You'll find out directly from Bruce.'

'How come?'

She pulled a face. 'No idea. Ask Bruce.'

'Look, I'm happy to tell you, Tanya. I don't want secrets between us. It's not good for desk relations.'

'Thanks. I'd appreciate it if you would, Nate.'

'No problem. Guess work might be part of KS' modus operandi, but it doesn't have to be part of ours.'

He sounds fed up. Maybe he'll leave.

She called Charlie, on his mobile.

'Are you coming in, Charlie, because I'm not telling you your bonus over the phone.'

'Oh, bonus day, is it?' He sounded groggy.

'Yes. If you had listened to your phone messages you would know that.'

'Is it worth me turning up?'

'I'm not telling you over the phone, Charlie.'

'That means it's not worth turning up, but why should I care? It's not my money anyway.'

'Pull yourself together, Charlie, and get your arse in here.'

'What time is it?'

'Nearly ten o'clock.'

'I'll be in by lunchtime.'

He wasn't, and at two o'clock Tanya called him again. He was in a bar.

'Sorry, Tanya,' he slurred. 'I think I'll give today a miss. I'll see you Monday.'

'Suit yourself, but... Look, it's nothing to do with me, Charlie, I know, but going on a bender isn't going to solve anything.'

He laughed. 'Another pint of John Smith's please, mate,' he shouted, 'and a double Glenfiddich.'

'Where are you?'

'Don't worry. I'm a long way from the City.'

'Scotland?'

'No, but I might mosey up there tomorrow, surprise Katherine on her birthday.'

Tanya sighed. 'Do yourself a favour, Charlie, and go home, and get some sleep.'

'I will, all in good time. See ya later, alligator.'

Peter rolled his shoulders back. 'They're taking the piss,' he said. 'Bruce and the rest of the top brass will fiddle the tax.' He put a hand under his T-shirt and scratched his stomach. 'That's a point, Darlin. There must be a way you can do that.'

'Fuck off, Pete. I don't want to be a tax dodger. I just want to be paid the going rate.'

'But it's not illegal. They're all at it. Everyone in your game avoids paying their full whack.'

'No they don't, and even if they did I wouldn't join them, because I'm not going to rob the sitting ducks. That's beyond the pale in my book. If I was starving, fair enough, but I'm not. I'll just get another job.' She sighed. 'Bruce stressed these are austere times, and obviously they are but—'

'Bollocks. They said on the tele the other night that four thousand City workers are each going to walk away with a million quid in bonus this year.'

'I know, but none of them work at KS, do they?'

'Ere, what did Nate get? You didn't mention him.'

He had asked earlier what her team were paid, and she had told him.

'That's because I don't know what he got, and don't ask me why because I'm in a bad enough mood as it is. Anyway, I don't care what he got, because I'm not going to be there much longer.'

Peter poured them both more wine, and sat down. 'Granted KS are taking the piss, but it's not the best time to leave, Darlin. The economy's in a right state.'

'I know but it's not going to recover overnight, and no way am I hanging around at KS until it gets better.'

'But didn't some IMF bloke just say a fuck-off size American bank is going to go under?'

He was referring to the IMF's ex chief economist.

'Yes. The markets went into a right tailspin on the back of what he said, but lots of people are spouting off at the moment. Don't believe everything you hear.'

'But he could be right, which means if you leave you could end up joining a place like Bear Stearns or Northern Rock, just before it goes to the dogs.'

'For God's sake, Pete, I'm not going to do anything stupid. And don't go confusing what happened at Bear Stearns with what happened at Northern Rock. Bear Stearns' prime brokerage business is worth billions, which is why J.P. Morgan Chase bought the firm. Northern Rock, on the other hand...' She rolled her eyes. 'Well, it don't fucking rock, does it? But we own the fucking thing. How clever is that?'

'But the bankers were being too greedy, weren't they?'

She laughed. 'Yes, because they had the upper hand, and got insulted. When you need tons of money, Pete, it's not wise to piss off the suppliers of it and act like you can learn their job in five minutes.'

Peter took a cigarette from his pack, broke the butt off and lit it. 'I know we've got to wait three years to get it all, Darlin, but that money's still ours, and if Bruce is right about the stock price trebling…' He didn't finish.

'I could be dead in three years, Pete. If I stay at KS, I probably will be.'

He sighed sympathetically. 'But wherever we work, we have problems, Darlin, and you have still been paid the most.' He paused. 'That bloke with the white eyebrows said we're in the worst credit crunch for sixty years.'

'For God's sake, Pete, stop believing everything you hear. It's propaganda. He's only saying it to divert attention away from Northern Rock.'

'You're probably right, Darlin, but gas and electric have just gone up, and if that IMF bloke is right,' he raised a hand, 'I'm not saying he is right, but if he is, banks will have to lay people off.'

'I know that, Pete, I'm not stupid, but I'm doing three peoples work for a fraction of the pay. Believe me, I'm aching for a basis upon which I can feel grateful.'

'Well think about those who worked at Bear Stearns then. They must have lost fortunes.'

She smiled. 'At last you've said something that actually makes me feel better.'

'See, I am trying, Darlin.'

'I know you are, but... The thing is, Pete, everything is relative, and I'm not sure I can tolerate KS for much longer. But don't start fretting, I'm not going to do anything stupid. If I do leave, I'll make sure it's for a good deal, at least a two year guarantee.'

'But Darlin, you can't trust anyone in your game, especially in a crisis. They're all out for themselves. They promise and renege for a living.'

Instinct had stopped her telling him about her upcoming interview with Olli Vermallen, for fear he would pile on the pressure, and she wasn't going to mention it now.

'Why do you keep going on about people in my game? There are horrible people everywhere.'

'Yes, but money corrupts, Darlin.'

'You're talking out your arse, Pete. I know more poor people who are corrupt, than rich ones.'

She yawned loudly and widely, and Peter got up, took her hands and pulled her to her feet. 'Let's get you into bed, clever clogs. I'll get up with the kids in the morning, so you can have a lie-in.'

'Will you really, Pete?'

'Course I will, Darlin.'

For the first time in ages she saw love in his brown hooded eyes, and welled up as guilt for how she sometimes treated him overwhelmed her.

He pulled her close, and she put her head on his shoulder and cried.

'Aw, Darlin,' he said, rubbing her back. 'You'll feel better once you've had a good night's sleep.'

That she yearned for it to be Spencer holding her, made her cry more.

'I know Bruce has had his pound of flesh, Darlin,

but he does have a point when he says times are bad for everyone.'

'If he appreciated me,' she blubbed, 'it wouldn't be so bad, but...' She didn't finish.

'I appreciate you, Darlin, and we'll get through this, don't worry. And I promise you that when we go on holiday, I'll make sure you have a really nice time.'

CHAPTER EIGHT

Hands dug deep in her coat pockets, Tanya stood in the cold drizzle staring at a sweet wrapper flitting in bursts across the grass, Fiona trembling by her side, as the hearse-led cavalcade ground to a crunchy halt. And as the pall bearers retrieved the casket, Fi's rakish frame convulsed with sobs. Tanya instinctively drew her into her arms, and hugged her tight.

The picturesque twelfth century church was packed, mostly with people from the market. One of Charlie's aunties read a poem about trains, which she said Charlie had loved as a child, and the Snowman song, one of his favourites apparently, was played.

Bruce gave an eloquent tribute. Charlie was a fine trader who understood team work and had served the firm with unswerving commitment. Charlie's eldest son spoke on behalf of all three children. '...We know you will still be there, Dad; in goal coaching us, at school chiding us, in bed hugging us...' Not much past fifteen, Tanya considered the lad very brave.

Katherine stood ashen-faced but dignified as the vicar performed the final blessing, her arms around her two youngest, whose bewildered expressions left Tanya feeling distraught.

As the coffin was lowered into the grave, Charlie's mother let out the most heart-wrenching wail and collapsed into the arms of Charlie's father. Tanya shuddered, and Steve gripped her hand.

'Tanya,' Spencer said in an urgent whisper, as the crowd began to disperse.

She turned and waited for him to catch up, her heart quickening as his swift virility strode toward her.

'How are you?' he said.

She pushed her damp curls off her face. 'I'm fine, just a trader down, that's all, but...' she swallowed hard, 'three children back there no longer have a dad. How heartbreaking is that, eh?' She dribbled tears, as they walked back to the car park.

'Suicide is such a heinous crime.'

She kicked at the gravel. 'I don't think you can generalise, but in Charlie's case I agree. It's some small mercy I suppose that he did it away from home, and chose a method that didn't leave anyone in doubt. Chucking yourself off Beachy Head at least shows clarity of purpose and a determination to succeed, whereas taking a thimble full of friggin dolly mixtures, like my mum did, is pathetic.'

'Gosh, this really has been a frightful year for you, hasn't it?'

'Just a bit, yes,' she said sarcastically.

'Any chance I can buy you dinner, before you go on holiday? I would obviously love to see you, but I also think it would do you good to talk.'

She thought for a few moments. 'I'm not sure I'll have time. If I do, I'll text you. If not, then maybe when I get back.'

He smiled. 'OK. Do you need a lift back to the office? We've a spare seat in our cab.'

'Thanks, but I've got Ted on hand.'

Fiona and Freddie travelled back with Tanya, while Steve and Joe joined the throng from the market for drinks at a nearby pub. Nate stayed at the office to cover the desk.

Lunchtime, the following day

'For once I think Charlie assessed the risk accurately,' Steve said. 'I mean, what was he going to do? Trade his coach house, Range Rover, and membership at Wentworth for a three bed semi, Nissan Micra, and subscription to bloody dateline? I don't think so.'

'Some men would have,' Tanya said. 'What he did was spiteful beyond comprehension – he had killed himself on Katherine's birthday – a wicked act of revenge that will haunt his kids for the rest of their lives.'

Joe and Nate nodded agreement.

Freddie returned from the cafeteria. 'White with sugar is the one on the end, Tanya,' he said quietly, holding out a cardboard drinks tray.

'Thanks,' she took the cup and put it on her desk.

'Good man, Freddie,' Nate said, relieving him of a small carrier containing his order of a coke, roast beef on rye sandwich, bag of crisps, and two Kit Kats.

'You're talking shite,' Joe said to Steve, irritated. 'Would you top yourself, and leave your kids without a dad for the sake of few quid, because I know I wouldn't?'

'Of course not,' Steve said. 'All I'm saying is that knowing Charlie as I did, I understand how he came to see his glass as half empty. He was an average bod in every way, in ability, looks, and outlook, and he knew at knocking forty, his best years were behind him.'

Nate poked his arm through a gap at the side of his computer, to offer Joe a crisp. 'I'd work my butt off in a soup kitchen for my kids if I had any, but I guess we're all made differently. Charlie was heading for Harlem as they say and couldn't hack it. The guy was weak.'

'I disagree,' Joe said. 'He survived this business for twenty years.'

Steve laughed. 'Yes, at everyone else's expense. Always last in with the drinks, first in with his order.'

Tanya narrowed her eyes at him. 'Charlie earned his keep, Steve. He wasn't the best trader but he certainly wasn't the worst.' She couldn't help but flash a look at Nate.

Joe nodded. 'He was no cracker jack but he was still a good, solid, steady-eddy who could easily have got ten more years out of this business. I don't know why, if he wanted more money, he didn't get a job in a place like Saudi Arabia. Cuts me right up it does that he couldn't see he had options.'

'With effort he could have done a lot of things,' Steve said, 'but he was lazy, except when it came to feeding his face, and I reckon if he'd made more of an effort with Katherine, she wouldn't have fucked off.'

'But laziness is a symptom,' Tanya said, 'not a cause. Charlie's main problem was a lack of courage, and in turn a lack of humility, which obviously affected his relationship.'

'How do you work that out?' Nate said.

'Well, it takes courage to acknowledge a lack of it, which makes us realise how human we are, which makes us humble. And when we're humble we connect more with others.' She gave a self-deprecating roll of her eyes. 'Or something like that.'

'I kind of get where you're coming from,' he said as he peeled the foil off a Kit Kat, 'but some people can't see what they lack, because they lack the IQ. I always found Charlie an OK guy but let's face it, he was intellectually challenged.'

She nodded. 'But you can't confuse intellect with intelligence.'

They exchanged a smile, shock and grief having induced, for the moment at least, a spirit of cooperation, before turning her attention to Fiona who looked upset.

'Are you alright, Fi?'

Fi was sitting at Charlie's desk, but had shunned his chair for a borrowed one.

'I keep thinking about how lonely Charlie must have been, which ties in with what you just said, and I wish I'd talked to him more. If I had maybe he wouldn't have felt so lonely, which might have made a difference.'

'Listen to me, Fi. There is absolutely nothing you or any of us could have done that would have saved Charlie. Not even Katherine is to blame for what happened. He chose to take his life because he lacked the courage to live.' She sighed heavily. 'Just make sure you don't get saddled with a bloke who doesn't have courage.'

'Tanya's right,' Nate said. 'You need a man who's capable of taking a risk in life.'

Tanya looked at him. 'You're assuming it takes courage to take a risk, but that's only true if the risk is at your own expense. Even then you may not be displaying courage. It depends on your base starting point in life, and general constitution.' She spoke quietly with no edge to her voice, and out of an urge to protect Fiona, rather than slap Nate down.

'Yes,' Freddie said, 'courage is...' He clammed up as all eyes fell upon him. 'Courage is…' His face turned bright red. An awkward ten or so seconds silence followed. Then he raced through what he had to say.

'Courage is doing something you're scared of doing, even if it's a small thing.'

God bless you, Tanya thought.

'That sums it up perfectly, Freddie,' she said.

Nods all round except from Nate who was reading, or pretending to read, something on his computer.

'Time to lighten up,' Steve said. 'Let me tell you this joke I heard yesterday. You'll die when you hear it. Forty Gypsies arrive at the Pearly Gates in their transit vans and caravans. St. Peter tells them to wait and goes into the gatehouse and phones up God. *I've got forty travellers here, God. Can I let them in?*

Sorry, God says, *but we're over quota on Gypos. We can only take a dozen. Tell them to choose the twelve most worthy among them, and just let them in.*

A few minutes later St. Peter is on the blower to God again. *They've gone,* he says.

What, all forty of them? God says.

No, I'm talking about the gates.

Everyone laughed, and Tanya admired Steve's courage in telling such a joke, courage much on her mind, especially her lack of it when it came to Spencer.

To her there were parallels between Charlie and Katherine, and her and Peter, yet her feelings for Spencer remained as strong as ever. When he'd invited her to dinner, her heart had done a flip, and she knew his invite would sustain her while she was on holiday, whereas she knew the right thing to do would be to use the break to get closer to Pete.

If I had a magic wand and I could get Spencer out of my heart, would I?

She barely had to think about the answer.

No, because I don't want to. That's the bottom line.

I can't give him up because I don't want to give him up. And that's a deliberate action, a choice I'm making.

She thought of Shakespeare's quote about destiny, and felt he was both right and wrong.

No one looks to the stars to create their destiny. We all create our own, by our actions.

*

'Of course Katherine's going to get his bonus. You'd get mine if I died,' Tanya snapped. 'She'll need every penny with three kids.'

'Yeah,' Pete said, 'the kids she robbed him of.'

She scratched her wrist. 'Charlie had his faults.'

'Don't we all?' He clutched at the thick gold chain lacing the neck of his T-shirt. 'He should have pushed her off Beachy Head instead, the slag.'

Tanya pushed her sunglasses onto her head and glared at him, her lashes almost touching her brows. 'You're such a chauvinist fucking pig, you really are.'

He prised a bit of food out of a back tooth with his little finger. 'I didn't mean that, Darlin, sorry, I just don't like to see a person wronged, that's all.'

'Yes, well Charlie more than got his own back.'

Peter made to reach for her hand but she nudged the plastic table forward and got up. 'I'm going to the loo.'

'OK, Darlin, I'll get the drinks in. I'm going to have a G & T. Shall I get you a glass of the house white?'

She flung her canvass bag onto her shoulder, and smacked one of her flip flops against the leg of her chair to shake off the sand. 'Get me a bottle.'

'Er, it's my holiday too, you know,' he said, touching his balls.

'I can see that,' she said, and pressed her hand firmly on his gelled hair, flattening it.

'Fuck off,' he said. 'What you doing?'

She laughed.

He took her arm and ogled her cleavage. 'You look really nice in those low cut halter neck things.'

She pulled away. 'I still want another bottle, but don't fret, I won't fall asleep.'

Vaguely aware of a pain across her eyes, caused by a shaft of super bright sunshine, Tanya turned over, and groaned in gratitude, thankful she was alone, her hand touching the edge of Pete's side of the bed. Then came an ear-splitting clack, as a window shutter flew open and hit the wall of the terrace, forcing her awake.

For fuck's sake!

She checked the time, eight o'clock, and could see enough of Peter to know he was already frying his flesh.

He's going to look like a six foot turd by the time we go home.

She pulled the sheet over her head and tried to go back to sleep, but shortly thereafter her mobile rang. Bleary eyed, she took the call. It was her corporate finance colleague, Pierre Dubois.

'Tanya, I am sorry to disturb you,' he said, in his thick French accent, 'but Banque Fouverie is ready to move. They want all bids in by noon, decision to be announced by five this evening, and Bruce wants us to win the deal.'

'Any change to the structure or size?' she asked.

'No. It's still a plain vanilla ten year, and one billion euros.' He meant Banque Fouverie wanted to borrow one billion euros at a fixed rate of interest for ten years.

'OK, give me about an hour and I'll call you back.'
She rang off, and rushed onto the terrace where Peter,
one leg either side of a lounger, his modesty covered by
a thong, was sitting up playing a game on his mobile
phone.

'Pete, you need to lose yourself for a couple of
hours, I'm afraid,' she said, tying a knot in her wrap.
'I've got to bid on a deal.'

He looked at her, disgruntled. 'I don't believe this.
You were on the phone most of yesterday, and you're
supposed to be on holiday.'

'I know, and I'm sorry,' she said, baring her palms,
'but without Steve to fall back on — he had quit the day
before her holiday — I've got no choice. I'll be as quick
as I can. Why don't you go to the beach with Alison and
the boys?' She paused. 'Oh, but I'm going to need your
mobile.'

'I can't go out without me phone.'

'Pete, don't be awkward. It's only for an hour.'

'No. I'll stay here,' he said sulkily.

'Suit yourself, but I still need your phone.' She
went to take it from his hands.

'Fuck off. You give out the number, and I'll give it
to you if anyone rings.'

Cursing, she walked back into the apartment.

About half an hour later, Peter came in and gave her
his phone.

It was Nate, and he asked Tanya what terms she
planned to propose. When she told him he noisily
sucked breath.

'Whoa, that's way too expensive. You won't even
be able to syndicate the deal on those terms.'

'With respect, Nate, I know what I'm doing. No

113

competitor is going to turn us down for a few basis points, and risk offending Banque Fouverie. It's a solid bank, a straightforward structure, and after the battering financials have taken, I think the sector is due for an upturn. I've had good feedback from Scott and Rich, the street is stupidly short in bank names, and the new issue calendar is thin. Trust me, by next week the bond is going to look cheap as chips.'

'Your call, Tanya, but Bruce will go ape if we end up long up the ying yang of the damn things, and we can't get rid of them.'

She breathed heavily down the phone. 'I know what I'm doing. Look, I have to go. Time's running out.'

'Prick,' she said, when she cut off, 'useless, nosey prick.'

Peter held out his hand.

'For fuck's sake, Pete. Andy and Freddie are going to be calling back on my phone, and I have to ring New York.'

'Don't get shirty with me, just because he got up your nose.'

She bit her lip. 'Sorry. Can I please use your phone? I promise I won't be long.'

'That's better,' he said, and returned to the terrace.

She had just finished a call to her colleague, Susannah Cordarosa, a corporate bond trader in New York, when Bruce rang to stress the importance of winning the mandate. She welcomed the call in light of Nate's comments.

'Don't worry, Bruce, everything's under control. I don't want to count chickens, but I'm confident we'll get this one.'

'OK, Kiddo. I'll leave it in your capable hands.'

When she gave Pierre her terms, he was almost gurgling with excitement.

'They said they will inform us of their decision by six o'clock, your time,' he said. 'I will call you as soon as I hear.'

'I shall be at dinner by then, Pierre. I'll choose a restaurant that sells decent champagne.'

He laughed and rang off, and Tanya sat on the bed, the sun streaming in, wallowing in the glow that accompanied big risky deals, that thrilling blend of anticipation and danger.

'Yes!' she said, with a single clap of her hands, and then checked the closet for what to wear for dinner. Having decided on a clingy white strapless dress, and white sandals with cork heels, she painted her toenails, and then joined Peter for a spot of sunbathing.

Peter looked at Alison and sighed.

'Come on, Sweetheart, eat your dinner,' Alison said to Jamie. 'Mummy won't be long.'

'Harry, no,' Peter said, 'mummy's on the phone.'

Tanya grabbed her bag and felt blindly in it for her cigarettes, snorting loudly upon hearing that BBI, short for Bay Brothers International, had got the mandate.

'Oh, Pierre, that's a brown envelope stitch-up, if ever I saw one.'

Peter flapped a hand. 'Tanya! Keep it down.'

'Shush, Mummy,' Jamie said, holding his index finger to his lips.

She waved the family to carry on and zigzagged her way out of the busy restaurant, too absorbed in what Pierre was saying to care about the frowns of tray-laden staff. And after a number of al fresco diners tutted on account of her pacing up and down outside the restaurant, ranting down the phone, she crossed the road onto the promenade, and perched on a tubular railing.

'...But Pierre, my bid was breathtakingly tight in the first place,' she said, head bowed, her curls almost touching the pavement, 'and you have to admit that BBI not just proposing terms identical to mine, but a half a basis point better does look pretty fucking dodgy.'

'Stranger things have happened, Tanya. Our bid simply wasn't the best. They were genuinely sad we didn't win the mandate.'

'Yes, but they're going to give that impression, aren't they? Let's be honest, they wouldn't be the first borrower to disclose the winning bid to a favoured competitor.'

'These are trustworthy people, Tanya. I can assure you they do not favour BBI. They wanted us to win the deal.'

She sighed heavily. 'How badly did Bruce take it?'

'I think you should call him,' he said, ominously.

Her stomach sunk. 'I will. Sorry for jumping down your throat, Pierre. It wasn't personal. You worked bloody hard on those guys, and you deserved that mandate.'

'We both deserved it, Tanya, but there will be other opportunities.'

She ended the call, and teeth clenched, rang Bruce. Lavinia, his p.a., picked up, and said he was on the phone and would have to call her back.

She smoked a cigarette while waiting, the irony of her visit to Belgium with Pierre to pitch for the deal on the day Nate bought NCA, not lost on her.

What an expensive trip that turned out to be.

She called Bruce again. Lavinia said he was now in a meeting, so she made her way back to the restaurant.

Meanwhile, Nate stood in Bruce's office, rubbing the back of his neck.

'...I admit, Bruce, that initially I thought Tanya's terms were on the tight side, but once I'd analysed the comparables and checked the new issue calendar...' He opened his hands. 'What can I say? It was pretty damn obvious our bid should have been swaps less six, govvies plus fourteen. Financials have taken one hell of a beating, and not many companies want to print at these levels.' He shook his head. 'If only she had listened to me, but she can be real stubborn can that one. I-know-what-I'm-doing, she said, so I stayed out of it.'

Bruce nodded sympathetically.

'I'm real pissed with myself I didn't come and tell you this earlier,' he continued, 'but I'm trying to work with Tanya, not against her.'

'You did good, Nate. I'm furious we lost the goddamn deal, but it wasn't your fault.'

'Don't let me off lightly, Bruce, I played my part. As Tanya's junior I was more concerned about not treading on her toes, you know how she is with me, when I ought to have been thinking of KS.' He blew his cheeks out and heaved a sigh. 'We live and learn, I guess.' He paused. 'Can I buy you a beer? You look like you could do with one?'

'You sure can,' Bruce said. 'It's been a long day.' He stood and put on his jacket. 'I'm in New York next week. I'll have a word with Dale, see what we can do to change the pecking order around.'

Nate grimaced. 'Hey, I don't want to cause bad

feeling, Bruce. I can live with the status quo. Tanya's been here a long time, and she's earned her stripes.'

Smiling, he gave Nate a pat on the back. 'C'mon, let's go and get that beer.'

'Cuddle, Mummy, cuddle,' Harry bleated as Tanya sat down.

She took him from Peter's arms.

Jamie promptly moved his chair next to hers. 'Shall I feed you, Mummy?' he said, picking up her fork and prodding a cold scallop.

'No, it's OK, Sweetheart. Mummy's not that hungry now.'

'You didn't get the business, then?' Peter said.

She shook her head. 'No. And you're right, Pete, we're on holiday, so aside from Bruce, I'm going to tell anyone else who rings to bugger off. I've had enough.' She drank some wine. 'Come on, let's pay the bill, and all go to the beach for drinks.'

'Whoopee,' Jamie cried.

But, given her debts and the fragile state of her industry, Tanya knew she was in no position to tell anyone to bugger off, and as the evening wore on her resentment toward Peter grew. And after Alison had taken Jamie and Harry back to their apartment, and with Bruce not having called, she picked an argument with him, about money.

'...and the amount you spend on your so called golfing pals is ridiculous. They're just a bunch of parasites.'

'Leave off, will you? Anyway, how can you begrudge me a pint and a game of golf when you're hardly ever around?'

118

'Don't twist it. You know full well I'd like to be around more, but I've got no choice, have I?'

'You're only having a pop at me because you lost the deal.' He paused. 'And what you're forgetting is that if I worked your hours, Jamie and Harry would be like a couple of orphans.'

'Fat fucking chance of that, and it's not as if you take the boys on the golf course with you, is it? They see more of me than they do you.'

'You're a nasty fucking bitch sometimes.'

'That's it, get personal, just because you're losing.'

He stood. 'Fuck you,' he said, and stormed off.

Glad to see the back of him, she turned her chair to face the ocean, and enjoyed the view, surf lapping gently at its edges, a moon that cast a triangular path of silver bubbles to the shore.

Focusing on a yacht twinkling in the distance, she imagined her and Spencer on board it, him shaking a bottle of champagne and showering her with its effervescence, as she stood naked except for a diamond choker, a Captain's hat, and black patent stilettos.

Then reality kicked in and tears rolled down her cheeks, as the stress of both being a working mum and not being at work made for an emotionally toxic trap. She sensed Bruce had expected her to cancel her holiday given Steve's resignation, but she felt that was entirely his fault, and anyway, she wasn't about to let her kids down. Yet now she wished she could explain her pricing rationale face-to-face, so that he could see the agony in her eyes at losing the deal.

Telling him by phone she didn't cut corners when she was on a beach was unlikely to sound convincing, that's if she got a chance to speak to him.

She returned to her apartment feeling fretful and low, and when Peter started groping her, she gave him the literal elbow. After using the loo in the middle of the night, she lay in bed awake, her mobile by her ear, until she knew Bruce would be on his way to the office, when she crept on to the terrace and phoned him. He answered and in an abrupt voice told her to cut to the chase. She apologised for losing the deal and attempted to explain, as quickly as she could, the extent of her due diligence, but about thirty seconds in, he interrupted her.

'Proximity matters, Kiddo. It wasn't a good outcome. The deal's quoted in early trading at issue price plus a quarter.'

Her legs suddenly felt like liquorice sticks, and she grabbed the balcony ledge, and lowered herself onto a cold wrought iron chair wet with dew, soaking her bum through her thin wrap.

Total fees on the transaction were 32 ½ cents which, on top of a price rise of 25 cents, translated into five million seven hundred and fifty thousand euros. Some of KS' competitors as well as investors would have shared in this fortune, but Tanya knew she could have conservatively banked half of it.

'I'll see you on Monday, Bruce,' she said quietly.

CHAPTER NINE

Walking to meet Steve for dinner, Tanya passed hoards of guys, jackets hooked over their shoulders, having a beer in the sunshine. But solemn faces abounded, conversations were quiet, and fewer men than usual cast an admiring glance at her. And she wasn't surprised, because tens of thousands of jobs were now at risk, people in the dark as to whether their employer would land them in the red.

In the space of a couple of weeks, the world of finance had undergone cataclysmic change that had proven the doomsayers right, and brought the banking system to its knees. Years of excess, wherein global banks routinely borrowed as much as forty times their capital, and shifted risky assets off their balance sheets so as to rinse and repeat and scale up their bets, had led to the inevitable: Flimsy economies and false wealth.

America's biggest mortgage underwriters, Fannie Mae and Freddie Mac, were on a respirator, only then courtesy of George Bush, and Lehman Brothers had gone bust, while Merrill had only avoided that fate by selling out to Bank of America at the 11th hour. And AIG insurance, which had provided credit default insurance on securities that were now worthless, and on which they had to pay out, but couldn't, had been taken over by the U.S. government. HBOS had been forced into a shotgun marriage with Lloyds TSB, and Morgan Stanley and Goldman Sachs were fighting for survival.

Losses and write-downs were now being discussed in terms of trillions of dollars.

'...All crimes have their roots in an inability to control one's impulses,' she said to Steve, 'which makes plenty of bankers criminals in my view. And their crimes are all the worse because they knew better and were paid shed-loads to do better. They've used their education to exploit the innocent. So have politicians and regulators.'

Steve nodded. 'What I don't understand is how anyone, let alone the top brass in banking and politics, could expect property prices to only go one way.'

'If you ask me, they didn't. They knew what they were doing. They're just lying now so they can keep their ill gotten gains. Conscience left this poxy business when firms sold out.' She paused. 'And what I don't understand is why Dick Fuld's assets haven't been seized.' This was the Chairman of Lehman Brothers. 'How come he can retire in luxury, while thousands have lost everything?' She snorted. 'I wonder how many duff securities went into his pension pot. I know what I'd do with him: Take all his money, and only give it back if he can prove he was not knowingly reckless, have him questioned by a panel of experts while he's hooked up to a friggin lie detector.'

Steve laughed. 'There's more chance of peeling a fucking snowball than anyone in power doing that.'

'I know, this is such a disgusting business. Talk about crimes against humanity. People will die over this, end up so in debt they'll top themselves.' She swigged some wine, and banged her glass on the table.

'I don't disagree, but there's no point stressing about things you can't control. You sound like you need another holiday.'

'I need another job, Steve, that's what I need. One like you've got, at a hedge fund, where what you see is what you get, where the guys are clever enough not to have to rig the books and lie through their friggin teeth.'

'I'm discreetly asking around. What's happening with Olli Vermallen?'

She shook her head. 'Nothing. I had to cancel the first interview because it fell the week of Charlie's death, then I was away, and now he's away.' She shrugged. 'Anyway, tell me about you. When do you actually start work at Barclay Gray?' He was on gardening leave, sitting out his notice at home.

'Next week, but I've been in a few times for lunch, and I don't want to make you jealous but the dress code is jeans, and they've got a courtyard with a table and chairs and heaters for the couple of guys who smoke.'

'A firm after my own heart. You certainly did the right trade, at the right time.'

He nodded. 'When you see Bruce, tell him thanks. If he'd upped his offer to two million, I might not have gone through with it.'

She did a double take. 'He countered you?'

He looked surprised. 'Yes. I thought he would have told you.'

'Bruce has hardly said one friggin word to me since I got back off holiday.' She told him about the Banque Fouverie deal. '...so how much did he offer you to stay?'

'One and a half million.'

There was no sex for Peter that night, and due to Tanya's tossing and turning, he went and slept in the spare room.

At four thirty a.m. she was in her lounge, punching the air as though giving someone a series of right hooks.

Bruce is not going to treat me like a piece of shit and get away with it. I had enough of that when I was a kid. He can stuff his job.

She recalled the worried faces she'd seen on her way to meet Steve, but her rage was stronger than reason. 'What am I, Boadicea or fucking Barbie?' she said, staring in the mirror above the mantelpiece. 'I deserve a life of dignity not degradation.'

Shaking with fury, she took her fags and lighter from her dressing gown pocket, and lit a cigarette.

Sit down and calm down.

She sat on the sofa.

Suddenly, Daphne's comment – When we love thy neighbour as thyself, guilt doesn't exist – came to mind.

Tanya was growing close to Daphne. About once every ten days, she would stop by her house after work for a quick glass of wine.

She pondered the statement, and while she wasn't sure she grasped its full meaning, she was sure she understood the first bit.

I'm supposed to love thy neighbour AS thyself, not INSTEAD of thyself. Jesus, why didn't I work that out before? For all my bluster, I've let Bruce take the piss out of me, loved him instead of myself.

She showered and dressed with a vengeance, choosing a red suit to match both her mood and her nails, and when ready to leave, shook Peter's shoulder hard to wake him.

'Wh-what, what's up? What's the time?'

'Quarter past five. Call a few estate agents, and arrange for them to value the house.'

He sat up with a start and rubbed his eyes. 'Why? What do you mean? What's going on?'

'Let's just say, I might not have a job when I get home.'

He vaulted out of bed and grabbed his jeans, but she left the room.

'Don't go doing anything stupid,' he shouted. 'I know what you're like.'

She peered up the stairs at him, as she put on her raincoat. 'Just ring the estate agents, OK?'

In three leaps he was standing in front of her. 'Whatever's happened, stay and have a cup of tea, and let's talk about it.'

'Fuck off, and leave me alone.' She opened the street door.

He took hold of her arm. 'Before you go wrecking our lives, think of the boys.'

'I am, and they need a mother who's got self-respect. No amount of money can buy that.' She pulled away, and walked down the path.

'You won't say that when we ain't got any,' he shouted.

Fuck off.

She climbed into Ted's car. 'Step on it please, Ted.'

'I'll get you there in no time at all, my Lovely.'

Seconds later Peter was ringing her mobile. She answered then cut him off, and switched off her phone.

Fuck him. Who's fucking life is this anyway?

'...So, Bruce, here's the deal,' she said, standing to show she meant business. 'I want a guaranteed minimum cash bonus for this year of two million dollars, and fifteen percent of the profit I make on the illiquid book, or I walk.' She shrugged. 'It's entirely up to you.'

Take it or leave it.

He remained seated and poised, as he set about trying to defend his offer to Steve. 'Steve was a special situation, Kiddo. Dale didn't want knowledge about KS' activities being exported to Barclay Gray. I don't have the scoop but there's history between Dale and Hugo Gray. It was out of my hands.'

'That's unfortunate.' *For you and KS.*

He asked her to sit down, which she did, and for about half an hour tried to dissuade her, soft soaping her with such gems as: *You've taken on a managerial role at an inauspicious time, Kiddo, and I'm aware of that, and of your dedication. It has not and will not go unnoticed. I'll personally see to it that your faith and patience is rewarded. You've got a fabulous career ahead of you here. I see you as family, and I know I can speak for Dale when I say that, too. You play a crucial role in the success of this organisation. Take it from me, Kiddo, your star is in the ascendant in this firm. Market conditions are not favourable to any of us right now.*

He didn't, however, put another cent on the table, because he knew she didn't have anywhere else to go. He had asked and she had told the truth. He also droned on about the austere climate and dangers she faced in leaving, which only hardened her resolve.

She stood. 'I sympathise with the firm's problems, Bruce, and I appreciate your concern for my well being, but I know my constitution and what I can and can't live with.' She paused. 'It's up to you. The markets are chaotic, spreads all over the place, and we've about one billion dollars worth of securities on the books that need managing, a responsibility I don't think you can afford to leave to Nate, but as I say, it's entirely your call.'

You're the one that started this, not me, and if you think I'm going to do you any favours, you can fuck off.

Favours were for fools, she decided, and she was done being a fool.

With his charm offensive having failed his smile became a scowl, and she detected anger in his voice when he asked her to wait outside while he rang Dale.

Lavinia made her a cup of coffee and as she sat drinking it, she again reflected on Daphne's statement.

Bruce is good at loving himself, and the likes of Nate, but not me, so all I'm doing is correcting that state of affairs. It's an act of self-love, and a way of helping KS to do the right thing.

She settled for a bonus of $1,250,000 and ten percent of the profit from illiquid trading.

'It wasn't personal, Bruce,' she lied. 'And thanks for fighting for me.'

He clasped his hands behind his head, and leaned back in his chair. 'You put the firm in an impossible bind, Kiddo.'

Good, she thought, quelling her urge to dance around his office.

'But the pressure's on you now,' he added.

'I understand. One last request, if I may.'

'What now?'

'The cut I get from illiquid trading. Can I get it paid separately, I mean into a different account and maybe a different name?' The idea just popped into her head as a way for her to give money to her mum without Peter finding out.

'As long as it's kosher with the British tax authorities, it can be paid to anyone you want. Sort it out with HR. And make sure you keep this quiet.'

On leaving Bruce's office she phoned Spencer, but on no pick up remembered he was at a conference with Rich Hillbrand, which she thought was maybe for the best. Even so, she left a message asking him to call her. She then sent a text to Peter, to say she was OK and had calmed down, which is all she felt he deserved to know for now.

Returning to her desk she felt torn about her triumph, hating she had been forced into forcing KS to play fair, and aware Bruce would never see her in the same light again.

So I'll have to watch my back, so what? What can he do that he's not already done?

Just then Nate arrived, and she beamed him a smile.

You're not the only one with a secret now, she thought, for he never did tell her what he got as a bonus.

Nearing ten o'clock that night
'It's alright, mate,' the cabbie said with alarm. 'I'm just helping her to the door.'

Peter watched, seething, from the porch as Tanya teetered up the path, with her right arm around the cab driver's shoulder, his left around her waist.

Inside her house, she sat on the stairs and gripped the banister as she told Peter her good news. '…I jusht had a few glasses to shelebrate, that's all.' Her head fell forward.

'A few glasses, a few fucking bottles, more like. Look at the fucking state of you.'

She slowly raised her head. 'Don't nag me, Pete. You should be happy for me, happy for us, happy for yourself. I promish you I'm not drunk, jush tired.'

'Yeah, right. Pull the other fucking one. I bet

you've been out on the piss all day, haven't you?'
She hiccoughed. 'We're not all like you.'
'You're a nasty fucking bitch sometimes.'
She hiccoughed again. 'Jush shometimes? I'm flattered, hic. I thought it was, hic, all the time.' Her head fell forward again.

Ponce. What does he care?

'Some self-respecting mother you are. If the kids saw you now they'd be disgusted.' He went into the lounge and slammed the door.

She took to her feet with the grace of a new born giraffe, and wobbled up the stairs and into the spare room, where she collapsed, fully clothed, onto the bed.

Where had she been? On her own mostly. After a quick drink with TJ, she had roamed the City waiting for Spencer to call to say he could meet her. He said he would try his utmost, but that it might be hard for him to slip away. As the conference he was attending was in a London hotel, she held out hope, although he had said Rich was shadowing him the whole time.

Her meanderings had ended on a bench outside the Royal Exchange where, the paper sellers gone, the rush hour march of the suit brigade over, she had sat gazing at the sky, a glorious raspberry ripple mix, and eaten a big bag of jelly babies she had bought from M & S. That was dinner. Thereafter, she had gone to an elite bar in the exchange, and bought a bottle of Bollinger, asking for two glasses. Half an hour later she got a text from Spencer to say he couldn't make it. But only when her waiter appeared to have acquired a twin, by which time her bottle was close to empty, had she called for the bill, because she was having a good time, a much better time than she felt she would have with Peter.

En route to work the next morning, Tanya had Ted stop at a greasy spoon on a shabby parade in Mile End, an unbecoming stretch of steel shutters, faded signage, littered forecourts, and pigeons fighting over scraps.

'What's it going to be, my Lovely?'

'A fried egg sandwich, white bread, brown sauce, please, Ted, and a cup of very milky tea, three sugars.'

'Coming up, my Lovely.'

While Ted got her order, from the luxury of his jag, she looked at the caff – with a linoleum floor, Formica tables, and plastic sauce bottles, it was hardly a cafe – and studied its hardy patrons, the real McCoy of market traders, munching their breakfast as they read tabloids.

There but for the grace of God, she thought, aware she could so easily have ended up with a money belt around her waist, tacking up wares on a stall, forced to smile come rain or shine.

Respect your luck.

Mid morning, she summoned Fiona to her office.

'Tell me, Fi, what is it you want out of life?'

'I'd like to get on, if that's what you're asking.'

'But what does that mean? Getting married, having kids, buying your own place? Your parents live in a council house, don't they?'

'Yes, but they're buying it,' Fiona said defensively.

'Is that your dream?'

'No. I want to own a pub, actually. I still work in one at weekends.'

Tanya leaned back in her chair. 'What's the score with you and Nate? Has he got into your knickers yet?'

'No,' she said, looking most put out.

'Good, keep it that way, because rules aside – KS prohibited relationships between colleagues where a conflict of interest could arise – if you gave in to him, he'd find a way to get rid of you.'

Fi looked hurt.

'Don't misunderstand, Fi, I'm not saying you're not good enough for him, far from it, but his interest in you is nothing more than infatuation.'

'It's not like that, Tanya.'

'You can't possibly know that. And remember, you're the one taking all the risk, not him. He's got no downside whatsoever. He can shag you and then toss you aside.'

Fi began pulling at her fingers.

'The suffragettes did a lot for us, Fi. And we owe it to them to make the most of ourselves. I'm just pointing out the risks. I'd hate to see you jobless living in some council flat, while Nate's on a yacht with his latest squeeze.' She paused. 'Now, let me ask you again. What do you want from life?'

'A lot more than I've got,' Fi said.

'Good. What do you think about learning to trade?'

Fiona gawped. 'What me? Trade?'

'Yes. But you'll need to give up the pub job, and forget about Nate, and there'll be no extra pay. Carry on with some secretarial duties, and basically work till your arches drop. But don't waste my time. If you accept, it has to be with all your heart and soul.'

Fiona crossed her arms, her hands tight to her waist. 'Can I think about it overnight?'

Tanya looked at her.

'OK. I'll do it.'

Tanya smacked the edge of her desk with her pen. 'Well done, Fi, well done. That was an excellent decision, the first, I hope, of many.'

Fiona gulped. 'What do I do now?'

'Read, listen, observe, just use your loaf and your common sense. Don't look so scared, Fi. The only thing at risk is—your entire livelihood.' She laughed. 'Come on, let's go and sort you out a desk.'

They went back to the trading floor.

'Fi has just been promoted to junior trader,' Tanya said to Nate, 'haven't you Fi?' She glanced at Fi, who was chewing her nails.

Nate's eyes lit up, and after congratulating Fi, he suggested she sit next to him.

Tanya scotched that idea on the basis she wouldn't be able to see or hear her, but of course she had other concerns. After a group desk chat, Joe offered to move up one and take Charlie's old desk, and let Fi have his desk. That pleased everyone. Fi was happy she didn't have to occupy a deceased person's work station, Nate that she wouldn't be sitting next to Freddie, and Tanya that Fi would get the measure of Joe's experience.

Tanya left them all chatting, and went to the cafeteria for another dose of fatty food, feeling proud of her decision, and her capacity to take a calculated risk. Of the traders she had interviewed in the previous weeks not one represented an adequate replacement for Charlie, let alone Steve. In her view they were all overpriced gob-offs, whereas Fi was cheap, honest, hardworking, and a known quantity.

*

'Time to get up Mummy, time to get up,' Jamie squealed, as he and Harry scrambled under the duvet, and started tickling Tanya.

'Oh, please don't do that, Darlings. Mummy's sleeping,' she said, coiling the duvet around her.

'Daddy said to do it,' Jamie said, giggling. 'He said it's time for you lazy bones to get up now.'

Jamie then started singing. 'Mummy's got no clothes on, mummy's got no clothes on.'

Tanya reached for her mobile, to check the time, nine fifteen. 'OK, OK, go and tell daddy you both did an excellent job at waking me. Now scoot you little monkeys, and Jamie, make sure you hold Harry's hand as you go down the stairs.'

'I will, Mummy.' Jamie propelled himself off the bed with a bounce on his bottom and turned to tend to Harry. 'Come to Jamie,' he cooed, stretching his arms to help his baby brother down.

A few minutes later Tanya stood in her kitchen, in a state of shock, the air thick with the odour of burnt food, a smoke layer, resembling fuzz in the morning sunshine, lingering below the ceiling. She marched to the patio door, unlocked it and slid it back to its limit.

A plate with ketchup smears, black pudding skins and a knife and fork lying anyhow was balanced on the drainer on top of two mugs, and a wooden spoon coated in baked beans, and a plastic jug were floating in the sink within a perimeter of scum. The grill pan, hosting a snarled piece of bacon, was on the breakfast bar, alongside a loaf of bread, the wrapper open, the remaining slices collapsed toward the air. And beside the pan was a margarine tub, contents finished, which had become home to some used tea bags, while on the hob was half a squashed tomato, a juice trail indicating a rescue attempt.

You disgusting pig.

She barged into the adjoining sitting room, where she found the curtains closed and Peter sitting, arms folded, in an unflatteringly tight pair of track suit bottoms, watching the sports channel, a tea towel on his lap, tabloid at his side, his bare feet resting on a coffee table, either side of a bowl of soggy cornflakes. Both boys were still in their pyjamas, and the seat of Harry's sagged with the weight of his unchanged nappy.

He looked at her fleetingly. 'Alright?'

Jamie was sitting beside his dad, slippers off, arms folded, while Harry was wandering around whimpering and pulling at his bottom.

She stood in front of the T.V. 'You disgusting pig,' she said in a quiet monotone, repressing her temper for her boys' sake.

He flapped his right hand. 'I'll clean up when this is finished, move out of the way.'

Fuck off, she thought, not budging.

'Come on, Tanya. I let you have a lie-in, didn't I?'

Only because you got your leg over.

'It's no wonder our au pairs leave. Cleaning up after you must make them vomit.' Leila, a sweet Spanish girl, their fifth au pair, had left after three months.

Harry hugged Tanya's leg, and she gathered him in her arms. 'You couldn't even be bothered to change his nappy, could you?'

Peter pulled a face. 'He's alright. He's been fed.'

She went to the window and drew the curtains, the swish sound as they retreated on their runners some compensation for how she was feeling.

'For effing sake,' Peter growled, 'I can't see a ruddy thing with that sun in my eyes.' He shot her an angry look. 'Weekends are for relaxing, you know.'

134

Every day of the week for you is like a weekend.
She made for the door and on her way out popped Harry in the crook of her arm, bent down and flicked the off button on the plug socket controlling the television.
'You bitch!' Peter leapt from the sofa, knocking the cereal bowl flying.
After she had changed Harry's nappy, he rejoined the men, and Tanya made herself a mug of milky sweet tea and drank it on the patio, sitting where she had a clear view of her willow tree, and could smell the scent of roses.
How can I love myself if I put up with this shit?
She spent an hour cleaning up, and executed the task as noisily as possible, slamming cupboard doors and banging pots together, and threw what was now, thanks to Peter, a badly charred frying pan onto the floor, not caring if she cracked the limestone (she didn't) before consigning it to the bin.
Apart from necessary chats about the boys, Tanya didn't speak to Peter for the rest of the weekend, and in bed on Sunday night, when he made a play for her pubic region, she pulled away, wrapped herself tight inside her bit of the duvet, and told him to fuck off.
'Don't get too cocky,' he retorted. 'You've still got barmy Barbara's genes.'
Too hurt to speak, she took to the spare room.

CHAPTER TEN

'Bruce, for you, on line two,' Joe said to Tanya.

Hmmm, it's early for him to be calling.

'Hi Bruce,' she said. 'Did you have a good weekend?'

'I got through it, Kiddo. I also got round to reading that report of yours.'

At last. Now he's paying me what I'm worth, he's taking me seriously.

'Get fed up with Bloomberg and Reuters did you?' She immediately regretted joking at her own expense. 'Anyway, you were saying, Bruce.'

'You've got some interesting ideas, Kiddo, but,' he paused, and she felt a sense of alarm. 'Why don't you swing by my office?'

'Now, or after the morning meeting?'

'Let's do it now.'

'OK, see you anon.'

She made haste feeling sick, aware something had to be up for him to want to see her right away, but she entered his office head up, shoulders back, and looking cheerful.

He smiled at her, and told her to take a seat.

'Thanks,' she said, and sat down.

'As I said, Kiddo, you've got some interesting ideas—but so has Nate.'

'What do you mean?'

He waved a few stapled sheets of A4 paper at her. 'Nate has a similar vision.'

'May I take a look?'

'Sure.' He gave her the document, which consisted of three bullet-pointed pages.

The first thing she noticed was that Nate's synopsis of a report was simply dated June, 2008, whereas hers was dated 10th June, 2008. And it seemed obvious to her as she read it that the ideas were hers, just summarised using fancier language. There was no mention of illiquid securities, about which Nate knew next to nothing, but all her other proposals, such as to expand KS' sterling activities, improve the firm's trading capabilities in the debt of smaller companies, and fine-tune the grading of clients, were included.

He's stolen my ideas and plagiarised my work, and the only way he could have managed that is if... No, she wouldn't have done. Or would she?

'I'm surprised by the similarities,' she said.

Bruce shrugged. 'Why? It's not unusual for two dedicated professionals to identify obvious areas of opportunity.' He paused. 'Anyhow, since you're both singing from the same hymn sheet, Dale and I feel you and Nate should be co-heads, and get to work to make this happen together. Do you have a problem with that?'

So that's what this is about, an excuse to promote the pillock. And a way for Bruce to get his own back.

She shook her head. 'Not at all, whatever's best for KS.'

'That's the spirit, Kiddo. It's time to draw a line in the sand. You and Nate are both working for the same firm.'

She smiled sweetly and left, but her face was like cracked ice when she got back to the trading floor.

'In my office, now!' she barked at Fiona.

Tanya sat impassively gripping her jaw, while Fiona

stood crying. '…I swear on my mother's life I never showed it to him.'

'In that case you must have left it lying around.'

'I'm sure I didn't. I was really careful with it.'

'Well how the fuck do you think he got hold of it?'

'I don't know, I really don't. I-I…' She wiped her nose with the cuff of her blouse.

'I take it you've never given him the password for your computer.'

'No, absolutely not.'

'Is it one that's easy to guess?'

'No.'

'When was the last time you changed it?'

Fiona didn't answer.

Tanya shook her head. 'Change it today, and make sure you change it on a weekly basis from now on.'

'OK.'

'Has he ever been near you when you've logged on?'

'I'm not sure.'

'That was a stupid question, because he must have been.' She heaved a sigh. 'Just go, and leave me alone.'

Fiona left.

I can just see it, him massaging Fi's shoulders early in the morning while she's logging on. Stupid cow.

Andy knocked, and she motioned him in.

'You won't believe what's happened, Andy,' she blurted. 'Nate's been promoted to my equal. He and I are now co-heads—friggin co-heads,' she threw her hands up. 'The slimy git also plagiarised my report, and Bruce, being the coward that he is, cited that as the basis for promoting the wanker.'

'Oh Darlin, that's terrible.'

She shrugged. 'Such is life, eh? It's who you know, not what you know.'

At least I'm getting paid for the abuse this place dishes up.

'Anyway,' she said, 'what's up?'

'This is not going to make your day any better, I'm afraid,' he said, and gave her the current edition of *Financial Insider*, a weekly rag.

Her mouth fell open as she read.

The Wrong Pryce

I hear Kohen Stanzinger's, Tanya Pryce, who was recently promoted to head of credit trading, was extremely wide of the mark in her pricing of the Banque Fouverie deal. (The mandate was awarded to BBI). The bond is now 101 bid. Ouch! In March, rumours were rife that Ms Pryce was wrong footed by a hedge fund, leaving KS nursing a loss of $5 million. OUCH! Knives are being sharpened as I write and there's no shortage of willing Mack's. Is this her Peter's pence? Are the doubting Thomas's who said she was only ever a mascot for feminists, about to be proved right? I hope not. Bruce Ghoff deserves better. You can tell an Essex girl anywhere, but you can't tell her much, not even how to eat asparagus! Psst: People tend not to eat the ends, Ms Pryce.'

Ludo Quagg.

'What a bastard,' she said, her voice faltering, pained, incredulous.

With his silly cravats and chauffer driven turquoise

Bentley, Ludo Quagg would be the markets' clown were it not for his pen and maverick attitude, a combination that saw him well taken care of by some of the biggest egos in the business. He was renowned for lumbering around London in his monstrosity of a car, alighting at the offices of mega-league investment banks, and the priciest restaurants. But Tanya neither liked nor disliked him, and they had always been polite to each other at industry gatherings.

Think of the money, she said to herself, but right then all she could think about was her peers speculating about her ability, and laughing about her heathen eating habits.

'Are you OK, Darlin?' Andy said. 'You look pale. Come and sit on the sofa.'

She did and as she sunk into the soft leather, anxiety spread through her like an ink spill on blotting paper.

'I need water, Andy,' she whispered.

He went to get some and by the time he returned, she was in the throes of a panic attack, soaked in sweat, her heart pounding, her mouth bone dry, and her fingers and toes full of pins and needles.

'Th-thanks' she stammered, shakily taking the plastic cup from him. He used his hand to steady hers, while she drank.

She began to calm down.

'Phew,' she said, fanning her face. 'That's better.'

Andy sighed heavily. 'I feel like bopping Quagg on the nose.'

I feel like murdering the cunt. That's what his name should be – Ludo Cunt.

'What do I do, Andy? I can't let him get away with it, can I?'

'It's up to you, but I wouldn't take him on. Quagg loves a spat.'

'But I've got to. A person's reputation is like a balloon, one prick and it's gone. I've got to fight.'

Freddie popped his head inside the door. 'The morning meeting starts in five minutes.'

Tanya glared at him. 'In future, knock. Go ahead without me. Tell Nate to run it.'

'OK, sorry, Tanya. Nate isn't in yet.'

Of course, it's Monday.

'Then ask Joe to run it.'

'Is there anything you want Joe to say on your behalf?'

'No!' She flicked her hand. 'Just disappear, OK?'

He hopped it.

'If you need to go to the meeting, Andy, go ahead. I'll be fine.'

'It's OK, Darlin, my guys know our priorities. I'll sit with you for a bit.'

'Thanks.' She sighed heavily. 'What distresses me most is that the market will directly link Nate's promotion with Quagg's article.'

'Some people might, but so what? Within a few weeks the story will be old hat.'

'Not to me it won't.'

At least now I'm getting paid a good whack.

That she was being remunerated fairly made Nate's promotion just about bearable, but Quagg was a different matter. His antics could put the kibosh on Olli Vermallen hiring her, and who knows how many others.

She pulled at her lip. 'I've got no choice, Andy, but to sue Quagg for libel.'

'Why give him the satisfaction of going to so much

trouble? OK, so the market might dine out on the story for a bit, but it will blow over.'

'It won't ever go away for me, though. All someone has to do is put my friggin name in Google and the article will appear. I'll be the object of gossip and derision forever more. Quagg's got to pay for that. If I had crossed him, fair enough, but I haven't.'

'Before you do anything, Darlin, make sure you take proper advice, and before you do that, talk to Bruce. I imagine he'll be as angry as you, because what Quagg's written makes KS look stupid.'

'You're right.' She sprang to her feet. 'I'll go and see him now.'

Andy wished her good luck.

Bruce's door was closed, and Lavinia innocently told Tanya he was in a meeting with Nate, whereupon Tanya knocked once on Bruce's office door and entered. To find Nate sat in the chair she had occupied less than an hour earlier, looking resplendent in a charcoal suit, white collared pink shirt, and coordinating Hermès tie.

A copy of *Financial Insider* lay open on Bruce's desk, and she instinctively felt Nate was Quagg's mole.

Nate smiled at her. 'Morning, Tanya,' he said, absently scratching the back of his neck, revealing a diamond encrusted cufflink.

'Morning.'

'We've been discussing the article, Kiddo.'

'I can see that,' she said, and turned to Nate.

'Did you feed the story to Quagg?'

He looked, with shock, at Bruce, who looked objectionably at her. 'Nate is goddamn furious about the article, Tanya.'

Guilty conscience, that's why.

Nate nodded. 'My suggestion is that we seek an apology, and insist that it appears on the front page of next week's edition.'

'I agree,' Bruce said. 'I'll call Rolf Peterson – the editor of *FI* – this morning.'

What am I, an ornament?

She took a deep breath. 'With respect, Bruce, it's not your reputation on the line.' She looked at Nate with contempt. 'Or yours.'

She looked back at Bruce. 'I'm sorry, Bruce, but an apology is not going to appease me. I'm going to seek advice, with a view to suing the scum bag for libel.'

Bruce and Nate exchanged sympathetic looks of despair.

So much for hoping Bruce would be an ally.

'Tanya,' Bruce said, 'we know Quagg's a parasite, no question, but legal action... C'mon, Kiddo, lawyers and all that prosecution-defence shit is messy. We don't have the manpower for you to be tied up in some court house.'

'Bruce's right,' Nate said. 'The desk needs you. We can't afford for you to become embroiled in a lawsuit.'

If Bruce had haemorrhoids, he'd be the cream.

She looked at Bruce. 'Would you overlook Quagg assassinating your character?'

Bruce scoffed. 'You're a big girl, Tanya. Quagg's joshing, having a bit of fun. These are miserable times. He's trying to raise a laugh. I hold with you that the article is in bad taste, but character assassination? I think that's a slight exaggeration.'

'Why devote time to discussing it then?'

He sighed. 'Quagg's clearly breached boundaries of

taste, for which he deserves, without question, a severe rap on the knuckles—but not a lawsuit, Kiddo. This is a tough business. It's not good to get emotional.'

She looked out of the window.

Stay calm and think of the money.

'If I tell Dale you're in a legal fight with Quagg,' he added, 'he'll have a seizure.'

In other words, I'm on my own.

She felt devastated at being hung out to dry, but at the same time stupid for expecting otherwise.

She turned to Nate. 'You avoided answering my question,' she said quietly.

He ran a bronzed manicured hand through his hair. 'We may have professional differences from time to time, Tanya, but it's an affront to my integrity to hear you question my allegiance to Kohen Stanzinger.'

'Why dance with the alphabet? Why can't you just say *No, I did not feed Quagg the story*?'

'C'mon, Tanya, you guys are co-heads now—in this together. This is not an auspicious start.'

'It's OK, Bruce,' Nate said.

'But why couldn't he have just said no?' she said to Bruce, her voice soft and sad.

'Look, why don't you go and get some fresh air, and have a cigarette?' Nate said.

Suddenly, in her mind's eye, she was screaming and running amok, taking the trio of delft plates displayed on the side cabinet and hurling them across the room. But she stood composed, if shaking inside.

'I don't want a cigarette—and don't you *dare* patronize me.' She held up her copy of *Financial Insider*. 'If you didn't feed this story to Quagg, how do you think he got hold of it?'

'I've no idea, but it's no secret the firm got caught out with the Belgian deal, and Krevamar could have told him about NCA.'

'Except hedge funds don't cavort with the Press, and Krevamar is especially secretive.'

'These things get out, Kiddo,' Bruce said.

'Try not to take this the wrong way, Tanya,' Nate said, 'but who has seen you eat asparagus?' I mean, do you eat it a lot, or is it a dish you order occasionally?'

It took all her self-control not to revert to her roots and punch Nate in the face. The question alone was humiliating enough, but she had also detected a fleeting warble in his voice. It was barely audible and only lasted a second or so but she had heard it. And Bruce's bald head was bowed, which left her mortified he could be hiding a snigger.

'I'm going to consult a lawyer, Bruce.'

'I can't stop you, but I would strongly advise you against taking a legalistic stance. Keep me informed. And don't lose sight of the bigger picture, either. These are challenging times, and you have serious professional responsibilities.'

She left without saying goodbye, and walked back to the floor wringing her copy of *FI* until it looked like a piece of rope.

She felt like buying herself a straight jacket and asking men in white coats to take her away.

Maybe what's known as madness is actually sanity.

Conscious of a gossipy undercurrent the moment she entered the trading floor, she strode through it with a fierce fuck-you-all look on her face, resolving not to let her feelings show.

But she ached to hear a friendly voice, and wished

she could call Spencer, but he was in New York where it was the middle of the night, and while Daphne crossed her mind, her hearing wasn't up to much. She rang TJ, but he said he would have to call her back. About to try Steve, Rich Hillbrand appeared at her side.

'I can hide, Tanya, I'm a salesman, but as a trader you can't, and as a cocky cockney, albeit a talented and loveable one, you're a tall poppy. A prime target for the Quagg's of this world. But, what goes around comes around.'

His charitable words brought a lump to her throat although she had never considered herself a tall poppy or a prime target.

'What would you do about it, Rich, if you were me?'

'Maintain a dignified silence, and keep Quagg guessing.'

'Thanks. I'll give that some thought.'

Joe came to cheer her up next. 'I've always eaten all my asparagus,' he said, with a chuckle.

She gave him a closed lip smile, and could feel herself blushing.

'Everyone has an Achilles heel, even Quagg,' he continued. 'I'll see if I can find out what it is. Then we can retaliate, and get him where it fucking hurts.'

She sighed. 'Who do you think fed him the story?'

'It could have been any number of people.'

'Nate?'

'Why would he do that? What's he got to gain from pissing all over KS at a time like this?'

'My job. Have you seen the memo?'

An email announcing that Nate was now co-head of the desk had already been circulated.

'Yep, and you've been shafted, but I still don't think he had anything to do with what Quagg wrote, because Quagg's facts are way off.'

Her emotions having calmed down, Tanya agreed, and regretted accusing Nate.

'Tanya, Ludo Quagg is on line three for you,' Freddie called out.

'Do you want me to take the call,' Joe said, 'and tell him to fuck off?'

'No, it's OK, I can handle it.'

She took a deep breath. 'Tanya Pryce,' she said sharply.

'Thank you for picking me up, Tanya, thank you. There was an editorial screw up. What appeared was a draft. The idiot hack responsible has been severely reprimanded, and I shall of course issue an apology. It is not often I feel remorse, but I certainly do today.'

Her muscles relaxed. 'It was an extremely cheap shot at my personal expense.'

'I realise that,' he said, 'and I am full of contrition.'

'You should be, because what you wrote wasn't true. You were way off about the hedge fund loss, and to say we missed the Belgium deal by a mile was a huge exaggeration.'

'I am more than happy to clarify if you give me the facts. I can do that discreetly, with no mention of you or KS.'

'What, and give you a story on a plate for next week, too? Thanks, but I'll pass. What are you going to write in your apology?'

He let out a little cough. 'If you would grant me the honour of having lunch or dinner with me, we could thrash something out together. It's more than I deserve,

I know, and I shall understand if you decline, although from a totally selfish standpoint, I would like the opportunity to apologise in person.' He paused. 'I don't have any commitment I can't break. I'll juggle my diary to suit you.'

Keep your enemies close.

'OK, let's do lunch tomorrow.'

'Thank you, Tanya, thank you. I shall book The Dam Club, for 12.15, if that's OK?'

'That's fine.'

CHAPTER ELEVEN

In a grey linen suit and lilac shirt, Ludo didn't look the spectacle Tanya expected, but it was august and hot, not the sort of weather for a cravat.

'Hi Ludo,' she said, her voice low, her smile economical.

He kissed her on each cheek, and told her she looked wonderful, which she didn't believe because she'd barely slept and felt dreadful.

They sat in a pair of worn Victorian armchairs, and when Tanya picked up her glass of champagne, Ludo raised his glass, as if expecting her to join him in a toast.

Piss off.

She took a sip. 'Who fed you the story, Ludo?'

He seemed not to hear her. 'Thank you for coming, Tanya. I know your time is precious.'

She raised her eyebrows at him, and reached for a crisp.

'I sincerely apologise, Tanya. Sometimes I get rather too zealous in my efforts to amuse. This time I overstepped the mark, as your fans in the market have been quick to point out. You're a highly respected lady.'

She asked who had called and he reeled off a list of names, including TJ's.

'...your new American boss, Nate Waltham, called too. Spitting angry he was. Very aggressive man. He certainly banged me to rights.'

She wolfed down some champagne. 'His surname is Walthak, not Waltham, and he is *not* my boss. We run credit trading jointly. Did he say he was my boss?'

Ludo almost spat out his drink in his haste to correct himself. 'My mistake, my mistake, Tanya, I was thinking of Bruce Ghoff when I said that.'

Mistake perhaps, but it had a horrible effect on Tanya's stomach.

'Yes, I remember now,' he added, 'your new chappy said you and he were partners in crime.' He paused. 'When did that happen?'

'Ludo, I'm not here to feed you information. Now, who was your source?'

'You know I can't possibly tell you that Tanya. What I can tell you is that it was the result of snippets from a variety of sources, which is the case with so much of what I write. I can't even be sure I remember.' He laughed. 'My address book is longer than the Thames, and I constantly forget who told me what.'

Liar.

She asked what he had in mind in terms of an apology, and he produced a piece of paper from the inside pocket of his jacket. 'It's only a draft,' he said, handing it to her.

I deeply regret my disparaging remarks [Issue 863] about Kohen Stanzinger's, Tanya Pryce, to whom I have apologised. On behalf of Financial Insider I would like to take this opportunity to apologise publicly to Kohen Stanzinger, in particular to Bruce Ghoff, and again to the delectable Ms Pryce for any injury caused to her feelings.

Distinctly underwhelmed, she gave it back to him.

'I think I ought to seek advice, because that doesn't do anything to restore my reputation, whereas what you wrote could have serious long term consequences. The industry could not be in a worse state. Who knows what's going happen to KS. And before you ask, I know nothing, but if Lehman can fail...'

His hair couldn't turn white, what little he had was already white, but he looked worried. 'Tanya, I want to sort this out amicably. I am sure I can come up with something that is to your satisfaction. I want you to be happy with what I write, really I do. However, I can't simply write *sorry, I made it all up,* because we both know that's not true. I mean,' he turned his right palm upward, 'if it wasn't you personally who lost out to the hedge fund, and you weren't responsible for the Banque Fouverie bid, why not let me set the record straight?'

She shook her head. Even if she hadn't lost the Belgian deal, she wouldn't dream of airing KS' dirty linen in the gossip leaves of *Financial Insider.*

'I'm not here to correct your wildly inaccurate stories, Ludo, but to give you the chance to correct your assassination of my character.'

'OK, OK, I have an idea, Tanya. You draft the apology. Write whatever you want, up to one hundred words. Get it to me by tomorrow morning, so we can iron out any crimps, and I'll make sure it goes in this week's edition. I can't be fairer than that, now can I?'

She leaned back in her chair and folded her arms as she considered his offer, which came as a welcome surprise. 'You're saying you'll print whatever I write?'

'Within reason, Tanya, within reason. It can't be defamatory.'

'I know that, I'm not stupid, Ludo.'

'Quite, quite.'

'OK,' she said.

He smiled and held out his hand, which she shook half-heartedly.

Over fish cakes and salad, he surprised her again.

'I could also demonstrate my remorse and make amends in other ways, Tanya, if you would let me.'

What's the snake got up his sleeve now?

'What do you mean?'

'Well, I know you're under enormous pressure, what with Steve Cranthorp's sudden departure and the tragic death of Charlie Pedroy,' he said, liberally buttering a thick cube of bread. 'Let me head hunt their replacements.' He smiled at her. 'My normal search fee, at thirty percent, is already highly competitive, but as a gesture of my not inconsiderable contrition, I will reduce that to twenty five percent. I'm on first name terms with the best money makers around. I can save you a lot of time and trouble.'

So that's why he wanted lunch.

'Money makers or gamblers?'

'Money makers, Tanya, money makers.'

'Why should I pass business your way?'

'Because I can have four of the best traders in London lined up for you to interview by Friday.'

She narrowed her eyes at him. 'Isn't it a conflict of interest writing in the industry's leading rag, and acting as a head hunter for the very people you write about?'

'You know as well as I do, Tanya, there are plenty of traders with stakes in head hunting firms, or spouses who are head hunters. They, more than me, have access to information they could misappropriate.' He topped up his glass. She declined a refill. 'It's the same with trading,' he continued. 'A potential conflict of interest arises when a trader has the same view as a client about a security. Who's to know if he puts his interests above those of his client? It's a matter of personal integrity.'

She smiled wryly. 'You've obviously had a lot of practice answering that question.'

He laughed.

Tanya hated the idea of using Ludo's services but she did need an experienced trader, and the search firms she'd checked out wanted thirty five percent of a candidate's first year's compensation. Head hunting fees came out of her budget.

'An alliance could be mutually beneficial, Tanya.'

She said she would think about his offer, and prepared to leave.

Ludo walked her to the lobby. 'Remember, Tanya, to make this week's edition, I must have your riposte by tomorrow morning. One hundred words maximum.'

'You'll have it this afternoon. I've got better things to do than spend a day on it. And it will appear on the front page, right?'

'Yes, yes.'

Two hours later, Tanya read through what she had written, and about to re-read it, deliberately pressed the send button. This is what she wrote.

I apologise unreservedly to Tanya Pryce for my unfounded attacks on her professionalism. Her track record is one of consistent profitability. She feels saddened by the attempt of my informant(s) to sully her reputation and that of KS, but recognizes their behaviour is rooted in cowardice, fear and jealousy. She would pit her wits against theirs any day, if only they had the gumption to show their face. She has also asked me to point out that she would feel thoroughly ashamed to waste good food.

All Tanya wanted to do when she got home was sit in her lounge with a large glass of wine, her cigarettes, and her thoughts. To be alone. But Jamie wasn't well, and as she was rifling in the airing cupboard in the upstairs hall, looking for some face flannels to use as cold compresses for his forehead, Peter came behind her and placed his hands on her hips.

'I was saying to Jack earlier, why go out for fish and chips when you've got steak at home.'

She hadn't told him about Quagg's article or Nate's promotion because he was still in her bad books. It also seemed pointless.

'If you can get fish and chips, Pete, take it.'

'Don't be like that,' he said, rubbing his lower region against her bum.

She tightened her buttocks, eased his hands off her, and slipped from his grasp. 'Jamie has a sore throat and a temperature. I think he's coming down with tonsillitis.'

Peter massaged his throat. 'Funny you should say that, because I don't feel so good.'

She gave him a withering look and went to tend Jamie, fanning him with a copy of *Private Eye*, her favourite publication, and bathing his forehead, until he fell asleep. He definitely had tonsillitis. She could tell by the stale sweet smell of his breath.

She slept in the spare room again that night, not that she got much sleep, because she was too wound up, too plagued by regret for accusing Nate of being Quagg's mole in front of Bruce.

Like Joe said, any number of people could have told Quagg about the hedge fund loss. Krevamar probably spoke with loads of dealers before calling Nate.

154

Three things in particular kept coming to mind. What Spencer had said about Nate not being in a position to know the NCA loss would escalate to three million dollars, Bruce's remark that it was not uncommon for two dedicated professionals to spot the same areas of opportunity, and what she had said to Andy about not being jealous of Nate.

Maybe Nate did make a genuine mistake with NCA. Maybe he didn't plagiarise my report, maybe it was just a coincidence, and maybe he didn't tell me what he got as a bonus because, as Bruce had indicated, it was peanuts. Maybe he was embarrassed. I said I wasn't, but maybe I am jealous of him.

She started crying, hit with the realisation that while she didn't want to be Nate, she would have liked his start in life, and to have a dad she could phone for advice and reassurance, a mother even. In the absence of both, it was hard for her to see how she wouldn't be jealous. She didn't want to be but logically felt she had to be, because it didn't stack up otherwise.

Everyone wants nice feelings, and to feel loved. If I didn't want a kind mum or dad, I'd be a robot. And since I didn't have either, I have to be jealous.

My fucking baggage is ruining my life, she thought bitterly, but firmly of the view the oh-woe-is-me route was a dead end, she quickly countered that thought. *Join the club. Everyone's got baggage. Even people who have had seemingly perfect starts in life, kind parents and a good education, still have issues. You're not the only one. Shit happens to the best of people. It's not all about childhood, either. Everyone makes mistakes. Like they say, to err is human.*

She bravely, for it was painful, mulled over all her

155

run-ins with Nate, and was left with an awful sinking feeling in her stomach.

I've misjudged him, because I'm jealous. I've been like a kid trying to force a piece of a jigsaw into a space where it doesn't belong. Yes, he can be cocky, but so can I, and his cockiness is probably a front, a way of covering up his inadequacies as a trader. If he was that confident, he wouldn't call his dad so often.

She suddenly felt pity for him.

Jesus, Bruce must think I'm paranoid.

Feeling awash with remorse she resolved to make amends, and considered the merits of apologising to Nate, Bruce and Fiona, but decided that would be overkill, and bad for her reputation. She would say sorry to Fi, as she felt awful having made her cry, but not to Bruce, on account of his sneaky behaviour with Steve, nor to Nate whose promotion she considered ample reward for any suffering he might have experienced at her hands.

I'll just be nicer to Nate, and make a point of giving him the benefit of the doubt, and I won't run him down to Bruce anymore.

She felt better with a plan of action in place, and as she settled down to sleep it struck her that not once during her deliberations had she drawn comfort from Spencer. TJ had crossed her mind and warmed her heart, as had Daphne, Joe, Andy, and her driver, Ted, whose oft quoted words of wisdom *Everything comes to pass but not to stay* had been especially comforting. *That's what I always tell my Eileen*, he would say. He and Eileen had recently celebrated their Ruby wedding anniversary.

It made her aware of the value of friendship, and

that Spencer wasn't a friend in the best and truest sense.

Pete's not my friend either, but who can blame him.

She recalled their tiff over Suzy's car, and their argument whilst on holiday, and felt ashamed.

I fancied him once, so maybe I can again if I try hard enough. He is the father of my children, after all.

*

'…I think we should up it to $825K,' Nate said to Bruce. 'Show the guy we mean business.'

'What's your call, Tanya?' Bruce said.

'I agree with Nate. If we raise our offer in dribs and drabs, we risk losing him to Farraday Levy.'

'I agree he's a good guy, but that's a heck of a hike,' Bruce said.

'This is his first job change,' Tanya said. 'Graduates are always underpaid until they change jobs, and on the basis his real worth is 625K the premium isn't that hefty. Our focus should be on the difference between what we offer and what Farraday offer, which I doubt will be more than one hundred and fifty thousand dollars.'

'Tanya's right,' Nate said. 'The question we need to ask ourselves is whether the guy's worth that extra 150. Whoever we hire will cost money.'

Tanya nodded. 'And don't forget that the 825K includes accrued bonus.'

'We need to be cognizant of the fact we don't have a back up either,' Nate said. 'If we lose the guy, we'll struggle to find the right combination of character and talent. There are plenty of traders looking, but not of the same calibre.'

Bruce shook his head. 'It's a colossal amount of money in this climate.'

'I agree,' Tanya said, 'but there's what the papers say and reality. Nomura has given Lehman's traders two year guarantees equal to what they made in 2007.'

Nate nodded. 'Hedge funds are still hiring, too, and let's not forget we're in competition here. Farraday has pretty deep pockets from what I hear.'

'What's the guy's notice period?' Bruce said, with a resigned look on his face.

'Three months,' Tanya said, 'but he's confident he can get it reduced to two, in which case he could start the beginning of November.'

Bruce sanctioned the offer and when Nate and Tanya got outside his office, they gave each other a high five.

'That's called teamwork,' Nate said. 'I just hope the guy accepts.'

'He will. You'll get your ride in his microlight,' she said, nudging his arm. Their prospective candidate, Sam Davenstaff, was a pilot and had his own microlight.

Nate laughed. 'Sam reckons flying one of those things in rough weather is a cross between riding a wilful horse and taking a cross-country motorcycle over rough terrain.'

'I don't even know what a microlight looks like.'

'It's like a large hand glider with a motor bike underneath, nothing between you and the ground but a lap-strap and a bar. When you fly those babies you can smell cities as you pass them.'

She laughed inside. *I bet he's never even seen one.*

They walked back to the floor nattering ten to the dozen, both expressing irritation that Ludo Quagg was going to get a big fat cheque for introducing Sam. He had sent Sam's CV to Tanya the morning after their lunch, stressing the need to move quickly because Sam was at a very advanced stage with an arch rival.

'Two hundred and six grand,' Tanya said. 'Nice work if you can get it, eh?'

'It's more than that, isn't it?'

How would he know that?

'I thought the going rate was a third,' he added casually.

See. There you again with your conspiracy theories.

'No. The creep gave me a discount for dissing me.'

'You should ask Bruce to split it with you,' he said.

'I'm sure he'd love that idea.'

'We're in the wrong business, Tanya.'

'Does seem like it. I suppose if all else fails we can always set up a head hunting firm.' She paused. 'By the way, I think I might have found us a permanent p.a. without the use of an agent, a woman called Helen Medley. Rich saw her as a favour to a friend, and passed her over to me.'

'What's she like?'

'Single, thirty one, curvy in all the right places, honey hair, big brown eyes... Do you want to know more?'

'Can she cook?

'I don't know about that but she can sing and dance. She's a member of an amateur dramatics society.'

'Call and offer her the job.'

Just then, as they were both laughing, Spencer appeared in the corridor a few yards ahead of them, having emerged from a side office.

'You two seem happy.'

'That's because I think Tanya's just found me a wife.'

'I hope she's single. I tend to find the best ones are married.' He glanced at Tanya, lust in his eyes, and she turned to jelly inside.

Nate laughed. 'You're obviously not looking in the right places.'

'So should we buy or sell, Spence?' Tanya said, to change the subject, 'and don't say we should do both.'

'Why not? It often pays to hedge ones bets,' he said ambiguously, and made off in the opposite direction.

She longed to run after him and throw herself into his arms, to feel his chest against hers, his breath on her face, and as the space between them increased, she felt crushing disappointment.

Her week had been going so well, until now.

If only you weren't married. I care about you. To borrow from Shakespeare, Princess: It is not in the stars to hold our destiny but in ourselves.

The downturn in her mood deepened as the day wore on, not helped by her having calculated it would be four thousand days before her boys were of an age where she felt they could handle her and Peter splitting up. Then, whilst on her way home, Spencer sent her a text: *Dinner? A drink? Please say yes, Princess. I miss you, dreadfully. OX.*

Her heart leapt as her stomach sunk.

From sacrifice comes strength. You have to say no. Think of Jamie and Harry.

But she couldn't bring herself to reject him. In the end she didn't reply, and she also saved his message.

I'm in prison. It's like I can see the sunshine but I'm not allowed to bask in it.

Barbara's voice entered her head. *What have you got to complain about? You should have had my life. I did, and only the bad bits, you old bag.*

All of a sudden she felt the urge to see Daphne and realising her cherubs would already be in bed, she had Ted drop her off there. Peter wouldn't be happy, but she was hardly up to facing him.

Over a glass of Beaujolais, after hearing Daphne's news and how much she had enjoyed her Dover sole lunch with her cousin at Claridge's, and the taxi ride to London and back, Tanya told her all about Ludo Quagg.

'...so in return for humiliating me he gets a cheque for 206,500 dollars. I must be mad.'

'Not at all, Dear. You acted responsibly.'

'That's my problem, Daphne. I'm too responsible.'

'But it sounds like this Mr Quagg has been useful.'

'He has, but I didn't... I didn't mean...' She shrugged. 'Let's just say my life is a bit of a mess right now. I'm OK when I'm making trading decisions, but with everything else...' She sighed. 'I need to count my blessings. I know I'm lucky, I just feel a bit trapped, that's all. Millions of others are in the same boat.'

Daphne played with a button on her cardigan. 'You must live your own life, Tanya, dear.'

'Yes, but that's easier said than done, especially when children are involved.'

'Shall we tipple up?' Daphne looked at the open bottle of wine on the table.

Tanya re-filled their glasses. 'Daphne, do you mind if I smoke?'

'Not at all, Dear. My Hector used to smoke cigars, and in my tea dance days I used to smoke.' She smiled dreamily. 'I had the most elegant cigarette holder, and I

161

used to feel awfully grown up puffing away on a Lucky Strike.' She gestured to the mantelpiece. 'There's an ashtray by that candle stick.'

'Thank you. That's really kind of you.'

Tanya put the ashtray on a low table beside her, lit up and drew heavily. 'That's better. I don't know what I'd do without my beloved cigarettes. I know smoking is a coping mechanism and all that, but I enjoy it.'

'I'm not judging you, Tanya, dear.'

Tanya's eyes instantly filled with tears. 'I'm sorry. It's just that no one has ever said that to me.'

Daphne's face was etched with loving concern, and Tanya was that overcome by her understanding she couldn't hold back her tears. She took a tissue from her bag and dabbed her eyes. 'I'm sorry, Daphne. I don't know what's got into me.'

Daphne rose from her chair, not easy for a lady her age, and came and sat beside Tanya, and began gently rubbing her back, whereupon Tanya dropped her head and began sobbing. 'Oh Daphne, I can't bear it any longer.' Her heart felt like it was breaking, and she sobbed for a good few minutes, while Daphne continued to rub her back without saying a word.

When she regained composure, she took Daphne's hand and kissed it. 'Thank you,' she sniffed. 'I'm OK now. Let me help you back to your comfy seat.'

'It's OK, Dear, I can manage,' she said, and returned to her dusky pink armchair.

'I love you for not asking me what's wrong, Daphne, but I want to tell you, if that's OK?'

'Of course it is, Dear.'

'There's this man at work called Spencer who likes me, and I know it's wrong but I like him too.' She gave her nose a blow. 'I don't love Peter, Daphne. I never have really, not in an intimate way, but I don't want to hurt my boys or, for that matter, Peter. If there was a pill I could take that would make me love him, I'd take it.'

'What, and give up the chance to play the role of a scarlet woman?'

Tanya laughed through her tears. 'Oh I do love you, Daphne. Maybe I should get a badge with Scarlet Woman on it, pin it to my lapel and be done with it.'

'That's better. To giggle in the face of fear is always a good sign.'

Tanya looked at her, serious. 'Jokes aside, how do I make a decision about what to do?'

'I think you have already decided what you are going to do, Dear. The only matter outstanding is when you are going to do it.'

Friday, I could do it Friday, it's a long weekend, she thought, and cried some more.

'Would you do something for me, Dear?'

Tanya nodded. 'Yes, of course.'

'On the third shelf,' Daphne pointed to her bookcase, 'on the left hand side, you will see a book with a yellow spine. Would you get it for me?'

Tanya obliged. It was an old paperback, with tanned edges and a lot of loose pages. She gave it to Daphne, and Daphne asked her to wait, found a page, and pointed at it. 'Would you read that sentence for me, Dear, the one beginning The sentiment?'

Tanya took the book from her, and coughed to clear her throat. 'The sentiment from which it sprung determines the dignity of any deed, and the question ever is, not, what you have done or forborne, but, at whose command you have done or forborne it.'

Tanya took it to mean she had to be true to herself. 'But I hate hurting people, Daphne.'

'It is not our place to play God, Dear. The Good Lord can manage very well on his own. And he cradles us all. He will watch over Peter, and your children, and you. He is doing that right now.'

Tanya noted the title, *Emerson's Essays*, as she put the book back on the shelf.

Friday would be perfect IF I am going to do it.

It was August bank holiday weekend, and ideal for a few reasons. She was off work Monday, and they had no plans to see Jim and Kay because Peter was playing in a few golf competitions.

I could have Alison take the boys to her parents overnight.

Upon leaving, she gave Daphne a long warm hug.

'You have helped me more than you can imagine, Daphne, and I can't thank you enough. I'll never forget tonight. I can now see the wood for the trees, and I feel OK. I know what I've got to do, and thanks to you, I now feel strong enough to do it.'

Daphne smiled. 'I'm glad I have been of some help, Dear, but it is the Good Lord who deserves the credit.'

CHAPTER TWELVE

Wearing a caftan and flip flops, her hair pinned up with a couple of knitting needle efforts, Tanya stood on the patio, and in between puffs of her cigarette, gulped from a large glass of Sancerre.

The door to her boys' play-shed was shut, their climbing frame, with its bright blue slide attachment, minus their energetic young bodies.

She put her glass on the table and yanked a spray from a Leyland cypress, a tower of a tree just beyond the patio, crushed the needles in her hand and sniffed.

The scent would forever remind her of family dinners in the garden, for she always sat in front of that tree and performed this ritual. A lump formed in her throat as she recalled their last.

They had dined on fine Chinese cuisine from a local restaurant, and she had stood Harry on the table so he could help open the parasol, and then given him the task of folding napkins. Jamie meanwhile had helped Peter drag the heater into position, and fetch chair cushions from the garage. And dinner over, Jamie had pushed Harry around the garden in his wheelbarrow, before the two of them had hunted for the family tortoise, while she and Peter had sat drinking wine and listening to a compilation CD.

In her head she could hear Peter's favourite track, Say You Love Me, by Simply Red, a song that always left her feeling sad, making her long for a man who loved her for who she was, rather than what she could provide.

Finding the silence disconcerting, she took a few deep breaths and noisily exhaled.

All around her seemed tranquilised, her weeping willow tree barely moving, ditto the geraniums, pansies and petunia's hanging in baskets affixed to a wall that ran the depth of the patio, and abutted the garage. This was the outside wall to a room that was now home for Florence, Tanya's new au pair, a petite girl with a boyish frame, who lived in jeans. Florence was not however at home. Tanya had asked her to lose herself for the night.

It's the fairest thing on Peter, she kept reminding herself. *He deserves a chance to find true love.*

All of a sudden she jumped, having heard him kick the street door shut, and drag his golf clubs into the hall.

Her heart racing, she quickly sat at the table, shakily refilled her glass, and swallowed a huge mouthful.

Keep calm. Life goes on. Nobody's died.

Upon entering the kitchen Peter took off his T-shirt and flung it on the breakfast bar, got a beer from the fridge, uncapped it, took a swig, and then came as far as the patio door. 'I thought the boys would still be up.'

'I need to talk to you, Pete. Come and sit down.'

'Can't it wait, I'm knackered?' he smelt under his arms, 'and I need a shower. But I'm quids up.' He took another swig of beer. 'Jack's the only guy I know—'

'Pete, stop. There's something I need to tell you.'

'What?' He felt his face stubble. 'You're not pregnant, are you?'

She drank some wine. 'No. I've had enough, Pete.'

He pulled a face. 'What, did you lose another deal?'

'I'm talking about us, Pete. I can't hack this marriage anymore.'

166

He momentarily scrunched his eyes shut. 'What are you talking about?'

'You know what I'm saying. I want out.'

He gripped the edge of the door.

'I'm not happy, Pete. I've not been happy for ages.'

He looked at her. 'Where are my boys?' he said, in a faint voice.

'They're with Alison.' Alison had taken them to stay overnight with her parents, David and Avril.

He walked as though drunk and slumped into a chair opposite her. 'What's brought this on?'

'It's not a sudden thing, and it's not about you. I just feel like I'm suffocating, like I don't know who I am anymore.'

He gazed at Harry's bike, a black and silver two-wheeler with stabilizers. 'Alison knows, does she?'

She looked into her lap. 'No. I just told her we had some things to discuss.'

'But we had sex last night. You can't have sex with your husband and then tell him the next day it's all finished. It doesn't add up.'

'I function like a machine, Pete. Sex is part of our arrangement, part of the deal.' She winced inside at how cold that sounded but she had steeled herself and there was no going back. Her heart was in lockdown. She was now in trading mode.

'But you come. I always make you come.'

Tanya's best orgasms were in fact self-induced and enjoyed privately, but she had never let on.

'It's not about sex. It's about everything else. My life feels like a silent movie. I feel—well most of the time I don't feel, at least not nice feelings. It's like I'm a clockwork doll. And I want to become real, to find out what makes me tick. I need to be on my own to do that.'

'I don't get what you're saying, Darlin,' he said, clenching and unclenching his hands.

'Like I said, Pete, this is not about you. You've not done anything wrong. I just want to be on my own.'

'But we've got a lovely life. The boys, this house, we love each—'

'I don't love you, Pete. I've stayed put and kept my mouth shut because of the boys.'

His chest caved. 'Is there someone else?' He stared at her through hollow eyes.

'No, I wouldn't do that to you. Where would I get the time, anyway?'

'Then let's go and see someone, get some marriage guidance. All couples have their ups and downs. We were happy once, and we can be happy again.'

Happy marriage was an oxymoron to Tanya. At best marriage was a bandage for the wounded, a shared crutch, at worst a prison sentence.

'I've never felt happy being married. I'm not sure it's possible for two people to be happy shackled to each other. It seems abnormal.'

'But I've seen you happy, seen you dance and sing and joke around, that's happy. You have been happy. Don't deny it.'

'Granted, I've had happy moments, but too few by far.' She ran a hand over her face.

'What about my boys?'

'You can see them as much as you want. I wouldn't dream of denying you access. They need you, and you need them, and you will always be their dad.'

He started to cry. 'Why didn't you say something before?'

'Because you can't fix what's wrong.'

'But you and the boys are everything I've got.'

She scratched at her wrist. 'People build new lives. We're both young.'

'But I don't want a new life, Darlin. I want this one. I love you.' He reached out to touch her arm, but she drew back, and stood up.

'I'm sorry, Pete, I didn't want to hurt you, but this is my life as well.'

He wiped his eyes with his arm. 'But you can't break up our family.'

'Couples get divorced all the time, Pete.'

For a few minutes neither spoke. Peter cried quietly, and Tanya stood on the patio staring at a dense grey sky ripped through with rich pinks, thinking it beautiful.

Peter got up and came toward her, his arms open. 'Can I have one last kiss, Darlin?'

She stepped onto the grass to get away from him. 'Don't make it harder than it already is.'

'Please, Darlin, just one kiss, that's all I want.'

She shook her head.

He came closer. 'Please, Darlin, please,' he said, his voice shaky, tears streaming down his face.

'Fuck off! It's over, OK? Over!'

He began to sob.

She felt wicked but also that it was the kindest thing to say. A final heartbreaking kiss goodbye would be excruciating for him, awful for her, too.

'Whatever's wrong, Darlin, we can sort it out, I know we can.'

'We can't.'

'We can. We can. I know we can.'

'Pete, I'm not interested in sorting anything out.

I've made my decision, and I've not made it lightly.'

She rushed past him into the house to use the toilet.

When she returned he was in the kitchen, putting his T-shirt back on. 'Jack's on his way round.' He blew his nose with a piece of kitchen towel. 'I'll be back in the morning. Make sure the boys are here.'

She nodded, and retreated to her lounge at the front of her house, opened a window and sat by it in a rocking chair, the twilit sky her only means of light. The scent of climbing honeysuckle wafted in, and the rich leafy trees lining her road swayed gently, as though nature sensed she needed soothing.

Jack's car screeched to a halt outside.

Peter pushed open the lounge door on his way out. 'I would have done anything for you.'

Except alter a golf game.

She didn't respond and kept her back to him.

'Why didn't you tell me you wasn't happy?'

She remained silent.

'It's the money, ain't it? Now you've got enough, I'm history.'

'No, but you'll get your whack, anyway.'

He left.

I did it. I finally did it.

Overwhelmed with exhilaration and relief, she burst into tears, and promptly opened a bottle of Bollinger, and toasted her freedom on the patio. *Here's to me*, she thought, as she took the first sip. Switching on her garden lights, she then took to the grass, kicked off her flip flops, and did a few twirls, before settling under her weeping willow tree, with her champagne and cigs. And as its delicate leaves swept tickles over her legs, she felt a child-like thrill knowing this was now *her* garden.

'Half of everything is mine, and that includes your pension, your bonus guarantee, the lot,' Peter said.

'I've no intention of stiffing you, but my pension's worth about three quid, and as for my guarantee, I'll have to talk to my solicitor, because that's a future thing, and dependent on KS still being around.'

'Don't give me that bollocks.'

'Please keep your voice down,' Tanya said, 'the boys have been through enough for one day.'

'Whose fault's that?'

His mobile rang. It was Jack.

Tanya sat expressionless listening to Peter's side of the conversation.

'Yes mate… Yeah, I know mate. Yeah. Yeah. Oh, don't you worry. Yeah, about to now, mate. OK, mate, see you in a bit.' He put his mobile in his back pocket, and rolled back his shoulders. 'I'm going for custody.'

She jumped up from the sofa. 'If you try to take the boys,' she said, pointing at him, 'I'll quit work, and you'll have to support us all.'

He smirked. 'I can't see you living in a prefab.'

'I'd live in a tent if that's what it takes to keep my kids. Try me, Pete. I swear if you go for custody, I'll stop work, just like that.' She snapped her fingers.

She went to the drinks cabinet, poured herself a brandy, and lit a cigarette. Although frightened, logic told her he was making an empty threat.

He loves his freedom too much to be tied down, and he's too lazy to look after them.

'That's floored you, ain't it?' he said triumphantly. 'They're not just your kids.'

'They're not fucking pawns either.'

Keep calm. He's bluffing.

She took a deep breath. 'You have a clear choice, Pete. Go quietly, and you'll get half of everything, and I'll even agree to a clean break order. That means I won't make any financial claims on you in the future, should my circumstances alter.' She paused. 'You'll have enough to buy a house outright, and two gorgeous children you can see whenever you want, but who won't cost you a penny.'

She knew giving him a clean break order was like throwing the kitchen sink at the problem, but her heart was driving her.

'Fuck off. Why should I dance to your tune?' he said, but she noticed a softening in his voice.

'You don't have to, but like I said, if you try to take the boys, chances are you'll end up penniless, because I'll stop work immediately.'

'Don't give me that. You'd go out of your mind staying at home.'

'Would I? Don't be so sure. I think I'd like it. I could do a degree, write a book, learn to play bridge. I'd still use my mind.'

She went and stubbed her cigarette out in the ashtray he was using, and then looked him in the eyes. 'Something tells me you'd find being broke a lot harder than I would.'

He didn't say anything, which came as a huge relief, the tension in her evaporating. She knew she had a deal.

'I'll leave you to think things through,' she said quietly, and left the room.

'I knew it!' Barbara said. 'Jackie saw it in my tea cup. Suitcases. A big pile of suitcases. Someone's leaving, she said. I saw them too. Clear as daylight they were.'

Tanya twisted the phone cord around her fingers.
She almost sounds cheerful.
'Do the boys know?'
'Yes. We told them yesterday.'
'Poor little sods. How are they?'
Fuck off. What do you know about parenting?
'They're fine.'
'What about that lazy git?'
'He's OK, obviously not jumping for joy, but OK. Anyway, I'd better go, Mum, I've got loads to do. I'll call you during the week.'
'Why don't I come over, give you a hand?'
Tanya felt a bolt of panic. 'You can if you want, but Alison's here.'
'Don't worry about that, not with all this going on. Anyway, Alison's alright, and with me around she can spend more time with Jamie and Harry.'
Half an hour later Barbara was on Tanya's doorstep with, to Tanya's consternation, two carrier bags full of clothes. 'You go and pay the cab, and I'll make you a nice cup of tea,' she said, and waltzed in the house, her skinny frame bobbing with energy.
A week tops, and she's going home.

*

With far more important things to worry about now, Tanya simply shrugged upon reading Ludo's email. Her apology had been rejected by *FI's* editor, and Ludo had come up with a revised version, which omitted her insults and challenge to his mole(s). Not over happy with it but busy she had OK'd it, and expected it to be in the latest issue, out today.

Tanya,

I do apologise, but it was out of my hands, totally out of my hands. The HBC arrests forced cuts all round. I had no say in what stories were axed or shortened. I have not had a wink of sleep all weekend. Rolf has promised me it will run next week.

On a more cheerful note, Sam has confirmed he can start work in November.

Yours,

Ludo.

HBC was Higgins Banking Corp., the crème de la crème of banks in the days of the British Empire, and two of its employees had been arrested for fraud, in relation to the collapse of a European food corporation called Carladeli. Despite good credit ratings Carladeli had defaulted on a bond repayment, subsequent to which the company was found to be broke, and in debt to the tune of billions. With numerous bond issues outstanding, the arrests were major news.

Her response was brief: *Thanks for letting me know. Good news about Sam.*

Ludo came back: *Thank you, Tanya, thank you. You are the epitome of grace.*

Foolishness, more like.

She sent Spencer a text: *An early dinner next week, my side of town?*

He replied immediately: *I would LOVE to but I'm away Thursday and Friday.*

Tuesday? She texted back.

Perfect - as are you! X

*

His brow furrowed, Peter scratched his chest. 'You want me to confess to adultery?'

Tanya's solicitor had unwittingly given her this idea, which would expedite her divorce.

'Why not? You'll earn out of it. It's over between us, anyway.' She looked at him through the mirror above the fire place – she was wiping away mascara smudges under her eyes with her fingers. 'You'll be quids up, and the lawyers won't know any different.'

Peter had already verbally agreed to a settlement of one million pounds, payable in two instalments: Half upon finalisation of their divorce, the rest when Tanya got her next bonus, the following June. With her guarantee and profit cut from illiquid trading, she hoped to have enough. Her bigger hope was that by the time of the second payment she would be working for Olli Vermallen and money wouldn't matter. She and TJ's first meeting with him had gone well.

He took a swig of his gin and tonic. 'You're a scheming bitch.'

She shrugged. 'I'm a trader, Pete. There's a price for everything. I'm not holding a gun to your head. You have the option to say no.'

If investment banking had taught Tanya anything, it was that human beings were self-serving.

When he asked how much, she knew she had another deal. All that had to be agreed was the price.

'I was thinking twenty thousand pounds.'

'Fuck off, that's fuck all.'

'If you don't want to play, that's fine.'

Peter came back with a counter offer, the next night.

'Fifty grand, and I'm only doing it for my boys.'

She shook her head. 'Forget it. I can't afford that much.'

'I've seen a house. The boys would have a bedroom each.' He handed her the particulars to prove he wasn't bluffing, and said he would need the money as soon as possible, if he was to secure it.

She wanted to tell him to get stuffed but concern for her boys dominated her thoughts. The house, a 1930's end of terrace, was only four miles away, and had a good size garden, big enough for Jamie and Harry to kick a ball around. 'Give me a few days. I'll see if I can get a loan from work.'

'Use our overdraft facility.'

'There's a short fall each month for Christ's sake, and we're heading for a recession.'

'Don't give me that. You can always borrow more on this place.'

'I've got to do that anyway. How else am I going to come up with five hundred thousand pounds?'

'Exactly! All you need to do is add fifty grand to the amount you borrow.'

She examined the hem of her jacket as she thought. 'OK. As soon as my solicitor's got your bit of paper confirming you're not going to contest my petition, the money's yours.'

He broke the tip off a cigarette, lit it, and held it between his thumb and forefinger as he smoked. 'I want it in cash. I don't want any trace.'

He sounded just like his tough-nut friend, Jack, who had clearly become his financial advisor.

She laughed. 'Cash? Marcus Rathbone will think I'm drug running.' Marcus was her bank manager.

'That's your problem.'

She smiled mockingly. 'No trace? What's that all about?'

'I don't have to explain myself to you. They're my terms. Take em or leave em.'

Technically his request made sense as it could be argued any cheque payment was an advance to be deducted from the divorce settlement, but it rankled that he doubted her word.

'OK, you've got yourself a deal. I'll call my solicitor in the morning. Now go and have a shave. You look terrible.'

'What do you care?'

'I don't, but it's not good for the boys to see you looking a wreck. After all, nobody's died.'

'You might be laughing now, but give it time. You'll get what's coming to you.'

'I wasn't laughing, Pete, merely stating the obvious. No one has died. But a part of Jamie did, when you balled your eyes out in front of him, and said I was making you move out. You'll pay for that one day.'

*

Spencer broke off a bamboo straw jutting out of his chair, and repositioned the cushion to protect his delectable bum. 'I feel like I'm sitting on a hedgehog.'

Tanya giggled. 'Don't be a wuss. This is salubrious for the East End.' She cracked a poppadom. 'Where are you off to, Thursday?'

'Moscow. Why, will you miss me, or has Nate won your affections? You two certainly seem to have reconciled your differences.'

She smiled inside, flattered by his jealousy. 'I loathe

him as much as ever. I just got fed up arguing. And as it happens I will miss you. Will you miss me?'

He took a gold pen from his pocket and drew a small heart on the paper table cloth. 'Need you ask?'

'Gosh, you devil, you. You'll be defacing the underground next.'

He laughed. 'It's lovely to see you in such a good mood. Are you leaving KS?'

'No. I'm just enjoying your company.' She paused. 'Tell me about Verity.'

His chin went down, his forehead forward. 'What would you like to know?'

'Tell me three things she didn't like about you, or the relationship.'

He picked up a spare glass and polished it with his napkin as he considered the question, his slender fingers revolving with a rhythm that made Tanya shudder.

'She was quite happy, but if I had to name three of her pet hates, they would have to be my travelling, my workout routine, and my mother.'

'Give me three more,' she said, since she wouldn't consider any of those a problem. Travelling she would understand, his routine, well discipline was no bad thing. As for his mother, no one in the world could be as bad as Barbara.

'I can't think of three more. Verity was quite content.'

'Did you argue?'

'We squabbled, naturally, but not very often.'

'Do you think she tried too hard to please you, because she wanted to get married?'

He had said her keenness – desperation, in Tanya's view – to get married was the main cause of their split.

'Possibly, I've not given it much thought.' He paused. 'I would much rather talk about you, Princess.'

'OK.' She picked a few grains of rice off the table and dropped them on her plate. 'I'm getting divorced.'

His eyes popped. 'Gosh, that's a quantum leap.'

'You're presuming I initiated it.'

'You didn't?'

She laughed. 'Of course I did.'

'What about your children, do they know?'

Her mask fell. 'Yes, and when we told them, Peter started crying, and told Jamie I didn't love him anymore, and that I was making him move out.'

He took her hand. 'How utterly heart wrenching that must have been for you.'

She nodded, her eyes misting over. 'It made me realise what scum I've been married to all these years. Believe it or not he then threatened to go for custody, until I paid him off.'

'What do you mean you paid him off?'

'I mean I've been extraordinarily generous. He's going to get half of everything, and a clean-break order which basically means I can't go after him for child support if my fortunes take a turn for the worse.'

'Is that wise? Far be it from me to interfere but the outlook for banking is less than encouraging. Policy makers are nowhere close to grasping the gravity of the downturn.'

She gave him a wry smile. 'Bless you for caring, Spence, but in all the years I've known you, I don't think you've ever been optimistic.'

He laughed. 'It's an occupational hazard.'

'Whatever happens,' she said, 'banks will still need credit traders. And even if KS laid me off, which is unlikely given that no one else in the firm can do my job, I'm sure they'd be a few people eager for my services.'

'Me for one,' he said, laughing. 'When will you be a free woman?'

'I'm hoping by the end of October.'

'That soon?'

'It shouldn't take long because Pete and I have squared things on the money front, and he's agreed to be the guilty party, to accept responsibility for the marriage irretrievably breaking down.' It didn't seem fair on Peter to mention their adultery deal.

'How magnanimous of him,' he said sarcastically. 'The USA majors, here we come.' He meant the golf championships.

Tanya shrugged. 'Up to him what he spends it on. I'm just glad to see the back of him.'

'That makes two of us.' He paused. 'I wish you had told me all this was going on. Who at KS knows?'

'No one except you, and I don't plan to tell anyone else. The more people that know the more I'll have to talk about it, and I'd prefer to just get on with work.'

He nodded understanding. 'May I ask if there was a particular incident that prompted you to action?'

She laughed. 'Well there was a certain someone on my mind.'

He pulled at his tie. 'Did Peter suspect anything?'

'He did ask if I had someone else, and I obviously said no, because I don't.'

'Yet,' he said, his face relaxing into a broad smile.

'Don't count your chickens. I've not agreed to go out with you yet.'

He laughed. 'Will I get a good night kiss?'

'No. First things first, Spence.'

He made a face. 'I understand, Princess, but I'm off to Asia on Thursday, back in London for a day on Saturday the 20th but only because it's my father's sixtieth, and then I'm off to New York for three days. It will be nearly a month before we can see each other.'

She felt a sudden sympathy with Verity, but hid her disappointment behind a smile. 'We'll live. My boys need me at home at the moment, anyway, so I couldn't get out much. We also need to lie low for a bit.'

Despite what she had said, once they were outside the restaurant Spencer took her hand, and playfully said he wasn't going to let go of it until she had kissed him, and she didn't argue. Seconds later they snuck into the deep doorway of a bank, and enjoyed their first kiss, while groping each other.

Spencer's arse felt gorgeous, his swollen cock a divine handful, and as he caressed the soft flesh of her inner thighs, she began to scream quietly, and when he pushed his velvety fingers up inside her, she nigh on fainted with the pleasure. Pulling her skirt up, she relaxed her weight against the wall of their small corridor, pulled her thong aside and begged him to tongue her, but fear got the better of him. 'Not here, Princess. I want to—God, I want to, but not here.'

Seeing his point of view, she straightened up and adjusted her clothing, and they had another long and passionate kiss.

'Wow,' she said afterwards, her body exhausted and limp, her head on his shoulder.

'Wow indeed,' he whispered. 'God, I wished I didn't have to go away.'

They stepped into the street.

She felt her face, which had suffered somewhat, albeit in the nicest possible way, from Spencer's five o'clock shadow. 'My poor lily white skin feels like it's got holes in it now,' she bleated.

'You look beautiful, and you taste delicious.' He sighed and tutted. 'This trip is such wretched timing.'

'Absence makes the heart grow fonder,' she said.

He smiled. 'Do you know the author of those words of wisdom?'

She rolled her eyes. 'What is this, Mastermind? No, but I'll take a guess.' She thought for a few moments. 'I'll go for Hitler.'

Spencer burst out laughing. 'Hitler?'

She shrugged. 'Well, he did want people to piss off, didn't he?'

'It was Shakespeare, Princess, Shakespeare.'

'Really. Hmmm. Smart bloke.' Glancing across the road, she suddenly gasped. 'Fuck! There's Peter,' she said, her voice full of panic.

Spencer froze, his eyes missing a few blinks.

She creased up laughing.

'That was not funny,' he said, blushing.

'Oh, Spence, your face... Sorry, but you'll have to get used to that side of me.'

CHAPTER THIRTEEN

Tanya banged her phone on her desk. 'Who did the trade in twenty million Credit Suisse bonds with shit-face Shinewater?'

'Not guilty,' Nate said.

'I did,' Freddie said. 'Is there a problem?'

'It depends on whether you bought the 5 1/8ths or the 4 7/8ths.'

'The 5 1/8ths,' Freddie said, looking at Fiona.

'I relayed,' Fiona said, 'but I wrote everything down.' She picked up her blotter and hurriedly flipped over the pages. 'I've got the 4 7/8ths written down.'

'For fuck's sake,' Tanya said.

'What are we doing talking to Shinewater?' Nate said. 'He's a client.'

'But you knew it was him,' Fiona said.

'Pardon me.'

'But, er, but you heard me shout it was Shinewater.'

'That sounds mighty like an ass-saving exercise.' Nate flung himself back in his chair and opened his arms. 'I can't believe you just said that, Fi. Tell me, who was I talking to? You should know, since Joe shouted the call over to me.'

'I-I don't know,' Fiona said, her face reddening, 'but when Joe told me to hurry up, and give him the price, you also told me to get moving.'

Nate massaged his jaw. 'Yes, because you need to move pronto when trading. I was simply reinforcing Joe's advice.' He shook his head. 'You've disappointed me, Fi. Seriously disappointed me.'

'Have we still got the bonds?' Tanya asked Freddie.

'No. I sold them to Jacob Robensteyn.'

'Fi,' Joe said, 'just because Nate knew you were doing a trade doesn't mean he knew who you were trading with. I didn't know it was Shinewater you were talking to either.'

'Thank you, Joe,' Nate said.

Fiona didn't say anything, just stood pulling at her fingers.

Tanya told Freddie to close out the resulting positions immediately.

He did, sustaining a loss of $54,000, and began to apologise to Tanya, but Nate stopped him.

'Save it for later. Tanya and I will see you and Fiona,' he glanced at Fi, 'in my office at the close of business.'

Fiona sat, arms folded, head slightly bowed, Freddie, upright and rigid beside her, blinking nervously.

'This meeting is not about blame, but learning,' Tanya said.

She looked at Fiona. 'Although you're not wholly responsible, Fi, if you had checked the price of the bond on a broker's screen, you would have spotted the error.'

'I realise that now. I'm ever so sorry.'

'Good. In future, write down every detail and put it under the trader's nose before you confirm a trade.'

Fiona nodded. 'OK.'

Tanya glared at Freddie. 'What have you got to say for yourself?'

'I screwed up. I'm sorry. I take full responsibility.'

'And so you should. Shinewater legging us over is friggin embarrassing.'

Nate stood. 'What saddens me most about this goof up is that it was an accident waiting to happen.' He rolled his tongue around his gums. 'Gossip, gossip, gossip, that's all I've seen you guys do just lately, and this is where it stops. When you're at the desk your priority is Kohen Stanzinger. Am I making myself clear? Gossip finito. End of. Period. You guys got that?'

They both nodded, and Nate sent them on their way. 'Goddamn bozos,' he muttered.

Although angry about what had happened, Tanya felt Nate's reaction was over the top, and rooted in jealousy, because Fiona, in revising for her FSA exam, often posed questions to anyone who cared to answer, and it was invariably Freddie who responded.

'That was a bit harsh, wasn't it?' she said, 'considering we're only talking about 54,000 dollars.'

Cheap as chips compared to the three million you lost. And Fi and Freddie have learned something.

'Not a bit. Freddie was long overdue for a boot up his jacksy, as you guys say.' He paused. 'How was your lunch?'

Tanya had been to see her solicitor.

'It was good, thank you.'

'Is everything OK?'

'Yes, why?'

'You look a little tired.'

It was now Wednesday, and Peter had moved out on Sunday, since when she'd hardly slept for worrying about Jamie, and painfully recalling his plea. 'Mummy, please don't make Daddy move out, he's my daddy and I love him and I want him to live with us.' He had given Peter his favourite teddy bear.

She faked a grin. 'I must confess I've not slept well

this week, on account of all the changes. I know what's happened is a good thing, but change is daunting, don't you think?'

She was referring to events at KS, which made for a plausible excuse. A Japanese bank, Hakatoshi Japan International, or HJI for short, had taken a big stake in KS, providing a much needed boost to capital. KS had also applied to the U.S. authorities to change its status from securities firm to bank, to enable it to take deposits, thereby reducing its reliance on the wholesale markets for funding. A Bloomberg news article also claimed KS was looking for a tie up with an American regional bank, but KS hadn't confirmed that.

'Relax, we're going to be in much better shape.'

'I'm sure you're right. In fact, I know you are.'

Nate smiled. 'Hey, why don't we have dinner one evening?'

'I'd love to, Nate, but I like to see my children before they go to bed whenever possible. How about lunch instead?'

For a split second he looked as though he'd sucked a lemon, but then he smiled. 'We can't both be off the desk at the same time, but lunch when Sam comes on board would be good. In the meantime, keep the dinner offer in reserve.'

'Thanks. I will.'

*

Upon hearing Jamie crying and stamping his feet Tanya jumped out of bed, threw on her dressing gown, and opened her door, to see him in a tug of war with Alison, trying to pull his skating trousers from her hands.

She kneeled down and gave him a cuddle, while looking up at Alison. 'What's Brendan doing here?' This was Tanya's gardener, and he usually came on a Friday, and it was the noise of him mowing her lawn that first woke her, spoiling her plans for a lie-in.

'He had a wedding to go to yesterday,' Alison said, 'so I said he could come today instead. Sorry.'

Jamie continued to cry on Tanya's shoulder. 'Sweetheart, those are special trousers for when you go skating, and they cost a lot of money.'

'But I like them Mummy, I like them.'

'That's why you must look after them, Sweetheart. If you spoil them you will have to wear one of my skirts to go skating, and then all your friends will see your knobbly knees.'

He cried louder. 'I want to see Daddy.'

I shouldn't have put him back in his own bed so soon.

'I know, Darling, and tomorrow you will see him, for the whole day. And when he moves into his lovely new house you'll be able to stay with him too.'

Tanya held him tight and kept reassuring him he would see Peter the next day, and after five or so minutes, he calmed down and went to his room, with Alison, to choose another pair of trousers.

Downstairs, Florence was playing snap with Harry in the sitting room, and Barbara was in the kitchen working her way through a pile of ironing. Tanya asked her if she wanted a cup of tea.

'Yes, please.' She paused. 'Do you think you'll have time to read my cup today?'

'Yes, Mum, but not right now. I'm still waking up.'

Barbara had introduced Tanya to tea-leaf reading as

a child. After virtually every cup of tea, she would turn the cup upside down on a saucer, and twist it three times to the left, before examining the leaves left in the cup, often until they dried to dust. Most of Tanya's predictions came to naught, and those that didn't were hardly unforeseeable, but Barbara still loved the ritual.

As Tanya took her first sip of tea, the doorbell rang.

'I'll go,' Florence called out. Moments later she came into the kitchen, carrying Harry, and said 'It's the bucket man.'

It was the window cleaner calling for his money. Tanya ran upstairs to her bedroom to get her purse, and paid him. When she returned to the kitchen Brendan was there, making himself a cuppa while chatting with Barbara about the weather.

He smiled at Tanya. 'You don't mind, do you?' he pointed to his cup, 'only Alison always lets me help myself.'

'You go right ahead.' She picked up her mug, and went into her lounge, but minutes later Barbara opened the door. 'He's gone now. You can come out.'

Tanya dutifully went back into the kitchen and sat on a stool at the breakfast bar.

'Ooh I like this,' Barbara said, holding up a cream linen top of Tanya's.

'It's new, Mum. Give me a few wears and you can have it.'

Barbara smiled. 'What are you doing today?'

'I'm not sure yet, but Alison and I will probably take the boys bowling this afternoon.'

Just then Alison and Jamie entered the kitchen.

'Yippee! Bowling,' Jamie said, having overheard. 'Mummy, can I go on the racing car afterwards?'

He meant a stationary racing car, in the amusement section adjoining the bowling alley.

'Yes, Darling, of course you can.'

'Yippee,' he cried again, and rushed to tell Harry.

'Do you want to come?' Tanya said to Barbara.

'No thanks, I think I'll put my feet up and do the crossword.'

Jesus, she's getting well comfortable.

Alison and Barbara exchanged a few quiet words, and Barbara giggled.

'Go on,' Alison said to her.

Barbara looked at Tanya. 'Vulay vu une tass der tay.'

Tanya burst out laughing. 'What the sod is that?'

'French, for would you like a cup of tea,' Barbara said proudly. 'Florence has been giving me lessons.'

The day passed quickly and Tanya felt it had been a good one, because Jamie and Harry enjoyed their outing, and Barbara remained in good humour. Sunday however was a different matter, on account of Tanya paying Daphne a visit, and foolishly telling Barbara she would only be half an hour, whereas she was out for an hour and a half.

'Sorry, I was so long, Mum. Daphne talks ever so slow.'

Barbara's mouth turned down.

Tanya pretended not to notice and said she would make her a cup of tea, but Barbara told her not to bother, that she had just had one, and went into a sulk.

Three hours later, having put her boys to bed, Tanya again tried to make up with her. 'I'm going to have a glass of wine, Mum. Would you like one?'

'You're definitely more like him, than me,' Barbara

said. 'I'll have a cup of tea.' She was referring to Tanya's dad, and his drinking.

'You like a drink,' Tanya said.

Barbara scoffed. 'I hardly ever have a drink. I can't, can I, because of my tablets?'

That didn't stop you when Kay and Jim came over.

Tanya made her a cup of tea and upon giving it to her, announced she was off to bed, which angered Barbara even more. Tanya knew it would, but felt opting out was better than losing her temper.

She's got to go home, but how can I tell her that? What do I say? It's not as if my house isn't big enough.

*

A hand on his mouse, head inclined to his computer, thick quiff nudging forward, Spencer looked pensively at the screen, unaware of Tanya's presence. She stole a few moments to watch him, to admire the strength of his jaw line, the definition of his permanent shadow, those dark lashes of his, and the shimmer of his suit.

She coughed.

He turned to look at her, his movements steady and sure, and grinned, showing his dimples. 'Good morning, Princess. To what do I owe this enormous pleasure?'

'Have you got a few minutes?'

'For you, yes.' He pressed a button on his phone.

She beckoned him with her finger, and closed the door. A minute later his back was up against it.

'No... no, Princess, no,' he said feebly, 'this is not a good idea...'

Ignoring him, Tanya unbuttoned her jacket, pulled her breasts out of her red bra, released the clip on his trousers, and slipped to her knees. Moments later she was murmuring pleasure as she brushed her face over his warm flesh, and nuzzled his blanket of rich brown curls. He kept saying stop yet held his shirt aloft, and as she licked and sucked his cock, while using her hand to force its load, his breaths quickened. Then his body jerked, and with a gasp and a grunt his spunk shot into her mouth—most of it anyway.

He looked at her, his eyes sweetly horrified, and rushed to restore an orderly appearance, while Tanya rose slowly, casually put her tits back in her bra, shook each of her legs in turn to restore feeling, and stretched her arms.

'For goodness sake, do up your jacket,' he urged.

'Stop panicking.' She buttoned up and wandered over to his desk. 'I can see you weren't a boy-bloody-scout. Mirror? Tissues? Water?'

He took a pressed cotton handkerchief from the inside pocket of his jacket, and gave it to her.

She winked at him, put her hand up her skirt, used it to wipe her pussy, and gave it back to him. 'Here you go, a soggy souvenir for you to sniff on the plane.'

He stared at her, the black seams of his eyes frames to a mix of admiration and torment. 'Now I know what I've been missing.' He drew a cross on her forehead with his finger. 'I hereby christen you Princess Minxy.'

'Thank you, I'm flattered. Right, I shall be off. I just wanted to give you a going away present.'

He followed her to the door, and held it closed. 'I shall miss you terribly.'

'How about a lovely wet goodbye kiss, then?'

As she expected, he hesitated. 'You're such a wuss, Spence. How can you not like the taste of yourself?'

'Female bodily juices are one thing, Princess, but...'
He didn't finish.

She kept a straight face. 'Take no notice of that research about gay people that was on the news. The statistics are really low. It's extremely rare for a man's sexual preference to change if he tastes his own semen.'

'Is that true?' he looked concerned, 'I didn't see that story.'

She giggled.

He shook his head. 'What am I going to do with you?'

'Just about anything you like, if you're a good boy.'

He laughed. 'Can I phone you while I'm away, I mean at home?'

She pulled a face. 'Text is better because my mum's staying with me at the moment, and she suffers from acute fucking nosiness.'

I've got to find a way to get her to go home.

'You have a wonderful way with words, Princess. Text it will be.'

*

Olli Vermallen sat with an arm draped along the back edge of his green Chesterfield, shirt open at the neck showing a tuft of ginger hair, with his freckly brow pinched, and baby blue eyes focused intently on Tanya.

'...if investment banks had had a mix of people of all ages and from all backgrounds at senior management level, there wouldn't be a crisis,' she said, 'but a diverse group makes for hard work when it comes to agreeing policies and practices. So they took the triple easy way, stopped anyone without a degree advancing from back to front office, which was my way in, restricted hiring to people from top universities, and heavily favoured those with science degrees.' She glanced at TJ. 'I have the utmost respect for TJ — he hailed from Trinity College, Oxford, achieving a first in PPE — but he's rare, because he has a conscience.'

TJ wiped an imaginary bead of sweat from his brow. 'I was considering getting my coat.'

They all laughed.

'Add in ageism,' she continued, 'sexism too, because while KS are great on that front most investment banks shy away from hiring women, and you end up with a highly skewed view.' She paused. 'At best that's social engineering, at worst a form of ethnic cleansing, and now the world at large is suffering the fallout of all that meddling.' Another pause. 'Sadly, too many bankers use their education to exploit. They don't care about shareholders, investors of any kind for that matter, and it's patently obvious all they learned from the collapse of Barings and LTCM was how to scale up on losses.'

Olli pinched his nose and sniffed. 'It's an interesting theory, but investors have also contributed to the industry's decline. No market can function for long without investor participation, and institutions have been more than happy to rely on rating agencies to validate their decisions.'

'I couldn't agree more. And rating agencies... Well, let's just say they should be second on the bonfire.'

That raised another laugh.

'How has Sky-Rise faired?' TJ asked.

Olli smiled. 'We were lucky enough to foresee the crash in subprime.'

'You mean smart enough,' Tanya said.

'Hey, there's always an element of luck to these things. We were in the right place at the right time, able to capitalise on one heck of an opportunity. We've never been into macro trading, or excesses in leverage, the economics don't stack up. Sky-Rise tries to go against the grain, in a modest way.' He again pinched his nose and sniffed.

He's definitely got something wrong with his sinuses. His laughs are like snorts.

'There are easier ways to make money than by competing in an already cramped arena,' he continued, 'where you have to leverage up to the hilt to achieve viable returns.' He paused. 'Anyhow, where do you guys see opportunities?'

TJ answered. 'Tanya and I both feel the trade to do at the moment is to go short the US and the UK, and long Argentina, Brazil, China and Russia, countries with natural resources and high foreign exchange reserves.'

Olli nodded and looked at the clock. Seven p.m. 'You guys want a drink?'

They both said yes, and he walked over to a fitted cabinet, which turned out to be a bar and a fridge. 'What will it be?'

Tanya and TJ both asked for a glass of white wine.

'Shit, no ice,' Olli said. 'I need to get the wine, anyhow. I'll be right back.'

When he left the room TJ and Tanya exchanged hopeful glances, and Tanya cocked an eye at the wall and a weird oil painting of a face, in two halves, one half higher than the other and one eye eerily large. She found it scary and felt it out of place given the antique furniture.

'Native American art,' TJ whispered, 'probably Potawatomi Indians.'

She cut the air above her head with her hand.

TJ smiled. 'Not important,' he mouthed silently.

Olli returned with a jug of ice, and a bottle.

'Is this OK for you guys?'

'Lovely, thank you,' Tanya said, glimpsing Torciano and Vernaccia on the label.

'1997,' TJ said, sounding impressed. 'Excellent.'

Olli gave Tanya and TJ their drinks, fixed himself a Gin Martini, and returned to his Chesterfield.

'Yes, opportunities in the credit markets,' he mused. He stirred his drink with a cocktail stick skewered with three olives, and ate one. 'If I was going to invest in corporate bonds, what would you guys recommend I buy?'

'Nothing at the moment,' Tanya said. 'If banks continue to hold the government to ransom by not lending to each other, the markets could end up paralysed.'

He looked at TJ.

'I agree,' TJ said. 'Right now the only certainty is fear driven volatility. In fact Farraday's doing a ton of business in structured products that enable investors to take bets on volatility, for that precise reason.'

Tanya nodded. 'If I had no choice but to invest, I'd buy long dated bonds and keep away from those due for redemption, because if the markets freeze, borrowers won't be able to refinance. If you're day-trading it's different, but to a first timer I'd say hold your fire.'

Olli smiled. 'When things settle down, if we take modest risk within the investment grade arena, what kind of returns do you think you guys can make?'

'We think thirty percent a year is a realistic target,' TJ said.

Ollie stroked his nose. 'That's not bad. Sure, I've made two, three, four hundred percent returns from private equity, but those days are over, in the near term anyhow.'

Thereafter they talked generalities until Olli brought the meeting to a close, and suggested they reconvene a month hence, adding that he'd like to make it sooner, but that he was out of the country in the interim.

Once Tanya and TJ had walked a safe distant from his office on Victoria embankment, Tanya did her first Olli impression. 'Hey, sure, what the heck,' she drawled, before sniffing and pinching her nose.

TJ laughed. 'A debrief over dinner at the OXO Tower?'

She looked across the Thames at the tower, and then at the London Eye.

Jamie and Harry would love a ride in the Eye.

'I need to get home, but let's have one drink.'

Peter was due round at ten o'clock that night to collect his money.

They walked along the river's edge absorbed in hopeful chatter, and stopped at the first boat bar they came to, and while TJ got the drinks Tanya gazed up at big Ben, and for a few sanguine moments imagined a debt-free life.

When she got home she had barely taken off her coat, when Barbara rushed into the hallway, slipped her hand into the pocket of her apron and pulled out a letter.

'This came for you today.'

Well why the fuck didn't you leave it in the letter rack?

Tanya snatched it from her, excited and hoping it was from Spencer, but she recognized it as clever spam, handwritten so as to look personal. Feeling annoyed and flat, she put it in the rack on the hall table.

'Aren't you going to open it?'

'No, not yet, and in future leave my letters on there.' She motioned to the table.

Barbara skewed her skinny face. 'That lazy git come round this afternoon to get his CD collection. New pair of trousers, smart shirt, he's spending your money like there's no tomorrow.'

'It's his money, Mum, not mine.'

'He said something about coming back tonight. Is that right?'

'Yes. We've got a few things to discuss.'

She hadn't told Barbara or anyone else about her and Peter's off the record deal.

'Like what?'

'Solicitor stuff. Don't be nosey.'

She's definitely going home by the weekend.

Tanya counted out the money on a sofa cushion in-between where her and Peter were sitting.

'I thought it would be bigger a pile,' she said, the fifty thousand pounds only standing about seven inches high.

Peter shrugged.

She stuffed the notes into two big envelopes, which Peter took and put into a sports holdall by his feet.

'Ta,' he said quietly.

'Are you OK?' He looked the saddest she had ever seen him.

'Not really, no,' he said, and started crying.

Tanya got up. 'I'm sorry, Pete. I didn't want to hurt you, truly I didn't.'

He looked at her. 'Could I have that last kiss, just for old time's sake?'

Too choked to speak, she just shook her head, and out of respect for his dignity left the room, and went to the kitchen, where Barbara was filling up the kettle.

'What's wrong? What's he said now?'

Tanya wiped her eyes with her fingers. 'He hasn't said anything. Divorce is just hard.'

'No good crying,' Barbara said. 'You just have to get on with it. I had to, and I had no money either.'

But you didn't get on with it. I was the one who got on with it, not you. All you did was eat tranquilisers.

'I'll be alright in a minute.'

CHAPTER FOURTEEN

When Freddie went and sat next to Fiona, Tanya could see Nate was annoyed, but with it being lunchtime and quiet, there wasn't much he could say.

'It works like this, Fi,' Freddie said, drawing on a piece of a paper. 'A hedge fund will typically earn between one and two percent for managing money, plus a performance fee on what they make over and above an agreed target, which can easily be twenty percent...'

Tanya tuned out of their conversation.

About ten minutes later Fi said, excitedly. 'Ah, I see. Whereas KS can reduce their inventory at whim by a billion dollars, if a hedge fund gave a billion dollars back to their investors, they would lose their ten or twenty million dollars management fee, and the chance to earn a performance fee. That would be like admitting they couldn't hack it, which would be stupid.'

'Exactly,' Freddie said.

'Well done, Fi,' Tanya said.

Smiling, Fi tightened the ruffle around her pony tail, and then rubbed Freddie's forearm, by way of thanks.

Tanya glanced at Nate. He was on the phone but looking in their direction, his chair slightly off centre of his desk, from where he could see them.

'Hedge funds can also take massive positions,' Freddie said. 'They're fiercely competitive and...'

Tanya again tuned out, but kept an eye on Nate. After finishing his call, he stood up, flexed his arms, rotated his neck, and then began screwing a sheet of paper into a ball. She could guess where it was heading.

'...the other thing to remember, Fi, is that hedge funds are free from the prying eyes—'

It hit Freddie on the head.

Freddie looked up and laughed. 'Good shot,' he said, and threw it back.

'As I was saying, Fi, hedge funds are free from the prying eyes of shareholders, and at arm's length from regulators. The difference—'

This time it was two balls, in succession.

Tanya looked at him. 'Nate, I've been reviewing Tarapet. Do you think we should tighten our terms?'

Tarapet was short for Tara Petroleum, an oil company that was a day away from raising 1.5 billion euros. KS was one of the banks bidding for the mandate.

'Maybe,' he said, 'it's a chunky deal. One and half billion euros would certainly help us in the league tables.'

'Hey, Freddie,' he snapped. 'What's your current thinking on Tarapet?'

Freddie looked up, startled. 'The same as it was, Nate, unless something's changed in the last hour.'

'Should we improve our bid?' Nate said.

Freddie started blinking.

Tanya tutted. 'He can't answer that, Nate. That's our job.'

Nate laughed.

'It's OK, Freddie,' she said. 'You carry on.'

He looked back at Fiona. 'The difference between a hedge fund and KS, Fi, is that KS is a public company, which means it has to answer to FINRA, the SEC, the FSA, and shareholders. But hedge funds...'

'Come and have a look at the profile of the deal,' Tanya said to Nate, which was on her computer.

He did, and stood looking over her shoulder at it.

'Hey, Freddie, What happened to BBI?' he said, perusing the list of bidding banks.

He meant Bay Brothers International and why they weren't on the list. Freddie had done the leg work, generating the profile, which included an analysis of the risks, and a rundown of hedging strategies and just about every conceivable trade the deal would throw up.

'They got dropped,' Freddie said.

Tanya elaborated. 'BBI's in the corner of the classroom wearing a dunce's hat as far as Tarapet is concerned. They've been selling Tarapet's debt in Asia, trying to force the price lower so they could buy this deal at a cheaper price. At least that's the rumour.'

Nate nodded. 'That sure smells like a BBI design.'

Freddie made to giggle but stopped himself.

'What's so funny little man?' Nate demanded.

Freddie started blinking.

'Don't get personal, Nate,' Tanya said.

He ignored her. 'Come on, don't be shy. Share the joke.'

Freddie's face reddened. 'That was a mixed metaphor. You can't smell a design.'

Tanya suppressed a laugh.

'It was a figure of speech, you idiot,' Nate said.

Freddie resumed playing teacher, and Tanya continued to chat with Nate about Tarapet but his responses were vague, so she decided to confront the situation, and asked for a quiet word.

They went to Nate's office.

'We're getting along well now, Nate, and I don't want that to change, so please don't read anything untoward in what I'm about to say.' She paused.

'You're making Freddie nervous, and if you keep digging him out he could leave.'

Nate laughed, and Tanya wondered if that was what he was hoping would happen.

'I'm serious, Nate. Freddie works bloody hard, and we need him, and by helping Fi he's helping us. We don't have the time to coach her.'

'Has he said anything, or filed a complaint?'

'No, he wouldn't, would he, he's too nice?'

Nate shrugged. 'So what's the big deal?'

'The big deal is that the way you're treating him is humiliating and disrespectful.'

'You mean you don't like my management style?'

She sighed. 'I didn't say that. I'm just sharing my observations.'

He looked at his watch. 'Are you done, because I have a meeting at three, with a client of Max's, and I need to prepare?'

She nodded. 'How long will you be, only we need to agree final terms for Tarapet?'

'We can do that in the morning.'

'Yes, but I'd prefer to get it sorted today, be ahead of the game. Personally, I think we should clip a few basis points off.'

'Double A, five years... I guess there's not much downside if we do,' he said.

'Except we can't afford to guess, Nate, and we both have to be in agreement. What time will you be back?'

'You sound real anxious.'

'I am. It's a big deal. Will you be back before six?'

He laughed. 'What's with the early exits?'

Fuck you.

'I'm in at seven every morning, Nate, including

202

Mondays, and I'm here until at least five thirty on Fridays. Not that you would know that,' she said, and walked out.

*

'...so with Fi acting as phone jockey,' Nate said, his backside perched on a radiator casing under a window, 'that chump Freddie buys Credit Suisse 4 7/8ths and sells the 5 1/8ths, and Tanya dismisses our $54,000 hit as chicken feed.'

'That's unlike Tanya,' Bruce said.

'I agree, but like I said, she's not herself lately, and she's looking real tired.'

Bruce clasped his hands behind his head. 'This is a tough business at the best of times. Even I'm feeling the pressure right now.'

Nate nodded, looking solemn. 'I think she might be seeing a shrink.'

'A shrink?'

'Either that or she's interviewing because these days she's gone by six at the latest. But a shrink seems more likely because,' he shrugged, 'well, it's hardly been one of her best years, has it? First NCA, which deep down she knows was her fault, then she loses us the Belgian deal, then Charlie checks out, and while that was clearly his decision, she did use to talk to the guy like a dog. Then Quagg has a joke at her expense, and she gets me as a co-head.' He folded his arms. 'She's a tough cookie, I give you that, but that's a hell of a roll call.'

'Gee, put like that... I've seen guys come unhinged in this business, let alone a woman. I don't want to see Tanya take a dive.'

'Me neither. When Sam comes on board, I'm going to insist she takes a break.'

'Good idea.' Bruce paused, took off his glasses and rubbed an eye. 'Why don't we take her out to dinner?'

Nate smiled. 'Great minds think alike. I already tried that, invited her to dinner last week, but she turned me down. But I'm sure she'd accept an invitation from you, although I doubt she'd want me along.'

'I think you should be there.'

'Don't worry about me, Bruce. It's Tanya we need to be concerned about.'

Bruce nodded. 'I appreciate the way you're handling things.'

'I'm just doing my job.' He looked at the row of clocks on the wall. 'Shit, I can't believe it's seven fifteen already. I gotta go. I've got a conference call with New York about Tarapet.' He dashed to the door.

'Go easy, Nate, and keep me informed as to how Tanya's doing.'

'You bet.'

*

Way to go, Kiddo! Well done. I owe you dinner. Go home and get some rest.

Tanya read the email about fifteen times, and sat soaking in the glory, Bruce's suggestion of dinner leaving her in raptures.

She gave Freddie a slap on the back. 'Who needs Nate, eh?'

'We did quite well, didn't we?'

'Don't be modest. We did fucking brilliant.'

Nate had called in sick with a stomach bug, leaving

204

Tanya to price Tarapet on her own. And with Freddie's help, she had not only won the deal but managed to sell two thirds of her allotment of bonds.

She glanced at Rich Hillbrand who despite the hour, six thirty, was still dialling for dollars. 'It's good to see his nerves are still wired to his bank account.'

Freddie smiled.

She threw a half eaten sandwich in the bin, and drank a mouthful of cold coffee. 'Yuk.'

'Would you like me to go and get you a fresh one,' Freddie said.

'No thanks, Freddie. I'm going home. I'm shot.'

The next day, a Friday, Nate called in sick again, saying he had a gastric bug.

Come Monday, however, when he showed up at eight thirty, he looked to Tanya as though he'd spent four days on a cruise instead of the toilet.

Food poisoning, my arse. The coward opted out and went on a jolly.

She updated him on Tarapet, and didn't hide the pride she felt at the job she'd done.

He gripped his jaw. 'Do you think we're going to be able to shift the balance at a profit?'

'I'm not Mystic Meg, Nate, but I think we've got a fair chance, and we've now got a profit cushion of well over a million euros.'

That he hadn't complimented her and had also focused on the negative really pissed her off, and she went to the privacy of her office to phone Spencer, who was in Tokyo, to have a moan.

'...He's such a prick, Spence. Not a crumb of praise. I was feeling great till I saw his face.'

'He's obviously jealous, but at least Bruce

recognized what a spectacular job you did. That's a lot more important.'

'You're right. Anyway, how are you? How's your trip going? And how close are we to the end of the world?'

He laughed, skipped over news about himself and told her what he thought of the global economy, the words recession, depression and stagflation getting frequent mentions.

The sombre tone of his voice sent Tanya into a fit of the giggles. 'Spence, have you ever thought of working for the Samaritans?'

He laughed. 'I wish I could see those eyes.'

'You will, if you're a good boy. Now tell me, is anything at all going up—apart from your gorgeous Georgy that is?'

'Gorgeous Georgy! I must say you do have a quaint vernacular, Princess.'

'How do you know, you've not seen it yet?'

They shared more laughter.

'I'm afraid I have to go, as I have to catch a flight to Kuala Lumpur. Can you call me tomorrow?'

'I'll try.'

'Is your mother still staying with you?'

'Yes, but she won't be for much longer, because she's driving me crackers.'

'I'm sure she means well.'

'You don't know her.' She heaved a sigh. 'Anyway, big kiss lover boy, and a special one for Georgy. I'll speak to you in the next day or so.'

'You are deliciously indecent, Princess.'

'I do my best. Byeee.'

Tanya remained light hearted, and deciding Nate

was a classic example of a poor little rich kid who needed reassurance, she found the goodwill to be nice to him. And it was a tactic that paid off, with him finally saying 'nice work' in relation to Tarapet.

He's not all bad, she thought, and complimented him in return.

'You did well to pick up those coal and steel bonds from Todd at 97,' she said. 'The cheapest offer I saw was 97.10.'

He smiled. 'It's called broker's poker. I gave him five seconds to fill or kill.'

'You bloody scum bag,' she teased.

'A man's got to do what a man's got to do, which reminds me,' he looked at the clock. 'I gotta go.' He took a comb from his jacket pocket and tended his hair.

'Are you off to Steve's cocktail party?'

He shook his head.

'A hot date then, is it?'

He rolled his eyes. 'Not exactly. I've a cousin over from the states, and she's a four hundred pound beach whale.'

Tanya laughed, 'That's definitely not good for your reputation.'

'You're telling me. I'm gonna head out of town and keep going.'

Promises, promises. I hear it's lovely in Vanuatu.

'I took her to a neat little place in Cromer last night, called Elderton Lodge.'

'Cromer in Norfolk? Blimey, that's miles away.'

'I know but it's worth the drive. The food there's excellent, and my cousin likes good food and lots of it. Boy, can she eat.' He puffed out his cheeks.

Tanya giggled, as she imagined Nate in his flash

207

convertible with the roof down, it being a warm September, with his fat cousin beside him.

He hooked his jacket over his shoulder. 'Are you going?' he said, meaning to Barclay Gray's party.

She shook her head. 'I need to get home.'

He touched her shoulder affectionately. 'You need to chill a little.'

She smiled, and wished him a good evening.

Minutes later she stood waiting for the lift, her raincoat draped over her arm, sighing heavily as she cheerlessly imagined Barbara's miserable face.

Fuck it. Nate's right. I do need to chill a little.

She called home. Barbara picked up.

'Hi, Mum, would you tell Alison I'm going to be late. I've got to go to a cocktail party.'

'The boys will be disappointed,' Barbara said.

'I know but I'll make it up to them tomorrow night.'

Barbara asked what time she would be home.

'I'm not sure, but it won't be too late.'

Tanya knew if she said a time and failed to meet it, Barbara would have cause to go on the turn.

'Shall I make you something to eat?'

'No thanks. There'll be food at the party.'

'Harry wet him himself again today. That's the second time in a week.'

Tanya's stomach knotted. 'I'll see you later, Mum.'

Barbara rang off without saying goodbye.

She is definitely going home at the weekend.

Tanya took a glass of champagne from the waiter's tray, and stood in the sweeping reception hall assessing the crowd. By her estimation under the roof of this sleek glass building in Chelsea Harbour were men and women who collectively controlled half a trillion dollars or more. Spotting Steve at the top of the galleried staircase with Denton Fenshill, hardly her favourite person, she mingled at ground level, knowing Steve would work the room and find her eventually, which he did.

'It's great to see you,' he said. 'I'm so glad you made it. How long have you been here?'

'About an hour. I saw you when I arrived, but you were with scumbag Fenshill, and I didn't want to talk to him, in case he mentioned NCA.'

'Neither did I but beggars can't be choosers. Krevamar's an investor in Barclay Gray's commodity fund.'

'You have my deepest sympathy.'

Laughing, he eyed her cleavage. 'You look lovely.'

'I can tell you've had a few,' she said.

He winked at her. 'Part of the job,' he said, and promptly took a fresh glass of champagne off a passing tray, 'unless you happen to be Denton Fenshill, whose a dead man if he so much as looks at a bottle of booze.'

Tanya's face lit up. 'I knew I was going to have a good time tonight. Quick, give me the scoop.'

Steve whispered in her ear. 'So the story goes, once upon a time Fenshill traded commodity futures and did a blinding job—until the pubs opened, when he also did a blinding job—of getting blind fucking drunk, which wouldn't have mattered if his wife was a nobody, but she's not. Her father's loaded, and I mean loaded, the bloke discovered oil somewhere in Africa. And he owns a chunk of Krevamar. Say no more. If Fenshill so much as sniffs a spoon of Tiramisu, his daddy-in-law will know about it, and chop his tiny little bollocks off.'

'I love it, Steve. I just love it.'

Someone caught Steve's eye. 'Don't go anywhere. I'll be back in a jif,' he said, and made off.

His jif was three quarters of an hour, but Tanya found lots of people to talk to, including, briefly, Denton Fenshill, who was hugging a glass of orange juice, which cheered her up no end.

The crowd was fast dispersing when Steve caught up with her again, by which time he was listing from the influence of alcohol.

He put a hand on the wall for support. 'Is Nate poking Fi yet?'

'I hope not, and I don't think so. I've done all I can to warn her off him, told her she's the one taking all the risk, and that when he's done with her, he'll get rid of her, by which time her career will be out the window. She didn't like it, but it had to be said. I couldn't sit back and watch her wreck her career for a loser.'

'She still might. Sense pisses out the window when it comes to a shag.'

She laughed. 'Eloquent tonight, aren't we?'

'My tongue is a natural gift.'

'By the way,' she said, 'how much did you pay Ludo Quagg to write that piece?'

A glowing write up about Barclay Gray had appeared in the latest issue of *Financial Insider*.

'It was payback for my job.'

'What do you mean?'

'Quagg helped get me this job.'

'But I thought you said you got it through FPS.'

FPS was short for The Finance Search Partnership, a head hunting firm.

'I did, but FPS and Ludo sometimes team up and split the fee, and that's what they did with me.'

'So what did Ludo get paid for, finding you or finding Barclay Gray?'

Steve shrugged. 'No idea, I just know he was involved, because I saw the invoice we paid FPS, which was reduced by fifty percent, with a note saying the other fifty percent was going to be paid to Quagg.'

'He's lower than fucking swamp life. We just paid him a small fortune for your replacement. The creep's banked money both ways.'

'Oops, I shouldn't have said anything.'

'It would have come out, Steve, these things always do. It's called divine justice.' She looked at her watch, gone ten o'clock. 'I need to make a move.'

He badgered her to stay longer, but she refused, and he walked her to the foyer, and helped her on with her raincoat, after which she opened her arms to give him a hug, only for him to kiss her. Open mouth stuff.

She pushed him away. 'For God's sake, Steve, I might not be married anymore, but you are.'

He grinned. 'I've always wanted to do that. Fancy another one at The Black Swan?' He paused. 'Or we could just go there and have a drink.'

She shook her head, laughing. 'You'll thank me in the morning for saving you from yourself.'

'No, I won't.'

Riding home in Ted's car, Tanya kept smiling to herself, flattered by Steve's attention. His kiss had also whetted her appetite for sex, albeit with Spencer not him. She sent Spencer a text: *I'm hungry, bleat, bleat, and in need of being seriously ravished!*

He replied the next morning: *Likewise, Princess. Missing you more by the minute. I shall text you later. X*

He didn't text her later though, and that night she

phoned him but the call went through to his voice mail. She didn't leave a message. She wasn't sure precisely where he was, somewhere between South Korea and Malaysia, but knew wherever it was it had to be morning, and so she fully expected to wake up to a text from him. But she didn't. And doubts began creeping in.

Is he a shadow or a real person? Is the paint of his portrait of oil, water or disappearing ink?

By the afternoon, she was fast coming round to the view that her declaration of need had been a mistake.

I was an idiot to show my hand.

Then he phoned to say he was in London.

'How come? I thought your dad's birthday bash was tomorrow.'

'A hungry princess needs feeding. I changed my plans, in the hope we could have dinner tonight.'

'Did you really, or did a client meeting get cancelled?'

'I'm not in the habit of telling lies.'

'Bear with me for a minute,' she said.

She raced through the practicalities in her mind. It was Alison's weekend off but she figured Florence could look after Jamie and Harry. (Barbara never had and never would baby-sit, at least not on her own.) She could put her boys to bed, change into something alluring, and if she was back home by seven on Saturday morning, her boys wouldn't even know she'd been out. Sorted.

'It will have to be late, Spence, as I need to go home first to see my boys.'

'That's fine. Why don't you come to my place, and I'll cook supper?'

'OK. I'll be with you by half nine.'

She was already mentally ripping his clothes off, her heart flipping with excitement.

To avoid speaking to Barbara, she phoned Florence on her mobile.

'Do you understand, Florence?' she said, after conveying her request a few times.

'Oui. I stay home tonight and look for children.'

Tanya laughed. 'Yes. Good. Thank you, Florence. Bye.'

Shortly thereafter Barbara called. 'You've got a cheek asking that poor girl to stay in on a Friday night, at five minutes' notice.'

You mean you're angry I'm not going to be at home reading your friggin tea cup.

'It's part of her contract, Mum, and this is the first time I've ever asked her to baby-sit.'

'Out Wednesday, out tonight, the boys won't know who you are.'

'I'm coming home first, so that I can bath them, tuck them up and read them a story.'

'Where are you going?'

'Clubbing, with a crowd from the office.'

'Clubbing? What's that all about? Some dance hall with drugs, I suppose.'

Tanya was too buoyant to engage in a spat.

'Mum, I have to go, I'm busy.'

'You're bloody selfish, if you ask me.'

'Well I'm not asking you,' she said, and rang off.

For the rest of the day Tanya's nerve endings were firing like a rocket, and in between every trade her mind leapt to her wardrobe, and what she was going to wear. She decided on her black bra with the gold chain linking the cups, and matching thong, stockings with lace tops, and black patent high heels. And a short pillar box red clingy cashmere dress, as that would show off her boobs and her legs, and was also lovely and soft to the touch.

When she got home she was treated to one of Barbara's blackest looks, but she took no notice and gaily concentrated her attention on Jamie and Harry.

A few hours later she was all set to rock and roll, as she saw it, her outfit concealed under a long cream coat, so that Barbara had no chance to pass negative comment on it. She looked in her cheval mirror in her bedroom, and smiled. 'Cinderella is finally off to the Ball.'

Downstairs, Barbara was drawing the curtain across the street door.

Tanya picked up her keys. 'I'm off now, Mum.'

'Off?' Barbara said, looking confused.

She heaved a sigh. 'I mean I am going out.'

Barbara furrowed her brow. 'But who's going to look after the children?'

'What are you talking about? Florence is.'

Barbara's eyes glinted. 'But Florence has gone out.'

Her body flooding with adrenalin Tanya rushed down the hallway to Florence's room and banged on the door. There was no answer, and the door was locked.

She stormed up to Barbara. 'You told her to go out, didn't you?'

Barbara didn't answer but her lips were turned down into a smug smile.

Tanya took her by the shoulders and started shaking her. 'You evil witch, you evil, evil witch, you. Get your things, and get out of my fucking house.'

Barbara didn't look smug anymore. Her face was chalky white, her eyes squinting with fear, shot free of the devilish joy they'd betrayed seconds earlier.

'I mean it,' Tanya said, 'go and get your things. I'm calling a cab right now.'

Barbara ran up the stairs to her room.

Sweating, Tanya opened the street door, and stood in the porch, grateful for the cool air, and when she heard Barbara coming down the stairs, she got her coat, and flung it at her. 'You've always said I ruined your life,' she said, quivering with rage, her voice thick with emotion, 'well let me tell you something, shall I? You've ruined mine too. But this is where it ends.'

When the taxi arrived, Tanya held out a twenty pound note.

'Stick your money,' Barbara said.

Tanya called Spencer and tearfully told him what had happened. He immediately offered to come to her house.

'Thanks, but I'd be on edge in case my boys woke up. It wouldn't be good for them to see a strange man in the house with their mum, so soon after Peter leaving.'

'Of course,' he said quietly. 'Never mind. I shall be back next weekend.'

'I'm sorry, Spence. You went to all that trouble for nothing.'

'It's OK, Princess, and I'm the one who ought to be apologising. I wanted to surprise you, but in hindsight I should have given you more notice.'

'Don't stop the surprises. What happened is not your fault. This situation has been brewing for a while, decades in fact. Even as a teenager my mum kicked up a fuss if I went out. I was fucked both ways, actually. If I went out I felt guilty, if I stayed in, I felt angry. She's always had a spiteful streak, has my mum.'

'Even the best of mothers can be difficult.'

215

'But you can have a rational conversation with most mothers. With mine I either fit in or risk an argument, where I end up feeling like the bad guy.' She sighed. 'What doesn't kill us makes us strong, I suppose.'

'That's the spirit, Princess.' He moved on to ask about her availability the following weekend, when he was back from New York, and with their having arranged a date for the Saturday night Tanya brought the conversation to a close.

Florence got home about midnight, and confirmed Tanya's suspicions. Barbara had offered to look after the boys and had encouraged her to go out.

In bed, Tanya reflected, and although angry, she also felt desperately sad at how her relationship with Barbara had ended, yet knew it couldn't have ended any other way. Barbara was incapable of negotiation. It was her way or the highway, always had been and always would be.

She painfully recalled Barbara's stock phrases when she was little. *I curse the day I ever had you. You're a bock on my life. You've made me ill.* And her reminding Tanya that she was an accident, always sure to add that she had never wanted children.

Her recollections made her realise that there was no way out, that no matter how hard she tried, she could never atone for the crime of her birth.

She began to see the positive side of events. At last she was free. She could see who she wanted when she wanted. No more hiding or explaining or defending herself. She had done her time, thirty seven years in all, but it was over.

She hated to look at it like that, but it was her only consolation.

That Sunday, however, she went to her local church, in the quiet of the afternoon. The only visitor, and thankful for the solitude, she knelt in a pew, on a small cushion, and put her forehead on her clasped hands. 'Ease my mum's pain, God, and let her know I love her,' she whispered, 'and that I am truly sorry she's had such a bad life.'

CHAPTER FIFTEEN

'Have you got a minute, Tanya?' Joe said.

About to make a call, she put her phone down. 'Of course, what's up?'

'Can we go in your office?'

She nodded, and they went there, her heart thudding, for fear he was about to quit.

'For Christ's sake, Joe,' she said, closing the door, 'please don't tell me you're going to resign on me.'

'Oh no, it's nothing like that, Tanya. I just need a bit of advice in confidence.'

She let out a huge sigh. 'Thank fuck for that.'

'It's Suzy. She keeps crying at the slightest thing. Last night, for example, when I said the curry she'd made wasn't as spicy as usual, it was waterworks. She says she's lonely, but what can I do? I've got to work. She calls me two or three times a day asking when I'm coming home. I don't know what to do.'

'Working here is without a doubt a bloody jinx on marriages.'

Tanya had told Joe she was getting divorced, Andy too, but no one else.

'Take a few days off, Joe, and spend some time with her.'

'No, that's not fair on you. We're too thin on the ground.'

Tanya thought for a few moments. 'Is Suzy eating and sleeping?'

'Yes, at least I think she is.'

'And she's not locking herself away, right?'

'No. She takes the kids to school, goes shopping, goes and sees her mum.'

'Does she have friends?'

He nodded. 'She's mates with lots of the other mums from the kids' school.'

'Then I'd say there's not much wrong with her that a bit of affection from you won't cure.' She checked her watch, half past four. 'Why don't you go home now, and pick her up some chocolates and flowers en-route?'

Joe smiled. 'Thanks, I'll take you up on that, providing you cover for me. I don't want Nate going anywhere near my trading book.'

Since becoming Tanya's co-head, Nate had rubbed Joe up the wrong way a few times, questioning his trades even though he knew virtually nothing about the sterling market.

She told Joe she would guard his book with her life.

Back at the trading desk, with Joe having left, Nate slid his chair closer to Tanya's. 'What's up with Joe?'

'He just wanted a word about a personal matter.'

He looked at her expectantly.

'It was personal.'

'Why has he left early?'

'He had something to do.' She looked at the small gap between their chairs. 'Give me some room, will you?'

He moved his chair back in line with his desk. 'We both run this division now. You can't make decisions autocratically.'

She sighed. 'If we discussed every decision we made, our output would collapse. Optimum productivity relies on synergy. As co-heads we have to trust each other.'

'In which case, you should trust me enough to answer my question.'

'Joe spoke with me in confidence. If you want to know what he said, ask him yourself.'

'I would but he isn't here, and I have a right to know why.'

She scratched her top lip. 'You're obviously bored, Nate, so why not make yourself useful and try and sell some Tarapet?'

'Let's discuss this in my office.'

'There's nothing to discuss. And unlike you, I've actually got work to do.'

He picked up his mobile and went into his office.

Prick.

The next day the markets plunged, after it became clear Henry Paulson – the U.S. Treasury Secretary – was in effect making things up as he went along. His plan to save the U.S. banking system which was called TARP, short for Troubled Asset Relief Programme, was being modified by the day, and he had admitted he had more or less plucked the number of $700 billion to fund it out of the air.

Bruce consequently told Tanya to sell the balance of her position in Tarapet the price of which, it being an oil company and the oil price plunging in anticipation of a decrease in demand due to a recession, was getting especially badly hit.

'I'm dribbling them out in ones and twos here, Tanya,' Freddie said, sweating, his copper hair flat with perspiration, 'but I've had a tip Jason could be looking for twenty five.' Jason was a competitor and Freddie was talking millions not literal ones, twos and twenty fives. 'I'm on hold for him now.'

'Whatever bid he gives you, hit it,' Tanya said.

She switched on her microphone. 'I want to see any bids for Tarapet, I mean any bids, no matter how low. You got that Rich?' Rich's hand shot into the air.

Nate, to her intense anger, was in the perimeter walkway, chatting with Doug Hutchinson, a lanky soft-spoken American, who ran KS' small Swiss office.

Come on, God, give me some help.

So far she had given back 400,000 euros.

Simon, Rich's deputy, rushed over. 'My guy will take ten million at 98.93.'

'Done,' she said, kissing goodbye to another twenty four thousand euros.

Max was next. 'I can sell five million at 98.95.'

She fired her finger at him 'Done.'

'Hey, Tanya,' Nate bellowed, 'over here.'

He sounded upbeat and she rushed to him, hoping he'd had a brainwave in relation to Tarapet.

He ran his tongue around his gums, glanced at Doug and smiled at her. 'You don't really think you can sell that shit, do you?' he said, and smirked.

She looked at him askance, and could feel herself shaking. 'Of course not,' she said, her teeth clenched, her voice dark, low and jittery. 'When I get up in the morning I think to myself, I wonder how much money I can lose for KS today. You stupid cunt!' With that she smacked him round the face.

She returned to her desk, grabbed her bag and went to the ladies room, where she splashed cold water on her face to calm herself down. She was dabbing it dry with a paper towel when Fiona came in.

'I saw what happened, Tanya. What did he say?'

Tanya told her.

'He's such a bastard,' Fi said. 'What I ever saw in him, I don't know.'

'Where is he?' Tanya said.

'In his office.'

'Phoning Bruce, no doubt.'

'If he does that, I'll back you up. I didn't tell you, but he threatened me over Freddie, said it wasn't good for my career to spend so much time talking to him.'

'Keep out of it, Fi. Go back to the desk, and carry on as normal. I'll be out shortly.'

Bristling with anger, Fiona stood heaving big sighs.

Tanya took her by the shoulders. 'Do you hear me, Fi? Stay out of it. I'm touched by your support but this is my fight not yours.'

Fiona left.

Tanya looked in the mirror. Her frown lines seemed to have disappeared, and she realised she felt peaceful, a somewhat strange sense of calm. She forced a smile. 'Life goes on,' she said, and returned to the floor.

Freddie looked at her. 'Are you alright?'

She winked at him and nodded.

'I sold thirty five million to Jason at 98.70. I hope that's OK,' he said.

She smiled. 'Good. What's the price now?'

'Todd's got a 98 ½ bid for five million.'

She told him to hit it.

Andy sidled over. 'Go and apologise, Darlin, while there's still time.'

She shook her head. 'On what basis, would I do that? I'm not sorry. I wished I'd fucking punched him.'

'Look on it as something you're doing for your kids. If you tell him about your divorce, I'm sure he'd understand.'

'Thanks for the advice.'

Tanya carried on trading, until she was clean out of Tarapet. The bid now stood at 97, reducing her net profit on the deal to a meagre 150,000 euros, not that Bruce would see it that way. All profit up to yesterday was history, accounted for, and in his eyes, secure. All he would see was that today she'd lost 1,309,000 euros.

What a note to quit on.

She sent TJ an instant message: *When you think it can't get any worse... Where the hell is OV?*

He replied: *Bad hair day? Joke. No yodelling here, either. OV's busy. A few weeks delay is neither here nor there. Fancy a drink later?*

Can't. Maybe lunch one day next week.

OK, meantime, chin up, powder dry and all that jazz.

Too late for that.

It's never too late, Gorgeous.

Wanna bet? I'll phone you shortly.

She resigned by email.

Bruce, I'm out of Tarapet, and I'm out of here. I slapped Nate, but he deserved a punch. He's bad for my constitution, but worse for KS' P & L, but that's for you to find out. I resign forthwith. I will phone you to discuss the paperwork. Tanya.

As she waited for Ted outside KS' building with archive boxes at her feet containing her belongings, she attracted furtive looks from passersby, such boxes now synonymous with *suddenly out on your ear,* as though badges of dishonour. But she refused to feel ashamed.

She called Spencer but had to leave a message. 'Spence, it's me. I've quit, but I would have been fired. I flipped, and gave Nate a long overdue slap. Call me.'

223

She called TJ and told him what had happened, and while she was on the line, he made an appointment for her to see a Percy Egerton, an employment lawyer, immediately.

A man of about fifty, with roguish good looks, Percy nodded sympathetically as Tanya gave him a chronological rundown of events since Nate's arrival.

'Where do I stand as far as my profit cut goes? Am I still entitled to the money?'

He explained that technically she had forfeited her rights by hitting Nate, but suggested she appeal to Bruce informally. 'On compassionate grounds and given your tenure, he may pay.'

He went on to say she may have grounds to sue for constructive dismissal if she felt harassed and bullied by Nate, and possibly sexual discrimination in that Kohen Stanzinger did not appear to have followed correct procedures when effectively demoting her. He added, however, that Nate could counter sue her on the grounds that she bullied him.

She asked him to summarise the risks of going the litigious route.

'Legal action takes months, sometimes years, and can have a seriously detrimental effect on a person's well-being and family life. And in my experience the baddies win as often as the goodies. Defying the law can be as effective as complying with it. If Mr Walthak was to counter sue and win, you could be liable for damages, as well as his legal costs.'

She smiled wearily. 'I thought honesty was dead, but you're proof it's not. How much do I owe you for your time?'

He told her not to worry about paying.

She phoned TJ to thank him, and learned that Percy was his uncle.

The next day Bruce phoned to try and broker a peace deal, and Tanya's verdict on hearing his proposal was *Thanks for fuck all.*

He had said if she apologised unreservedly to Nate, agreed to report to him, and got anger management therapy, KS would have her back.

She remained polite. 'Thank you, Bruce, but I could not accept one of those conditions, let alone all three.' She then broached the subject of her profit cut.

'I'll have to consult with our lawyers, Tanya. If we owe you the money, we will honour our commitment.'

Two can play that game.

'If KS won't pay, I'll sell my story, Bruce. I'm sure one of the tabloids would love it. I can just see the headline. The Mess at KS: How Shareholders Money Is Really Spent.'

'What's got into you, Tanya? Calm down,' he said brusquely.

'Actually, Bruce, I am calm, calm enough to know that what's happened would make a great story in this climate. The press are clamouring for scoops about failed banks and failed traders, not that I'm saying KS is a failed bank, but I do consider Nate a failed trader, and therefore someone who is being subsidised by a public company.'

Poke that up your arse.

'Take it from me, Kiddo, you do *not* want to get embroiled in a lawsuit with KS.'

'Why not? The publicity could help me get another job.' She paused. 'In fact I think you should tell the new

225

Japanese members of KS' board what's going on, so that they won't be shocked if they suddenly see their mug shots in the newspaper.'

'I'll call you back,' he said.

'OK. In the meantime I think it's only fair to tell you that I will be making discreet enquiries, to find out the going rate for my story.'

'I'll call you back,' he said again, and rang off.

He didn't but power-mad Stella Hornston, head of KS' HR division, did. Tanya loathed the woman, considering her a useless box-ticker; politically correct, commercially inept, and incapable of original thought.

'Tanya, Stella Hornston here. I have just had a meeting with Bruce Ghoff, who tells me you plan to speak to the press regarding the nature of your departure.' She waited, but Tanya didn't say a word.

Stella huffed. 'I would like to remind you, before you embark on such a potentially ruinous course of action, of your legal—'

Fuck off, bitch-face.

'I know my rights, Stella. As long as what I say is true, I can say *exactly* what I like, and that's precisely what I'll be doing. If KS want to sue me, good luck to them. They'll have to prove what I've said is a lie. Oops, my other phone's going,' she lied, 'must be my lawyer. Must dash.' She hung up.

Tanya figured that if defying the law could be as effective as complying with it, even if she was to say something that gave KS grounds to sue her, they could lose. And even if she was at fault, it would take months if not years for KS to prove it and meantime they would suffer unwanted publicity.

I've got a lot at stake, but so has KS.

Tanya's next call was from Stella bitch-face's assistance, to check the amount she felt she was owed. When she rang off she punched the air.

'Cinderella WILL go the Ball!'

A cheque for £175,000 arrived by courier the following day, and Tanya felt the rush of the trade pulse through her as she held it in her hand. It was proof of her potency, a sign she had what it took to survive.

*

Tanya sat on Spencer's bed caped in a towel, looking at a framed caption on the mantelpiece: *Each Moment, Only Once.* In the hearth was an array of candles, their flames dancing, as though to music.

I've just had thousands of new moments.

Spencer had given her a massage which had reduced her to tears, in part because he had been mindful to avoid her intimate areas. To her that showed genuine concern and consideration.

He called to her. 'Supper's ready.'

She sat opposite him at his small square dining table, wallowing in the joy of his caring. Classical music, the volume pitched just right. Bollinger, chilled to perfection. Fresh flowers, a glorious autumn mix with a non-intrusive scent. Homemade Crab linguine, not too much and delicious. And him!

'The Magic of Mr Rivington's Hands, by Tanya Pryce,' she said. 'Has a ring to it, don't you think?'

He laughed.

'Or,' she said, 'The Riveting Magic of Rivington. Hmmm, actually I like that better.'

Dinner conversation remained light and simple,

about music, and his visit to Harrods' food hall. No talk about KS, or collapsing markets, or Nate. Or sex, which was still to come.

Having taken her plate, he gave her a small silver dish. 'I think that's an ashtray, Princess. It was a gift from the wife of the Turkish Chargè d'affaires in Malaysia. I stayed at his house when I was there, and she gave it to me when I left. I'm sure she won't mind if it isn't.'

Of all the evening's wonderful moments this was the defining one, the moment she felt she could fall hopelessly in love with Spencer.

Verity must be off her head.

From the comfort of an American size cloth sofa, she took long slow puffs of her cigarette, and as she did so Daphne came to mind, and she thought how nice it would be to have an elegant cigarette holder. It had been that kind of evening. Spencer had treated her like a lady.

Give him a chance. He was probably nervous.

Her head on his chest, a chest now fragrant with ylang ylang massage oil, he wove a strand of her hair around his finger. 'God, you're sexy, Princess—and loud.'

She laughed. 'By my standards I was quiet. You'd better tell your neighbours you've got a lodger called Gorgeous Georgy, who gets up to a lot of hanky panky.'

Sex had been quick, and Spencer had kept telling her to 'shush', and as a result she hadn't got remotely close to any kind of an orgasm. It was not the dessert she had been hoping for.

To ease her disappointment she thought about the night's positives, but that didn't assuage her ache for an orgasm. She badly wanted to masturbate but felt too embarrassed, as well as concerned about the noise she would make. If Spencer thought her mutterings during sex were loud, how was he going to cope with her orgasmic scream?

She roused him during the night for another session, and while she found it enjoyable, a climax was as far away as the North Pole, his hang up about noise hardly a relaxant.

His technique, she concluded, needed polishing. He knew his way around but lacked a dedicated focus, which she felt was at least partially due to his fear they would be overheard.

When she emerged from his en-suite the next morning and began putting on her bra, he threw off the duvet to exhibit his wares.

'No good doing that, Spence, I've got to go. But I could come over late tomorrow night, get to you by, say, ten, and be out of your way by six, so that I'm back before my boys wake up.'

He sprang from the bed, and put on his robe. 'Make it ten thirty, as I have a dinner.'

For the next three weeks for the most part this became Tanya's nightly routine. Spencer's technique did improve, and he lasted longer, but she still sensed a constraining undercurrent at work, with him continuing to worry about disturbing his neighbours.

So they were having what she saw as respectable sex, not something she would boast about, but being needy in that area she counted herself lucky. And while an orgasm was still a hope rather than a reality, she still enjoyed their sessions, and being in his arms.

Her days were less pleasant. If she wasn't on the phone scouting around for leads, she was having a drink with a broker, often the first ones to know of trading vacancies, or meeting a head hunter, or having an informal chat with a firm who might, sometime before the third millennium, have an interest in hiring her.

Steve was already seated at Centriko's when Tanya arrived for lunch with him, which was his treat.

'Don't get up,' she said to him, popping her bag on the carpet by her chair.

'Try stopping me.' He rose and gave her a very affectionate hug. 'I'm still dreaming about that kiss,' he whispered.

She laughed. 'Has Tess gone off you or something?' Tess was his wife.

He gripped her waist. 'No, she still finds me as irresistible as ever and be honest, so do you, don't you?'

'Your job's gone to your cock,' she joked, prising his fingers off her waist.

'Tanya!' It was Spencer.

She spun round. 'Spencer! How lovely to see you.'

She gave him a peck on the cheek, and he and Steve shook hands, and the three of them exchanged a few friendly words, before he went to his table, at which point Steve and Tanya sat at theirs.

'Looks like I've got competition,' Steve said.

'What do you mean?'

'Spencer fancies you.'

She threw her head back and laughed. 'Don't be ridiculous.' She didn't feel it would help her job search to say she and Spencer were in a relationship. Nor did she feel they were, not yet. They were just having sex.

'He does. Didn't you notice the way he undid his jacket, and smoothed his hair.'

'You've been reading too many girls' magazines.' She paused. 'That said I could do a lot worse.'

'What than Spence the fence? I'm not sure about that.' In his view Spencer always sat on the fence, and lacked the conviction to stick to a permanent view.

'But he called this downturn accurately,' she said.

'Yes, but he wasn't the first economist to do so, more like number thirteen.'

Tanya moved on and told him about her final hours with Bruce, Nate and Stella bitch-face, and how depressed she was feeling about the job market.

'...the problem is that there's not many, if any, senior enough jobs out there, not that I care about seniority. I'd be happy to just trade, but trading heads won't take me on, because they feel threatened.'

'You can't blame them given the climate, but once Christmas and bonuses are out the way, the musical chairs will start, and you'll get snapped up.'

'But that's months away.'

He gave her a sympathetic look. 'What's happening with Sky-Rise and Olli Vermallen?'

'Nothing, but it's not dead, at least I don't think it is. The guy just travels a lot. I sent him an email to say by choice I am no longer at KS, and he replied thanking me for letting him know and said he would be in touch soon.' She shrugged. 'But when, who knows?'

'Don't get disheartened, Tanya. You've loads going for you. You just have to keep punching.'

'I know, and I am, and I know something will turn up eventually, but the problem is that I owe Peter half a million quid, which I've got to pay by the end of next

June. I know that gives me eight months, but time flies when you're in the shit. I had to increase my mortgage to pay him the first lot, and what with school fees and the cost of Alison, my overheads are now nudging eighteen grand a month. I can't keep that up, which means if I can't get a job, I'll have to sell my house.' She heaved a sigh. 'At least I've got an asset to sell.'

Steve put his hand on hers. 'I forgot about your debt to Peter. I've asked around already, but I'll ask again. I know a lot more people in the hedge fund industry now. One of them must need a trader. I wish Barclay Gray did.'

'That's really kind of you, Steve, thanks. But don't ask Krevamar.' She shuddered. 'Ugh. Fenshill's definitely one man I'd never work for, however much he offered me.'

'Never say never in this business.'

'Trust me, I'd sell my body before I'd work for that creep.'

'How much?' he said, slipping his hand in his jacket, as though to get his wallet.

She laughed. 'What am I going to do with you?'

He leaned toward her. 'I don't know, but I'd love to find out.'

Realising she had borrowed this line from Spencer she sneaked a look in his direction, hoping to catch his eye, but he wasn't looking her way, and she felt a tiny stab of disappointment.

That became a big stab when he bade her and Steve goodbye with a polite wave from a distance, rather than stop by their table.

He's with a client, for God's sake. I'm seeing him later anyway.

Tanya felt more awkward than usual when they had sex that night, and she blamed it on their absurd routine, mutual oral, missionary, her on all fours, and finally astride him, but without her making much if any noise.

She wasn't sure when or how it had happened but knew she had sacrificed her own sexual preferences in favour of his, as if his controlled quiet approach to love-making was somehow better.

His cock still inside her, and having ejaculated, he gazed into her eyes. 'God, I adore you.'

No you don't, you just adore my body.

He rolled onto his back, took her hand, and began drawing circles in her palm with his finger. 'Walky round the garden like a teddy bear, one step, two step, tickly under there!'

She clamped her arm to her rib cage to stop him tickling her armpit.

'You don't seem as relaxed tonight, Princess. Is anything wrong?'

'No, I'm fine, just tired, and concerned about work.'

No orgasm aside, she was also pissed off that when she had told him Steve was going to ask around for jobs on her behalf, he didn't offer to do the same. He had asked whether she had tried this that or the other, all obvious steps that she had taken, but that was all. It made her wonder whether Steve had a point, whether he was the sort of person who always sat on the fence.

'Something will come up,' he said.

She cuddled into him. 'I hope so.'

'It will. I'm certain of it.'

He was soon fast asleep, his breaths even and peaceful, which also annoyed her, because unless she was drunk it took her time to go to sleep, with her needing first to go over the day's events, until she felt OK, and as though she'd made some kind of progress.

At an ungodly hour the next morning, Spencer buttoned her coat and pulled up her collar.

'How am I going to manage?' he joked.

He was off to Eastern Europe for four days.

'I'm sure you'll find a way.' She picked up her overnight bag, and then slipped her free hand inside his bath robe and cupped his balls. 'Just tune in to the porn channel when you're in bed, and give Gorgeous Georgy lots of strokes.'

Find out how it's done.

He tutted, and she laughed.

'Better still, check out the real thing. There must be loads of strip clubs in Moscow, where getting carried away is encouraged. I'm sure a bit of dingy velvet and burlesque would do both of you good.'

'What am I going to do with you?'

'Why don't you give that some thought?' she said, and kissed him. 'See you on Friday.'

CHAPTER SIXTEEN

Tanya put a plastic milk bottle in the recycle box in her porch, kicked a pile of frosted leaves from the front path onto her lawn, and peered up at the black sky. 'Brr,' she uttered, rubbing her shoulders, and returned to the warmth of her house.

Who wants to go out in this weather anyway, she thought, her diary for the rest of the week empty. Spencer had only been gone a day but she was already missing her nightly excursions.

She made herself a mug of coffee, and took refuge in her lounge, where the gas fire was on full blast, and sat on the sofa, her lap top on her left, a tray providing a firm base for her coffee mug and ashtray on her right. And glancing at the tray she suddenly felt very sad.

It was etched with a wigged couple in regency costumes, the lady seated with her hand outstretched, the man bowing to take it. Tanya had bought it whilst away on a dirty weekend with Peter, who had said on seeing it that she had illusions of grandeur. 'Predictions, Pete,' she had said. 'Predictions of grandeur.'

That was eight years ago.

Her debts and future weighing heavily on her mind, she kept checking her mobile, just in case she'd missed a call. And when she heard the click sound her laptop made when an email arrived she tended to jump, Tesco now a bastard that could fuck off on account of theirs.

Come lunchtime and with it the realisation that no one, if anyone, would contact her until mid afternoon, she went upstairs and into her boys' bedroom.

She picked Harry's talking phone up off the floor, and put it on a shelf next to Jamie's toy Mini Cooper. Then, sitting on Jamie's bed, she cuddled one of his pillows while looking at the wall she'd had an artist paint to resemble constellations of the northern sky. The result was an intricate expanse of midnight sparkle, and a treasure of a storybook. Her boys now believed Father Christmas lived in the Milky Way, because that was closest to earth, that Peter Pan's house was the square of Pegasus, and that all of it was heaven, that anyone who died would be able to fly from one star to another.

She slipped off her shoes, crawled under the duvet, and closed her eyes. The next thing she knew Alison was standing over her, smiling, Harry's Thomas the Tank Engine bed linen like a collapsed tent in her arms.

'I thought you were out, Tanya. Can I make you some lunch?'

She swung herself into a sitting position. 'No thanks. I'll have something later.'

'You're losing weight, and there was nothing of you to begin with. Let me make you a fried egg sandwich.'

'I'm fine, honestly.'

Alison gave her a maternal frown.

The deafening silence continued throughout the afternoon and at five o'clock, with all hope gone that anyone important would be in touch, Tanya went to see Daphne.

'...I'm scared, Daphne. It looks like I'm not going to have a choice about selling my house.' She scratched at her wrist. 'I've paid the ultimate price for a moment's madness, and put my kid's livelihood at risk.'

Daphne drew her shawl tight around her shoulders. 'Do you regret hitting that man?'

'No. In fact I still wished I'd punched him instead of giving him a silly slap.'

'But that's good, Dear.'

'It doesn't feel like it to me.'

'Perhaps you wanted time with your children.'

'I did, but not like this, with me worrying myself sick about whether I can get another job.'

'Can't that new man of yours help?'

'No. He works in a different field.' She heaved a sigh. 'What would you do if you were me, Daphne?'

'I can't answer that, but I know what I would do if I were in your situation.'

'Which is?'

'Say a prayer of thanks as if I already had what it is I wanted.'

Daft cow.

Tanya smiled out of politeness.

'It's all the rage in America,' Daphne added. 'They call it the power of positive thinking.'

'I know what you mean, Daphne. I've read books on it, but I need to do something a bit more practical than dance round the room singing I'm in the money.'

Tittering, Daphne looked at her piano. 'What a lovely idea. My fingers are not what they were, but I could have a go, and you could sing along. Oh, but you need the lyrics. I think you might find them in the piano seat, Dear. The song is actually called We're In The Money.'

She's off her tiny tree.

'Another time, perhaps, Daphne, but right now I need to get back to my boys.' She got up, pulled on her fur jacket, and went and gave Daphne a kiss on the cheek. These days she let herself out.

Daphne smiled. 'He always knows the way through, Dear, but you must tell him what it is you want, and allow him to help. He's not a mind reader, you know. Not one to meddle.'

Tanya squeezed her hand. 'I will do some affirmations, Daphne, I promise. Thanks for listening to my moans.'

'Any time, Dear. Now take good care of yourself and don't forget,' she was speaking like a mother hen, her eyebrows raised in concern, 'you are more than a job and your house. You have earned money before, and you will again.'

'But what if my luck's run out?'

Daphne scoffed. 'Luck is a spurious figment of one's imagination, Dear, a way of diminishing one's worth and disowning the right to enjoy life. We all have that right, you know, to enjoy life.'

'You're so sweet, Daphne. I will give serious thought to what you've said.'

Tanya did and that night went to sleep silently reciting over and over *I have the job of my dreams.*

But it didn't appear on Tuesday or Wednesday, and on Wednesday night a group of teenagers out on the make for Halloween knocked on her street door.

'Trick or treat,' one said, skateboard under his arm.

'Bugger off.' She closed the door. Seconds later a couple of eggs were thrown at it, and she heard the hooligans laughing and running away.

'Little bastards,' she kept saying, as she cleaned up the mess.

The next day, fed up chasing people and going stir crazy waiting for someone to chase her, Tanya went shopping, and took Harry with her.

The supermarket shelves had been swiftly emptied of Halloween paraphernalia, and aside from a few fireworks were already screaming Christmas, tinsel, trees and toys as far as her eye could see. She stood zombie like in the aisle, contemplating it without Peter, Kay and Jim, or Barbara. Or a job.

Harry pulled at her sleeve to get her attention, and pointed to a small guitar.

'Sorry, Sweetheart. Mummy was miles away.' She looked at the guitar. 'If you're a good boy Father Christmas will bring you one.'

'That too, Mummy.' He pointed to a trio of drums.

'Yes, OK, Darling.'

I'll call Peter. Maybe he can join us on Christmas day. Perhaps Kay and Jim could come too.

She knew these were crazy ideas, but her sadness was such that they still gave her a grain of hope.

The heavens had opened when she left the store, and she had forgotten her umbrella, so it was a splash dash to her car. She strapped Harry in his safety seat and dried his face with a tissue, before putting her shopping in the boot, rain managing to find its way down the back of her neck as she did so. That job done, she left the empty trolley where it was, and got in her car.

Bugger, I forgot my cigarettes. I'll have to go back.

Harry fought with her as she tried to undo his safety strap, and when he started crying she decided to leave him where he was, telling him where she was going and that she would only be a few minutes.

He was happy. 'I'll be a good boy, Mummy.'

Inside the store Tanya joined a long line of people, the lone cashier handling sales of newspapers, sweets and lottery tickets, as well as cigarettes.

I hope this store goes fucking bankrupt, she thought, angry at the length of her wait.

Her purchase made, she headed quickly back to her car, and as she did so she saw that there were some people by it, whereupon she raced to it, her stomach plunging as dread gripped her.

Thank God, she thought, upon seeing that Harry was fine, albeit crying. She opened the door and gave him a kiss. 'It's alright Darling, Mummy's back.'

'It's dangerous to leave a child alone in a car.' The statement came from a middle age man in a brown uniform, the word Security written in red across his breast pocket.

'It was securely locked,' Tanya said, 'and I was only gone a few minutes.'

The guard looked at her disbelievingly, and then at his colleague, a lad Tanya had seen earlier, collecting supermarket trolleys.

'He was screaming his lungs out for about twenty minutes,' said the lad.

You fucking liar, Tanya thought, estimating it had been ten minutes at most.

She noticed an elderly couple and two women exchange frowns, and glared at them. One woman glared back at her. 'Breaks my heart it does to see a child in distress,' she said loudly, to her friend. Her friend nodded.

'Well he's not in distress now, so you can all go back to your little lives.' Tanya opened her driver's door. The guard grabbed the top of it. 'I'm afraid you can't go anywhere, Madam. The police are on their way.'

'The police?' Tanya started to shake.

'Yes, Madam, the police.'

'But this is ridiculous.'

'You can tell that to the police.'

Two special female constables turned up minutes later, and to Tanya's rage spoke first to the trolley attendant. And when they turned their attention to her, one simply took her contact details, and car registration, and the other told her to expect a visit from more senior colleagues within a few hours.

Back at home, she got Florence to supervise Harry – Jamie was at school – and summoned Alison into the lounge and told her what had happened.

Alison put her arm around her. 'Why don't people mind their own business? Anyone can see that Harry is loved and well cared for.'

'I know, and it wasn't like my car was unlocked. The guard could easily have issued a message for me over the tannoy, but no, he had to go all out and call the fucking police, as if their time couldn't be better spent.'

Alison told Tanya someone had called while she was out and had left a message.

'I'll listen to it later,' she said, too shocked to concentrate on anything.

Two police officers arrived within an hour and after listening to Tanya's version of events, gave her a piece of their mind as to the dangers she had put Harry in by leaving him unattended. They then asked to be left alone for a few minutes.

She paced her hallway, her heart pounding, and when she was invited back into her lounge, the elder of the two officers, a man, informed her they would let the matter rest with a caution. He added, however, that it was a borderline decision; that she had only narrowly escaped prosecution for child neglect. Tanya thanked them and showed them out, and again summoned Alison.

'...Child neglect, Alison, child neglect... They haven't got the first fucking clue about child neglect.'

Alison shook her head and sighed. 'Whatever happened to common sense,' she mused.

'Harry was strapped safely in his seat and my car doors were locked for Christ's sake. And the odds of a paedophile lurking in a busy car park at two in the afternoon, while it's still daylight, looking in car windows for signs of a child alone...' Tanya threw out her hands. 'Even if that happened, the paedophile would have had to smash open my car. I mean, it's a Land Rover, not a Reliant fucking Robin.'

Tanya said the same thing various different ways over the following hours, and Alison kept reminding her she was an excellent mother, and had simply fallen foul of a bored trolley attendant, who was desperate for some drama and to feel important.

Tanya agreed, but her guts remained knotted, and she ghosted her way through the evening, her mind tormented by the term Child Neglect.

But by the next morning fury was her dominating emotion, her attitude *Fuck them all*. As far as she was concerned all the people she had met the previous day, including the police, were small minded and deluded, of the view they were making a difference, when they were really just serving themselves, trying to achieve the feel-good factor without effort or risk, and so always looking to pick the low hanging fruit.

She listened to her phone message. It was from a head hunter asking if she would be interested in a job as a junk bond trader. Feeling a frisson of excitement she called the head hunter and said yes, and he arranged for her to meet with the bank that afternoon.

Feeling more than deserving of a break after the previous day's events, she dearly hoped this was it, but yet again the meeting turned out to be another fishing expedition for information about KS.

She tried to look on the bright side. She had made some more contacts, always useful. But as she walked to the underground, she felt as though she was the only person in the world without a job, the quiet City streets a reminder that the rest of her ilk were working.

She phoned Spencer, who was in a taxi on his way home from the airport.

'Sorry for the short notice, Spence, but I can't make tonight.'

He sounded devastated. 'Why? Are you OK? You sound different.'

'I'm fine, but it's been a very shitty week, and I've just had my time wasted with a pointless interview, and I'm not in the mood for socialising. I just want to stay home tonight with the boys.' Her voice was hollow of emotion. She felt too ashamed and guilty to tell him about the incident with Harry.

'Are you sure you're OK?'

'Yes, I'm just tired and fed up.'

'Can you come over tomorrow, or on Sunday? I have lunch with my parents on Sunday, but I'll be home by six.'

'I'll come on Monday. I've got a lot to do this weekend.'

'I have a long day on Monday, Princess, and a dinner.'

'I'll come on Tuesday then.'

'I see.' He wished her nice weekend and rang off.

She could tell he had the hump but she didn't care.

On the tube on her way home, an unkempt young mother, with purple hair and three sets of earrings in each ear, bounced a pushchair into Tanya's carriage, while yelling at her two equally unkempt daughters to hurry up. Tanya watched as the little girls innocently pole danced, swinging their bodies every which way, showing their grubby knickers, while their mum argued with someone on her mobile, swearing shamelessly.

And they think I'm neglectful.

Spencer phoned her twice that evening, and both times she diverted the call to her voice mail. At gone midnight, when she was in bed, he phoned again.

Why can't he just fuck off and leave me alone.

She picked him up. 'I'm in bed, Spence. What do you want?'

'Please don't ignore me.'

'Just because you ring, it doesn't mean I have to pick up.'

'It is good manners.'

'Don't take the moral high ground with me, Spence. Why should your needs come above mine?'

He was quiet for a few moments. 'I apologize. I simply wanted to make sure that you were OK.'

'I told you I was fine, and I am. Anything else?'

'Will I still see you on Tuesday?'

'Yes. Now please let me get some sleep,' she said, and rang off.

He's so predictable, it's boring.

*

On Monday Tanya received notification that her decree nisi had been granted. In six weeks and one day she would be a free woman. That meant a few days before Christmas.

Maybe then my luck will change.

She did not agree with Daphne's take on luck. To her it was hard to have hope without believing in luck. She had also read somewhere that the atom occasionally jumped, didn't conform to rigid behaviour, which made surprising events possible. Given that she felt in great need of hope, her view on luck gave her just that: Hope.

By Tuesday she was looking forward to seeing Spencer and telling him about her decree nisi. She hoped the news would give him a sense of power, perhaps make him reckless in bed.

Incredibly, however, he cancelled their date, and by text: *I can't make this evening.*

She immediately called his mobile and got his voice mail, and then the office but his secretary said he was out. She left a message on his home phone. 'Spence, darling, I just got your text, and I'm really disappointed. Hope it's not tit for tat. I'd love to see you, and I can come over late if you have a dinner. Give me a call back.' She texted the same message to his mobile. The delivery report said it had been sent successfully.

As the evening wore on and with still no word from him, her concern grew. The weather was bad, icy, and she wondered whether he had had an accident, perhaps while out for a run. Or been kidnapped by Russians mistaking him for a spy. As ludicrous as that idea seemed, it had crossed her mind. And made her giggle.

But she was genuinely worried. It was so unlike him to be curt with her, and while she knew she had been rude to him, she had told him she wasn't feeling great, and why, and felt he ought to understand her situation.

She kept trying both his phones and finally, at a little after eleven p.m., he answered his landline.

'Spence, what happened? I've been worried sick.'

'How could you, Tanya?' He repeated the question, slowly. 'How—could—you?' He hung up.

What does he mean, how could I? How could I what?

His tone infuriated her. She called him again and was put through to his answer phone. She left a message. 'Pick me up, Spence, I know you're there, and I've no bloody idea what you're talking about, and I don't appreciate being spoken to like a dog either.'

He picked up. 'I did not speak to you like a dog.'

'I think you did. Now, what is this about?'

'I can barely speak about it.' He paused. 'I had lunch today with Nate and Denton Fenshill.'

'That's not my fault, is it?'

He ignored her quip.

'And I had to feign amusement as they speculated about how long you and Steve Cranthorp have been having an affair.'

'How can you believe crap like that, from crap people like that?' she said angrily.

'Denton Fenshill said he saw you and Steve in a passionate embrace, at Barclay Gray's cocktail party.'

'That's absolute rubbish. What happened was that Steve was a bit drunk, and when I went to give him a goodbye peck on the cheek he tried to kiss me, and I immediately pushed him away.'

'Denton Fenshill said you were eating each other, in full view of clients.'

'That is a complete and utter lie. Are you certain Fenshill said that, or did it spring from Nate's gob? And how much have you embellished what you heard? That you can believe what those two say is worrying.'

'You both seemed to be enjoying yourselves in Centriko's.'

'So we flirted, so what? Steve's happily married.'

'Flirting leads to things.'

'Only if you want it to.'

'You held hands with him at the table.'

Jesus, he must have been looking at us the whole time to catch that.

'We did not. Steve took my hand for a few seconds as a show of concern.'

'That you let him could be construed as egging the fellow on.'

'For God's sake, Spence, what do you want me to say?'

'I don't know.' He paused. 'Actually, yes I do. When he kissed you, did you enjoy it?'

'I'm disgusted by that question, and I've no intention of answering it.'

'So you did enjoy it.' He hung up.

She smacked her phone on the coffee table. 'Go to fucking hell,' she shouted, and then burst into tears.

She ended up crying her heart out, curled up on the sofa under a throw, after which she fell asleep.

'Mummy,' Jamie said, shaking her arm, 'why did you sleep in here?'

She pushed her throw to one side and sat up. Her face felt tight, as though it was covered in dried honey. 'I wasn't feeling well, Sweetheart, and I needed the warmth of the fire.' She opened her arms. 'But I'm better now, and a cuddle from you guys – Harry was by Jamie's side – will make me even better.'

Tanya waved her boys off to school, with yet more tears in her eyes, and she was glad it was weekly shop day as it meant Florence had gone with Alison, and she had the house to herself for a few hours.

When she closed the street door she looked in the mirror in the hallway, and was met with a piteous sight, a face with as much sparkle as a mushroom. Her eyes were puffy, her complexion pale, and her usually lustrous curls were dank about her shoulders.

Her life was a mess and it showed, and for the sake of her boys she knew she had to do something about it.

After a cup of coffee and a cigarette, she phoned the British Association of Psychotherapists' referral service, an organisation she had once contacted on behalf of Barbara, and obtained the names and numbers of a few therapists who lived near her. Within an hour she had made an appointment with a lady called Jess Larance for the following day.

For the first time in ages she felt peaceful, and therefore as though she had done something right.

Spencer can go fuck himself, and if I have to sell my house to pay my debts, so be it. As long as I've got my boys, and the health to look after them, I'll be happy.

CHAPTER SEVENTEEN

Tanya flicked up the brim of her hat so that she could see well enough to drive, tightened her seatbelt, and switched on the engine.

I suppose we'll end up talking about that crap again.

She meant her childhood, and was on her way to the fifth of an agreed twelve sessions with Jess Larance.

I'll pay her what I owe her, and call it a day. It's a pointless exercise delving into the basement.

Folding her tissue into a small square, she wiped her eyes. 'All this therapy stuff is making me anxious, and it makes me wonder if I'll end up like her.' She was referring to Barbara.

'Anxiety is not genetic,' Jess said. 'It's a learned response. What are you most afraid of right now?'

'How much time have you got?' she said sarcastically, 'having to sell my house, not getting a job, not having enough money. It all comes down to money in the end. Money buys freedom.'

'Freedom from what?' Jess asked.

'I don't know but,' she sighed. 'Look, I'm not sure raking over the past is doing me any good.'

'If something hurts on the way in,' Jess said, 'it usually hurts on the way out. It takes courage to heal.'

She's talking her own book.

'I was listening to some idiot on the radio the other day preaching forgiveness,' Tanya said, 'as if it's that easy. He never said anything about the process, just banged on about how we should all forgive. Some people are so thick. I wonder if he'd forgive someone who kept deliberately smashing into his car.'

'The word forgive means to give up, as in to give up one's negative thoughts and feelings about a person.'

Tanya appreciated the clarification. 'So if someone gets robbed, for example, you're saying that once they've come to terms with what was stolen from them, they can forgive.'

'Forgiving occurs naturally upon the completion of grieving.'

'You mean if a person grieved for everything that had ever upset them, they'd become serene and tranquil.' Tanya slowly lowered her head and opened her arms, as though taking a bow. 'And they would live happily ever after,' she said softly, and then laughed.

Jess smiled. 'Forgiveness does bring peace.'

'That makes a lot of sense, but I bet that fucking pillock on the radio didn't know that.'

'You sound angry.'

'I am, he annoyed me. But I take your point. I know I've got a lot of anger in me. In fact, I'm sure I could kill, if I had to. I'd certainly kill to save my kids, but I wouldn't do it for a living, because I love my freedom too much.'

'Would you say you enjoy life?' Jess said.

She glanced out the window, at some trees. 'I love nature.' She thought for a bit. 'There's always room for improvement, but in general yes, I do think I enjoy life. Although I wouldn't say no to a quick-grieve pill.'

Jess smiled. 'I'm afraid I don't sell those.'

'In that case I'll have to go home and stab the cat.'

'Punching a pillow might be less bloody.'

They both laughed.

'We have to stop now,' Jess said.

Tanya drove home on the brink of tears, and felt emotional all evening.

That's it. I'm not going back to see Jess. A chat with Daphne is more helpful. What good does crying do anyway?

She put the question to Google and learned that tears release toxins and aid healing, which came as a relief and made for a better night's sleep.

But when she got up, at the luxuriously late hour of seven a.m., she felt worse than she had the day before, and stood in the shower crying, feeling bitter that no one had yet offered her a job.

The problem wasn't that she had given Nate a slap, but that she was over-skilled and therefore a threat. No amount of humouring could hide the knowledge she possessed, and to be punished for knowing too much felt unjust. She was also coming to despise head hunters for their idiotic suggestions. Would she consider broking or a position in sales?

The idea of being a broker made her want to puke. To her, broking was a bloke's arena and one that required a great love of booze and lap dancing clubs.

And that she could become a salesperson was in her opinion too friggin silly for words. It would take years for her to build a client base and, like broking, a sales role would involve a lot of entertaining.

A trading job was the only job that would give her a degree of control over her personal time, enable her to see as much of her children as anyone who worked in investment banking could. That's why she was a trader.

She took a jumper and a pair of jeans from her

wardrobe, casting a forlorn look at all her suits hanging there forgotten like Billy no-mates, and dressed slowly.

Come on, buck up. No one's died. Like Daphne says, you've got to think positive, and expect better.

But she was empty of ideas, and by lunchtime she felt as though she was going round the bend. Another cigarette, another cup of tea, another trip to the loo, another peek out of the window, another look in the mirror, another check of her computer for emails, another tot up of her finances, another scan through her address book, another look at the news on TV. It was a depressing routine, her version of a hamster wheel, and as the minutes passed her mood darkened until, out of desperation to do something, she dressed up and drove to the West End, to do a spot of Christmas shopping.

'I'll take it,' she said, handing the white gold key ring back to the male assistant.

'Would Madam like it inscribed?'

It looked like a miniature book, and it opened to reveal a heart one side and a tiny photograph frame the other.

She hesitated. 'No, thank you. I want to think about what to say.'

'If Madam would like to leave it here and—'

'No, that's quite alright. I don't live locally.'

The mature salesman didn't press the matter.

He knows, knows I haven't got anyone to give it to.

She gave him an exaggerated smile and put her left hand in her pocket, as if the nakedness of her ring finger was a sign she wasn't lovable.

Having been subjected to romantic songs for a few hours, courtesy of every big store on Oxford Street, her heart was churning, and this was the result, an impulse buy for Spencer. But to get it personalised in some way when they had not spoken for weeks seemed stupid.

What if he's back with Verity?

She suddenly felt sick, not having considered that possibility until now.

'Thank you, Madam. Merry Christmas.'

She returned the greeting, and went through the same ritual with another man who stood guard by the door and let her out.

If he is back with her, he was never the one for me in the first place. Her next thought was even less palatable. *What if he's agreed to marry her?*

She inhaled deeply, and gathered a brutal pace.

What doesn't kill us makes us strong.

As she cut through the icy air, the corner of one of her stiff expensive carrier bags kept stabbing her calf, but she didn't do anything about it. Nor did she stop when her coat flew open. Instead she let it try to tear itself from her and tipped her face to the biting wind, as if defiantly challenging God to strike her down.

*

Jess sat with her hands resting loosely on her skirt, as Tanya talked about her latest disappointment: Being cut out of the frame for a job due to a spat between two head hunters.

'My problem is that I don't have friends in high places,' she said. 'Then again, I don't think I'd like strings to be pulled. Nate Walthak got his job at KS because of his father. Hey, Pop, how you doing?' She mimicked Nate's voice. 'The slightest bit of pressure and he was on the phone to his dad, sometimes that was two or three times in one afternoon if things weren't going his way. What a fucking baby.'

'What's Nate's father like?'

She shrugged. 'No idea, never met the man. All I know is that he's rich, and friends with the President of KS. One cosy little clique, of which I was never a part.'

'Things aren't always what they seem. Appearances can be very deceptive.'

Tanya laughed. 'I know. Look at me. People think I'm living the life of Riley.'

'What people?'

'My mum, Peter, my dad too, probably.'

'Something for us to discuss next time,' Jess said. 'We have to stop now.'

Stuck in traffic on the way home, Tanya watched as a woman of about her age wearing a pashmina over her coat, and carrying a briefcase, strolled across the road.

She looks happy enough but who knows what's going on inside her head and her heart. We all put on such an act. Jess' right. To compare how I feel on the inside, with how someone else looks on the outside is stupid. For all I know, Nate might not be happy.

Who am I kidding? Don't think about him.

When she reached her festively lit high street she parked up, and checked out the Christmas trees lining the railing outside her local fruit and veg shop.

She'd always left buying a tree to Peter, considering it a chore, but she didn't rush the task. To buy an inferior one that faded in colour and went bald before Christmas was over, could she felt have a detrimental effect on her boys. She wanted a tree that was bigger and more spectacular than anything Peter had chosen.

She had a salesman remove the mesh on three trees, so that she could inspect them closely, and plumped for the biggest, a seven foot Viking, and also bought a bronze cast iron stand.

It was delivered by two cheerful men in white overalls, who kindly set the tree up in the stand, and took their time positioning it, concerned to make sure it stood bang centre of the bay window in her lounge.

Touched by their efforts she gave them a fiver each as a tip, and on their way out one asked her if she would like to 'go out for a drink sometime'. As he didn't tick any of her boxes, she said she already had a boyfriend.

Dressing the tree made for a fun time with her boys. After Jamie held up a carved wooden Father Christmas and a reindeer, and said they were his favourites, Harry promptly tipped a box of decorations onto the sofa, gathered as many as he could in his arms, and claimed them all as *his* favourites.

Her boys in bed, Tanya and Alison shared a bottle of wine in a lounge that now glowed and glittered, and was rich with the scent of pine needles.

'Here are their letters to Father Christmas,' Alison said, laughing. She and Tanya read them together.

Jamie had asked for a Scalextric Le Mans race set, a pair of skates, a 4-in-1 games table, a Nintendo Wii Console and Wii sports, and an electric scooter.

Harry's orange crayoned list was just about legible thanks to Alison's guiding hand. He wanted a Lego airport and castle, and a Thomas the Tank Engine road and rail set, games consul and magic canvas.

'I have explained to them,' Alison said, 'that Father Christmas has a lot of children to buy presents for, and that his piggy bank might not have enough money in it.'

Tanya poured more wine. 'Whatever the New Year brings, Alison, we're going to have the Christmas of all Christmases. One my boys will never forget. There will be presents galore and enough champagne to bath in.'

'Now don't go wasting money on me or my parents, like you did last year. You haven't got it.'

Tanya smiled. 'Special people deserve special gifts.'

Alison and her parents were coming to stay with Tanya for Christmas, and Daphne was also coming to lunch on Christmas day. Peter was having Jamie and Harry on Boxing Day.

As they discussed gift ideas and menus, Tanya got quite excited, able to push thoughts of her debts from her mind and to appreciate the smallness of the moment. Spending hours buying and dressing a tree and nattering about the trivialities of Christmas were firsts.

But then she put on some music, and in the process her heart sank, because she found, already in the player, Andrea Bocelli's Toscana CD. Spencer had played it when giving her a massage, and had gifted it to her in memory of their first night.

'I wished I had put the radio on instead,' she said to Alison.

'Why don't you write to him?'

Tanya shrugged. 'What am I going to say that I've not already said?'

'That you love him.'

'I could never do that.' She got up, rearranged the cushions and sat back down. 'Jess thinks I'm scared of my feelings. Maybe she's right.' She sighed. 'Anyway, I think he's back with Verity.'

Alison shook her head. 'I doubt that very much. I

think he's just angry and jealous, and waiting for you to make the first move because he feels humiliated.'

'That's plausible, I suppose. Image does matter to him, and he does take himself seriously.'

Tanya's landline rang, and in her haste to get to the phone she spilt wine on the sofa.

It was a wrong number.

Cursing herself, she mopped up the spillage with a paper napkin.

Alison looked at her sympathetically. 'Write to him. I'm sure he'd be thrilled to hear from you.'

She recalled his warm flesh against hers and sighed. 'I'll think about it.'

Alison smiled. 'Good.'

The next day Tanya did write him a letter.

Spence,

I care not one jot for Steve and <u>never</u> have. What happened was at his initiation not mine. And I <u>swear</u> I pushed him away.

How could a silly incident, an unplanned fleeting kiss from a drunken and <u>married</u> associate, drive such a wedge between us? It doesn't add up.

Am I missing something? If so, at least tell me, and give me a chance to make amends.

Tanya. x

After weighing up the pros and cons of sending it, however, she tore it up.

Yes, she wanted a happy Christmas, but not at any price. To crawl to Spencer was beneath her, and to do so when she felt low was in her view dangerous.

No such thing as a free lunch or a free anything. He might well rescue me from a miserable Christmas, but he'd then see himself as the hero and me as a vulnerable weakling. At some point he'd use that knowledge against me. Anyway, he could write to me. He knows my address. Come on, Spence, get over your hissy fit, and get in touch. Maybe he will. After all, men feel soppy this time of year too.

*

'Hey, Tanya, it's Olli.' His quack tones needed no introduction.

'Hi Olli, it's great to hear from you. Can you hang on one second?' She turned off the tap, closed the dishwasher and dashed into her lounge.

'How are you?' she said.

'I'm good, thank you. Any chance you can swing by my office later? I apologise for the short notice, but I'm only in town for a few days.'

'Yes. TJ, too?'

'For the moment, no. I'd just like a one-to-one with you.'

'That's fine, Olli. Name the time and I'll be there.'

He suggested six thirty.

She dolled herself, her best black suit, a pink silk blouse and high heels, and had Ted drive her there. An indulgence given her circumstances but she wanted and needed to feel the part, and did not want to turn up hair askew or with a nose red and runny from the cold.

Upon arrival Olli asked her if she would like a glass of champagne.

258

'Yes, please,' she said.

As he stood at his drinks cabinet uncorking the bottle, Tanya noticed his belly, not helped by a thick fleece checked shirt, had grown a few inches.

'You're looking great,' he said, as he gave her a flute filled almost to the brim.

She smiled. 'Thank you, and thank you.'

'Today's my birthday,' he said.

She kissed his glass with hers. 'Congratulations. Happy Birthday.'

'Why, thank you.'

He sat on his Chesterfield, Tanya in an armchair opposite, and after apologizing for not being in touch sooner, told her about Sky-Rise's new premises in St James's Square. He said the trading room, which overlooked the statue of William III, was in the process of being kitted out and would consist of thirty trading positions. Then he asked about Nate.

She sat forward, and gave him a blow by blow account of her and Nate's history, opening up about the NCA loss, and the circumstances that led to her departure.

'...He goaded me, and I blew. It was the last straw.'

Olli pinched his nose, and snorted. 'The guy sounds like a real asshole.'

'To be fair it was mutual dislike from the outset. I felt cheated he was dumped on me, and he felt, I think, jealous of my experience.' She took a sip of her drink. 'So, are you still on track to set up this fixed income fund, or have market conditions scared you off?'

He smiled. 'What would you buy right now?'

'Hmmm, well spreads have widened massively in corporate bonds, so there's probably fair value to be had there, although not in the best names, on account of the CDO machine, and synthetic portfolios.'

'What do you mean?'

'I mean loads of the best quality bonds have been used to make up the safe portion of an artificially created bond such as a CDO, or an entire artificially created portfolio. Once a bond is used for that purpose it's essentially taken out of circulation, and suffers from a lack of supply which drives up its price. This has happened on a massive scale, but there are no official statistics, so knowing which bonds are affected or when they might come back into circulation is a guessing game. Knowing one big buyer could drive a stupidly high price even higher, while one big seller could knock it down dramatically is not good for the heart. Throw into the equation capital-rich equity sponsors looking for targets and you have the perfect nightmare.'

'Go on,' he said.

She could tell he was part testing her but also enjoying listening to her, and watching her movements, for she had a habit of using her hands when she spoke.

'Well let's say you own a CDO containing a bond you consider a safe name, and a firm such as KKR (Kohlberg, Kravis, Roberts, a major American private equity firm) launch a leveraged buyout for the company. If they succeed the company will become highly leveraged with loads of debt, and as a consequence its bonds will get downgraded and collapse in price. When that happens, a yield increase of 250 basis points in as many seconds is not uncommon.'

'You sure know your stuff.'

She shrugged. 'It's my job to know, at least it was.'

He smiled 'I've more questions, but I need to eat.

Would you care to join me?'

'Yes,' she said, without hesitation, 'but do you really want to talk shop on your birthday?'

'My folks are in Chicago, along with my soon to be ex wife. Talking shop is better than staring at the wall.'

'That wall perhaps,' Tanya said, looking at the one that sported the eerie eye.

Olli looked at it. 'You don't like that?'

'It scares the wits out of me.'

A loud nasal laugh followed. 'You British women are so funny.'

They went to a lively unassuming restaurant in Soho and Olli queued along with everyone else and waited his turn.

'Sure, twenty minutes is cool,' he said to the waiter. They stood at the bar and had a drink, Olli a Gin Martini with a twist, Tanya a glass of white wine.

Over dinner he asked if she was chatting with many other firms.

'A few,' she fibbed, 'but the job I want is the one you're looking to fill, and I can start tomorrow.' She paused. 'Can I ask how many people are in the frame?'

'Two, including you. There's a guy I have to see, who's been highly recommended.'

'Well if he's working he'll have to complete gardening leave, whereas I can start tomorrow.'

He laughed. 'You're one sassy lady. What were you making at KS?'

'In dollars, my base salary and bonus last year was a million dollars, this year it would have been one point five. I also got a ten percent cut of the profit I made from illiquid trading. KS paid me what I was owed in that respect, even though they weren't obliged.'

While she had forfeited most of last year's bonus, having quit before it vested, her figures were accurate.

'That's not bad for a lower middle tier firm. How much would you be looking to make, if you came to work for me?'

She had to think quickly. Hedge fund traders tended to earn modest base salaries but they got a slice of management and performance fees, often a substantial amount given the vast sums of money they typically helped to manage. But the EZE fund she hoped to run for Olli was his personal money.

'I've told you what I was earning so I'd rather leave it to you to come up with a sensible figure. But I would happily compromise on the cash element in return for an equity stake in Sky-Rise.'

He roared with laughter, and the heads of a few fellow diners turned at the sound.

It was cheeky but she felt she might as well float the idea, since even a tiny stake, say an eighth or a quarter of one percent, could make her rich if he sold out.

'You're cute, you know that. Hell, I'd have queues around the block, if I added an equity kicker.'

She grinned. 'Perhaps, but you'd be hard pressed to find someone as loyal as me.'

He laughed, glanced at his watch and called for the bill. 'I guess you need to get home to your husband.'

'I don't have one anymore.'

He frowned. 'What a bummer.'

'Not really, it was my decision.'

'A woman who knows what she wants. I like it.'

'More a case that I knew what I didn't want.'

'Isn't that the same for all of us?'

'I suppose it is.'

He threw down his napkin. 'Are you ready to head out?'

'Yes.' She got up. 'Thank you very much for dinner. I've really enjoyed it.'

He winked at her. 'Me too.'

He said he would be back in touch shortly, and with a handshake, they went their separate ways.

Yes! Chin up, and frock on, Cinderella—Ball here we come.

She treated herself to a black cab home. And as the taxi crawled east on a busy Victoria Embankment she sat, her feet resting on the seat opposite, dreamily admiring the floodlit South Bank. All the buildings looked immaculate even though some were run down, their silhouettes on the water most grandiose, and a few boasted prettily dressed trees. She glanced at revellers on a nearby boat and felt pleased for them, glad they were enjoying themselves.

I shall always remember the tenth of December.

She smiled at how that rhymed.

Now it really does feel like Christmas. Thank you, Oliver Vermallen.

*

Squeals erupted at silly-o'clock Christmas morning, and by five fifteen a.m. Tanya, Alison, Avril, and David, sat bleary-eyed in Tanya's lounge, emitting gasps of joyous surprise each time the boys tore open a gift.

By nine thirty Tanya was all glammed up: Freshly washed tumbling hair, mascaraed lashes, red lipstick, long diamante earrings, and a forest-green dress topped with a red cardi, and black patent shoes. She always glossed up on Christmas day, but as this was her first as a single parent, she made an extra effort, determined, for the sake of her boys, to paint it happy.

'That'll be daddy,' she called out when the phone rang, but she pounced on it all the same, in the faint hope it was Spencer.

'Hi, Pete.' She paused. 'Merry Christmas,' she added quietly.

'Don't insult me.'

'You're welcome to come round for a drink.'

'I can't, I'm going out. Put Jamie on the phone.'

To Tanya's relief, Jamie and Harry were full of smiles as they chatted with him.

Well done, Pete. Thank you.

In the digestive phase of the afternoon, while the adults listened to the Queen's speech, Jamie picked up the game of Mah Jonng that Daphne had bought him and carried it to Tanya.

'How do you play this, Mummy?' he said, climbing on her lap. Tanya looked at the instructions, but couldn't make head nor tail of them. *Bless her,* she thought, glancing at Daphne. 'I'll show you later, Darling,' she whispered.

He looked at Harry, who was snuggled in Alison's arms, against her ample bosom, awake but tired, and started fidgeting. 'I want to see Daddy.'

Tanya's stomach knotted. 'You will, Sweetheart, in the morning,' she whispered. 'Come, I'll give you a game of tennis on your Nintendo.'

He beamed and rushed from the room, Tanya fast behind, smiling.

At tea-time the doorbell rang, and Tanya's heart ground to a halt, again in the hope that it was Spencer.

She knew it was mad to think he'd turn up unannounced on Christmas day of all days, when he had never been to her house, but she couldn't help having the thought.

It was Ted, looking festive in one of Eileen's knits, a cream pullover with a Christmas tree on it, bearing stockings stuffed with sweets for the boys, and a box of Belgian chocolates for Tanya. He stayed for a cup of tea and a mince pie.

'It was so thoughtful of you to call round, Ted,' Tanya said, as she showed him out. 'I hope I'll see more of you in the New Year.'

'I've no doubt about that, my Lovely.' He turned as he walked down the path. 'Oh, and don't bother sending those cheques. I only tear them up.'

'But, Ted,' she ran after him, 'I want you to have that money. You have to live as well as me.'

He patted his stomach. 'Me and my Eileen don't starve. You've enough on your plate.'

God bless him.

By eight o'clock Harry was curled in a ball on the end of a sofa with a blanket over him, unconscious to the music playing and conversations going on around him, his Lego castle, half finished, thanks to David, on a board in the middle of the room. Jamie was face down on the floor playing with some coloured cubes.

Time for another drink.

'Another Snow-ball, Avril?'

'Yes, please, Tanya.'

'You sticking with the red, David, or are you going to help me and Alison out with the champagne?'

He smiled. 'I'll stay with red, if you don't mind. If I change colours I'll suffer for it tomorrow.'

'No problem,' Tanya said.

'Are you sure you want to open another bottle of champagne, Tanya,' Alison said, 'I'm happy with a glass of anything.'

'Shush,' Tanya said, 'any more talk like that and you're going to bed.'

Alison laughed.

While Tanya made Audrey's drink, she thought of Kay and how she'd get squiffy at Christmas and dance around the lounge, singing, to Jim, You Won't Find Another Fool Like Me. And it brought tears to her eyes. For all his faults, she realised she even missed Jim.

Stop it. It's been a perfect day, and the boys have had a brilliant time.

She blinked away her tears.

Fill your glass up, if it feels half full, she thought, and laughed to herself as she did just that.

I'm bloody lucky to have Alison and her parents here. Were it not for them Christmas would have been bleak.

Tanya enjoyed the rest of the evening, but come bedtime, when she was in her en-suite looking in the mirror above the washbasin and about to cream off her face make-up, she burst into tears.

She knew she had looked lovely today, and it seemed such a waste that she had no man of her own, no man to whom she could show off her lace top stockings, no man to share a Christmas kiss with, no man to notice her in an intimate and sexual way. Not that she wanted any Tom, Dick or Harry.

Perhaps he'll get in touch on New Year's Eve.

CHAPTER EIGHTEEN

We're born on our own and we die on our own. And when we're in a hole we're definitely on our own.

Tanya sucked hard for nicotine, and watched the smoke curl its way into the crisp air.

The doors overlooking her back garden ajar, she was sitting by candle light, in a recess in her bedroom, a blanket over her legs, and had already downed half a bottle of champagne.

'If you're there, God, show your face, because right now I feel as if I'm the only one pulling the sledge. And it's FUCKING hard. And I'm FUCKING tired.'

It was mid January, and she still hadn't heard from Olli Vermallen, or made headway elsewhere.

Fuck Barbara. And Nate. And Bruce. And Spencer. And Peter. And Him (she meant her dad). *Aliens, the lot of them. And Jess, too. What good did she do me? Who wants to spend their life crying?*

Anger plus alcohol however often led to tears with Tanya, and she was soon in floods of seemingly endless ones. No sooner had she taken one tissue from the box beside her to blow her nose or wipe her eyes, so she needed another. And as though wanting tangible proof of her sadness, she threw the used ones onto the carpet; in front of her, to her side, over her shoulder, anywhere but in the waste bin, less than a foot away.

Cried out, she sat drinking and smoking, and staring at the moon, which to her looked like a dull, deformed egg, a symbol of a misshapen and murky world.

What hope is there? Everything and everyone is

fucked up. The system sucks you in, tries to turn you into a Dalek, and if you don't conform, does its best to rip your soul out. What a poxy life this is.

She looked skyward and stuck two fingers up.

'If there is anyone there, you're fucking useless, totally fucking useless.' She shrugged. 'Who cares, eh? No one, that's who—*fucking* no one.' Her bubbly all gone, and keen to sleep, she still sat there.

Oh, to be carried to bed. That would be so lovely.

Suddenly, she felt a stab of concern, realising that of late she had felt increasingly drained, as though she was walking up the longest escalator in the world, the wrong way.

She got up, closed the balcony doors, and stared at her handiwork, the filled ashtray, drained bottle, and candy coloured tissues around her feet. 'Maybe I'm dying. Woohoo. That would solve a lot of problems.'

She staggered into bed.

When her alarm sounded, she silenced it and turned over, and groaned as she did so, finding the simple movements a strain. Her body felt as though it was sixty percent bricks instead of water, and her head throbbed.

She worked out how many hours sleep she'd had, and calculated it to be seven, which surprised her because she still felt tired. But then she remembered how much alcohol she had drunk, and how much she had cried. And what she had to do today.

Stop being pathetic. Nobody's died. You're just dehydrated. Drink some water.

That was breakfast, a litre of water, followed by a mug of strong coffee and four cigarettes while staring blankly at the front page of her FT.

At nine thirty she was sat on the stairs dragging on

her boots, and she used the banister to haul herself to her feet.

Pulling up the hood of her duffle coat, as much to hide her swollen eyelids, as to shield her from the cold, she trudged to the High Street eyes to the pavement all the way, aware but not caring that Daphne was probably sitting at her window and would welcome a wave.

After checking out four estate agents, she arranged for two to visit that afternoon.

The first valued her house at £2.2 million, the second £2.4 million. Given the fragile state of the housing market these were good valuations, but her house did tick all the boxes, and there were no similar properties for sale. Nonetheless, she knew market forces were against her, and that one seller could encourage others. Even so, she went with the highest price. If she could achieve that, she calculated she would have about £600K after paying Peter, her mortgage and her debts. She refused, however, to have a board outside, and gave strict instructions on viewings. Potential buyers had to be accompanied by an agent, and could only view her house between the hours of ten in the morning and two in the afternoon.

She spent the next few days numbly having a clear out, thinking about nothing but the immediate task of what to dispose of and how. If she was going to move she wanted to travel as light as possible. When she was done her garage was full of tat, piles of bric-a-brac, books, bedding, clothes, furniture and toys.

Having loaded up her Land Rover with stuff she deemed unfit for charity shops, she drove to the local recycling site, where smells reminiscent of a mangy wet dog shot up her nostrils.

A friendly gold-toothed council worker with skin like a rhino pointed to the relevant skips as he explained the system. *Talk about organised,* she thought, for there were designated areas for gardening waste, general waste, textiles, green glass, clear glass, newspaper, and magazines, cardboard, metal, hardcore, and electrical items. There was also a shop, where items considered too good to throw away could be left. Who knew where the proceeds went, but Tanya felt the staff deserved it all, for the dirty job they did.

Parked in the bay for General Waste, she donned a pair of leather gloves and began unloading her wares, declining an offer of help from an attendant because she didn't want to feel like a wimp. Then, in case he was watching her, she quick-footed up the metal steps, and hurled two collapsed sun beds into a skip as though they were a couple of cereal packets. It nearly pulled her arm out of its socket, but pride kept her going, and next into the huge crate, with great strain on her biceps, was a slab of marble, followed by two boxes of tiles. *Fuck,* she thought, suddenly realizing they ought to have gone in Hardcore. She looked around, no one seemed to have noticed, and carried on, covering her crime with some carpet remnants, and a shade from a standard lamp.

'Phew!' She stopped for a breather, before sprinting back up the steps with a near-full tin of paint in one hand, and a box of crockery under her arm. A split and unruly hosepipe went in after that, then a small rickety bookcase, a curtain pole, a wicker chair, and a sack of broken toys. Only at the recycle shop did she accept help, to off-load a gramophone.

Back in her car, she took off her gloves, swigged from a bottle of water, and then lit a cigarette. It had been an experience she wouldn't want to repeat, but she was also grateful for it, relieved to know her physical stamina was not disappearing.

They say use it or lose it. Maybe I need to go to a gym, get some regular exercise. I mean, it's not as if I even have sex these days.

The idea of joining a gym, however, slipped from her mind as quickly as it had entered, for a gruelling routine workout didn't strike her as being much fun.

I could take up yoga though, or go swimming or dancing.

Driving home she thought of the outfits she would need for each pursuit, filling her mind with whimsical thoughts to keep it off reality.

That night she sat cross-legged on the floor in her lounge, with tears in her eyes.

You only miss the water when the well runs dry.

She was admiring the architrave edging the ceiling, which to her resembled embroidered lace, and the reflection of her chandelier on one wall, which created a dappling of tear drops when the light was dimmed, as it was now.

She sniffed and sighed.

I fucked up, simple at that. But I'm still young. I'll make it all back. Somehow, I'll make it all back.

But she wasn't convinced by her thoughts, because they were just thoughts, and lacked energy, as did she.

She switched off the fire and got up. 'Argh, ooh, ouch,' she whined.

It's my own fault. I shouldn't have done all that running around. That was stupid. I'm not used to physical exertion.

She looked at her baby grand piano.

271

That's going to require specialist movers.

Daphne knocking out the tune to We're In The Money came to mind, and she smiled.

It's not over, yet. I could still get a job. Olli could still come through. Anything is possible. Daphne's right, I've got to think positive. She heaved a sigh. *Easier said than done though. Maybe I should go to the doctor, get some happy pills. No, I'm not taking tablets. They didn't do Barbara any good. If anything, they made her worse.*

The next day Tanya edged her way through the morning still in her dressing gown. Her head felt like it wasn't attached, her body one dull ache.

'Why don't you go back to bed?' Alison said. 'It's been an emotional few months, and that takes its toll. You need to rest, and stop pushing yourself.'

'Maybe you're right. It's not like I'm up to much, so I might as well try and get some sleep.'

But then Barbara's voice entered her head.

There's nothing wrong with you, you lazy cow. You're just feeling sorry for yourself. You should have had my life.

'I don't like giving in to tiredness, though.'

'You're not a robot, Tanya.'

Tanya felt that zonked she took Alison's advice, and slept for three hours, but when she woke up she didn't feel any better physically, and mentally she felt worse, angry with herself for having given in.

Get up, get moving and pull yourself together. Most of the world's starving. All you have to deal with is a bit of debt. A house is only bricks and mortar. You'll get a job eventually. Nobody's died, for fuck's sake. Or do you want to end up like Barbara? Loafing on the sofa, moaning and groaning, dragging the world down with you? Is that what you want? Sell your house, pay your debts and be done with it. It's NOT the end of world. You're being dramatic. There's nothing wrong with you that a few quid can't solve.

Upon using the bathroom, however, she realized something was wrong. And lacking the strength to go downstairs or shout for Alison, she shuffled back to her bedroom, and called her on her mobile.

'Alison,' she whispered, 'can you come upstairs?'

The nurse pulled a floral screen around Tanya's bed.

'There's a chance we can save this baby,' the doctor said, having estimated Tanya to be thirteen weeks pregnant.

'Take it away.'

The gentle faced Asian, his white coat open, ventured to dissuade her from aborting, but she cut him dead. 'I DON'T want it. If you don't take it away, I'll go to an abortion clinic.'

Her eyes were dry, but her heart felt as if it had been sliced in half.

No one would dare meddle with my decision if I was in a private hospital, she thought, such care having been a perk of her job. Both her boys had been born in a private clinic, in Hampstead, courtesy of KS.

Everything felt surreal. It had never crossed her mind she could be pregnant, because she was fitted with a contraceptive device, yet for three months she had been carrying Spencer's child.

In the middle of the night, as she reached for a glass of water, a nurse appeared and relieved her of the task.

'Are you in pain?' she asked in a whisper.

'No. I'm fine.'

The nurse checked her pulse, felt her forehead, and took her temperature, before going on her way.

Unable to go back to sleep Tanya lay reflecting on all that had happened, and while relieved to have found out before it was too late, she felt bitter she had been forced to make a life or death decision. She thought of the unkempt young mother on the train.

More kids than brain cells. And skint. Probably no partner either.

She knew that could easily have been her, had she not fought for better, that history could so easily have repeated itself had she not sacrificed her longings. It made her decision to terminate feel like the right one.

At teatime the next day Alison and the boys came to visit, Jamie holding out a bunch of freesias, Harry a box of Maltesers, which he and Jamie scoffed while she and Alison chatted.

'How is it in here?' Alison asked.

'Excellent. I never realized how hard nurses work. They all deserve a medal.'

Alison nodded and smiled. 'A Mrs Johnson came to view the house this morning. She wants to come back one night this week, with her husband. I told the agent I would check with you, if that was alright.'

'It's not,' Tanya snapped. 'Tell the agent to tell Mr Whatever-his-name to take time off work.'

'OK,' Alison said quietly. 'Joe called earlier. I didn't say where you were, just that you were away for a few days. He sounded keen to talk to you.'

'If he calls again, tell him I'm in hospital for a very minor procedure. I don't want him to think I'm ignoring him.'

'OK.'

When Alison was about to leave, Tanya returned to the topic of her house sale. 'Sorry for jumping, Alison. Tell the estate agent Mr and Mrs Johnson can view the house up to seven thirty, but no later as I don't want it interfering with the boys' bedtime.'

Alison smiled. 'OK. Now remember what I said about your dinner. You need to build up your strength.'

'I won't leave a crumb, I promise.'

That evening Tanya was gob-smacked to see Joe being escorted in her direction. He was smartly dressed, black suit, striped shirt, but his shoulders were drooping and his face lacked a smile.

'I hope you don't mind me coming, Tanya. I called round your house, and Alison said you were in here. I had to see you.'

She sat up. 'Not at all, Joe. What on earth's wrong?'

She suspected he'd either been fired or lost a vast amount of money.

'I'll tell you in a second, but are you alright? I don't want to pry. I just want to make sure you're OK.'

'I'm absolutely fine, truly I am.'

He pulled up a small wooden chair and sat down. 'Suzy's been having an affair—'

'Oh Joe.' She made to touch his arm, but he pulled away and raised a hand. 'Hang on, Tanya. I'm not finished. She's been having an affair with Peter.'

Tanya gasped, and clamped a hand over her mouth.

Memories of weekend lunches at her house or Joe's, when frivolous and saucy banter had dominated, came thick and fast. And it was like a bundle of discarded jottings suddenly became an award winning script.

She took a glass of water from her bedside cabinet, and sipped. 'When did it start, do you know?'

He nodded. 'Just over a year ago.'

A year ago! He's robbed me of fifty grand.

'A year ago? Are you sure?'

'Yes, unless Suzy's lying, and it's longer than that.'

Longer?

'How did you find out?'

'I hired a private detective, to stake out my house. Peter was round two days running. Once I had the photos of him coming and going, I confronted her.' He shrugged. 'She had no choice then but to confess.'

Tanya struggled to make sense of the attraction. Suzy was pretty, but scrawny, and quiet, nothing like her, and while Peter was good-looking, so too was Joe.

'What made you put a private detective on to her?'

'I knew something was up, didn't I? And I asked her outright if she was playing around, but she swore blind she wasn't, even went as far as to say I was imagining things.' He paused. 'The next bit would be funny if it wasn't my life. I bought her a spa break for her birthday and she came back with bald pubes, said a bikini wax came as part of the deal.'

Tanya broke eye contact and sipped more water. Peter liked bald pubes.

'Given we were hardly having sex,' he continued, 'I thought that was a bit odd, but not implausible. Then on Suzy's actual birthday, while I was at the gym, a bouquet turned up, a gift, she said, from the mothers at Sarah's school (Sarah was their daughter). But there was no card and I just knew she was lying, so when she went asleep, I went through the bins and found it.'

'What did it say?'

'Nothing. It was blank, except for kisses.'

As they talked they realised that all the times Suzy

276

or Peter had phoned either of them at work, it was to ensure they were indeed at the office.

'...It's amazing how much information private investigators can lay their hands on. I could have got Suzy's bank statements, if I'd wanted. That said, it all costs.'

'How much did they charge?'

'Two and a half grand.' He shook his head. 'Waste of money in a way. I should have rumbled it.'

'Don't blame yourself for that, Joe. I didn't suss it either.' She paused. 'Do you still love her?'

He gave a hollow laugh. 'Love her? I don't know the woman. How can I love her? She loves Peter now, anyway.'

'You don't know that, Joe.'

'I do, Tanya. I asked her.'

'Oh, Joe, I am sorry.'

He shrugged. 'What can you do? Shit happens. Life injures the lot of us in the end.'

That's so true.

'What now, Joe? Are you going to file for divorce?'

'Yes, and that's going to cost a fortune.'

Peter and Suzy are going to end up wealthier than me or Joe.

'Work's terrible, too,' he added. 'December was our worst month on record.'

'Did Nate lose money?' she said.

'Do bears shit in the woods? He still read us the riot act though. I swear the guy's schizophrenic. He's on holiday this week, thank God. And he's put Sam in charge.' He shook his head. 'As if I care.'

'How's Spencer?' She couldn't help but ask, and her heart pounded as she spoke his name.

'He's alright, does his rounds as usual.' Joe looked a bit surprised at the question, and she hastily asked after Andy, Rich and a few others.

He said everyone was fine, and got up to leave.

'This is far worse for you than it was for me, Joe. I didn't love Peter, but I know you love Suzy.'

'I don't feel any love for her now.' He rubbed an eye. 'I just feel like a fucking idiot.'

'You're not an idiot, Joe, no more than I am. We were sitting ducks for two cheats. And I know it might sound trite, but what doesn't kill us makes us strong. At least we can face ourselves.'

He gave her a kiss on the cheek. 'Yep, but who gives a shit?'

She squeezed his arm. 'You do, Joe, and so do I. That's why we're friends.'

On saying that she felt a big pang of guilt, realizing that if they weren't, he and Suzy would still be together.

Joe smiled but his hazel eyes were glazed with tears, like pebbles just washed ashore.

'I'll ring you tomorrow, when I get home,' she said.

'OK, thanks.'

As she watched his dejected frame, hands in his pockets and head down, disappear through the swing doors, a big lump formed in her throat.

She burrowed down the bed as far as her nose, closed her eyes, and found herself staring intently into her eyelids, at whirls, dots, bubbles, and fluffy clusters all merging and pulsing around in a busy greyness. She found solace in the images, because they made her feel less alone.

Jess is right. Appearances can be VERY deceptive. Pete's tears were for himself, not me. What a bastard.

Joe's right, too. Life injures the lot of us in the end.

Pondering Peter's treachery, she began to feel lucky in as much as she would hate to be him. Yes, he had deceived her and effectively robbed her, but he had to live knowing he hadn't played fair. He wasn't just a liar but a coward too, a gutless, morally corrupt dreg.

Everything happens for a reason. I was supposed to get shot of the creep. Who knows, maybe I was supposed to be in here when I heard about it, in a place where I'm being looked after. Anyway, what's fifty grand? A few months pay once I get a job.

She thought long and hard about work, and decided to ask Olli Vermallen outright to employ her, because notwithstanding her predicament, she instinctively felt she was the best person for the job.

If he turns me down, so be it, but for the sake of Jamie and Harry I've got to ask. If he says no, I'll badger TJ, Steve, and everyone I know. OK, so the markets are diabolical but there are still plenty of firms making money, and I only need one.

Her thoughts returned to what she had just done.

I could never have coped with another child. And at least I now know I've not got some wasting disease. Spencer's obviously OK, and I'm obviously not on his mind. Cunt. I'm best rid of him, too. Never in a million years will I tell him I carried his child. Never.

*

Tanya got her wish but Olli Vermallen was a shrewd businessman, securing her services for a relatively modest sum that would not enable her to keep her house. But that no longer seemed important. No way though was she going to sell it to Mr and Mrs Johnson, whose offer of £1.9 million she considered so derisory she turned down flat.

Her new work environment, however, was taking some getting used to. An elegant room in a Georgian house, and quiet, it was a far cry from KS' trading floor.

Tanya reckoned it had been a reception room in its heyday, a place where the likes of Dukes, Counts and Lords, and their other halves had fun.

She sometimes imagined men in tail coats and shoes with buckles, and women in bolstered dresses carrying fans, entering through the imposing double doors to the left of where she sat. Doubtless to the sound of a gong and announcement of their names. And their horse drawn carriages laced around St James' Square.

But Tanya knew she was being romantic, and that London was known for its stench in those days, the air thick with soot and the cobblestone streets strewn with manure and all manner of sewage. That back then the vast majority lived in squalid, stinking hovels infested with bugs and cockroaches, lice and rats, and died from the cold or hunger or exhaustion, or a disease such as TB or typhoid, or a combination of these and worse.

To forget the less glamorous side didn't seem right to her, because her lineage was marked by destitution, her ancestors the workhouse poor, some criminals who had been sent to America and Australia. All mongrels, they were slaves in one form or another for their entire lives, and no doubt some as children were put to death or deported for stealing a morsel of bread.

It made her feel lucky. But, everything is relative, and while she felt blessed, grateful to be working and in such grand surroundings, the lack of noise in Sky-Rise's trading room was a problem for her, almost like a noise that itched in her ears.

She had colleagues, but they were about thirty feet away at the rear of the room, and most were foreign. They also worked in markets about which she knew little, so when she did chat with them, conversations tended to be brief, and confined for the most part to pleasantries.

Thierry, a slightly goofy Frenchman, together with Fritz, and Janek, a Hungarian with white curly hair, managed a pan European equity portfolio. China Paul, so named not to be confused with British Paul and Sanjay specialised in Asian equities. The commodity team, comprising British Paul, Alex and Jeremy, were responsible for funds invested in oil, gas, cocoa and coffee, while Brian, Carlos, Dimitri, Julian, and Ricardo specialised in convertible arbitrage.

In a way she had the best desk for she was able to see everyone who came and went, and beyond the wall to the left of the doors was Olli's office, so she was closest of anyone to the boss.

However, with little more than the sound of her own voice and her fingernails tapping her keyboard to keep her company, she often felt lonely, and as though she was working in a library.

CHAPTER NINETEEN

Tanya took off her shoe, and removed the object of irritation, a flat gray button with a logo on it. 'Hmmm,' she uttered, for she didn't recognize it as belonging to any garment she owned.

Then, remembering she had kept this pair of shoes at KS, and had not worn them since leaving the firm, she wondered if it was Nate's. If so, she knew the only way it could have found its way into her shoe was if he had been snooping in her drawers.

So what if it is Nate's? So what if he was snooping? Makes no difference now.

Even so she was curious, and en-route to work, and nearing KS' offices, she called Fiona. 'Can you nip out for a minute, Fi? I want to show you something. I'll be parked outside, in Ted's car, in about two minutes.'

'I'll be right down,' Fiona said.

Fiona strode toward Tanya, her blonde pony tail swinging from side to side, looking very smart in a pinstripe skirt suit, and almost as tall as Tanya in her platform boots.

As it was still dark out, Tanya borrowed a torch from Ted, and shone it on the button, in the palm of her hand, so Fiona could get a good look at it.

'I found it in a shoe I kept in my filing cabinet, which I know for certain I haven't worn since I left, and I think it's come off one of Nate's shirts. It's not a big deal, but I do like to solve a mystery, me.'

'I think you're right, because he wears gear by that designer. He was probably looking for your report.'

'Or maybe he's got a shoe fetish.'

They both laughed but Tanya was only half-joking, now acutely aware how deceptive appearances could be.

She put the button in her pocket and gave Fi a hug. 'Thanks, Fi, you're a doll. Mystery solved.' She paused. 'How's Sam getting on?'

'He's doing well, works really hard, and hustles the sales force just like you used to, whereas Nate still waits for business to come to him, and then grumps when it doesn't.'

Tanya smiled. 'Give Sam my best, and say hallo to the rest of the crowd for me.'

'I will, and if you're looking to hire a junior trader, you've got my number, right?'

'I know it off by heart, Fi, and you're on my list.'

They said goodbye, and went their respective ways.

A few hours later, Tanya got a call from Andy.

'I was wondering whether you were still alive,' she joked.

'I'm sorry, Darlin, I've been busy. Fi said she saw you earlier.'

'Did she tell you why, what I found, that Nate is now officially a snoop?' she said light-heartedly.

'Yes, and it reminded me of something. A few weeks before Quagg wrote that piece about you, I thought I saw him and Nate going into a restaurant. I can't be certain, as I was in a cab and we were going fast, which is why I didn't mention it at the time. And I obviously kept shtum once the article came out because you and Nate had just become equals, and I didn't want to stir up trouble.'

I was meant to find that button.

'Well, well, well. So he was Quagg's source.'

Nate gave Steve's details to Ludo in return for Ludo rubbishing me.

'Don't know about that, but he could have been, if it was them I saw, but as I said I can't be certain it was.'

Tanya's guts told her otherwise, and a lot more besides, enough for her to get Nate fired if she could prove her assumptions, but she wasn't about to share her thoughts with Andy.

'Even if he was Quagg's mole,' she said casually, 'it wouldn't have made a difference, because I wouldn't have been able to prove it.'

'That's what I thought, Darlin, that's why I didn't say anything. So how's life treating you?'

Tanya stayed chatting for about a minute, before using work as an excuse to wrap up the call. She then rang Joe and got the number of his private detective, saying it was for a friend. The man's name was Jeremy Pinkton, the company, Quick-Speed Investigations.

Calm down. Don't be hasty. You could be wrong.

She scratched at her wrist.

Nate got a back-hander for tipping Ludo off about Steve being unhappy, plus a cut of what KS paid Ludo for introducing Sam. That's why he pushed hard to get Sam a good deal. He was on the take, robbing KS. If I can get his bank statements, and telephone records...

Her logical reasoning left brain told her to leave well alone. *It's illegal. You've got enough to do. You haven't got the money.* But her right brain was screaming *Go for it. Get the bastard.*

She had already worked out what to say to Jeremy Pinkton: Nate had conned her out of money, leaving her heavily in debt, and she wanted to find out where her money had gone, which didn't feel like an entire lie.

Feeling pumped up and in a fighting mood, she wanted to phone Jeremy immediately but doing that from the office carried a risk, and she had work to do. It would have to wait until she got home.

But, itching for some action, she felt it was a good moment to phone Spencer, and ask to be put on KS' mailing list for his economic briefings, something she had been putting off.

'Spencer Rivington,' he said.

Her legs turned to jelly when she heard his voice, and she was glad she was sitting down.

'Hi Spencer, it's Tanya. Can you add Sky-Rise to your mailing list please?'

'Yes. Yes, of course. I'll take care of it straight away.'

'Thank you.'

'Congratulations.' He meant about getting a job.

'Thank you.'

'I'm sorry I haven't called, but my mother passed away, and I haven't been the best company.'

Fuck!

'I'm so sorry to hear that, Spence. Is it too delicate a question to ask what happened?'

'It's OK. She had a heart attack, sadly on New Year's Day.'

'Spence, I am really sorry. That's an awful day for something so terrible to happen.'

'It is rather, but we got to spend Christmas with her, I mean my father and I.' He paused. 'I'm afraid I must go as I have a meeting, but it would be good to see you. Perhaps we could have dinner one evening?'

His mother's passing considered, she could hardly say sling your hook.

'I'm really busy at the moment, but I'll call you when things calm down.'

'I've missed you, Tanya. I was going to phone you, but I've been doing a lot of travelling lately. My way I suppose of dealing with things.'

'I'll call you,' she said quietly, and rang off.

Fair enough, his mum dying is terrible, but actions speak louder than words. He had nigh on two months to call me before she died, but he didn't. Translated, he chose not to. And it's closer to two months than one since she did die. And being away is no excuse either. He could still have phoned, could have even sent me a Valentine's Day card. She heaved a sigh. *Don't be so hard. The poor guy's lost his mum. And maybe he was being honest, maybe he didn't get in touch because he didn't want to burden you, because he knew you had your troubles, too.* Another sigh. *Didn't I, just. How have you been, Tanya? Moi? Great. It was a hoot being skint and unemployed, and Christmas was just dandy without a shag. Oh and then I had a little stint in hospital getting rid of your kid. Now I've got to sell my house.* She snorted. *He can fuck off.*

But the next minute she was staring at her diary, trying to work out when she could see him, IF she wanted to see him.

'Hey, what's that pensive look for?'

Startled, she looked up at a smiling Olli. 'Sorry, I was miles away, mentally organising my dairy,' she fibbed. 'I'm being invited to lunches and dinners left right and centre.' That bit was true.

'Anything in your diary for tomorrow lunchtime?'

'No.'

'Great. I'll take you out for a bite to eat.'

'That will be lovely,' she said, but alarm bells sounded, for this would be their third lunch in as many weeks, and there was no such thing as a free lunch. She sensed he was growing fond of her, and while she liked him as a boss she wasn't the tiniest bit attracted to him.

'What information are you looking for?' Jeremy Pinkton said.

'Ideally, I'd like to get my hands on his bank statements, find out where my money went. I wouldn't mind seeing his telephone bills either. Is that sort of thing possible?'

'Yes, but obtaining someone's personal records is complex and can take time, but you'll need to speak to my colleague, Miles, who deals with crime. He'll be in the office tomorrow.'

'Can you give me a rough idea of the cost?'

After extolling the virtues of Quick-Speed Investigations – the firm apparently used the best electronic gadgetry, computer experts, and operatives (spies) – he hastened to add that while they invariably achieved success, they could not guarantee it.

'As far as cost goes,' he continued, 'it really does depend on how long it takes. Your man could be a serial fraudster, in which case he'll be adept in the art of espionage. He'll have numerous bank accounts, each safeguarded with a series of passwords that he changes regularly. And his computer will be like Fort Knox. I might be barking up the wrong tree. This man could be a dope, and it might be easy for us to tap into his affairs. We won't know until we try.'

'I understand. Assuming he's smart, how much do you reckon it will cost to come up with what I need?'

'As I said, crime's not my area, and you'll need to talk to Miles, but if I had to take a guess, if he's a lower league player, not a member of the Mafia, somewhere between fifteen and twenty five thousand pounds might get you what you want.'

Tanya gulped. 'How much for just his telephone bills?'

'It doesn't work like that, and I doubt his phone records will tell you much anyway. An educated man with a crooked bent of mind is not going to have his telephone calls itemized. A person with something to hide is going to be secretive. If this man is a fraudster, you're unlikely to be the only one he's defrauded, in which case you're unlikely to be the only person after him. Given that scenario, he'll be in to counter-surveillance in a big way. His phones, cars, houses, yachts, and anything else he owns will be regularly swept for recording devices. People like that invest heavily in not getting caught. I'm not trying to put you off, I just want to put you in the picture as to what you might be up against. But Miles will be able to tell you a lot more than I can.'

She let out a big sigh. 'I'd love to use your services, but sadly I can't afford the sort of money you're talking about. I've been done out of most of what I had.'

He was quiet for a few moments. 'Look, there's a man I've come across in the past, who might be able to help you. He goes by the name of Wagsy. He uses methods we might not employ here, but his rates are reasonable, and I gather he gets results.'

He gave her Wagsy's number.

'Thank you, Jeremy, that's really kind of you.'

'No problem. Good luck. I hope you get your man.'

288

She very much doubted Nate was a professional criminal. In her view he wasn't that sophisticated, and was more likely to just be making a few extra quid on the side to fund his jollies. On that basis she felt this man Wagsy was worth a call.

She looked at his number, feeling slightly unnerved.

Phone him. You don't have to follow through, if you don't like him.

She rang the number.

'Wagsy ere,' the deep, low voice said, 'leave a message, and I'll call ya back.'

She left a message, said Jeremy had recommended him, and that he could call back up to midnight.

He didn't.

Olli glanced at a passing diner, a pretty female with fulsome boobs to rival Tanya's but which, with her push-up bra and tight blouse, looked enormous.

He needs to get out more, she thought, smiling to herself.

He stirred his coffee. 'Information is a big responsibility. And bankers are *very* easily tempted. I paid close attention to the collapse of Amaranth.'

He was responding to her question as to why Sky-Rise had three Prime Brokers, instead of the usual one or two. And by Amaranth, he meant Amaranth Advisors, a hedge fund that collapsed in September 2006, the biggest failure of its kind at the time.

Prime Brokerage is a service provided by all major investment banks, ostensibly for the benefit of their clients yet they earn billions from prime broking, and actually created both sides of the trade so to speak.

In the 90s they invested heavily in electronic trading

systems, as a way to both reduce risk and increase income. And to give themselves a fighting chance of success, they withdrew liquidity in about ninety percent of bonds in existence, and concentrated on jumbo size deals, bonds that were highly liquid and therefore easy to trade electronically. At least, that's how Tanya saw it.

Their plan worked well for a while, well enough for them to give up their riskiest activity of all, Proprietary Trading, which involved buying and selling securities for their own account. As a consequence they had no need for prop traders, which meant hundreds of super smart traders suddenly found themselves out of work. The majority set up hedge funds. Investment banks then became service providers, that is, prime brokers, to this new breed of fund manager. Whatever hedge funds needed, be it money, trade execution and clearance services, and any kind of ancillary service, investment banks fell over themselves to provide.

The irony was that as competition forced prime broking fees lower, investment banks returned to proprietary trading to boost profits. They were back, except now hamstrung by the inability to trade head-to-head, and to boot they were in competition with all the hedge fund whiz kids they had axed.

Tanya was glad such wide scale manipulation of what had been a free market had backfired, but angry shareholders and Joe and Josephine Public had to pick up the tab. Many of the bonds that became illiquid were packaged up into CDO's, creating another money spinner for the banksters.

Her relationship with investment banking was very love-hate. She was good at trading and enjoyed it, but steering a path that felt ethical was a constant challenge.

Working for a hedge fund, and Olli, a man who had contributed to the wider world via his health clinics, record business and dot.com systems, made her feel a lot cleaner than she had when working for KS.

She laughed. 'So you spread the business around to stop the greedy buggers exploiting you?'

'You got it. No one bank knows enough about Sky-Rise's activities and positions to pose a danger, and I intend to keep it that way.' He paused. 'Would you use KS as a prime broker?'

'No way. In 2007 their cost-to-income ratio was a whopping sixty five percent, while their ROE (Return on Equity) was a pathetic eleven. What a claim to fame, eh? The firm is very badly run.'

'How come you stayed there so long?'

'Because I had obligations, family responsibilities and all that. But it was also a great place to work, until Nate came on the scene.'

He nodded. 'What's Dale Stanzinger like?'

'He's obviously clever, but in my opinion lazy. I could count on one hand the times he called me to find out what was going on in Europe, whereas he should have phoned me on a daily basis. I'm sure he spoke to Bruce, but Bruce spends too much time in his office to know the detail of what's going on. His biggest problem is that he likes the women. Can you believe he once asked me to do a twirl? Do a twirl young lady, he said.'

Olli smiled. 'Did you?'

'Yes, I'm ashamed to say, but I was only twenty five at the time.'

'He's married, right?'

'Yes, but he's always played around. Not good for his jam tart, if you ask me.'

Olli laughed. 'You mean heart, right?'

She drew a tick in the air with her finger. 'Correct, but on a serious note, Dale is not doing KS any favours. The firm could probably double its earnings with the right leadership.'

'Why don't you buy a controlling interest, and do a leveraged buyout?' She added, tongue-in-cheek.

What a brilliant boot in the face that would be for Nate. And Bruce. If only. Still, I've planted the seed.

He grinned. 'Hell, I was just curious.'

'I know, but if you ever get bored...'

He laughed. 'What's rhyming slang for drink and cheque?'

'Tiddly and Gregory,' she said, mimicking Olli's accent, minus nasal affectation that is. 'Tiddly wink, drink, and Gregory Peck, cheque.'

He let out a cheerful boyish giggle, which she found endearing.

'Right, let's finish our Tiddly's and get the Gregory, shall we?'

On collecting their coats Tanya couldn't help but admire Olli's. 'That's really nice, very stylish.' It was chocolate brown leather, long, single breasted, with a back vent.

'Why, thank you,' he said, slipping it on. 'Feel it. It's real soft.'

She felt the sleeve. 'Mm, it's lovely.'

As they walked back to the office, they passed a florist's van, back doors open, and Tanya glanced at a bouquet being retrieved from it by the delivery person.

'Do you like flowers?' he said.

She nodded. 'But roses are my favourite, the smelly sort especially.' She then told Olli about Peter's gift of flowers to Suzy. '...the most I ever got was a card, and one year he gave that to me just before I went to bed. Actually, he didn't even give it to me. He just pointed to it and said *there's your card.* And one Christmas he bought me a string of fake pearls, and that wasn't when we were skint either.' Suddenly embarrassed, she added. 'Don't say it. I know I was an idiot.'

Olli shook his head. 'No, you weren't. The guy's an asshole.'

'Yes, he is. Sadly, there's a lot of them about, present company excluded of course.'

He smiled. 'Why, thank you.'

That afternoon, Wagsy called Tanya back.

'I'm at work, so it's a bit difficult to talk,' she said. 'Can I ring you later?'

'Do you want to meet up?' he said, although it came out as ja-wanna-mee-up.

'I see you. You see me,' he added. 'I don't do business over the phone.'

She thought for a second. 'OK. What neck of the woods are we talking about?'

'Bethnal Green. Do you know it?'

'Yes,' she said, not letting on just how well.

'There's a pub called the White Hart, in the Roman Road. Why don't we meet there?'

'OK. When?'

'Tonight. Tomorrow. You tell me.'

For a split-second she considered backing out, but the potential reward was too great to resist. 'Tonight? Nine o'clock?'

'I'll see you outside,' he said.

'OK. What do you look like?'

'One arm, one eye, a scar across me face, a limp.'

He paused. 'That was a joke.'

She laughed, finding his slow way of speaking and baritone voice funny, but she was also nervous.

'I'm a regular looking bloke, about five ten.'

'OK. Shall I phone you and let you know what I'm wearing?'

'Nah. You'll be the only one loitering with intent. I'll find ya. Oh, and I only deal in readies.'

He rang off.

Tanya parked her car in a side street, and walked the last hundred or so yards to the White Hart pub, the hood of her duffle coat up, a thick scarf around her neck, and her jeans tucked in her boots, for it was freezing cold. The strap of her shoulder bag, containing one thousand pounds in cash – an amount she considered enough to get started, if she wanted to go ahead – was secure across her chest, and hidden under her coat.

Feeling more excited than scared, the icy mist added to the thrill as she trod what was for her home turf. Although the odours had changed, curry, chow mein, and cannabis replacing that of fish and chips, and cockles and mussels, she still felt a sense of belonging.

Her earliest memory of the Roman Road was of standing outside The Railway Tavern with a bottle of coke, and glimpsing the glamour inside as people came and went: The laughing heads, bright lights, and smoke. And of listening to her dad belt out ballads, and to the applause and rowdy encores that always followed. Of smelling perfume, beer and gin, as men in suits and ladies in high heels stood at his fish stall, devouring such delicacies as jellied eels soaked in vinegar with crusty clumps of white bread. Of watching wavering bodies slur goodbyes before zigzagging into the distance, and men pissing in shop doorways.

Wagsy wasn't at all regular looking in Tanya's view. To her, his swarthy pock-marked complexion and deep set eyes made for a distinctive and dramatic look. His eyes in particular told a story. They were tired, sad eyes, with big dark bags underneath, eyes she imagined had seen a lot of action, not all of it pleasant, and which along the way had missed a few years sleep.

They shook hands, went in to the pub, and found a discreet corner. Wagsy took off his overcoat and carefully folded it, before laying it on the padded bench, and going to the bar. Clean shaven, solidly built, and quite smart in a turtle neck sweater and grey suit, Tanya estimated his age at about forty five.

'One lime soda, one pint of beer,' he said, putting their drinks on the table.

'Thank you.' She took a sip of her soda. 'Were you ever a singer?'

He smiled. 'Done a lot of shouting in me time, but no singing. Why?'

'Your voice. It's low and,' she didn't want to say frightening, so she said, 'interesting.'

'I used to be a fire eater.'

Her mouth fell open.

'That was a joke.'

She laughed.

He moved on. 'Let's talk turkey. What is it you're wanting?'

'Info on a bloke I used to work with who did me wrong,' she said, reverting to her roots and adopting his vernacular.

'What sort of information? His shoe size? What

time he goes to bed? Where he keeps his safe? You need to be more specific.'

'I'm hoping you can help me on that score. I think he's double dealing, getting kick-backs from a journalist, for giving the journo inside information which, if I can prove, would be enough for me to get him fired.'

'Why do you want to do that?'

'He got me fired, and robbed me of a professional fortune.'

Wagsy nodded.

'I thought his bank statements and phone records would tell me all I wanted to know but Jeremy Pinkton wasn't so sure. Basically, I'd like your advice, bearing in mind I don't have that much to spend.'

'I don't give credit, and like I said, I only deal in cash. I'm a wunner – he meant one hundred pounds – an hour, day or night, plus expenses. But I don't take liberties with expenses. What's your budget?'

She absently massaged a knife scar on her left palm, inflicted by a thug from her secondary school, as though connecting with Wagsy's world. 'I could stretch to a couple of grand, maybe three.'

He asked a few questions about her enemy.

'So this geezer's got a bit upstairs, but he's flash and can't keep his mouth shut?' he said.

'Yeah, that sums him up well.'

Wanting to give him time to think, Tanya used the bathroom.

'We're going to need the kid,' he said, when she returned.

'The kid?'

'One of me little helpers,' Wagsy said. 'Brainy like

Einstein, he is. Hack into anything. Went to one of the best universities.'

She got goose bumps. 'We're not going to get caught, are we?'

'I don't know your last name,' Wagsy said. 'I don't want to know your last name. You are not going to tell me your last name. I don't know where you live. I don't want to know where you live. You are not going to tell me where you live. You are not going to get caught.'

'Thanks,' she said, with a sheepish look on her face.

'Five days, I reckon, and we'll have a good read of this bloke, but it's going to take all of your three grand, and I don't give guarantees. We do our best. You buy our time. You OK with that?'

She nodded.

'What you do with the information is your affair, but it won't be of any use officially. Coppers won't touch it, except for what we might find on public records.' He looked at his watch. 'I've got to go. Think about it, and let me know.'

Tanya unzipped her bag, and put her hand inside. 'I want to go ahead, and I can give you a grand right now.'

'Not in here,' Wagsy barked in a whisper. 'Let's go to my car.'

They walked a few yards, before turning into a quiet side street, and Tanya suddenly felt nervous.

He knows I've got a grand on me.

But aware that if she showed fear it would indicate mistrust, she carried on walking, and calmly got into the passenger seat of his Audi.

'Shall I shut the door?' she said.

'Might be a good idea.'

She closed it.

297

He spread an atlas over the steering wheel, took a notebook from his pocket, a pen from his glove compartment.

'Right, what's his full name and his full address?'

'I know he lives in Onslow Gardens, South Kensington, but I'm not sure of the number.'

'We can find that out. What's his full name?'

She frowned. 'Hmmm, I know he's definitely got a middle name, and I'm pretty sure it begins with H.'

Wagsy's dark eyes looked amused. 'The kid's clever but he ain't fuckin psychic.'

She laughed. 'Hang on, let me think. Henry, Herbert, Harry... Harvey. That's it! Nathan Harvey Walthak.'

He went on to fire lots of questions at her about Nate, all of which she was relieved to be able to answer.

She was astounded by the speed with which he was taking notes, until she saw he was writing in shorthand.

'You know Pitman's shorthand?' she said, with an expression of incredulity.

He gave a small nod. 'Comes in handy.'

Instinct told her not to ask where he had learned the art, her gut feeling being that it was whilst serving time.

He finished by asking her whether she knew where Nate banked.

'I know he's got an account at Citibank, but I don't know the branch, or if that's the only bank he uses.'

Wagsy penned a squiggle, and closed his notebook.

She gave him the one thousand pounds, and arranged to meet him the following night to hand over the balance.

'Same place, same time, tomorrow?' she said, levering the car door open.

'Same time, but meet me outside The Camel in Globe Road. Do you know it?'

'I'll find it,' she said. 'Goodnight.'

Feeling a mix of exhilaration and fear, she stood trembling as she watched Wagsy's car disappear from view, and then shakily lit a cigarette.

As Percy Egerton said, defying the law can be as effective as complying with it. All I'm doing is a bit of snooping on a shady character who has already done me harm. It's not as if I'm trying to get him done in. Anyway, what I'm doing is no more corrupt than KS breaching their duty to employ fit and proper people. If they had, Nate wouldn't be there, I would still have a job, and shareholders would be quids up.

Needs must. It's only temporary.

Tanya was in Hatton Garden and had just pawned her only asset aside from her house, a ring, a three carat diamond solitaire to be precise, for five thousand pounds.

She had felt sick handing it over, but had maxed out on her significantly reduced overdraft facility, which had been cut after she became unemployed. Her bank manager had cited the credit crunch as the reason, but she knew he was worried she could become a bad debtor.

Tanya had bought the ring as an act of defiance when she was married, and only because Peter had infuriated her. Having mentioned to him in passing that she'd quite like a diamond ring, he had said 'I should cocoa'. In other words, forget it; over my dead body will you ever have one of those.

As she was the one making the money, his retort

had incensed her, so much so that she made buying one a priority. She knew nothing about diamonds, still didn't, but had found a friend of a friend, a lady who was into antique jewellery, and given her a blank cheque, with instructions to buy the biggest diamond ring she could find. And she had come up trumps, sourcing Tanya's sparkler from Phillips Auctioneers.

Who would have thought I'd be using it for this purpose. On the other hand, it's an angry ring.

She laughed inside at her last thought, because she did now wear it on her right rather than left hand, but then she heaved a sigh.

I'll get it back when I've sold my house.

CHAPTER TWENTY

'You won't believe what came for you today,' Alison said excitedly.

Tanya followed her into the kitchen where on the breakfast bar sat a green china bowl, similar in shape to a chamber pot, with a red bow around the neck, filled with deep red roses and lush foliage.

She gasped.

'They're from a florist in Kensington, no less,' Alison said. 'Don't they smell lovely?'

Tanya nodded, and opened the attached card.

A token of what you're worth, Olli, X.

She told Alison about her passing remark to Olli.

'...I wish I hadn't said anything, because now I feel awkward.'

'He's obviously sweet on you.'

'I know but I don't like him in that way.' She pulled at her lip. 'And I know this is going to sound ungrateful, but I wish they were from Spencer.'

'You deserve better than him, Tanya. Besides, I doubt he could afford a bouquet like that.' She chuckled. 'How much did you say Olli's worth?'

Tanya laughed. 'Stop it. I'm not a prostitute.'

She went into her lounge and called Olli.

'Olli, what can I say? They're absolutely beautiful, thank you, but I feel hideously embarrassed.'

He laughed. 'Why? I just wanted to bring a smile to that beautiful face of yours.'

'But you shouldn't be buying me flowers. It's not right.'

'Hey, if it makes you feel better, look on them as a thank you for the CPC trade you did today.'

Her trade was more luck than judgement and it was far from a big deal. She had bought some bonds issued by CPC Holdings, a European bank, which had spiked in price, and sold them for a profit of twelve thousand dollars.

'That does make me feel a tad better, but I bet Thierry doesn't get flowers when he makes money.'

He laughed. 'Hey, I've another call coming in. I'll see you in the morning.'

'OK, bye.'

She resolved to be more careful about what she said to him in the future.

*

'…Someone else has tried to hack into his accounts and made a pig's ear of it,' Wagsy said, 'and now the bloke's made sure that unless you're working for MI5 you'll never get into them. They're zipped and stitched and cross-coded like no tomorrow.'

Tanya blew out her cheeks. 'I'd be lying if I said I wasn't disappointed.'

Wagsy had not been able to obtain Nate's telephone records either, and his surveillance of Nate's flat had yielded nothing of consequence. A cleaning lady had entered the main door of the house, as had a pizza delivery guy, but as Nate's front door was inside the house he couldn't even confirm if these people were calling on Nate. And to know Nate had left and returned home at times consistent with work, dressed in a suit, was hardly of any help.

'I'm choked,' Wagsy said. 'I watched the geezer for a total of twenty four hours, and the kid put in more time than that on the internet.' He paused. 'It's not good for business when we hit brick walls.'

She nodded understanding, and gave him a closed lip smile, and his tired eyes seemed to light up.

'Never mind,' she said. 'You did your best.'

He took some folded A4 sheets of paper out of the glove compartment, and gave them to her. 'They're yours, but like I said there ain't much there.'

She read the first page, which was a typed recap of Wagsy's findings, and noticed two things he hadn't mentioned, that Nate wasn't a bad debtor, in as much as he didn't have any CCJ's (County Court Judgements) against him, which came as no surprise, but also that he owned his flat.

Property of residence purchased by Mr Walthak in May, 2008.

She pointed at the sentence. 'That must be a mistake, because he rents his flat. He did move into it about that time, but I know he was renting because I heard him tell his boss as much.' She clearly recalled him telling Dale.

'The kid don't mess up. Have a look at the next page.'

She did. It was a photocopy of an official document from the Land Registry. Her stomach tightened. 'Can we be certain this is accurate?'

He nodded. 'That bit's public information. That don't get on there unless it goes through a solicitor. Has to be right.'

'But why would he lie about owning his flat to his boss,' she mused.

'Perhaps he wanted the bloke to think he was poor,' Wagsy said, 'or perhaps he wasn't saying it for the benefit of the boss.'

Tanya shook her head, dismissing both possibilities. If anything she felt Nate would want Dale to think he was rich and used to the high life. Nor did she think he'd lied for her or anyone else's benefit, because he had only revealed he was renting by way of a response to Dale asking if he'd found himself an apartment.

So why did he lie? He had to have a reason.

She folded the papers up and put them in her bag. 'It's an academic question since I'm broke, but what would it cost to go through his bins?'

'You're talking heavy money if you want us to crawl up his backside. It would take a few weeks of non-stop surveillance of him and his gaffe just for me to work out the best ways and times to gain access. I can do it, can bug his phones, his house, put a tracker device on his car, but we're talking in the tens.'

He meant the tens of thousands of pounds.

She shook her head. 'Forget it. Champagne taste and lager money, that's me.'

He looked at her sympathetically.

With a resigned smile, she opened the car door. 'Thanks for your help. At least what you've come up with proves he's a liar.'

'Mind how you go, Tanya. Look after yourself.'

'You too, and enjoy the rest of your weekend.' It was Saturday.

She drove home cursing under her breath, angry she didn't have the money to find out why Nate was lying, and when she got home it was to a final bill from Jess Larance, accompanied by a note: *If you are unable to*

*pay the full amount immediately, please telephone me.
I'm sure we can come to some arrangement.*

Oh, what a lovely day, she thought sarcastically. *All
I need now is for the house to fall down. Actually, I
wished it would, as then I wouldn't have to worry about
selling the friggin thing.*

She wasn't annoyed with Jess. In fact, she felt
guilty she hadn't bothered to turn up for her last three
appointments, and immediately wrote a cheque for all
she owed her, and a note of thanks. Then she drove,
with her boys, to Jess' house, and popped it through the
letterbox.

On her way home, having bought Jamie and Harry
enough sweets to keep them quiet for a week, which
they were scoffing merrily, her mobile rang. She
answered via her earpiece.

It was Spencer.

Her head said tell him to fuck off, but her body was
already agitated at the prospect of a bit of fun. Her heart
didn't seem to care.

'Hi,' she said, 'what's up?'

'Nothing. I was simply calling to say hallo.'

'Hallo,' she said.

'You sound like you're having one of those days.'

'I am.'

'Is there anything I can do?'

'Such as?'

'Buy you dinner, tonight?'

'I'm not sure that's a good idea. Look, I've got the
boys in the car. I'll call you when I get home.'

'I would dearly love to see you, Tanya. I know it
was remiss of me not to call, but my mother's death hit
me very hard.'

'I can appreciate that, but what about November and December?'

'I wanted to call, many times.'

'So why didn't you?'

'The longer I left it, the harder it became. You know how these things are.'

'No, I don't actually. I'll call you when I get home.'

'Please don't be cross with me, Tanya. You were constantly in my thoughts.'

She sighed heavily, and thought for a few moments. 'What the hell. I've had a pig of a day. Going out will probably do me good.'

'Excellent. I don't mean excellent you're not having a good day. You know what I mean, I hope. Where would you like to go? I'll make a reservation.'

'Why don't you cook, and I'll come to yours?'

'Perfect. What would you like to eat?'

A triple decker pecker. Your cock, followed by your cock, followed by your cock.

'I can't say because I have the boys in the car,' she said, with appropriate intonation. She couldn't see any point beating around the bush. If she was going to see him, they both knew what would happen.

He laughed. 'Now I shan't be able to concentrate. I can't tell you how wonderful it is to hear your voice.'

'I'll be with you at eight thirty,' she said.

'Perfect.'

On hanging up, she switched on the radio and tuned in to a music channel, something she hadn't done in months.

You romantic fool, you. I know. I can't help it. But you know what he's like; chatty today, incommunicado tomorrow. Yes, but who else have I got to go out with?

306

He really hurt you, don't forget that. I'm not. I just want to step off the planet for a few hours, get pissed and have a bit of fun. Fair enough, but there's no such thing as a free lunch, or a free dinner. Yes, but I'm used to him, and I'm not going to let him get to me. Make sure you don't. Don't worry, I won't. Perhaps he does care, though. I mean, he did sound sorry. And his mother did die, which must have been terrible for him. He may have desperately wanted to see me but felt too embarrassed to let me see him distraught. Men are like that, and appearances really matter to him. He probably cried his eyes out for weeks. Stupid sod. Why didn't he tell me? I would have been at his side in a flash. But what about November and December?

Her emotions blew hot and cold all afternoon, but she needed sex. Being single had its drawbacks.

About to leave, she picked up her gift to Spencer, from her bedside cabinet, and took the key ring out of its box. 'A belated merry Christmas to me.' She swung it gaily from her little finger. 'You're the one with a heart of gold, not him.'

Spencer took Tanya's coat, hung it haphazardly on a nearby hook, and turned to her, his eyes travelling the length of her body. 'My God, it's good to see you.' He pushed her long curls off her face, and took hold of her by the small of her back and drew her to him.

Her heart was thumping but she merely brushed her lips across his, and reclined into his hands, and met his adoring gaze with a glacial stare. It was a look usually reserved for the trading floor, when she didn't want to show her hand.

She took a deep breath, and noticed him glance at

her breasts, her cashmere cardigan accentuating their shape and fullness as they rose provocatively.

'So,' she said, 'we meet again.'

'We do indeed. Thank you for coming.'

That's better. Show a bit of respect.

She tapped his chest with her clutch purse, and pulled away. 'I need a drink.' Walking along the hallway ahead of him, she swung her hips so that her sexy black rah-rah skirt danced around her thighs, to reveal, she hoped, glimpses of stocking lace.

Spencer poured them each a glass of champagne and they sat on the sofa, him in the centre, her at a slight angle to face him, with one knee over the other.

'I'm sorry if the place looks a little untidy, but I only got back from New York yesterday.'

She glanced around. 'Looks fine to me.'

He smiled. 'I wasn't there entirely on behalf of KS.'

'So where are you going?'

'It's not done yet, but we're at the final stage.' He paused. 'Piper Kline.'

'Wow. Good for you,' she said, for this was a top tier American investment bank. 'How senior is the job?'

'I'll be reporting directly to the global head of international economics, who reports to the chief economist and the global head of investment research.'

'Well done. That's a big deal at a firm of that size.'

'I know. I had a two hour meeting with them all on Wednesday, and the vice chairman and head of emerging markets also decided to sit in.'

'That must have been nerve wracking.'

'No, I rather enjoyed it, although I could have done without the monstrous child behind me on my flight over. I had a whole pile of stuff to read in preparation, and the little brat kept bouncing his tray and kicking my seat.' He shook his head. 'Children should be confined to a separate section on long haul flights.'

'Like in kennels?'

'You know what I mean, Princess. The child was a little wretch with a howl that would frighten a dinosaur.'

She laughed. 'How old was this little wretch?'

He shrugged. 'I don't know, three, four perhaps. He could talk—a little bit.'

'And I suppose you think a toddler should have been doing the *Times'* crossword for eight hours?'

His laugh turned her legs to jelly. She had missed that sound, and his gorgeous face.

'You wait till you have kids and everyone's looking at you in disgust,' she added.

'I shall teach my children good manners.'

So he does want them. Well, that counts him out, because I'm not having any more, not after that.

'Good luck,' she said.

He smiled. 'Did you know that last year Piper Kline was in the top three in every major league table?'

'No, but they have got seventy five billion dollars in capital, which sort of helps. Have they put a firm offer on the table?'

'Yes, but I'm negotiating.'

'It's not like you to play hardball.' It was a deliberate put-down, because she was fed up with him banging on about himself.

'I wouldn't call it hardball exactly. I will be giving up seniority, after all.'

'Yes, but Piper Kline is much bigger and much better run than KS. If they match your current package, it's not a bad trade, if you ask me. What does your head hunter think of the offer?' She raised a hand. 'Please don't tell me it's Ludo Quagg.'

'I'm dealing directly. Satoshi called me and set the ball rolling. You remember Satoshi, don't you?'

'Yes, but not fondly.'

Satoshi, now at Piper Kline, used to work for KS in Tokyo. And while at KS he once had Tanya mark up the prices of two bonds to be swapped, by 25 cents, and then informed her she had only done one half of the trade: Bought bonds 25 cents higher without selling any. She got the trade unwound but it took a fight.

'He's a nice fellow once you get to know him.'

She rolled her eyes. 'If you say so. Anyway, what's for dinner?'

'Penne with a tomato and beef sauce, followed by chocolate mousse.'

'Well Spenceroni Salvatori needs to get a move on,' she said, in an Italian accent.

He laughed. 'Come and keep me company, and tell me what's been happening with you.' He took her hand and led her into the kitchen. 'I was so pleased when I heard you had joined Sky-Rise. That you landed sweetly on those pretty toes,' he flashed a look at her feet, 'is justice indeed. Are you enjoying the work?'

'Yes, but the office is very quiet, but after nearly four months out of work, I shouldn't complain.'

'You must be learning a lot about the hedge fund business.'

'I am, and that part's great.' She held up her glass. 'Can I have some more shampoo?'

'Of course, Princess.' He wiped his hands on a tea towel, refilled her glass, and then excused himself to go and put some music on.

I don't think so, Tanya thought, when she heard Andrea Bocelli's voice. *If he thinks we can pick up where we left off, he's dreaming.*

She went into the lounge. 'Do you mind if we have something else on? I'm not a great fan of Bocelli.'

'Er, no, not at all.' He looked surprised. 'Would you like to choose something?'

'OK.'

He left her to it, and she put on a classical mix, and immediately felt better.

When she returned to the kitchen he was at the sink, with his back to her, and she stood staring at his arse, which looked more round, plump, and grabbable than ever. Unable to resist, she went up behind him, placed a hand under each cheek, and squeezed.

'Mm,' he uttered.

She slipped her arms around his waist, moulded her body against his, and nuzzled his neck. 'I'm ready for a kiss now.'

Moments later they were locked in a luscious snog, while feeling each other up and rubbing groins.

She tugged at the belt of his cords, managed to undo it and unzipped his trousers.

'No, Princess,' he said, breathless, 'not here, we're overlooked.'

She cast her eyes to the window and laughed, and then squatted.

He wagged his finger at her. 'If you do that, you will most certainly be the loser. Come,' he pulled her to her feet, 'I want to be naked with you.'

Lust, however, took over, and next thing her skirt was up around her waist, her cardigan around her neck, and she was yelling, 'Yes, Yes, Yes,' as they fucked.

But shouting worked against her, causing him to ejaculate far too quickly.

'Sorry, Princess,' he said breathless, his forehead on the pillow beside her face, his cock still inside her.

'It's OK,' she whispered.

He pulled back. 'Open your eyes, Princess.'

She did, but immediately covered his eyes with the pads of her fingertips.

'Don't do that,' he chided.

She let him look at her.

'God, I've missed you.'

No, you haven't. You've just missed my body.

She smiled, and nudged him off her. 'Sorry, but I need some air, and the loo. And a cigarette.'

During dinner she became increasingly irritated because he talked virtually nonstop about Piper Kline, telling her what questions he'd been asked by the firm's big shots, and the answers he had given.

He only called because he was in a good space.

The evening now felt wrong, and she wished she hadn't come.

If I was a man, I would have bought sex and done away with all this aggravation. Our personalities and lifestyles are miles apart.

She consoled herself with champagne, and mounds of pasta. 'That was delicious, thank you.' She patted her stomach.

He smiled. 'Your appetite is astonishing. I don't know how you manage to keep so slim.'

You would if you saw my bank statements.

'Tonight's an exception,' she said.

Since there's fuck all else on offer, I'm comfort eating.

He took her hand. 'Will you be able to stay tonight? I would love to wake up with you beside me.'

Just then her mobile phone, which was on the arm of the sofa, started ringing. 'Sorry, but I need to get that in case it's Alison.' The caller ID said OV. 'It's Olli. I'd better take it.'

Spencer looked at his watch.

'He's in Chicago,' she said, and answered the call.

'Hi Olli, how's the Plush House?' This was the most expensive hotel in Chicago.

'Why don't you come see for yourself? I'm here for another four days.'

She burst out laughing, lost for what to say to such a loaded invitation, especially with Spencer listening. Twirling her hair, she crossed the room, and knelt on Spencer's chaise longue under the window, and peered into the street below as she chatted, well aware she was flaunting her scantily clad bottom.

'Hey, sorry I didn't get back to you yesterday,' he said, 'but I was jammed solid. Is everything OK?'

'Everything's great. I just wanted to know what you thought about us buying some subordinated perpetual floating rate notes. Allied Capital (a European bank) did a deal last year. It was too expensive at launch, so not many investors bought it. Then the market bombed. Most of the deal is still in professional hands, and it's now quoted in the sixties, but that's not a real price. I reckon we'll need to pay up to seventy five, but even at that price the bond still represents incredible value.'

Spencer started clearing the table—noisily. Tanya turned around and gave him a pleading look, but he carried on, his face tense with annoyance.

He's such a child. Mr nice-when-it's-easy.

313

She was on the phone for about ten minutes, during which time Olli sanctioned her purchase, and when she finished the call she tossed her mobile in the air and caught it with one hand. 'Sorry, Spence, I couldn't ignore the boss.'

'It didn't sound as though you wanted to.'

'Not true,' she said, her tone indifferent.

He motioned to her to sit down for dessert. They ate in silence, and she cleared her bowl despite feeling full.

'Mm, that was yum,' she said.

He looked up briefly. 'Good.'

Fuck him, she thought, and got up and went into the kitchen, returning with a new bottle of champagne.

'Do you mind if I open this?'

'Be my guest.' He folded his napkin and retired to the sofa, with his glass of red wine.

He's not got green eyes for nothing.

Standing at the dining table, she removed the foil top and wire, but when she tried to twist the cork, it wouldn't budge. She muttered about it being stuck, but Spencer didn't offer to help.

It's official. Petty warfare has been declared.

She took it back into the kitchen where, with the help of a damp cloth and a few almighty twists fuelled by frenzied pride, she got the bugger to pop. To calm her temper she drank half a glassful straight off the bat and refilled her glass before returning to the lounge.

Spencer was now sitting at one end of the sofa, staring at a TV that wasn't on.

She sat the other end, ashtray on her lap, and lit a cigarette.

I've got two choices. I can go home, or try and make peace, in the hope of getting some half decent sex.

Opting for the latter, she kicked off her shoes, turned lengthwise and put her feet on his lap. 'Please, Sir, may I have a foot massage?'

He distractedly rubbed her left foot. 'Is he fond of you?'

'Who, Olli? I don't know.'

'You *must* know.'

She blew a plume of smoke into the air. 'Yes, he does like me, but that's not my fault, is it?'

'It is, if you wear skirts like that to the office.'

She glowered at him.

He heaved a sigh. 'You just seemed awfully happy when you were on the phone.'

'Yes, because I was talking about a trade. You know what I'm like when there's a deal to be done. Don't punish me for a crime I haven't committed. If you were on the phone with your boss, I would have massaged your shoulders, or something.'

He stroked her leg. 'I'm sorry, Princess. I'm behaving like an oaf.'

'Apology accepted. Now let's get back to being friends, shall we?'

He looked at her. 'You didn't answer my question about staying over.'

She rubbed the ball of her foot over his cock. 'I would *love* to stay, but I want a smile first, because I'm not enamoured with your Mr Misery Guts impression.'

His eyes creased like punched pillows.

Ladies and gentlemen, I am pleased to announce the restoration of self-serving peace.

'Ouch, ouch, not so hard, Spence.' She flipped onto her back. 'Come and kiss my mouth instead.'

315

His playful grabs had turned into earnest mauls, and the pleasurable scrape of his teeth over her thighs and bottom into painful bites. Initially excited by what she felt was his pent up jealousy coming out, she had murmured encouragement, but now it was hurting.

He began biting her belly, which felt OK, until he delivered a sharp little pincer-like nip that made her wince, and caused her stomach muscles to contract.

'Stop it, Spence. That fucking hurt, and your beard feels like a cheese grater. Come and give me a kiss.'

This time he did and simultaneously entered her—like a bullet train, and as he fucked and kissed her he grabbed hold of a great load of her hair, pulling it hard.

That's when it struck her he was being driven by more than just jealousy, that he was trying to expel the pain of losing his mother. To get rid of his grief and achieve a connection to make up for the one he'd lost. Whether she was right she didn't know of course, but she sensed more than just jealous passion pouring from him, and had never seen him this highly charged. Not that he was making much noise.

When he was done he slumped onto the bed and conked out, and she felt a strange satisfaction, almost privileged she had been able to help him discharge some of his hurt. As per usual she hadn't managed to have a decent orgasm, but for once it didn't bother her. Nor was she that bothered that she hadn't enjoyed sex, had actually found it painful, especially when he had entered her, because he had been too rough and aggressive.

Maybe the point of life is just to feel, whether that's pain or pleasure. Maybe any experience is better than no experience. Hmmm. But would I say that if he had really hurt me, or if I had been scared? No.

She gave his furry chest a soft kiss, before turning onto her side, and going to sleep.

In the night she got up to use the loo, and to return to warm bed and snuggle up to Spencer felt great. And more in the mood for sex than sleep, she slipped under the covers and began licking his genitals.

Minutes later his cock felt hard as marble, and he sprang into action, forcefully encouraging her onto all fours, and locking his hands onto her hips with a vengeance. Feeling the tip of his cock pushing on her anus, she raised her buttocks and manually guided his erection into the right opening, bracing herself for the surge.

This time he came up trumps, and her head high like a cat, her hair like garland on her bare shoulders, she screamed and wailed like a wolf as he rammed into her. And lo and behold, he didn't tell her to shush.

But still no orgasmic flood tide, for her at any rate.

Nine thirty next morning and he was back to his composed self, sitting at the dining table spreading marmalade on his toast. Looking the archetypal moneyed weekender, in Chinos, polo shirt and a sweater tied loosely around his shoulders, while she was in the previous night's clothes.

'What are your plans for today, Princess?'

'Why, do you want to go back to bed?'

He grinned. 'Sadly, I can't. My desk is a veritable shambles, I've a report to write, and I have lunch with my father.'

Your loss.

'I've got loads to do as well, anyway.' She sipped her tea. 'How is your father?'

'He's OK. He's not yet returned to the marital

317

bedroom, but it's still early days.' He paused and looked at a china cruet set on the table. 'I was with her when she bought that. We were at a craft fair. I was about six, I think.'

'Aw. Did it get used?'

'Yes, all the time. It was a permanent fixture on our breakfast table.'

She picked up the salt cellar for a moment. 'It's a blessing to have those memories.'

'I know. I feel very lucky.'

He took her hand, and she smiled.

'Have you made up with your mother?'

'No, and to be honest I don't want to.'

He nodded understanding. 'Do you miss her?'

'No. My life's a lot easier without her in it.'

'But it must still be distressing to be estranged from her. She is your mother, after all.'

'But she's a different sort of mother to the one you had. Yours enhanced your life, whereas she went out of her way to torment me and make me feel bad. Life's always been about her, and always will be. It's not that hard to turn your back on a spiteful person.'

'But even the best of mothers can be difficult.'

'Difficult is different from spiteful. Look what she did when you and I were going to meet up. That was downright evil.'

'Why do you think she did that?'

'She didn't want me to go out, because she wanted me to stay in with her.'

'In other words she wanted to spend time with you?'

'Spence, I can see where you're trying to go, but I know where I stand, and why I stand there, OK? Life has always been about her and what she wants. What I want has never come into it.'

He tutted sympathetically. 'But we only have one mother, Princess.'

'I know, and more's the pity.'

'I'm sure you don't mean that.'

'I do. This might come as a shock to you, Spence, but not all mothers love their kids, you know.'

'I'm sure in her ow—'

Tanya withdrew her hand as though she had just got an electric shock. 'Don't even go there.' She rummaged in her bag on the chair next to her, and took out her cigarettes. And as she lit one, like a leopard noticing one blade of grass flicker in the brush, she caught fleeting disapproval on Spencer's face.

Fuck him. He's sure of this, He's sure of that. He doesn't even know me, let alone her.

He went and got her an ashtray, and put it on the table.

She mumbled thanks.

For about a minute her noisy sucks for nicotine, and breaths thick with annoyance were the only sounds.

'I was only thinking of you,' he said. 'If something happened to her, you would never forgive yourself.'

She shook her head. 'You really don't get it, do you? First you try and lay a guilt trip on me, then you say you're thinking of me, and then you try and lay *another* guilt trip on me.'

'Don't be ridiculous. I did no such thing.'

'I think you did.' She paused to take a puff of her fag. 'You're sure of this. You're sure of that. You don't even know my mum. Or me, for that matter.'

'There is no need to be like that.'

319

'Well don't stick your nose in where it's not wanted, OK? You had a good mum who loved you, and that's great, that's really lovely. But I didn't.'

'I understand that. I suppose I'm just concerned for you. I can't imagine you'd be jumping through hoops if you found out she was seriously ill.'

'She's been seriously ill her entire fucking life.'

He snorted. 'You know what I meant. And there is no need to swear,' he said sternly.

I'm off.

She stubbed out her cigarette and stood. 'I'll get my things.'

He saw her to the door. 'I'll call you later, shall I?'

'Don't bother.'

'Please, let's not part on a sour note. I had a very nice time last night, and it's been wonderful to see you.'

She thought for a few moments. 'Look, I'll call you, OK?'

'When?'

'Don't try and pin me down. That was one of my mum's favourite tricks as it happens.'

'You can be so exasperating, Tanya.'

'And you can be so... ignorant,' she said, and left.

That afternoon she went to see Daphne, who was in raptures because her son, Humphrey, had called to say he was coming over from Australia in June.

'That's super news, Daphne.'

'I know. I'm so excited I can hardly sleep,' she said, sounding like a little girl. 'I haven't met William yet but knowing my Humphrey, I'm sure he's delightful. You must come to tea while they're here.'

'I would love to,' Tanya said.

'Now tell me, Dear, how you are?'

Tanya told her about Olli sending her flowers, and that she had seen Spencer.

'...so he made me feel guilty about my mum, and then had the cheek to call me exasperating. Plus he made me feel uncomfortable about having a cigarette.'

'That was very naughty of him.'

Tanya nodded. 'The thing is, even though I feel weak having slept with him, and really wished I hadn't, I can't be sure I won't again. Pathetic, isn't it?'

'We all need affection, Dear.'

'I know. I just wished I could get it from someone who didn't have a habit of putting their big foot in it all the time. I can't begin to imagine what he'd have said if I'd told him about my termination.' She shook her head. 'He tries to be helpful, I can see that. It's just that he fails miserably.' She shrugged and sighed. 'Or maybe it's me. Maybe I'm just too sensitive.'

'Nonsense! He's simply not good enough for you.'

'You say the sweetest things, Daphne.'

'I speak from my heart. You are a remarkable and beautiful young woman, who deserves a prince on a white horse, not some little scraping of boot polish.' She looked over the rim of her tea cup. 'Seriously, Dear, what are this young man's good points?'

'Well, he's clever, handsome, hardworking, solvent, keeps himself fit,' she paused for thought, 'and he's available.'

'I think my ears may be troubling me. I didn't hear you mention any virtues.'

Tanya laughed.

'Is he kind, patient, thoughtful?' Daphne said.

'On balance I'd have to say no. I think he's too into himself to worry about others.'

'He isn't kind?'

Tanya made a face. 'He's not cruel, but I'm not sure I'd say he was kind either, whereas Olli definitely is.'

An impish smile spread across Daphne's face. 'Why don't you go to bed with this kind man, Oliver, and see what you think?'

Tanya burst out laughing. 'You're not serious?'

Daphne's skinny body bobbed gently with laughter. 'That's what people do these days, isn't it? Try before you buy, I think it's called.'

'I'm all for that, Daphne, but I can't sleep with someone I'm not physically attracted to.'

'Why ever not?' Her eyes lit up. 'It's commonplace in arranged marriages, Dear, and I think you'll find most of those work out very well.'

Back at home, after washing her smalls and polishing a pair of boots, Tanya made a cup of coffee and sat in her lounge, looking at Olli's roses, which showed no signs of wilting. For the briefest of moments she thought of Daphne's suggestion, and him naked, and it gave her goose bumps. *Ugh. No way.*

She tipped the contents of her bag onto the sofa, and began putting everything in its proper place. Hairgrips in her cosmetic bag, pen tops back on their pens, loose coins in her purse, and grubby tissues and unwanted receipts in a waste bin by her feet. Then she re-read the papers Wagsy had given her.

What I know for certain is that Nate's a liar. But what I can't be certain of is that someone else has tried to hack into his accounts, as the kid could have used that as an excuse, because he hadn't managed to do so. But what if someone has? What does that tell me?

She checked the time. Her boys were due back from their day with Peter.

Get your act together and stop playing diversions.

Using the calendar on her mobile, she counted the weeks until the end of June, in case there were more than thirteen, even though she knew there wasn't.

I'll give it one more week, and if nothing comes up, I'll have to hit Mr and Mrs Johnson's bid.

She felt bitter at the prospect of them getting her beloved house at a knock down price, but Peter had to be paid, and she needed to free up cash to keep going.

Her plan was to rent for a year, until she could afford a house that didn't represent too much of a come down. She glanced at her roses.

I need to keep this job, whatever happens. And Jamie needs to remain in the same school.

She was concerned about Jamie, who had become prone to outbursts of tears. Divorce had hit him hard, and so would a house move. She couldn't impose a change of school on him as well.

CHAPTER TWENTY ONE

Ludo opened his arms and smiled broadly. 'The vision of you makes me weep.'

'I'd like to return the compliment but...' She jokingly grimaced at his fuchsia pink cravat, and matching hanky sprouting from his top pocket.

He laughed, his body buckling, thrilled, she felt, that he stood out.

Once seated, he ordered a pricey bottle of Puligny Montrachet, which he invited Tanya to sample. She sniffed its bouquet, before swirling it round her glass and tasting it. 'Very good,' she said to the waiter.

She had told Ludo she was looking to hire a trader, so lunch was his treat and she had chosen Centriko's, but in truth she just wanted information about Nate.

'Ah, there's Steve,' she said, feigning surprise and standing as he approached their table, for his presence was no coincidence, but her idea.

'Hiya, Gorgeous.' He gave Tanya a hug, before shaking hands with Ludo, who greeted him like a mate.

'Am I blessed or what?' Ludo said, gesturing to Tanya.

'Why don't we swap?' Steve said. 'I'd much prefer to dine with this delicious creature. Uh, my guy's just walked in, I'd better go.'

When they sat back down, Tanya asked Ludo how he knew Steve.

'How do I know anyone? How long is a piece of string?' He spread his napkin on his lap. 'It's my business to know people.'

He moved on to ask her about Sky-Rise and Olli Vermallen's character, and she took great pleasure in telling him how fabulously clever and wealthy Olli was, and how much she loved working for him.

He raised his glass. 'To you, Tanya. You deserved a break.'

She tapped her glass against his. 'I certainly did.'

'I was both sad and shocked to hear about your departure.'

Liar.

She smiled. 'It didn't turn out so bad in the end.'

'Even so, I imagine it was a hellish few months.'

'I've been through worse.'

'I admire you, Tanya. That's why I didn't write about what happened.'

'Thanks,' she said, although she felt that was rubbish, and it more likely that Bruce, fearing she'd follow through on her threat to sell her story, phoned Rolf Peterson, Ludo's boss, and asked him not to run any stories about her departure.

They spent lunch discussing various candidates, and when they got to the brandy, Tanya returned to the topic of Steve.

'I need to ask you a question, Ludo.'

He made scoops with his right hand, by way of encouragement.

'I know you played a role in getting Steve his job at Barclay Gray, so why didn't you tell me, when I asked how you knew him?'

He nonchalantly turned his palm to the air. 'I must err on the side of caution with such information, Tanya. If a candidate wants to divulge it, all well and good, but it's not my place to do so.'

325

'Good answer. Another question. Did Nate get a kick back?

Ludo's eyebrows shot up. 'A kick back for what? What are you suggesting?'

'The obvious, Ludo, that Nate tipped you off that Steve wasn't happy, and that you compensated him for his troubles.'

'That's an insult to my integrity, Tanya.'

What integrity?

'It's plausible,' she said.

He leaned forward. 'Nate might not be pencil straight, Tanya, but I am.'

He knows something.

'So he didn't play any part in you finding Steve?'

'Absolutely not.'

Her heart sunk because he looked genuinely aghast and spoke emphatically.

She shrugged. 'Case closed, Ludo. I believe you. But since I might use your services, I had to ask the question.'

'I quite understand.'

'What are you hearing about KS?' she said.

'That your old division is limping badly. I gather January was their worst month on record and February not much better.'

'That's what I've heard, not that I feel smug, because when you spend nearly half your life at a firm it becomes like family.'

'Do you think Nate is to blame for the losses?'

'I could say a lot, Ludo, but I'm not into muck spreading. All I'll say is that I wouldn't hire him.' She paused. 'God knows how he ever got into Harvard.'

'You mean Princehaven.'

Her heart missed a beat, but she remained calm.

'Oh,' she said casually, 'I always get confused when it comes to fancy American universities.'

She wasn't confused. Nate had boasted more than once about his time at Harvard.

'Anyway,' she added, 'how come you know what Uni he went to?'

'It's my job to know these things.'

Thank you Ludo.

'If he's looking for another job, don't bother sending me his CV,' she said, laughing. 'In fact, if you want to keep your clients, don't send it to anyone.'

He didn't say anything but he did laugh.

'Not that it matters anymore, Ludo, but was Nate your source for that article you wrote about me?'

He blushed. 'I deeply regret writing it.'

It was an admission of sorts, with which she was satisfied.

She gave him a wink. 'I'm beginning to think you're alright, Ludo.'

He laughed. 'I try to be. I try to be.' He checked his watch and summoned the waiter. 'One more for the road?'

'I can't, much as I'd like to,' she picked up her bag, 'but thank you for lunch. It's been great.'

'My pleasure, and I look forward to our next one.'

She smiled. 'Me too.'

Ludo decided against another drink and asked the waiter for the bill.

'Would you like a lift,' he said. 'I've got Ben outside.'

Ben was Bentley. Very Tourqoise Bentley.

'Thanks, but I'll get a cab, as I need to make a call.'

It wasn't true, but she wouldn't be seen dead in his car. The colour, the company... She had standards.

She got up, as did he, and they had a hug.

'I'll send you those CVs this afternoon,' he said.

She smiled. 'Great.'

As soon as she returned to her office she brought the Harvard Business School website up on her computer but not having attended, couldn't gain access, so she called TJ and sought his help.

He said he had some Harvard chums, and would get one of them to check for any record of Nate, and call her back. He did so in less than hour. Nate was not on the alumni and TJ's friend had checked five years either side of his supposed attendance.

When she put the phone down on TJ, she called her estate agent. And before the afternoon was out she had agreed, on the basis of a quick sale, to sell her house to Mr and Mrs Johnson for £2.1 million. This would leave her with just £300,000, but with her deadline for paying Peter drawing ever closer, and with no other buyers on the horizon, she knew she had to act. This way round she would also have money in the bank, and more than enough to put Wagsy back on Nate's case, which she fully intended to do.

Needs must. It's only money. I'll make it all back.

On her way home, she dropped in on Daphne, and told her she was selling up.

'How exciting, Dear,' she said, clasping her hands.

'I suppose it is in a way, but I wished I wasn't being forced to sell. It's always nice to have a choice in life.'

'But you have chosen. You've chosen self-reliance. What could be more satisfying?'

'That's one way of looking at it, I suppose, but I'm

worried about the effect moving is going to have on Jamie and Harry, Jamie especially.'

'With you as their mother, they will thrive wherever they live.'

'Bless you, Daphne.' She paused. 'I just hope I can find somewhere decent enough to rent.'

'Of course you will. And I must say I think renting is a very good idea, as it will give you freedom, and the opportunity to think about where you want to live.'

Tanya nodded. 'I also think it's the right course of action given the state of the economy.' She paused. 'By the way, that man Ludo Quagg has turned out to be a very useful contact, and he's not the scumbag I thought he was either.'

Daphne's eyes sparkled. 'Tanya, dear, that's wonderful news. I'm so pleased you told me. It proves you were supposed to meet him.'

'I think you may be right.'

'I know I am, Dear, although please don't think I'm being full of myself when I say that. I am simply speaking the word of the Good Lord. It's the Good Lord you know who arranges these things. He always makes sure we are in the right place at the right time, doing exactly what we need to do. It's all part of the process of becoming conscious. And the more conscious we become the more we become aligned with His love.'

Tanya smiled, but not in the mood for a discussion about God or consciousness, prepared to leave. 'I must go, Daphne, but can I get you a drink first?'

'Yes, please. There's a bottle of red wine in the kitchen.'

Tanya put her drink on the mobile table across her lap, and kissed her on the forehead. 'When I move, I'll still come and visit you. In fact, I don't know what I'd do without our chats.'

'Please don't worry about me, Tanya, dear. You have more than enough to deal with at the moment.'

'But I will, I promise, and once I'm settled, wherever that is, you're obviously more than welcome to visit me. I can easily pick you up and take you home.'

Daphne took her hand and squeezed it. 'That would be lovely, Dear. I shall look forward to that very much.'

Tanya gave her another kiss and left.

*

Tanya's phone rang and she saw it was Peter calling.

What the fuck does he want at this hour?

It was half past ten Saturday evening, and she was scanning the local papers for properties to rent. She answered.

'About my money,' he said, 'any chance of getting it a bit earlier?'

'Don't tell me you're broke.'

He laughed. 'Don't be stupid. There's an investment I want to make.' He didn't elaborate and she didn't care to ask.

'No.'

'Come on. You must be minted now, working for a hedge fund.'

'Fuck off, Pete. If you think hedge fund means easy money, you should try working for one. Come to think of it, you should try working, but of course you don't have to now, do you? Thanks to me and Joe you and Suzy have a great life.'

She heard ice cubes being swirled around a glass

and Peter utter a satisfied 'Ah' after gulping whatever he was drinking. 'As my dad says, if you marry into money you end up earning it.'

'He would say that wouldn't he, the lazy git. Well since you're on the phone, I might as well tell you. I'm moving, downsizing and renting, so that I can pay you.'

'Don't give me that.'

'It's true.'

He sounded like he was wheezing, something that happened when he got anxious, the residue of childhood asthma. 'You can't expect me to feel sorry for you.'

'I don't, but that's not even a possibility, because you're incapable of feeling sorry for anyone except yourself. You've proven that in spades.'

'I don't want to argue with you. Where are you moving to?'

She glanced at the crumpled gazette beside her. 'I'm not sure yet, but it won't be far.'

'Do the boys know?'

'Yes, I'm making it sound like an adventure for them.'

'Good, best way.' He paused. 'I suppose I'll just have to wait till the end of June for my money then, won't I?'

Sensing he was panicking about getting it on time, she didn't answer.

'You still there?' he said.

'Mm, but I'm going now.' She put the phone down.

He rang back.

She picked up, and could hear Suzy whispering in the background.

'A contract is a contract,' he said.

She laughed. 'Panicking, are we?'

'Don't worry, Pete,' Suzy said, loudly enough for her to hear. 'She's legally bound. She's got to pay you.'

At that Tanya hung up, and silenced both her landline and mobile phones. Then, donning a pair of leather gloves, she stomped into her garage, took one of Peter's forgotten golf clubs from its cobwebbed bag, and whacked the concrete floor with it.

'You fucking, cunting ponce,' she shouted.

She said the same thing over and over again, while beating the ground as if trying to pulverise it, tears of rage soaking her face.

I've a good mind to renege and let him sue me for the fucking money.

Exhausted from the strain, she flung the club down on the floor. 'Bastard.'

The next morning, and Peter's day with the boys, Tanya was coming down the stairs when he pressed the doorbell, and she saw him, through the glass door panels, make haste back to his car to wait for the boys.

You lazy, lying, spineless, friggin wimp. Without that fucking troll, Suzy, or Jack at your side, and a big drink, you're an out and out coward.

Once her boys had left she phoned some letting agents that had advertised properties which appeared suitable, obtained the addresses, and went and viewed their outsides. They were all shabby, and one looked positively frightful, a curtain knotted in the centre of a window that was so dirty it didn't need a curtain.

She also realized they were all too small to take all of her furniture. Much of what she owned would have to go in storage, unless she disposed of it altogether.

I'll live. It's only temporary.

She spent most of her afternoon crouching in her attic, in the miserable dull glow of a low-watt light bulb hanging from a bit of flex above the loft hatch. Clueless about support structures, she gingerly negotiated joists and insulation wadding, as she set about emptying it. She made countless trips to her garage, with boxes and bin bags of books, clothes, and yet more old toys and general tat. It was sweaty work for her light frame, especially after her golf practice, and by the time she was done her body ached, her eyes itched from dust, and her black cords were coated in what looked like yellow candy floss.

But at work the next morning, when Olli arrived moments after her, and asked how her weekend had been, she smiled broadly and said 'Wonderful'.

'How was yours?' She handed him a coat hanger.

'Not bad. I caught a movie, ate, slept, did some work, spoke to my folks.'

'Sounds pleasant enough.'

He shrugged. 'I guess. What did you do?'

'Usual stuff, took my boys bowling on Saturday, and yesterday I went to see a friend.'

He smiled. 'Hey, that's a nice suit, goes with your hair.'

Tanya shot a look at her dark green suit, which was smart but conventional. 'You mean I look like an upside down tree?' she joked.

He laughed. 'The colour suits you.'

'Thanks.'

He walked off in the direction of the kitchen.

'CNN, guys, Carladeli!' Tanya yelled to her colleagues, as the headlines flashed across her computer screen.

Thierry waved acknowledgment.

Bay Brothers International implicated in collapse of food corporation, Carladeli, while Higgins Bank executives are charged with fraud.

She read the revelations with mounting excitement. BBI was allegedly complicit in the fabrication of documents showing non-existent assets, which they had used to raise capital for Carladeli, thereby misleading investors. And some senior employees from BBI had personally benefited from the cover up.

She checked the price of BBI's most recent ten year bond – down eight points – bought five million bonds, and quick-paced to Olli's office, knocking and entering at the same time. He was on the phone but smiled and asked the person he was chatting with, to hold.

'Sorry to disturb,' she said, 'but did you see on CNN that two thieving gits from HBC have been done for fraud over Carladeli, and that BBI has been implicated?'

'Yes, I caught it. We're not long any of BBI's bonds, are we?'

'No, believe it or not we were short. I just banked four hundred grand. Someone up there,' she pointed to the ceiling, 'obviously likes us. I had a look at their recent ten year deal last week and figuring it was expensive, shorted a few. What a stroke of luck, eh? I could have run the short but I reckon it will bounce, in which case I might short some more.'

He made a circle with his thumb and forefinger. 'Excellent.'

Tanya went back to her desk feeling grateful, most respectful of her luck, and called the trading desk at KS to have a gossip with Sam, who used to work for BBI.

Freddie answered, sounding rushed off his feet. 'He's on the phone, Tanya, do you want to hold?'

'Yes.' While waiting she sat reading Bloomberg's report on the story, when Nate came on the line.

'Sorry about that, Pop,' he whispered.

She froze.

'Pop?' He sounded alarmed. 'Shit.'

She slammed the phone down, raced back to Olli's office, and burst in.

He looked up, startled, from his computer, and flicked his hair away from his eyes.

'Sorry for barging in again, but I think I just stumbled on something big.'

He grinned at her exuberance. 'Go on.'

'I was on hold for Sam at KS,' she said breathlessly, 'when Nate came on the line whispering to someone he thought was Pop, who I always assumed was his dad.'

'And?'

Taking a deep breath, she tapped her watch. 'It's eight thirty in the morning. His dad lives in the States.'

Olli looked perplexed. 'What's your point? His father could be finding it hard to sleep, or he could be in London.'

She shook her head vigorously. 'I know Nate, and I could tell from the inflection in his voice that he's up to no good, and...' She stopped mid sentence, suddenly hit by a road to Damascus moment, recalling the time Jess Larance had asked her what Nate's father was like. 'Look,' she continued, 'this might sound off the wall, but now I'm wondering if Pop is his dad. And even if he is, it doesn't mean he's not up to no good as well.'

Olli pinched his nose. 'What sort of no good are we talking about?'

She flicked her pen between her fingers. 'I don't know, but I'd love to put a private detective onto him and find out.'

Olli snorted, quacked and laughed all at the same time. 'Hell, we're traders, not sleuths.'

Me and my big mouth.

'Look, forget I said that. I got a bit carried away. I'll catch you later. You must have heaps to do.' She headed for the door.

'Do you think he's involved in the Carladeli scandal?'

Her heart skipped a beat as she turned around. 'Who knows? With Nate anything is possible. People lie and I know for an *absolute fact* that he does. For all we know he could be right in the centre of it.'

'Did you watch an episode of Columbo last night?'

She bit her lip. 'No,' she said curtly.

'Just jesting, Tanya.'

'The thing is, Olli, I know Nate, and I've got a sick hunch about him, and not just because we clashed.'

Olli stared at his rolodex and twisted the wheel. 'Why don't you sit down and tell me what you're not telling me, Tanya,' he said gently.

She knew by not looking at her while accusing her of hiding something, he was sparing her the embarrassment of eye contact, which she appreciated.

And as she wrestled with telling him her secret, he continued to play with his rolodex.

'I'd rather not,' she said. 'You said yourself that information is a big responsibility.'

He leaned back in his chair, took hold of the arms and looked at her. 'It is—in the wrong hands.'

He thinks I don't trust him.

'It's not…' She heaved a sigh. 'Do you really want to know?'

He nodded, and she pulled up a chair.

'Can this be off the record, Olli? Like I'm telling you as a friend?'

'Sure.'

She told him everything.

'…Why would Nate lie to Dale about his flat? And to Ludo about his education? And why are his bank accounts zipped, stitched and glued?'

Olli rubbed his face with both hands. 'Who else knows about this?'

'No one. I come from the East End. I don't blab.'

'You're one heck of a player, I'll give you that.'

'Do you wish I hadn't told you?'

'Not at all.'

'In that case would you lend me twenty five thousand pounds against my bonus, so that I can get Wagsy back on Nate's trail?'

He frowned, tilting his head toward her. 'Are you familiar with what happened to Roberto Calvi?'

In June, 1982, after Banco Ambrosiano, of which Mr Calvi had been chairman, went bankrupt, he was found hanging under Blackfriars Bridge, in London.

She nodded, and laughed.

He drank from his mug. 'I'm serious, Tanya. If Nate is involved in the Carladeli scandal, he's a heck of a lot more dangerous than you think.'

She pulled each sleeve of her jacket up slightly, showing her wrists. 'Don't worry about me, Olli. I can look after myself. I was born into danger. Literally.'

His eyes softened. 'Are you saying your folks were abusive?'

She folded her arms. 'No violins, but some parents should be shot.' Her lips pursed and puckered, eyes cast down, she absently gave a couple of small nods.

He was quiet for a few moments. 'You must have real good reasons for saying that.'

She smiled, pleased he hadn't judged her harshly. 'Thank you. I do.'

He returned to the topic of Nate. 'Run me through everything again, chronologically, from the day Nate arrived in London.'

She left nothing out, not even remarks she had deliberately made to wind Nate up. '...Now will you give me the loan?'

'What, and risk you ending up in a box?'

'Like I said, Olli, I can take care of myself. But I'll respect your decision, whatever it is.' She paused. 'Actually, now that I've told you, it's probably best if I just get a loan, and keep you out of it.'

He pulled a face, which made her nervous, and while he was thinking, his phone beeped. He answered on speaker. It was Isobel, his p.a., who told him that his visitor had arrived.

Fuck it.

'If you'll excuse me, Tanya, this should only take fifteen minutes. I'll come and get you when I'm done.'

She got up. 'I'll leave you in peace.'

He glanced at her hand. 'I did wonder about your ring.' He had once admired it, said it was 'stunning— like its owner'.

She shrugged. 'Needs must. I'll get it back.'

An hour later, and with no word from him, her heart was doing the dance of death. Had she blown it by telling him about her flirt with gangland? Perhaps she shouldn't have revealed what she knew. Had she crossed an invisible line by asking him for a loan?

What if he fires me?

Her anguish rose as another half an hour passed, and then finally he appeared at the double doors to the trading room and beckoned to her.

Her stomach churned as she followed him into his office and closed the door.

He scribbled on a post-it. 'This guy goes by the name of Lennie. He's waiting for your call. He's a private investigator.'

She did a double take, shocked he was involving himself. 'I can't let you do this, Olli. It's not fair. I'll be fine with Wagsy.'

'You don't know that.'

'But—'

He pushed the note in her hand.

She swallowed hard. 'What does Lennie charge?'

'Let me worry about that.'

She shook her head. 'No. That's even less fair.'

He looked at his watch. 'Ring Lennie. He's waiting by the phone. Use the office at the end of the corridor.'

She peeked at the post-it. 'How do you know him?'

'You don't need to know that,' he said firmly.

'Of course I don't. Sorry. I'll go and call him.' She made for the door.

'And Tanya.'

She turned around.

He drew his fingers across his mouth. 'This stays strictly between us.'

'You've got my absolute word.'

Tanya could tell immediately that Lennie, who had a slight Irish accent, was a lot more sophisticated than

Wagsy. 'I'm going to ask a lot of questions about our target, Tanya,' he said. 'Please answer as fully as you can. Any repetition on my part is only to make sure I understand.'

His interrogation lasted close to two hours, and by the end of it she felt sucked dry. And scared at the amount of information she'd divulged, much of which she didn't realize she possessed.

Lennie now knew everything she did about Nate, from what he looked like and where he lived, to his habits, routines, possessions, social network, and even potential enemies.

'Sum up his character in one sentence,' Lennie said.

'He's arrogant and flash, and loves what money can buy, but he can also be charming.'

'Thank you,' Lennie said. 'I have everything I need for now.'

The line went dead.

Parched and desperate for a cigarette, Tanya made herself a mug of milky sweet coffee and took it outside, where she smoked two cigarettes, one after the other.

I've crossed the Rubicon, haven't I? All I can do now is hope my instinct was right, that this isn't all going to come back to haunt me. No other choice now. I've dealt.

CHAPTER TWENTY TWO

Tanya stood in the doorway of Olli's office. 'Isobel said you wanted to see me.'

'Come on in, and take a seat. And close the door.'

She did.

He held up a stapled document. 'Nate's mobile calls for the last month.' He slapped it on his desk, in front of her.

'Jesus, that was quick,' she said, seizing it. 'How did Lennie manage that?' It was less than two days since she'd spoken with him.

'What do we care?' He gestured to the log. 'Take a look.'

She began scrutinizing it. 'Fuck!'

Olli put his forearms on his desk, and leaned forward. 'What is it?'

Two telephone numbers stood out for the frequency with which they appeared, and the time of day. One was a landline number which Tanya recognized as BBI's trading desk, the other a mobile which Lennie had scribbled in the margin as being registered to BBI.

'Nate's used his mobile to call someone at BBI on their mobile during office hours, when KS has a direct line to BBI's trading desk,' she said, her stomach tight with excitement. 'Why would he do that?'

'A lady friend?'

'Could be, but I can't think of any woman at BBI who would be Nate's type.'

He turned his phone around so Tanya could use it. 'Call the number. See if you recognize the voice.'

The Texan dialect was unmistakeable. She dropped the handset back in its cradle, and gasped. 'It's Taylor Friezegeld,' she said, her eyes fired with intrigue. 'He's American, fairly new to London, and a senior credit trader. Just like Nate. Sam Davenstaff hates him, that's why he left BBI to join KS.' She threw Olli a dramatic knowing look. 'These two have Carladeli written all over them.'

'Let's not jump to conclusions. Could they be a couple of fags, or just real good friends?'

'No way. Nate's as heterosexual as they come, and if Taylor was a friend he'd call him on a KS phone line. The only reason he wouldn't is because those lines are recorded.'

'Not necessarily,' Olli said.

'OK, I agree he could have made some of the calls when he was away from the desk, but not all of them. There are too many. Besides, he often used KS lines to make personal calls.'

He nodded. 'Nice work, Lennie,' he mused.

'So what do we do now, boss? Tap his phones, put a tracker on his car, burgle his house, have him kidnapped?' she joked.

He winked, picked up his mobile, and pressed a few buttons. 'We need Lennie's platinum service.'

'Hey, Lennie, good work on the log. What's it going to cost to get this guy's DNA?'

She sat chewing her lips as they talked.

'Are you trying to bankrupt me, or what?' He sniffed and pinched his nose.

A short while later he smiled. 'I like that figure a whole lot better. Keep me posted.' He rang off.

'You must let me give you something toward the

342

cost of all this. I can't imagine Lennie comes cheap.'

'It's cool. Don't worry about it.'

'But I do. When I get my bonus I'll give you some money.'

He smiled and rose from his chair. 'We can argue about that another time. I have a lunch appointment.'

She stood and picked up the phone log. 'Can I borrow this for a more thorough read?'

'Sure, but keep it safe, and don't take it out of the building.' He got his jacket, which was on a hanger suspended from the knob of a cupboard, and put it on.

'Thanks. I'll guard it with my life.'

In the glare of the sun, for it was a beautiful day, Tanya spotted a strand of Olli's red-gold hair on his jacket. 'You've got a long hair on your left sleeve, just at the top, near the shoulder.' She touched the same area on her jacket.

He looked, but couldn't see it, so she went to him and removed it. 'And there's another one,' she said, plucking it off his jacket collar.

'Why, thank you. I need a haircut. It's getting way too long.'

She smiled at him. 'It looks good long. It's funky.'

'Why, thank you.' He paused. 'You got great eyes, you know that?'

She averted her gaze. 'Thanks. They come in handy do eyes, very useful for seeing things,' she said, unnerved by the sudden intimacy.

He made a funny little quack sound, a half laugh.

She blushed. 'I'll see you later. Enjoy your lunch,' she said, and left.

Too excited to work, Tanya also went out, for a walk, and while glad of the sunshine and crisp April air,

343

she wouldn't have cared if it was chucking it down in sheets. Her inner smile was wide as a flip top bin, her strides confident, as she headed up St James Street, took a left into Regent Street, and veered into Carnaby Street. Where she settled, at a table outside a restaurant, and over a glass of wine and a few cigarettes collected her thoughts.

To have Olli at her side felt amazingly good, but she doubted he would have taken up the baton on her behalf if he didn't fancy her. Concerned not to lead him on, she resolved to pay him twenty five grand, as soon as she had sold her house. What percentage that might be of Lennie's charges she had no idea, but it was the figure she'd mentioned. TJ then came to mind as she was due to have lunch with him the following week. Given his help in establishing Nate had not attended Harvard, he would no doubt expect an exchange of conspiracy theories.

I'll have to act like I'm too busy with work to be bothered about Nate anymore.

She hated the idea of lying, to TJ of all people, but her pact with Olli to keep her mouth shut was sacrosanct, and cancelling lunch could arouse suspicion. Besides, lunch with TJ was always fun.

She eyed up a black guy walking past, and suddenly felt an urge for sex, and began fantasizing about him. And then TJ and Steve, even imagining sex with the three of them at once. As her daydream took hold, everything in her midst with a phallic-enough shape became a potential dildo – the sugar shaker, a bottle, the case in which she kept her sunglasses, her mobile phone – and she found herself with her hand under her coat caressing the triangle of her lap.

Moist, and feeling desperate for a shag, she brought Spencer's number up on her phone.

Don't. Anyone is better than him.

She went through her wallet, and took out a dog-eared shiny black business card, with red writing on it.

Remember
US
Unforgettable Services
For Beautiful Unforgettable Women
Carlos Julio Rodriguez
073373003

A dish of a guy, who she presumed to be Carlos, had slipped her the card more than a year earlier, when she was in Soho, on her way to the Groucho Club for dinner. She rang the number to see if it still worked. It did, and Carlos answered, whereupon she said she had misdialled and cut off.

It felt tough being single.

*

Much to Tanya's disappointment there was no further news from Lennie for the rest of the week. And contrary to her expectations and hopes BBI had not imploded, which left her feeling most uneasy. The bank had fired two nobody's and one man had resigned but that was all, and yet its stock price was well off its lows.

She listened for a second time to a news interview with BBI's Chairman. 'Crisis, what crisis?' he said, which on the one hand made her laugh for its absurdity, yet he categorically denied any wrongdoing by BBI.

If Nate isn't mixed up in Carladeli, what's Olli going to think of me?

A new explanation for his and Taylor's têtes-à-tête suddenly sprang to mind.

They could have been organising a party for a mutual friend. That could take a lot of phones calls.

Now she felt sick, more so because it was late Friday afternoon. It was as though she'd started the week in a Ferrari and ended up in a Pedalo.

Keep your nerve. As Jess said, appearances can be very deceptive. BBI's Chairman could be lying. People smile to camera and lie to camera in a crisis. It's not as if he swore on an affidavit before speaking. He may genuinely not know what's going on.

For distraction and a sense of control she made a list of things to do over the weekend.

Sort out shed. Order skip. View properties. Call removal firms for quotes. Make list of who to notify about move. Take boys ice skating, and cinema? Pop to see Daphne. Pay electric and gas bills. Pick up postal redirection form. Collect suits from dry cleaners. Buy Florence a birthday present. Get car cleaned. If Peter calls about his money, tell him to fuck off!

She went to the office kitchen to make a cup of coffee, and while there Olli came in.

'Just the person I want to see,' he said, flicking his hair from his eyes.

Her heart stopped.

'Do you know any good secretaries?' He took a side plate from a cupboard, a fork from a draw, and opened the fridge. 'Isobel has just resigned on me. She's going back to school to do a degree.'

She hid her disappointment behind a smile. 'Yes,

Helen Medley at KS. She's top notch, and I'm sure she would be very interested, because the poor woman works for Nate.'

'Excellent.' He slid two wedges of cheesecake onto his plate and shut the fridge door. 'Give her a call, and ask her to call Isobel.'

'OK.' She put the kettle on just to hang around, hoping he might mention Lennie.

'Mm, this is good,' he said, in a creamy coated voice. 'Hey, if you want some, help yourself. There's plenty left.'

'Thanks, but I'll pass.'

'Your loss,' he joked, and left.

Helen was ecstatic to hear about the vacancy.

'...and you won't meet a more decent man than Olli, at least not in finance. I've no idea about the pay. You'll have to ask Olli or Isobel about that.'

'Thanks, Tanya. I'll be forever in your debt if this comes off. I'll ring Isobel now.'

Tanya wished her luck and hung up, and as soon as she had she felt very down: Disconnected, lonely, and worried. The office was quiet as usual, her colleagues beavering away in near silence in the distance.

I hate this room.

As it wasn't late enough for her to go home, she set about reading a prospectus for a bond issued by a company that made eco friendly trucks. The purpose of this exercise was to satisfy herself with regards to the firm's pension liabilities, to make sure their pension pot was adequately funded. But, neither her head nor her heart was in the task, and after reading the same paragraph about ten times she gave up—and in to worst scenario imaginings. Nate would turn out to be clean, her relationship with Olli would be irreparably damaged, and she would lose her job. Meanwhile, Spencer and Verity would get married, as would Peter and Suzy, while she would be on her own. And although she knew it was stupid, Olli's 'Your loss' remark kept coming to mind, accompanied by a sense of foreboding.

*

'I read a really depressing article today about the dangers of heavy drinking,' Tanya said, 'and I thought to myself, that's it.' She paused. 'No more reading.'

Jake, a tanned, flaxen-haired Australian salsa-dance teacher, and the hotel bartender, burst out laughing, showing off a great set of teeth.

He can dock his cock up my frock any day.

'It's quite an old joke, actually,' she said. 'You must be quite young.' She peered over the bar and gave him the once over. 'I'd say you're about twenty four.'

'Eight,' Jake said, 'and only for two more months.'

That'll do nicely.

'I've got one,' he said. 'Two female terrorists are at a bus stop, and one points to her rucksack and says to her friend *Does my bomb look big in this?*'

Tanya giggled and sipped more of her bubbly. 'My turn. A man walks into a delicatessen, and says to the female assistant *Could I have a steak and kiddle-I pie please? Don't you mean a steak and kidney pie?*, she says. The man says *That's what I said, diddle-I?*'

Jake grinned. 'You are one crazy lady.' He looked at her near empty glass. 'Can I get you to a refill? Or whatever else you might want.'

'Hmmm, let me see, what do I fancy?' She ran her

tongue slowly around her slightly open mouth. 'Can you rustle up a long thick cocktail, something with a kick that's frothy, and feels good in the mouth?'

Laughing, he glanced at the optics behind him. 'What do you know? We're clean out of the cream I need, unless,' he slipped a thumb under his belt buckle, 'you'd like me to improvise.'

She looked at his groin, the contours of his manhood temptingly visible, and licked her lips. 'Let me think about it.' She eased herself off her stool. 'In the meantime, I'd like a bottle of this champagne,' she held up her glass, 'personally delivered to my room.'

'One glass or two?' Jake said.

'That depends.' She stared into his eyes.

He smiled. 'I'll make it two.'

Suddenly noticing a man in a dinner suit at the other end of the bar, Jake straightened his bow tie and excused himself. Tanya watched lustfully as showed off his mixology skills, blending sherry, rum, crème de cacao and angostura bitters. The result was a bronze coloured cocktail which he decorated with an orange slice. He then picked up a silver tray, put the glass in the centre of it, and spun once on his heels, without spilling a drop.

Cocky fucker.

He shot her a look, and wiped imaginary sweat from his brow.

But a nice cocky fucker.

She clapped silently, with her fingertips.

Upon his return, he performed another spin. 'Where were we, Miranda?'

'I can't remember,' she lied, testing his desire, and laughing inside about her new persona. Tonight she was

Miranda Sheringham, girlfriend of Guy, a property developer, who was out of the country on business.

He clicked his fingers. 'You were about to give me your room number.'

'So I was. Have a guess.'

He quipped sixty nine.

She shook her head and laughed.

'Shall I start low and go higher, or higher and go lower?' he said mischievously.

'Why don't you do both?'

'What, here? Far out.'

'I'm teasing you,' she said. 'It doesn't have a number. I'm in the Marigold Suite.'

'Crikey! I finish my shift in a quarter of an hour. Can you wait that long—for your champagne?'

She peeked at her cleavage. 'I'm sure I can find a few things with which to amuse myself.'

She gaily scrawled Miranda Sheringham across her bar chit and gave it to him.

Twenty minutes later, she was sitting on the side of her bed staring at his genitals.

Best sports kit I've ever seen.

She stroked his balls. 'What's your recovery time?'

'A sneeze.' He coaxed her mouth over his cock. 'You'll flag long before I do.'

Two hours later and Tanya realised he was right. When she went to use the loo she could barely walk for the pumping he'd given her.

Back in bed, she sat astride him. 'So you like your nipples pinched, too,' she said, squeezing them.

He grinned. 'Are you sure you're not a hooker?'

'I'm something ending with er but it's not hooker, and it pays better.'

'Am I supposed to guess?'

She shook her head. 'No. I don't want to talk about work.'

She gave him a lingering kiss, and then collapsed her side of the bed.

He turned onto his side and looked at her. 'I like you, Miranda.'

She smiled. 'Good, I like me too.'

Jake shook her gently. 'Miranda, I have to go,' he whispered. 'Can I have your number?'

She rubbed her eyes. 'What's the time?'

'Ten thirty and I'm teaching a class at eleven.'

'Fuck!' She jumped out of bed.

She had wanted to see her boys before they left for the day with Peter, but it was too late.

Fuck, fuck, fuck.

She threw on her blouse, minus her bra, and began buttoning up, guilt galloping through her.

'What's the rush?' Jake said. 'I thought you said Guy wasn't back until next week.'

Guy? Who the fuck is Guy?

She suddenly remembered, and smiled. 'I've a friend coming to lunch.'

He picked up a tablet of hotel stationery, and a pen. 'What's your number?'

'Write yours down instead.'

He looked disappointed.

'I would give it to you, but even when a girlfriend calls me Guy gets jealous.'

'You said last night you were going to break up with him.'

Blimey. What else did I say?

'I am,' she said. 'I'll give you an email address he doesn't know about.'

She took the pad from him, wrote it down, tore off the leaf and gave it to him.

He read it out. 'Liquid Lively Red at hotmail dot com. Very sexy.'

She held out her hands. 'It's the colour of this nail polish.'

He folded the bit of paper, kissed it and put it in his shirt pocket. 'I'll email you.'

She smiled. 'Attach a photo, of you in the nude, full frontal.'

He put a hand under each of her breasts. 'Will I get the same in return?'

'Maybe,' she said. 'It depends what I think of yours, whether it moves me, if you know what I mean.'

He laughed, and then kissed her. 'I'll email you later,' he said, and left.

She finished dressing and looked in the mirror. At a face streaked with mascara, at eyelashes unflatteringly stuck together, at bloodshot eyes, and wild hair that was matted in places.

Jesus, I might as well have a note stuck to my forehead saying fucked all night.

After settling her bill, in cash, she slunk out of the hotel, and stepped straight into a taxi, courtesy of an extremely efficient porter who plainly wanted to see the back of her, which both amused and embarrassed her.

No harm done. I'm only human. Everyone has needs. I can't be goody two shoes all the time.

But then her inner critic joined in.

You more or less bought sex. You might as well have bought Carlos for the night.

352

A mental debate ensued over whether she was a good or bad girl, and Daphne came to the rescue.

Daphne wouldn't even think in terms of good or bad, only glad or sad. I'm sure she'll laugh her socks off when I tell her what I've done, applaud me even, so how could I possibly be bad? As she said, we are always in the right place at the right time, doing exactly what we need to do. Hmmm. That means we always make the right decisions. And that there aren't any mistakes. Hmmm. I like that. We always make the right decisions. There aren't any mistakes. Cheers, Daphne.

CHAPTER TWENTY THREE

'Lennie just called,' Olli said. 'He wants to see us. Can you free yourself up this evening?'

Thank God.

'Absolutely,' she said, and got up from her desk.

He flashed a look at her outfit, a chic rose wool suit – lunch with TJ demanded feminine colours.

'We'll meet at my place. You can ride home with me.'

'Great.' She placed a hand on her stomach and took a deep breath.

'Nervous?'

She laughed. 'Excited more like.'

He smiled. 'Do you want to catch a bite at lunchtime?'

'I'd love to, but I've got lunch with TJ.'

'Some guys have all the luck. Give him my regards.'

'Thanks, I will.'

She felt sad as she watched his corpulent frame amble back to his office. It wasn't his fault he fancied her or her fault she didn't fancy him.

'Is it too late to change my mind?' She stood at his open office door an hour later. 'TJ just got a mandate for a new deal and had to cancel.'

He flicked his hair from his eyes, and pressed a button on his phone.

'Yes, Olli,' Isobel said.

'Call Morgan Fulbright and cancel my lunch, you know the routine, and see if you can get me a table for two at Green's for one o'clock. If not, try Langan's, Brown's, and the Wolsely, in that order.'

Tanya was shocked he was cancelling lunch for her, in front of her. To her that showed great confidence.

'OK,' Isobel said, and disconnected.

'Gosh, I feel bad now.'

'Don't. Morgan's a good buddy.'

Lunch was at Langan's Brasserie, a popular haunt of financiers, celebrities and Joe public alike.

Tanya snapped a thin breadstick in half. 'What's Lennie like?'

Ollie made a face. 'I'll tell you later.'

'Sorry.'

He smiled. 'Not a problem, Hon.'

Hon! HON!!!

During lunch she worked hard to ensure their conversation remained about business, but over coffee, as she was spooning froth from her cappuccino into her mouth, Olli grabbed his chance to get personal.

'You got a new man in your life?'

'No, and I don't want one at the moment. Thanks to Peter, I'm off men, except for my two little chaps at home. A relationship is not even on my radar. I've decided I need at least a year to recover.'

She felt bad being so defensive but didn't know how else to ward him off.

'That schmuk must have really hurt you.'

'It's not so much that he hurt me. I just want some time to myself.'

'Hey, I can understand that, but don't you get lonely? I sure know I do.'

Bless him. He's so affably transparent, she thought, compassion sweeping through her.

'Not really, because I've got my boys, but I imagine it must be ever so hard being single without a family.' She paused. 'Why don't you register with a high class agency?'

'Prescription dating is not my scene. Anyhow, I don't have time. That's my problem, lack of time. Too busy doing deals.'

'Is that why you and Loretta broke up?'

'Partly, but it's a long story. I won't bore you with it.'

'I'm sure it isn't boring,' she said, sensing he needed to talk.

He offered her a petit-four, which she declined, and ate two himself. 'Time was certainly a factor. Loretta had too much of it, whereas I had too little, and when I look back I can see she needed a lot more attention than I gave her. But I don't think however much I gave her it would have been enough. It's not that I didn't try. I covered nine cities in four days once so I could make it home for the weekend.' He paused. 'In the end she became convinced I didn't love her. It wasn't true, but hey, what control do we have over what another person chooses to think?'

'I know what you mean. A man convinced against his will is of the same opinion still. Dale Carnegie.'

He nodded and smiled. 'Smart guy.'

'What a shame, though,' she said. 'Any chance of a reconciliation?'

'Not now. Her mind's too affected.'

'What do you mean, if you don't mind my asking?'

'It's OK. Two months after we came to London, she cut her wrists,' he sniffed and pinched his nose, 'but luckily, she phoned me.'

So that's why he stepped in to help me. The idea of me ending up in a box reminded him of Loretta.

'Oh my God. How awful.'

'It was pretty unpleasant, I must admit—sure as hell scared the heck out of me when I got that call.'

'I bet it did.'

He blew out his cheeks. 'When something like that happens you do a lot of soul searching.'

'But it wasn't your fault.'

'Hey, who knows whose fault it was?' He sighed. 'I don't understand life sometimes, Tanya.'

'Me neither.' She paused. 'Did Loretta not like London?'

He laughed. 'She was the one who wanted to come here, but no, she didn't like it. I guess she thought it was going to be different, that I was going to metamorphose into a different personality.'

'I take it she went back to Chicago?'

He nodded.

'Did you think about going with her?'

He shook his head. 'Anyhow, she didn't want me to and if I'm real honest about it, I was relieved. There's only so much chasing and running a guy can do, and after what she did...' He shrugged. 'She could never be the mother of my children.' He ate the last of the chocolates.

'That's a sad story, Olli. I'm sorry to hear you had to go through all that.'

He smiled. 'Hey, no harm done, and I learned a few things. In future I'll steer clear of women with too much time on their hands. I think I need a career girl, someone who understands my work.'

Alarm bells started ringing. 'I'm not sure I agree.

Two workaholics would have no time for each other. I don't think you can generalize. There are plenty of intelligent women without careers, who lead full lives.'

'Let's head out. We can argue about that some other time.'

To her relief, when they got outside Olli received a phone call, and told her to go on ahead.

Tanya had been to lots of cocktail parties in fine London homes, and wasn't usually intimidated by wealth, but Olli's period house in Belgravia took her breath away.

The five-story white mansion, floodlit from the basement, with its balconies and shuttered windows, pillared porch and black railings, was sheer opulence.

His housekeeper, Annie, a well-spoken white lady of a motherly age and demeanour, greeted them at the door, and took their coats.

'May I use the bathroom, Olli,' Tanya said.

'Sure. Annie will show you where it is.'

Annie led her along the marble-floored hallway, past the majestic staircase with its fancy iron balusters, and an eclectic array of art.

Maybe Olli's got bad eyesight, she thought, noticing a plain painting of dense purple next to one of a bright tribal scene of people with their eyes rolled to the sky.

Levering the brass handle of an oak door, Annie pushed it open and on came the light. 'The reception room, where you will find Mr Vermallen, is back down the hall, on the right hand side.'

'Thank you,' Tanya said, and closed the door.

The next second she jumped and then laughed at her reaction, the cause of her alarm being a painting of woodland with ghostly shapes creeping between trees.

What on earth possessed him to put a picture like that in the friggin toilet? Maybe he gets visitors he wants to frighten the fuck out of.

She was in there only as long as necessary, and entered the reception room to find Olli, standing by a mantelpiece nearly as tall as him, throwing a cashew nut into the air, which he caught in his mouth.

'Well done,' she said.

He smiled. 'Is champagne OK, Tanya?'

'Yes, thank you.'

He took a black control, about the size of a cigarette packet, off the mantelpiece and pressed it. 'Take a seat.'

She sat on one of two sizzling orange sofas, and cast an admiring glance at curtains of the same colour, which billowed like parachutes, and a pair of figurines of demure oriental women either end of a black and gold consul table. Then she noticed a game of Solitaire on the low table in front of her, and felt sad.

Annie came into the room. 'Yes, Mr Vermallen?'

'Champagne is fine, Annie,' he said.

'Yes, Mr Vermallen,' she said again, and left.

'You have a very nice house,' Tanya said.

'Why, thank you. Come and see the kitchen. I just had it refurbished.' He paused. 'You may want to bring bring your bag, as we'll be holding the meeting in the conservatory.'

She picked it up and followed him to the far end of the room, through double doors into a dining room dominated by tasselled tapestry chairs, and out into a small corridor. Then into a kitchen resembling a 1950s American milk bar: Shiny chrome appliances, powder blue walls, a two-tiered crescent bar, and red stools.

Hmmm. Each to their own, I suppose.

It was not to her taste. 'Wow, how refreshing,' she said. 'It makes me want to order an ice-cream soda.'

He grinned. 'I'm sure Annie could fix you one.'

Annie, who was by the fridge filling a champagne bucket with ice, looked up and smiled.

Tanya laughed. 'Thanks, but I'll stick to alcohol.'

'Hey, Annie, I'll take over,' Olli said, walking toward her. 'You go home.'

'But what about dinner, Mr Vermallen?'

'I'm sure I can manage for one evening, Annie.'

She looked concerned. 'I could rustle up a jambalaya before I leave.'

'I'm sure there's food in the fridge, Annie.'

She nodded. 'There's cold chicken, smoked salmon, foie gras, and I had Paula bake an app —'

'Thank you, Annie. That will be all.'

'Yes, Mr Vermallen.' She whipped off her apron and put it in a cupboard, bid Olli and Tanya goodnight, and disappeared.

Olli opened the French doors to the conservatory and turned on the lights. 'Come on in and make yourself comfortable, while I fix the drinks.' He looked at his watch. 'Lennie will be here in ten minutes.'

Olli's sunroom was more to Tanya's taste: Stone floor, oak refectory table to seat twelve – she counted the chairs – and a selection of leafy plants. Of special appeal to her was a portrait of a Native American Chieftain, his war bonnet dripping feathers.

Mm, wouldn't say no to him.

Below the chief, on the floor, were three colourful drums with skin tops, and above those, on a shelf, some Native American dolls in traditional dress. One, of a young woman in a white fringed dress and matching moccasins, and vibrant blue and white headdress, stood out to Tanya as the prettiest.

Olli sat at the top of the table, Tanya to his left, and they made small talk about interior design, until a shrill bell signalled Lennie's arrival.

'Excuse me,' Olli said.

He went into the garden and unlocked a side gate, and Tanya got her first view of Lennie, a muscular man, with a crash helmet under his arm.

'Good to see you again, Ol,' she heard him say.

Olli slapped his back. 'And you. Come on in and meet Tanya.'

She stood, and they shook hands. 'It's good to meet you,' she said.

'Likewise,' Lennie said.

Olli offered him a drink.

'No thanks, Ol.' He unzipped his jacket. 'I'd just as soon get started.'

Olli smiled and sat down.

After removing a folder secured across his chest by an elasticised body strap, Lennie sat down, and took three large photographs out of the folder and laid them on the table.

Tanya gasped and pointed to a picture of a house. 'That house was advertised for sale in *Country Life*, and Nate earmarked the page.' She pointed to the second photo, of a man waiting at a cash machine. 'And that's Taylor Friezegeld.'

Look to the left of the picture, Lennie said.

She did and there was Nate's car, parked on double yellow lines, in a side street.

'That was taken in the Kings Road on Saturday night,' Lennie said, 'before they went to the house.'

The third photo was a direct shot of Nate sitting in his car.

'Take a look at this one,' Lennie said, pulling out a fourth print.

It was an aerial view of the house, which was totally secluded, set within what looked like miles of field.

'It's in Norfolk,' Lennie said. 'Good flat terrain, hard to spot and,' he pointed to a grey patch, 'it comes complete with an old World War II runway.'

'Oh my God,' Tanya said. 'Nate once told me about a restaurant in Norfolk, where he'd taken his cousin, a place called Elderton Lodge as I recall.'

'When was that?' Lennie asked.

She thought for a bit. 'Last September.'

Lennie made a note.

'Did you by any chance find anything out about a man called Pop?' she said.

Lennie smiled. 'I did indeed. Pop is not one person but two. It's what Friezegeld and Walthak call each other when they talk on the phone.'

She punched the air. 'Yes!'

Olli smiled at her. 'Well done.'

'Thanks,' she said, smiling broadly.

'If you ever fancy my line of work, Tanya, give me a call,' Lennie said.

She laughed. 'I'll keep it mind.'

'Who owns the house?' Olli asked.

'It's registered in the name of Strovitch Enterprises, and a man called Ivan Siperivsky.'

Olli looked at Tanya. She opened her hands and shrugged. The names didn't mean anything.

'Does anyone live there?' Olli asked.

Lennie nodded. 'We've not been able to get a shot

of her, but locals say it's a young half-caste woman who speaks little English. She's a looker by all accounts, but you know those farmers. Anything with two legs is better than a sheep.'

They all laughed.

'So how does this all tie in to the Carladeli fraud?' Tanya said to Lennie.

'I was just coming to that,' he said, 'and the short answer is that it doesn't. As far as I can make out from their coded conversations, Nate Walthak and Taylor Friezegeld are not embroiled in the Carladeli scandal.'

Her stomach sunk.

'But,' he added, 'they are involved in something. And it's far from kosher. They're trafficking goods of some kind.'

Olli let out a low whistle. 'Drugs?'

'Could be, Ol, then again it could be a lot of things. Alcohol, caviar, diamonds, arms, money, people, who knows. Bearing in mind the location of the house, it could even be insects or birds. All I know for sure is that it's not birdseed.'

Tanya sat dazed and speechless, and when she did speak all she said, in a shocked whisper, was 'Fuck'.

Olli looked at her. 'Hey, Tanya, we knew he wasn't playing by the rules, right?'

'Yes, but trafficking.... I mean, it's not as though he's that bright.'

'He's bright enough,' Lennie said. 'You don't need a PhD to traffic goods.'

She pulled at her lip. 'So what happens now?'

'You're going to call in the cops, right?' Olli said.

Lennie nodded. 'This is beyond my remit. If the police want to investigate, that's up to them.'

Tanya suddenly felt empty of bones.

If Nate's smuggling drugs or arms, and he finds out I got him nicked, I'll have a price on my head.

'Tanya and I are out of it, right?' Olli said, as if tuning in to her thoughts.

'For sure,' Lennie said, nodding. He put the photos back in his folder.

How sure can he be?

'Won't the police want to know how you came by the information?' she said.

Lennie cocked an eyebrow, his eyes alive with humour. 'If they did, I'd be out of business, and pushing up a few daisies, I think.'

She laughed. 'Sorry, that was a daft question. My head's a bit of a scramble.'

He smiled. 'That's understandable.' He picked up his folder, stood, and slipped it under his body strap.

'It's nice to have made your acquaintance, Tanya.'

'And yours.' She got up and shook his hand. 'Thanks for all your help.'

'My pleasure.' He zipped up his jacket, pulled a balaclava out of a side pocket, and picked up his crash helmet. 'I'll be in touch, Ol.'

Olli showed him out.

'Hey, I think we both need a stiff drink after that,' he said, upon his return.

'You can say that again. Make mine a treble.'

'How about a Gin Martini? That's what I'm having.'

'That sounds great.' She picked up her bag. 'Do you mind if I go into the garden and have a quick cigarette?'

'You can smoke in here.' From the table drawer he produced an ashtray. 'I might even join you.'

She smiled. 'I didn't know you smoked.'

He winked. 'There are a lot of things you don't know about me.'

She turned her chair around to chat with Olli while he mixed the drinks in the kitchen. 'So, Lennie will tell the police what he knows, and they'll take over, leaving him to fade into the night—just like us. Is that it?'

He finished filling a tumbler with ice from the ice dispenser before answering. 'I guess so, but hey, I'm as unfamiliar with this type of crime as you are.' He put the tumbler on the table, along with a dish of olives, some napkins, and cocktail sticks. 'Nearly there.' He went back to the kitchen, and returned with a bottle of martini, a bottle of gin, two glasses, and some plastic stirrers.

As he made their drinks, he reminded Tanya of a lovable chubby school boy carrying out an experiment.

He gave her her drink. 'I hope it's not too strong.'

'Thank you.' She downed a large mouthful. 'Wow!' Her eyes started watering.

He laughed and helped himself to one of her cigarettes.

After briefly competing to create smoke rings, which neither of them succeeded in doing, Tanya held up her glass. 'I forgot to say cheers or thank you, Olli. Forgive me. You took a huge risk on my account, and I owe you a serious debt of gratitude.'

'Hey,' he touched her glass with his, 'you owe me nothing, Tanya. I chose to get involved, and I'm sure glad I did.'

'So am I.' She paused. 'I just hope after all this that the police do investigate.'

'They will. Lennie's got a good track record.'

She knew better than to probe.

'In which case,' she said, 'Nate might end up in the slammer. Woohoo. Wouldn't that be a result? If he does, I might just pay him a visit, take him a nice bunch of weeds, and a bottle of piss water.'

Olli burst out laughing. 'You're terrific, Tanya, you know that?'

'I try my best.'

'But your attitude's cool, seriously,' he said. 'Even though we don't have anything to worry about, a lot of people would be worried right now.'

As if to prove her fearlessness, she took an even bigger swig of her drink. 'I'm not a fan of fear, me, although I'll tell you what would have worried me—if Lennie had drawn a blank. If that had happened, I would have been very worried about my future at Sky-Rise.'

Olli nodded. 'I can understand that.' He paused. 'Hey, do you want to catch a bite to eat? There's a great Italian a few blocks from here.'

'I'm sorry, Olli, but I must get home.'

'Sure,' he said, 'maybe another time, eh?'

'Definitely. Let's fix a date tomorrow.'

He smiled. 'That's a deal.'

He walked her to the hallway, helped her on with her coat, and saw her to the door.

She touched his shoulder. 'Thanks for everything, Olli. You're a great boss.'

He stared at her. 'Do you think you could you ever see me in any other light, Tanya?' he said gently.

She swallowed hard, and thought for a few seconds. 'I can see us becoming close friends, but —'

'Hey, that's a start, right?'

She felt for him, but knew she had to be straight.

'Olli, I think you are possibly the most decent, generous-hearted man I have ever met in my entire life, but the chemistry isn't there for me.'

He forced a smile. 'At least our feelings are out in the open. Got to be a good thing, right?'

She also forced a smile. 'I hope so. I'll see you tomorrow.'

Head up, back straight, big smile, Tanya said to herself, knocking on his office door the next afternoon. She hadn't seen him that morning, and didn't want to go home without having broken the ice.

'Come in,' he said.

She did but on seeing that his desk was covered in papers, held the door open. 'I was wondering about dinner. Can you make next Thursday?'

He rubbed his eyes. 'I'm not sure, check with Isobel. She has my diary.'

'OK. Sorry to have disturbed you.'

He smiled, but avoided eye contact. 'No problem.'

She closed the door quietly.

He's taken umbrage. It was stupid of me to be so blunt. Now I've hurt his feelings.

He kept his distance until the end of the week, when he stopped by her desk to thank her for introducing Helen, who had accepted his offer of employment.

She smiled. 'You're welcome. It's the least I could do after all you've done for me.'

He then praised her, for adding to her position in Allied Capital. 'Keep buying. It's a well-run bank, which is more than I can say about the company I'm dealing with at the moment.'

'That doesn't sound good.'

367

'It's not, but hey, life's full of problems, right? Anyhow, I'm confident of solving this one.'

He went on to say he was leading a shareholders revolt, to oust the CEO of a medical device company, who in his view had strangled distribution because he was a control freak. 'I had to do something.' He ran his fingers through his hair. 'After a three-year stock market rally the share price was down seventy percent. Now it's halved again. The guy should have stuck to medicine instead of share price destruction.'

In telling her this she felt he was trying to make up for being off with her, which relieved her.

'I hope you succeed in getting rid of the idiot.'

He sighed. 'Me too, I hate it when investments let me down.' He walked off. 'Have a good weekend,' he called out, raising a hand.

'And you. Try not to work too hard.'

He looked back at her. 'Work keeps me sane.'

Poor Olli. He badly needs a girlfriend.

CHAPTER TWENTY FOUR

Showered and ready for bed in her dressing gown, a cigarette on the go and a glass of wine at her side, Tanya was filing her nails, when the dramatic sounds heralding the news emanated from the TV.

'Police bust sex trafficking ring operating from Norfolk mansion. More than a dozen young women rescued. Eight men arrested.'

She sat bolt upright and watched transfixed as the crime scene filled the screen. As a male reporter stood windswept in front of a house – the very same house she had seen in *Country Life* and Lennie's photograph. Its vast frontage was teeming with ambulances, squad cars, sniffer dogs, and police armed with automatic weapons, and helicopters were flying overhead.

'It was shortly after seven p.m. this evening,' he said, 'when the Metropolitan and Norfolk police raided this mansion, tucked away in the Norfolk countryside, and made their shocking discovery.... ...all the young women are of Eastern European origin... ...various states of undress...clearly distressed...speak little English.... ...medical examiners are likely to refute at least some of those claims. Sixteen is the age of sexual consent here in the UK... ...viewers may find the next scenes disturbing.'

The scenes were of female police officers guiding victims, their faces blurred and each caped in a blanket, into ambulances, Alsatians pulling hard on their leads as they sniffed the ground, and police in white plastic overalls exiting the property carrying boxes.

The reporter continued, shouting to be heard above the din of helicopters. 'We gather none of the men involved are British, and while police have not yet disclosed the nationalities of those arrested that aircraft — he motioned to a plane in the distance — is a Lear jet with U.S. markings. That suggests at least one person is an American citizen. As you can see, forensic teams are busy at work, and we gather they have already removed a number of computers from the property, as well as a substantial quantity of cocaine, and a variety of X rated DVDs and literature. Allegedly, a host of equipment still remains in the house, equipment that would corroborate suspicions these young women were forcibly subjected to acts of a sexual nature. According to a local farm-hand who did not want to be identified, the property is rumoured to contain some kind of a dungeon, a room in which there are body harnesses, cages, and shackles. Whether that's the case remains...'

Trembling, Tanya picked up her mobile to phone Olli only to discover six missed calls from him. She had silenced the ringers on her mobile and landline so that she could read her boys a bedtime story in peace, and, not wanting to hear from Peter, hadn't restored sound.

She called him.

'Olli, the news—'

'I know. I've been trying to reach you. Hang on.'

She could tell he was listening to the same news channel as her, and they continued to listen, while remaining on the phone.

'...The trafficking of adolescent females for sexual purposes is a highly lucrative business, with tens of thousands of pounds paid for virgins. In 2007, a nationwide campaign was launched aimed at tracking down the criminal gangs behind the sex trade, leading to more than three hundred arrests. But this barely scratches the surface. The exploitation of vulnerable women and children, smuggled into the UK illegally is a growing problem. They are unwittingly lured with promises of jobs and money, and then forced into prostitution. If the girls found at this house tonight are under the age of sexual consent, and willing to testify against their abusers, the men involved could face charges of Paedophilia. Social workers say the average paedophile will abuse between fifty and one hundred children during his lifetime, but to catch such a person in action is rare. For police to have snared this gang of evidently wealthy predators is a major coup. Melvin Prince, Little Broadland, for News Today.'

Tanya and Olli both muted the sound of their TVs.

'Lennie rang about an hour ago to forewarn me. I was trying to reach you, to do the same. Are you OK?'

'I'm fine, obviously shocked, but OK,' she said, and quickly swigged some wine.

'You'll be more shocked when I tell you what else Lennie told me.' He paused. 'The jet belongs to Dale Stanzinger. He's involved in this up to his eyeballs.'

On hearing that Tanya's stomach caved as if she had been punched.

'No!' she gasped.

'I'm afraid so.'

'Have the police arrested him?'

'Hell, yes, and they've got Nate and Taylor Friezegeld and, Lennie says, some Ukrainian guys.'

'Thank God,' she whispered. 'Do you know if Nate or Dale were among those caught in the act?'

'Lennie didn't say.'

A few moments silence followed.

'KS' stock price will crash, big time,' Olli said.

She was looking at the TV where the story was being re-run. A few of the girls were much shorter than the female police officers tending them.

'Are you still there?' he said.

'Er, y-yes, sorry, sorry, I was just looking at the TV.' She shook her head, and inhaled deeply. 'You're right. Shareholders are in for a big fright on Monday. I can't imagine anyone will want to own KS stock once they hear the word Paedophilia. It's going to kill the KS name stone dead.'

'I don't know about that, but the firm is certainly in for a rough ride.'

He's going to try and buy it.

'Are you going to mount a bid to buy it?' she said.

'Possibly.'

Under any other circumstances Tanya would have been overjoyed at that prospect, but her heart felt black.

Olli carried on talking, said he had contacts, a few people he felt would want to join him in a bid for KS.

'That's great,' she said quietly, her voice flat. 'If you need any information, I'd be glad to help.'

'Thanks.' He paused. 'Are you OK?'

'Mm, I'm fine.'

'God, I'm a klutz. This has to be one hell of a shock for you.'

Not wanting to dampen his spirits or hurt his feelings again, she forced an upbeat tone of voice. 'It's OK. I'm alright. It is a shock but I'm getting over it as we speak, although I must admit I could do with some downtime to take it all in. Look, do you mind if I give you a call tomorrow?'

'Sure. You go and get some rest.'

Tanya switched off her phone, and within minutes she had locked up, turned off the lights, checked on her boys, creamed off her makeup, and cleaned her teeth, all in a state of suspended reality, oblivious to what she was actually doing. It was only when she was in the shower, clean forgetting she'd had one earlier, and the water began to run cold, that she reconnected with who she was, where she was, and what had happened. But, not yet ready to engage, she absently dried herself, put her dressing gown back on, sat at her dressing table, and began cleaning out its side drawers. An hour later and her waste bin was full of stuff she didn't like or use: Soaps, perfumes, bottles of nail varnish, an assortment of cosmetics, and various tubes and pots of hand and body creams.

That's a mess, too, she thought, looking at a basket in which she kept her hairbrushes. She put it on her lap, and took out each brush in turn and removed every dead hair, using a small pair of nail scissors and tweezers to get at stubborn ones. Thereafter, she decided to clean the bath, and before she knew it she had cleaned the whole bathroom, even washed the wall tiles.

She moved on to her bedroom, tidying the drawers in which she kept small items, until all her belts, gloves, scarves, bras, knickers, socks and stockings, were organised by colour, and arranged in neat rows.

Oh, I didn't wash my hair. I should have washed it when I was in the shower. I need a shower anyway.

She subjected her flesh to another scrub and washed her hair, and rough-dried it knelt on the bedroom carpet by the hearth, turning her gas fire on beforehand because she felt cold. She didn't bother using a mirror.

That done, she finally stopped chasing herself in circles, throwing her damp towel to one side, rather than rushing to hang it over the radiator in her bathroom.

Hugging her knees to her chest, she bowed her head and sat tight and compact listening to her breaths, as she recalled the smell of potato dust and rotting cabbages.

Decades on and yet, as she now realised, she was still being stalked, the emotions fresher than yesterday, the images like a grease smear over her eyes.

She remembered how the sunlight used to creep from the edges of the flattened cardboard boxes used to cover the windows, casting shadows on the walls and bare floorboards. And sitting on an old banana box, and feeling frightened because she had torn her dress on a nail. How leaden and rigid her body felt as his rough hand stroked her thigh, and how her nostrils filled with the smell of bryl cream.

Incest has been around as long as man. I'm not the only one. There are thousands, probably hundreds of thousands, millions even, in the same boat.

Jittery and shivering she crawled into bed, and lay in a foetal position trying to look on the bright side. She had been pivotal in putting an end to some suffering. If she achieved nothing else in her life, that made her existence worthwhile. Nonetheless, she knew she still had to deal with the harrowing memories engulfing her, that no one else but her could put the black cloaks and white faces back in their coffins.

If she slept she didn't remember, and shortly after six a.m. she was back in the shower. And once dressed, until it was time to wake her boys, she sat in the kitchen drinking coffee and smoking, and, drawing on Daphne's philosophy, scrawling an affirmation in her journal.

Healing love attends me now.

The statement seemed to come from nowhere but it felt right and she felt grateful for it. She wrote it over and over, until the pads of her fingers were numb from holding her biro, and her pen blobbed from overuse.

She hid her angst from her boys, and for their sake managed to keep her cool with Peter when he came to collect them.

'I just heard on the news the private jet at that house belonged to Dale Stanzinger,' he said, spilling over with glee. 'Just goes to show, don't it?' He shook his head. 'What a pervert. I could tell when I met the fat bastard he had a cruel streak.' He hadn't met Dale, but Tanya saw no point in correcting him. He was referring to the one and only time he had seen him, which was at a KS Christmas party five years earlier, and it had been at long range, because Tanya had pointed him out.

She pulled at her lip. 'Jamie needs to finish his maths homework. I've put it in his rucksack. Make sure he does it.' She turned around and looked up the stairs. 'Jamie, what are you doing up there?'

'I can't find my football shirt,' he bleated, from the top of the staircase.

'Have you looked in your chest of drawers?'

He raced back to his bedroom.

'I told you what those pen pushers were like, didn't I? One of those kids only looks about twelve.'

'Don't exaggerate.' She crossed her arms. 'Anyway, I'd rather not talk about it, especially in front of Harry.'

Peter was holding Harry's hand and glanced at him. 'He don't understand, he's too young.'

'Even if he doesn't understand the words, he will still absorb the emotions. He's a very sensitive child.'

375

Peter tutted and pulled a face. 'Come on little fella, let's get in the car.'

Tanya bent down and kissed him. 'Bye, my Darling, have a lovely day.'

'Bye, Mummy, love you.'

'I love you too, Sweetheart.'

She called up the stairs to Jamie. 'Jamie, for goodness sake, daddy's waiting.'

He eventually bounded down the stairs, gave Tanya a kiss and ran down the path, dragging his cotton sports bag on the ground.

On closing the street door Tanya suddenly felt alone. Realising she wanted to see people, but not to talk, she went for a drive. An hour later she was parked in Epping, in a lane with over arching trees illuminated with shards of sunlight. She opened the windows and took some long deep breaths. The crisp air was shot through with the scent of burning wood, moist earth, and dung.

A group of children on horseback, topped and tailed by grownups, trotted by. The fresh faced youngsters, in their breeches, smart jackets, and riding hats, made a fetching site to Tanya, and she found the lazy clip clopping of hooves very soothing.

One day I'm going to learn to ride a horse.

She took her journal and a pen from her bag, shoved her seat back to give her more room, opened the journal on her lap, and smoked a cigarette. Then she attempted to draft a letter to her dad.

I've changed my mind. I am going to report you to the police.

That's all she wrote before lapsing into a daydream wherein her short, stocky, no-neck dad, stood in the

376

dock, head down, while she gave evidence against him
—and every member of his family hissed at her.

If she did go to the police she felt certain she would
become the subject of a hate campaign. Both her parents
and their relatives would be on one side, her alone on
the other. She would be massively outnumbered. And
the emotional toll on her, and in turn her boys, would be
heavy. Not a good idea, especially given her financial
situation.

*Life is logical if not fair, and given what's happened
it's logical for me to feel anxious, and to want to get rid
of my shitty feelings. But that's not an overnight job.
Jamie and Harry need me. If I went to the police I'd be
risking their livelihoods. That would be like letting him
and Barbara win. I'll confront him one day, her too, but
now is not the right time.*

The bark from a black and white Border Collie
nosing in the adjacent hedge startled her back to reality,
with her nearly jumping out of her skin.

'Fergus! Come here.'

'That's not nice, Fergus. You frightened the lady.'

The voices came from a man with a walking stick,
and his female companion, both of whom were wearing
identical Barbour jackets.

'He didn't mean to frighten you,' the man said.

Tanya laughed. 'It was my fault. I was in a dream.'

They smiled and walked on.

Tanya drove home, with the windows open, silently
reciting *Healing love attends me now.*

Once there and settled with a cup of tea, she
switched on her mobile to find that just about everyone
she knew at KS had called, bar Bruce and Spencer.

She deleted all messages without listening to them,

and switched her phone to silent. Then she pondered how to pass the time until her boys came home.

I'll do some packing. Oh bugger, I forgot to call the letting agent. I need to call Olli as well.

The previous day she had viewed a house she rated borderline adequate, and had asked the letting agent to reserve it for her overnight. But the agent closed at one o'clock on a Sunday, and it was now one thirty.

I'll call first thing tomorrow. It's hardly Blenheim Palace. I'm sure it will still be available.

She rang Olli. 'Hi Olli, how are you?'

'Hey, Tanya, great to hear your voice. I'm good, thank you, sitting here crunching numbers as a matter of fact. How are you?'

'I'm fine, thanks.'

'Did you sleep OK?'

'Yes, thank you,' she lied.

'That's good to hear. Are you free this evening? I'm hosting an early dinner at my house for a few key people, to discuss KS. If you feel up to coming, I'd love you to be there.'

'Count me in.'

As ragged as she felt she wasn't going to give up the chance to meet some seriously high powered people. She also knew if they were to buy KS she would push for a job there, in which case they would be her bosses.

I'll call Alison and ask her to come home early. Florence can look after the boys in the meantime. And I'll try and take a nap.

'Terrific. It will be six for six thirty. Shall I send Geoffrey to pick you up?' This was Olli's chauffeur.

'Yes, please.'

She didn't nap because she feared a nightmare and

anyway, there was no time. Instead she trawled the internet, for news about KS and the markets in general.

And at five forty-five she was on her way to Olli's, all glammed up in a royal blue dress and jacket, and a fair amount of face paint to hide signs of fatigue. Not that she felt tired. Having something to focus on had revived her.

Olli's friends numbered four and turned out to be Arabs of high order: Dr Mustafa Al-Nazir and his colleague, Mr Farouk Abididi, from Egypt, and Prince Al-Wahabi and Sheik Al-Albarak from Saudi Arabia.

'Aleykum Salam,' she said, glad she knew the correct greeting.

Olli introduced her as the best trader in London, which she laughing dismissed as a wild exaggeration.

Pre-dinner drinks were served in the reception room, where Olli sat across from her on a sofa, between the bandannas and sheets, who occupied higher individual armchairs that were placed at a slight angle either end. She sat between the silk suits, uncomfortably aware she was the object of attention.

It came from her sofa partner, Mr Abididi, a weighty man with a moustache, as much hair on his hands as his head, and a gold Cartier wrist watch with diamonds around the face. He sat forward, cracking pistachio nuts with his teeth and spitting the shells into a bowl whilst, too frequently for Tanya's liking, flashing his black eyes at her. And as they proceeded to the dining room he put his arm around her, and muttered something in Arabic, which raised laughter.

She smiled nervously. 'What was that? My Arabic's a bit rusty.'

'Mr Abididi thinks you're very beautiful,' Olli said.

She faked a smile. 'Thank you.'

At the dining table, Mr Abididi seated himself beside her, and once conversation got under way, she suddenly felt his hand on her knee. After a few seconds stunned paralysis, she discreetly pushed it away.

'I'm sorry, Olli,' she said. 'I didn't catch that. What was your question?'

If I make a scene, Abididi will lose face, which could have dire consequences for Olli.

In the Arab world saving face was everything, and whoever caused it to be lost, suffered.

'What's your view of Tom Fischer?' Olli asked her. Tom was on KS' board and global head of equities.

'Tom's a good person but not best qualified for his current job. He worked in repo trading, money market sales, and structured products, which was a disaster, before he moved into equities, so he's had a bit of a chequered career.' She paused. Mr Abididi's hand was back on her leg. She pushed it away, and sipped some wine. 'What's helped Tom,' she continued, 'is his speaking ability and love of the stage. His presentations are full of amusing anecdotes and impersonations, which clients love. He's the joker on the board, and has got where he has because he makes people laugh.'

'How about Greg Bromfern?' Olli said. Greg was global head of structured products.

The hand was back. 'Greg's problem is that people don't trust him, and for good reason.' She paused and glanced at Abididi. 'He can be very underhanded, can Greg. His knowledge of structured products is excellent, but he has to be top dog, and he loves the sound of his own voice. Another annoying trait is that he likes to mystify people by using long complicated words. His first priority is himself,' she looked again at Mr Abididi, 'which is the wrong way round.'

Tanya was asked various questions, from her opinion of key individuals to which of KS' businesses she would eliminate and why. That meant she did a lot of the talking and had to concentrate, not easy knowing the tarantula could land on her at any moment, which it did, twice more before the main course arrived. She could tell by Mr Abididi's smiles that he was enjoying himself, treating his assaults much like a game of dare.

This fat git deserves a fucking slap. But Olli needs his backing, and I need to keep my job.

While the main meal was being served she used the distraction to move her chair a few inches away from him. It made no difference. Covert touches continued.

After coffee the white robes left, and with them seemed to go the last of Mr Abididi's inhibitions. Over brandy and cigars, in Tanya's case a cigarette, taken in the reception room, where she sat in an armchair, he invited her back to his hotel for a nightcap, while shamelessly ogling her.

She covered her mouth and yawned. 'Thank you, but I'm very tired, and I need to get up early.'

Mr Abididi laughed. 'You will sleep better afterwards,' he said, his eyebrows dancing.

Olli looked at Mr Abididi and said something in Arabic that drew sounds of sympathy and nods.

'It's OK, Tanya,' Olli said. 'I've explained to Mr Abididi that while I don't want to spoil your fun, I do need you present and alert in the office by five thirty in the morning.'

Tanya smiled at Mr Abididi. 'Perhaps we can have a drink another time.'

By the time Messrs Abididi and Wahabi left, Tanya had a blinding headache, and sat rubbing her temples

'Hey, I'm sorry about Abididi's behaviour, Tanya. I've never been with him around women.'

She gave a weary sigh. 'I wished I'd worn a friggin burkha. He put his hand on my knee about six times during dinner.'

Olli looked aghast. 'Mother-fucking asshole!' He helped himself to one of Tanya's cigarettes, which were on the coffee table. 'Persistent mother-fucking asshole. I'll deal with the son of a bitch, Tanya.'

He paced the floor as he smoked, and said angrily every now and again, as though he had Tourette's syndrome, 'mother-fucking asshole.'

Tanya laughed to herself. 'Olli, relax. It's not a big deal. I'm fine. It was just annoying.'

'It sure as heck is a big deal to me.'

She stood. 'Look, there is no upside whatsoever in you saying anything. In fact, if you do, it will make my sacrifice in keeping my mouth shut pointless. Let's just look on it as one of those unforeseen events that couldn't be helped.'

He pulled at the collar of his shirt. 'I'll never let anything like that happen again. I'll think of a silent code of alert you can use, and next time we see Abididi I'll make sure he doesn't get within ten feet of you.'

'OK, but no harm has been done. I've been closer to strangers on the tube, and it's not as if I let him get away with it. I did keep removing his hand.' She yawned. 'Look, I hope you don't mind but I need to get going. I'm dead on my feet.'

'You're welcome to stay over. I've got plenty of spare bedrooms.'

'I'm tempted,' she yawned again, 'but I've no change of clothes, and I'd like to get home to my boys.'

'Sure, not a problem,' he said, and immediately phoned and summoned Geoffrey to take her home.

He helped her on with her coat. 'Take tomorrow off.'

'I can't. The markets will be rocking over KS. I don't want to miss opportunities.'

'It's not going to be over in a day, Tanya.'

She smiled. 'I could do with the morning off, to catch up on some packing, but not the whole day. I'll come in at lunchtime.' She intended to sleep but didn't want to say that in case he thought her weak.

'Packing?'

'Yes. I'm moving house.'

He pinched his nose and sniffed. 'Why?'

She shrugged. 'There are too many memories where I am. I want a fresh start.'

'Is that the only reason?'

She broke eye contact. 'Yes.'

'Hey, if you need money — she began shaking her head — I'd like to help.'

'That's very kind of you, Olli, but I can manage.'

'OK, but the offer's there should you need it. And it's an offer without strings.'

She gave him a peck on the cheek. 'Thank you.'

He smiled, surprised. 'You're welcome,' he said, and opened the street door.

'I'll see you tomorrow,' she said.

He nodded, suddenly pensive. 'You know, you don't have to go it alone all the time, Tanya.'

She swallowed hard, his words touching her deeply, and resonating on many levels.

'It's the only way I know,' she said softly, and shrugged.

He looked at her with sadness.

'I'll see you tomorrow,' she said again, and retreated down the steps and into Geoffrey's car.

Olli's kindness so moved her that she sat weeping quietly all the way home.

His decency made up for so much indecency, his caring for so much neglect.

'Fi, take some deep breaths, OK?' Tanya said, 'and stick by Freddie. He'll look after you.'

Fi was very emotional, crying for the most part whilst telling Tanya what was happening, frequently digressing to thank her for warding her off Nate.

KS was crawling with police, and Nate's office had been stripped bare, as had his trading desk, all his files and computers removed, and no one was being allowed to access their computer, until they'd been interviewed. The press were apparently pitched ten-deep outside the building, while one journalist had wangled his way onto a window cleaner's platform to get pictures.

'...People are just walking around in a daze, or crying,' Fi said. 'Even Rich has been crying.' She shed a few more tears. 'Thinking about what I'm going to say to the police is making me feel really sick.'

'You don't have to think, just tell them the truth.'

Fi couldn't answer for crying.

'Fi, listen to me. Even if you had slept with Nate it would not make you guilty of anything. Do you understand? You haven't done anything wrong.'

'But what if I have to go to court and testify?'

'If you have to go to court, I will come with you.

And I'll buy you a large drink before and afterwards. Now go and find Freddie, OK? I'll phone you later, when I get to work.'

'OK,' she sniffed. 'Thanks, Tanya.'

When Tanya arrived at work, Thierry, China Paul, Janek and Alex made their way to her desk clapping, and Thierry jokingly asked for her autograph.

They had found out through market friends that she had slapped Nate.

'I am going to write to your Queen and recommend you for a knighthood,' Janek joked.

She burst out laughing. 'I think you mean the Prime Minister and for women it's a Damehood, but if that happened it would definitely mean knife crime was out of control.' He understood the quip and laughed.

Her new found friends asked lots of questions about Dale and Nate, which she answered with relish. Flash bulbs and a few microphones shoved under her nose and she would have thought she was on TV. Her fame was short lived, however, because Olli appeared.

'Hey guys, this is not a good time to abandon ship.'

They immediately returned to their desks.

He came to Tanya. 'How are you feeling?'

'Good, thanks, better for a decent night's sleep.'

He smiled. 'Abididi will be calling you to apologize.'

'But —'

'It's cool. He's still on board vis a vis KS.'

'I hope so, Olli, because if you've jeopardized your chances on my account, I am going to be very upset.'

He winked at her and changed the subject. 'Jacob Robensteyn. Do you know him?'

'Yes. He's one of KS' best clients, at least he was.'

'He's also one of their biggest shareholders. His support will be crucial to any bid we may make.'

'Do you want an introduction? I know Jacob well and we've always got along.'

'Thanks, but there's no need. I'm meeting him tomorrow.'

Stupid cow. As if Olli needs me to introduce him.

'If it's appropriate, give him my regards.'

He nodded and smiled. 'What's he like?'

'He's an honourable man, very decent, but quiet and circumspect, the sort who keeps his cards close to his chest. He's also teetotal, so don't offer him any alcohol. And extremely Jewish, wears a skullcap.'

He laughed. 'Sounds like I'm in for some fun.'

'He's actually very nice, just a bit shy, I think, and while he drives a hard bargain he's fair, not the type to double deal or lie.'

'That's good to hear. Thanks for the low-down,' he said, and walked away.

Tanya sat speechless for a few seconds as she digested what Susannah Cordarosa had just said. Susannah was a veteran of KS, based in New York.

'Nina Stanzinger, Nate's mother? You're not joking with me are you, Susannah?'

'Would I joke at a time like this, Babes?'

'But... How the fuck did that come about?'

'You know Dale and Harvey Walthak – Nate's father – were at grad school together, right?'

'Yes, I knew that much.'

'OK, well, they were good mates, but competitive, went head to head all the time. But Dale's a helluva smart guy whereas Harvey, from what I can make out, is a real dipstick, so he always came last. And that trend continued after they graduated, with Harvey, poor guy, left doing diddly-squat, while Dale gets a job at KS. If you ask me that must a had something to do his parents being loaded. Anyway, when Dale finds out his buddy's living in some mud-hut apartment in Brooklyn, he helps him out, and gets him into KS, which is when the shit-balls really started flying, because they both got the hots for Nina—'

'Ah, so Nate's mum also worked at KS?'

'You got it, Babes. Nina was a floor secretary, and to cut to the chase for once Harvey came first, beat Dale to her boudoir, and got her pregnant with Nate.' She paused. 'Now we both know how much Dale likes being outdone, right, so he gets him fired? But not Nina, who had to hang around to pay the bills. The rest is history. By the time Nate was six months old, she'd shacked up with Dale, but part of their deal was that Dale had to take care of Nate and Harvey, which he did, in return for Harvey keeping his mouth shut.'

'So what you're saying is that Nate doesn't know that Nina's his real mum?'

'Don't know, Babes, but unless he thinks you can buy a place in the Hamptons with food stamps, he has to know his dad's got a benefactor, because Harvey's like a number three in some research department for a two-bit broker.'

'Does Bruce know this?'

'No idea, Babes, probably not, he's not really part of the inner circle, if you know what I mean.'

'Jesus, I need a stiff drink,' Tanya said.

'Have one for me. It's only eight o'clock here. Listen, Babes, I gotta go. Catch you later.'

Tanya was still taking all this in, when TJ sent her an instant message: *Clara just called. She wants to interview you about KS. She'll pay. What do you think?*

Clara was a close friend of his, and editor of a national tabloid.

Forget it. I'm not making money out of those kids.

She replied: *Tell her thanks, but no. I'm too busy, and Olli would hate the publicity.*

Understand, TJ wrote back. *How's biz?*

Good. How's it with you?

We're making a merry mint! It's yuk scandal pays, but... Chat later, Gorgeous. X

Tanya looked for Olli, to tell him the latest about Nate, but he was out, so she carried on betting some of his money, trading bonds issued by banks impacted by the crisis, or rumoured to be impacted. The use of derivatives obscured the real picture in terms of which ones were most exposed to KS. The firm's stock price had now fallen sixty percent, while its bond issues were trading between thirty and forty cents on the dollar. Meanwhile, brokers and traders were taking personal bets on who from the market had partaken of Nate and Taylor's hospitality, and who was peddling drugs.

Tanya loved the buzz of trading in a crisis, of being in the thick of rumour and panic, and trying to guess it right, even though it made for some scary moments. So far she was up a few hundred thousand dollars, not that she felt proud as much as lucky, because this wasn't serious trading but punting.

That she was enjoying herself made her aware of how much she missed a real trading floor.

*

Never mind. It will be OK. I'll just have to explain to Peter what's happened, and offer him interest for late payment. I'll find a buyer eventually. It's not a big deal.

Her solicitor had just phoned to say Mr and Mrs Johnson were pulling out of buying her house, because Mr Johnson had lost his job.

She stared at the lights flashing on her dealer board. *Nobody's died. There are loads worse off than me. At least I've got a job, and a house to sell. OK, so it will take a bit a longer, so what. What can Peter do?*

What sprang to mind by way of an answer was force her to sell her house, at a price that left her with close to nothing.

He wouldn't do that, surely.

But she wasn't so sure, and in any event she knew she would now have to crawl to him for a favour.

Suddenly she felt sick, genuinely sick, and she made a dash for the loo, and locked herself in a cubicle.

She was still there forty minutes later, on her knees, head over the toilet, her throat stinging from having vomited what seemed like half her weight. When she had nothing left to expel, she dragged herself to her feet, lowered the toilet lid, and sat on it, rubbing her knees.

If only you weren't married.

She started crying. 'I was a stupid fucking idiot. He didn't take any risk whatsoever.'

No good crying. You just have to get on with it. Anyway, you've still got seven weeks.

She rinsed her mouth and sluiced her face, and looked in the mirror above the hand-basin. 'Smile. I *said* smile. Nobody's died. Get some perspective.'

She managed a grimace, and returned to her desk, where her dealer board was throbbing.

She picked up each light in turn, said 'I'll call you back', and cut off. But she didn't succeed in clearing the board.

Fucking opportunists.

Then an outside line began blinking, which she had to answer.

If this is a trader trying to catch me out, so he can flog me some crap, I'll pull his line.

It was Bruce Ghoff. 'Please don't hang up, Kiddo.' He sounded almost in tears.

'I wouldn't do that, Bruce,' she said quietly.

'I owe you an apology, Kiddo, and I've just found out something you deserve to know.' He paused. 'I can't tell you over the phone. Are you by any chance free for dinner tonight?'

'No, but I can do tomorrow, although it will need to be early and quick, otherwise next week.'

'Tomorrow's fine, Kiddo, thanks. I can meet whatever time suits you. Is Flowers OK?'

This was a spacious dimly-lit restaurant in Covent Garden, with tables far enough apart to ensure privacy.

'Flowers is fine. I'll see you there at six fifteen.'

CHAPTER TWENTY FIVE

Neck forward, shoulders slouched, Bruce sat as though his jacket was made of lead, one chunky forearm on the red tablecloth, alongside a crumpled *Wall Street Journal*.

'Don't get up.' Tanya put a hand on his shoulder.

He made a feeble attempt to lift his weighty frame and sunk back on his chair. 'It's good of you to come, Kiddo.'

'No problem,' she said, and sat down.

Jesus, he looks dreadful.

She hardly expected him to look great, but he'd piled on the pounds since she had last seen him, and his complexion was dry and flaky. And the delicate skin around his eyes looked red raw.

He folded his newspaper and put it in his briefcase, which was on the floor beside him. 'Journalists...' He shook his head. 'Goddamn parasites.'

'It's their job. Try not to take it to heart.'

The press were baying for his blood, for failing in his duty of care to shareholders, and Tanya had been reliably informed by moles within KS that the bulk of his wealth had also been invested in KS stock. So not only was his career hanging in the balance, but his fortune had gone down the plughole.

She picked up a menu. 'Shall we order first?'

He nodded and stopped a passing waiter.

Tanya ordered a glass of red wine, the lamb, and a glass of water, Bruce 'another' large gin and tonic, and a double steak burger with cheese, and extra fries.

'It's good to see you, Kiddo. You're looking well.'

If only I felt it.

'Thanks,' she glanced at her watch. 'I don't have much time, Bruce, so we need to get started.'

He nodded and loosened his tie. 'First off, Kiddo, I didn't want Nate in London any more than you did, and I made that clear to Dale, told him we could hire our own guys. But he said the office needed some fresh stateside blood, someone current on how things were done at HQ. So I came up with some alternatives, four guys in all, each of whom I know wanted to come here, but he ruled them all out for one reason or another. And when he dismissed my fourth choice, I realised there was no point in trying to find a substitute, because he'd made up his mind.' He paused. 'It was tough, because I kind of felt like I was being asked to groom my replacement.'

'You probably were.'

He shook his head. 'No, that wasn't his motive. I take it you know Nina Stanzinger is Nate's mother?'

Tanya nodded, this now having been reported in the newspapers.

'Well, according to Chuck Dickson – Chuck was a KS board member – Dale wanted to fire Nate, but Nina wouldn't hear of it.'

The waiter arrived with their drinks.

'How long have you known Nina was Nate's mum?' Tanya said.

'Days, Kiddo, days. I had no idea.'

'Do you know if Nate knows?' she said.

'My understanding is that he does, but I don't know when he found out.'

'Years ago, I reckon, because you don't become

that fucked up overnight. He obviously hates his mum for leaving him, his dad for selling his soul, and Dale for being the puppet master.'

'I guess so. I always liked Nina, thought she was a good woman, but she has a lot to answer for.'

'You're not blaming her, surely?' Tanya said stiffly.

'History plays a part in everybody's life, Kiddo.'

'Yes, but there are loads of people in this world who have been crapped on, but they don't go around crapping on others because of it,' she said angrily. 'Nate had a choice about how he reacted, and he chose destruction over redemption, pure and simple.' She drank some wine. 'If you want to start apportioning blame, try Dale. Not only did he screw Nate's life up by screwing his mum, but he's been screwing other women ever since. And not that it excuses Nate's actions, but that can't have been great for him to witness.' She paused. 'When it comes to blame, Bruce, Nina comes way down the list, way down.'

He rubbed his forehead. 'Gee, I didn't mean to be controversial, Kiddo, and you're right, Nina can't be held responsible for Nate's actions, any more than she can for mine.' He swallowed hard. 'And I've let a lot of people down, you especially.'

'I can't pretend otherwise, Bruce. I always tried to do the right thing by you and KS, but you crapped all over me once Nate arrived, discarded me like I was a friggin broken toy.'

There was an awkward silence.

'I'm sorry, Kiddo,' he said, his voice cracking with emotion. He slipped a finger under his glasses and wiped his eye. 'I got something from the doc to help me sleep. I shouldn't really drink. It gets me emotional.'

Her anger turned to pity.

He's weak and he's been a prat, but he's not evil.

'I've said my piece, Bruce, and that's the end of it.'

Noticing he was fiddling with his wedding ring, she suddenly remembered he and his wife, Marylyn, didn't have children.

Fuck. Maybe they can't have kids. Maybe he's impotent. Maybe that's why he's pissed off with Nina Stanzinger.

She put a hand on his forearm. 'It takes a lot to apologize, Bruce, especially in person. I respect you for that, really I do.'

'That's something, I guess.' He paused. 'If you'll excuse me, I need the rest room.'

He used the support of the table and his chair to aid him in standing, and it pained her to see how slowly he moved for a man of forty seven.

And as she watched him walk to the bathroom, a saying came to mind: *There's the person you think you are, the person other people think you are, and the person you really are.*

The poor guy's finding out who he really is.

Their food had arrived by the time he returned.

'I've more to tell you, Kiddo, but let's eat first.'

A few forkfuls and Tanya felt full, but Bruce swept his plate clean and quickly, and it struck her that food to him was what cigarettes were to her, that he wasn't greedy as much as needy.

He dabbed his mouth with his napkin and pushed his plate to one side. 'OK. Now until all this comes out, Kiddo, keep it under your hat. Do you get what I'm saying? I don't want you getting into trouble.'

She smiled. 'I'll keep my mouth shut.'

'You were smarter than the goddamn lot of us, Kiddo. Aubrey Young – Bruce's counterpart at BBI, and Taylor Friezegeld's boss – had an interesting visitor yesterday afternoon: Denton Fenshill. The jackass confessed to acting as front man on NCA. Taylor apparently gave him some baloney about having had a fall out with Nate.'

Her heart leapt. 'Well, well, well... Do you know how much the slimy git made on the trade?'

'Twenty cents,' he said. 'The jerk flouted FSA rules for a lousy thirty thousand bucks.' He paused. 'That's not all. Friezegeld bought the bonds from Hasseen.'

'No!' The vigour of her breath blew out the candle on their table.

Mr Hasseen had not done anything wrong by selling some of his company's bonds into the market. If an issuer has a view on the market, they can use their own securities to punt, but Denton Fenshill's involvement suggested fraud.

'You mean Hasseen gave Nate and Taylor a kick-back?' she said.

'It certainly looks that way. Aubrey said Hasseen was in London visiting BBI a month before the trade, and six weeks after it, when he also had dinner with Friezegeld. And according to Friezegeld's expense form one other person was at that dinner, and Nate submitted a taxi chit for that evening from the same part of town.'

'So they made a million dollars each,' she said.

He shook his head. 'Aubrey and I think they got something, but not an even split, and they wouldn't have got a million apiece anyhow. The market going south as it did was just a stroke of luck for Hasseen.'

'Scumbags. But never mind, maybe they'll share

the same cell, go back to the good old days.' It had transpired Nate and Taylor used to share an apartment in New York. 'And with any luck,' she added, 'it'll be for a long time. Fraud, drugs trafficking, sex with underage girls,' she held a finger up for each offence. 'They'll get at least ten years each.'

'Who knows, Kiddo? It all has to be proven, and that's going to be tough. Aubrey said there's zilch on tape of Taylor and Hasseen's conversation when they did the trade, and Hasseen is not returning Aubrey's calls. We're just hoping the authorities spot something when they examine Nate and Taylor's transactions. Chief Inspector Roberts, he's the guy in overall charge of the investigation, seems to know what he's doing, but we'll have to wait and see.'

'I'm sure they'll find something, because Nate's clumsy.' She glanced at her watch. 'Look, as riveting as all this is, Bruce, I need to make a move, unless you've more heart-stoppers in store.'

'That's it for the moment, Kiddo, but I'll keep you posted. You get going. I'll get the cheque.'

'Thanks.' She picked up her bag.

He looked at her with affection. 'How's the job? I meant to ask you that earlier.'

She shrugged. 'It's OK, although the pay could be better, but it's hard to negotiate a decent whack when you're unemployed. That's not a dig, it's all water under the bridge, but financially life could be better.'

'I'm sorry, Kiddo. I've been a goddamn fool.'

'Don't worry about it, Bruce. It's not all your fault. You were also manipulated. Anyway, what doesn't kill us makes us strong.' She paused. 'I just hope Nate and Dale, and Friezegeld all end up in Wandsworth.'

'Is that a tough gaol?'

'It's known as the hate factory,' she said with undisguised joy. 'If those three fucking Amigos end up in there, they won't know what's hit them.' She threw back the last of her wine and stood. 'They asked for it.'

Bruce laughed, and then stood and gave her a hug.

'I know it's a bit late in the day to say this, Kiddo, but if there's anything I can ever do for you, let me know.'

'Thanks, but for now just concentrate on yourself, and,' she pointed to his briefcase, 'stop buying friggin newspapers. You know they're only going to write garbage about you.'

He smiled. 'Thanks again for coming, Kiddo. At a time like this, it's hard to find a friend.'

'You need to toughen up, Bruce, learn to stick two fingers up to the world and say fuck you all.'

'He smiled and nodded. 'Take it easy, OK?'

'I will, and make sure you do the same.'

*

Tanya sat in Olli's office scratching her wrist. 'I'll get to the point as I know you're busy.' She took a deep breath. 'I answered truthfully the other night, but now I am in a fix. I owe Peter five hundred thousand pounds in final settlement of our divorce, which I've got to pay by the end of the June. And my house sale just fell through, which means I haven't got it, I mean none of it. I've got more than enough equity in my house to cover it, and I'm obviously doing all I can to find a buyer, and I know I will, but I doubt I'll get a deal done and dusted in six weeks.'

She had been refused an increase in her mortgage, at least for the full amount, because it would have reduced the equity in her house to, in her lender's opinion, a 'dangerously low' fifteen percent at best.

Olli opened his desk drawer, took out his cheque book, and began writing a cheque.

'I'll pay it all back, with interest, as soon as I've sold my house.'

'Is that enough, or do you need some float?'

'Well another ten thousand would be a great help.' She paused. 'I could ask Peter to wait.'

'I know you could, but I also know how that would make you feel.'

He held out the cheque.

She looked into his eyes as she took it. 'Thank you, Olli, very, very much,' she said, spacing her words to convey the depth of her gratitude.

'You're welcome,' he said casually.

'You make it sound like you just lent me a fiver.'

'Hey, I said I would be glad to help, and I am.'

'Yes, but how can you be this trusting?'

'Give me one reason why I shouldn't trust you.'

She smiled. 'We need to put something in writing, in case I fall under a bus or have a heart attack.'

'I'll leave you to draft something.'

His reaction almost made her thankful for her predicament. When she got up that morning she felt like the world's biggest loser, whereas now, thanks to Olli, she felt special. His faith in her felt like validation, proof she was a good person.

'You're an amazing man, Olli. Thank you.'

*

Tanya put the lever arch file, in which she kept her bank statements, back on the shelf in her study, and then struck through and scrawled *paid* on the last of her bills, and filed those away.

Now let's go and see what my little chaps are up to.

She found them in the kitchen, sitting at the breakfast bar drawing, a wad of white paper and a box of crayons between them, while Alison sat a few stalls up, sewing a name label into the collar of Jamie's new school jumper.

'Why aren't you little chaps in the garden?'

Jamie gave Alison a black look.

Alison looked at Tanya. 'I've said they can go back out to play when they've digested their lunch.'

'Alison's right, you'll be sick otherwise.' She went and stood between them and put an arm around each.

'We're drawing scary monsters,' Harry said.

Peering at their efforts, she recoiled in mock horror and gave a little scream.

Harry laughed, but not Jamie.

She looked at Alison and smiled. 'I'm going to pop and see Daphne for an hour.'

'OK, have a nice time.'

'While I'm out, why don't you guys draw me a picture of a car? They can't be the same style or colour, because I want two very different cars to put on the wall in my bathroom.'

'That's boring,' Jamie said, but he took a clean sheet of paper and set to work. Harry did the same.

She kissed them both, said bye to Alison, and left.

On her way out she treated herself to a sniff of a honeysuckle shrub in her front garden, albeit a brief one due to the sudden appearance of a huge bumble bee.

And as she strolled to Daphne's, all she thought about was what colour to paint her toenails.

'Oh,' she said, taken aback when a tall man with a moustache opened Daphne's street door. Then she realised from photos she had seen it was Daphne's son.

She proffered a hand. 'Gosh, forgive my rudeness. You must be Humphrey. I'm Tanya, a friend of your mother's. It's lovely to meet you at long last.'

He smiled briefly, and shook her hand. 'Please, do come in.'

Hmmm, the reserved type. William must be the loud one in the relationship.

'I don't want to impose,' she said, following him into the lounge, 'I can come back later, if I've caught you all at a bad time.'

When Tanya entered the lounge her heart plunged for there was no sign of Daphne, and she noticed two copies of the *Telegraph*, both folded and unread, on the mobile table that would ordinarily be across her lap. And then she remembered Humphrey wasn't due to visit until June, whereas it was late May.

'Where's Daphne?'

Humphrey clasped his hands and looked at her, his eyes sad, his expression sympathetic.

'No. Please don't—'

'I'm afraid so. She died on Thursday.'

She kept shaking her head and saying 'No'.

'Please, take a seat.'

She sat down. 'Did she suffer?'

'No. She died very peacefully, in her armchair. She had just had a cup of tea and a biscuit. Her care worker actually thought she was resting, because mother always enjoyed a snooze before lunch.'

'Thank God,' she whispered. 'Thank God.'

'Can I get you a cup of tea?'

She nodded, too choked and devastated to speak, and he left the room.

Her hands crossed around her waist, tears soaking her face, she stared at Daphne's dusky pink armchair. That she would never see her delicate features and sparkling eyes again seemed inconceivable.

'I loved you, Daphne,' she whimpered, 'I really loved you.'

Humphrey gave Tanya her tea, and sat down.

'Mother often mentioned you. She enjoyed your visits immensely.'

'Thank you for telling me.' Tanya pulled a tissue out of the pocket of her jeans and blew her nose. 'Your mother enriched my life no end, Humphrey, and I loved her, I really did.'

'I can see that.'

'Do you know yet when the funeral will be?'

He nodded and explained the arrangements. There was to be a service at St. Mary's Church, where she had once prayed for her mum, at two p.m. the following Thursday, and Daphne was going to be cremated.

'May I come?'

'Of course. Mother would love you to be there.'

'Thank you.' She pointed at a lilac shawl draped over the back of Daphne's armchair. 'Humphrey, would you mind if I had that?'

'Not at all.' He got it, and gave it to her.

'Thank you.' She held it to her face and let out a loud sob. It smelt of roses. Daphne's favourite fragrance was a Tea-rose eau de toilette. 'I'm sorry. I should be the one consoling you.'

'Please, there is no need to apologize. I'm touched by your feelings for my mother, and I know she thought an enormous amount of you.'

'She was my best friend, Humphrey,' she said, her chest juddering with emotion, 'my very best friend.'

Tanya stayed another few minutes, and on her way out plucked a Tea-rose from Daphne's front garden. She walked home holding it to her nose, Daphne's shawl clasped to her chest.

On hearing what had happened Alison took the boys out, and Tanya took to her bed. Lying fully clothed she hugged the shawl and wailed, every so often screaming 'NOOOOO!' as grief and fury overwhelmed her, as her powerlessness to bring Daphne back hit her.

I'll never be able to look at her lovely face, kiss her soft cheek, or hear her sweet voice, ever again.

In her mind's eye, she saw Daphne sitting in her armchair, her table across her lap, her shawl around her shoulders, sipping tea from a pretty cup and saucer.

'Oh, Daphne,' she sobbed, 'my precious Daphne. I loved you. I love you! I will always love you. I want you back, Daphne. I want you here. I want to see your face, and hear your voice, and cuddle you. Please come back, please, please, come back, pleeeeease, Daphne, pleeeease.' Her cries were like those of a tiny, lost child, which is how she felt.

That she had been so upset about losing her house made her feel ashamed. That could be replaced, but Daphne was gone forever, her warm fluid blood dried out for good.

CHAPTER TWENTY SIX

The squeaky rip of binding tape being yanked from its reel, as Tanya sealed another batch of compressed cardboard boxes together, ready for recycling, gave her a feeling of satisfaction. It signalled another job out of the way, and fulfilled her need to notch up successes, however small, as she adjusted to the disappointment of where she had ended up.

She had sold her house to a Brett Hogarth, a cash buyer, for two million pounds. With no other buyer in sight, and prices coming off by the day, she felt she had no choice but to bite the bullet. To have hung on could have left her with less than zero, whereas she had just shy of two hundred thousand pounds in the bank. It seemed a fair price under the circumstances. She was currently off work moving in.

Keeping busy and narrowing her focus was for her the best antidote. The house had seemed big enough, but that was minus furniture and people. *It's my own fault,* she thought, feeling more in control by blaming herself.

She was working out in which cupboards to put the crockery she'd just unpacked, when Alison called to her from the living room. 'Olli's on the business roundup.'

Three strides and Tanya was in the room, watching, on a TV that now looked stupidly big, taking up half the wall, a scowling Olli. Flanked by lawyers, who Tanya recognized, he was emerging apace from an office in Mayfair, his hair trailing in the breeze, his pale, freckly face on full show. Jacket cast back, hands in his trouser pockets, his red braces were the only sign of cheer.

Tanya bit her lip as she listened. Recovery Partners, the Arab/American consortium, for which Olli was front man, had pulled out of bidding for KS. And Olli had issued a statement, citing two reasons for RP's abrupt withdrawal. Competition had driven the price too high, and they had lost the backing of Jacob Robensteyn.

She felt very disappointed because returning to KS had crossed her mind more than once, even though she knew it was foolish to be having such thoughts.

Alison began winding the vacuum cleaner flex around its brackets. 'Is that bad news for you, Tanya?'

'No, but I would have liked Olli to have succeeded, as he worked really hard on the deal.' She paused. 'I think I should go and see him. He looks like he could do with seeing a friendly face.' She also wanted to get out of her rabbit hutch of a home for a few hours.

Alison smiled. 'I'm sure he'd appreciate that.'

Annie showed Tanya into a study-cum-lounge, a room where Olli obviously hung out as it was littered with paperwork and newspapers. And Olli, minus his shoes, reclined in a comfortably-worn tawny leather armchair, one of a pair either side of a small table.

His long face gave way to a smile when he saw her, and he quickly drained his glass, put it on the table, next to a bottle of scotch, and got up. 'It's good to see you. I was glad to get your call.'

She had phoned him to check it was OK to visit.

She smiled. 'And you.'

'Make yourself at home.' He gestured to the other armchair, beside which, on a drinks trolley, was a bottle of champagne in an ice bucket.

How generous and thoughtful of him.

404

'Thanks.' She sat down, and put her sun glasses, which were hooked in the cleavage of her silk shirt, in her bag, and popped it on the floor by her chair.

He poured her a glass of champagne, and gave it to her.

'Thank you.'

He then poured himself a refill, a good inch of scotch, threw in a few ice cubes, and settled in his armchair. 'Here's to a bummer of a day,' he said, and took a large swig.

She sighed sympathetically. 'But you know better than me, Olli, no trade is better than a bad trade.'

He turned his glass in his hand. 'Yes, but I'm not sure it would have been such a bad trade.'

'In that case, why not make a fresh offer?'

'Because we'd need Jacob Robensteyn onside, and that's not going to happen because the mother-fucker hates RP. It was clear from the outset he wanted CRW (Cabowitz, Rosen and Weinstein, a private equity firm) to win, and with his votes and influence, he's going to make that a reality. But hey, what can you do? CRW boast an all-Jewish line up.'

Tanya tutted yet doubted Jacob Robensteyn would be influenced by history.

'How did he get along with Abididi?' she said, suspecting it wasn't well.

'That was a bit of a problem,' he said.

'Look, if you want me to talk to Jacob, act as a sort of emissary for Recovery Partners, I'm happy to give it a go. As I said, he and I have always got along.'

'Thanks, but I think we've wasted enough man-hours on this one.'

Nonetheless, they went on to discuss the deal for

about an hour, during which time Olli admitted RP should have increased their offer. He said he had wanted to but Abididi hadn't, and that Abididi had played politics to get the Saudi's to back him over Olli.

'So Abididi ganged up on you? What a creep. I bet he pissed Jacob Robensteyn right off, didn't he?'

Olli looked mildly amused. 'They didn't exactly get along.'

'That guy should come with a health warning.'

'Don't worry. He's not going to get anywhere near you again.'

'I wasn't talking in the context of me. I can take care of myself. I just think it's a shame he messed up what could have been a great deal.'

'It happens.'

'Yes, but it's not pleasant to get shafted by one of your own.'

'I'll live.'

'I hope so. I don't want another funeral just yet.'

'How was that?' he said, referring to Daphne's. 'I meant to ask you, but—'

'It's OK. You had far more important things to think about. It was a lovely service, but...' She shrugged. 'Tears can be so annoying.'

'Hey, if you care, you cry.'

She nodded, suddenly sad, and recalled what she had done a few days earlier, on the day she had moved. Once the removal van had left, and so had Alison and Florence, she'd walked to Daphne's house, and up to her street door. And drawn a cross on it with her finger, and whispered. 'Goodbye, Daphne. It was a privilege to know you, and you will always be in my heart. I hope the Good Lord's looking after you.'

You came here to cheer him up, remember?

She smiled. 'Let's talk about something a little merrier, shall we?'

'Be my guest.'

'Do you want to see my impersonation of the Egyptian saboteur?'

He smiled, and she began mimicking Abididi's gestures and accent. Her finale was to spread her legs – she was wearing jeans – and push out her stomach, and re-enact the time he invited her back to his hotel.

It earned her a belly laugh. 'You're terrific, Tanya, you know that.'

I wish I felt it.

She laughed, and absently twisted her hair into a top knot, and let it fall about her shoulders.

He stared at her, his eyes soft verging on dreamy.

Bless him.

'Your turn,' she said. 'Have a go at taking off Jacob Robensteyn.'

He snorted. 'Acting is not my strong suit. Anyhow, I need to go and get my cigars.'

'Ooh, does that mean I'm allowed to smoke in this room?' she said, longing for a cigarette.

'Sure. You can do anything you want.' He sat forward, pushed a pile of papers by his feet out of the way, in Tanya's direction, and reached for his shoes.

'In that case, may I have an ashtray?'

He glanced at the table. 'Shit, that's Annie. I don't know why she hides the damn things. I'll fetch one from the kitchen on my way back.'

In his absence Tanya looked idly around and, glancing at the papers on the floor, noticed among them a familiar cream and green letter-head.

When Olli came back, she pointed to it. 'I thought Stamford & Stamford solicitors only serviced the hoi polloi,' she joked. 'I would have thought corporate finance was way above their provincial heads.'

He put an ashtray on the table between them and sat down. 'Have you read it?'

'God, no. What sort of person do you think I am? I wouldn't read someone else's mail.'

He grinned, and began clipping his cigar.

She lit a cigarette, and seeing that he didn't have a lighter, passed him hers, which he took with a wink at her, and gave back to her with a 'Thanks, Hon.'

Ten minutes, and I'm off.

He sat back in his armchair, and savoured his cigar.

Tanya loved its chocolaty smell, which brought back memories of being in pubs after hours as a child.

'It is,' he said, about a minute later.

Given the time lapse and that she was feeling a bit tipsy, it took a few seconds for her to twig that he was talking about Stamford & Stamford, and meant that corporate finance work was above their heads. 'Oh,' she said, 'so you use them in a personal capacity, too?'

He focused on the trail of his cigar smoke. 'I bought your house.'

You did what?!

'W-what?' She emitted a nervous laugh. 'What did you say?' She hoped she'd misheard but a powerful shot of adrenaline surged through her, which was not a good sign.

He smiled at her. 'I had my property company buy your house. Brett Hogarth manages that side of my business.'

Oh. My. God.

'I fully intended to tell you, as soon as I got a free moment,' he added, 'but things have been a little hectic.'

She was now on her third deep breath. 'Gosh, I don't know what to say. I'm grateful, of course I am, and thank you. If it wasn't for Brett, I mean for you, I'd still be running to stand still. But, I must admit, I am shocked.'

He smiled. 'You can move back there, if you want. Brett wants to use it as a corporate let but I can take care of that with one phone call, and I'm sure we can work out something favourable as far as rental rates go.'

A childhood image of the rent collector, who used to peep through the letter box for signs of life, sprang to her mind. When Barbara saw him turn into their street she would drag Tanya into the walk-in pantry, clamp a hand over her mouth and warn her to keep quiet. She couldn't forget the shame of having to hide, or the fear she witnessed in her mum's eyes.

He's trying to control me, lock, stock, and barrel.

'I'm deeply touched by the offer, Olli, but it will yield far more as a corporate let.'

'Hey, forget about the money. If that's what's worrying—'

She gave a dismissive wave of her hand. 'It's not just about money. I wanted a fresh start. The house has too many memories. In fact,' she picked up her bag, 'I purposely brought my cheque book so I could repay you. To me, that's a milestone, my way of letting go of those memories.' This was a lie, she had intended to pay him via a bank transfer, but panic had taken over.

Olli's smile collapsed. 'There's no rush, Tanya.'

'I know, but I'm here now, and I've got my cheque

book.' She wrote the amount in capitals, and scrawled her signature large, feeling both angry and disappointed. With Daphne gone, she had hoped Olli would become more of a friend, but now she had to keep her distance.

She gave him the cheque. 'Thank you very much indeed. I've made it out for five hundred and fifty thousand, to cover interest, and a contribution toward the cost of Lennie's services, but by all means, tell me if I owe you more.'

You can buy my house, but you're not buying me.

He sighed and put the cheque on the table. 'That's too much.'

'I'm sure it isn't. Anyway, I think you've earned any surplus.'

He gave a wry smile. 'What is it with you and men, Tanya?'

Cheeky bastard. Mind your own business.

But she knew she had to be careful how she answered, because he was still her boss.

'It's a long story, but in a nutshell, and in general, I'd rather not rely on them.'

'We're not all bad. For every Nate Walthak and Dale Stanzinger out there, there are ten thousand good ones.'

'I didn't mean you. You've been kinder to me than anyone, and I couldn't be more grateful. As I said, I was talking in general.'

He shot her a quizzical look. 'What's the deal with your father?'

She absently crossed her legs. 'Why do you ask?'

He shrugged. 'If a woman has issues with men she usually has issues with her father, and you did once say yours ought to be shot.'

She had forgotten saying that, and felt pissed off he was trying to make her wrong because she didn't fancy him. But, in the interests of her career, she felt she had no other choice but to make light of it.

'What are you, a closet psychoanalyst?' she joked.

'Hell, no. What I know, I know from Loretta. She saw a therapist for a while.'

Of course, Olli's got his own baggage. This is not about me, but him.

She helped herself to a refill of champagne. 'My dad was alright. We just didn't get along, that's all.'

He sniffed and pinched his nose. 'Is he dead?'

She shook her head. 'Not as far as I know.'

'When was the last time you saw him?'

Time out.

'With respect, Olli, do you mind if we talk about something else?'

'Sure. Did you hear on the news that Walthak's likely to get bail?'

She gave him a hard stare, sensing he was deliberately trying to needle her by mentioning the one man he knew she abhorred. 'No, but Nate is someone who should definitely be shot.'

He did a double take.

She heaved a sigh. 'I'm sorry. It's been a bit of a crap day for me as well. Not on the same scale as you, of course, but moving house isn't a lot of fun.'

He smiled forgiveness. 'It never is when you're on your own.'

'But I love being on my own. I'm just fed up with unpacking, that's all. I'm the sort of person who likes to learn from what I'm doing, and there's a limit as to what anyone can learn from shoving cups in cupboards.'

'You and I are so alike.'

She nodded and smiled. 'Well, we are both traders.'

'We'd make a terrific team, you know that?'

'We are a team,' she said, aware it was a disingenuous response.

'You know what I'm talking about, Tanya.'

She pushed her hair behind her ears and looked him in the eyes. 'I can't force feelings, Olli. I just can't.'

'I know I could make you happy.'

She cast her eyes down.

Not true. He knows he could make himself happy.

'I realize I'm not what you want—right now, but I know I'm what you need,' he added.

He spoke gently, a self-serving tactic in her view.

'How can you possibly know what I need? I'm not a friggin dog.'

He gazed at her.

'I'm not looking for a man, Olli. My independence has been hard-earned, and I've come to like it. In fact, standing on my own two feet is the best feeling in—'

'I'm in love with you.'

She shakily picked up her drink, and took a gulp.

'Olli, you're not being fair,' she said, her heart racing. 'You can't just spring stuff like that on me.'

He snorted. 'Are you saying you didn't know, because if you are I don't believe you?'

Her veil of self-deception dissolved instantly, for she had always known. How could she not? He had always been upfront about his feelings.

'And if you're really smart, Tanya, you'd marry me.'

She sat speechless, the hairs on the back of her neck standing on end.

412

'I know I'm a jerk sometimes, but hey, I'm a rich jerk. You'll never have to look at a price tag again in your life. And I would look after your children as though they were my own.'

His face was fixed into a happy clown expression.

She swallowed hard. 'I'm sorry, Olli, but I'm not in love with you.'

'I understand that, but feelings can grow. They're like flowers, Tanya. You feed them, they respond.'

I'm not a fucking flower.

She shook her head. 'It doesn't work like that with me.'

'It can, if you give it a chance.'

In need of some space she got up and walked around the perimeter of the carpet, the sound of her shoes on the oak floor better than awkward silence.

Olli stubbed out his cigar, stirred in his chair and took hold of the arms. 'Think about what I'm saying, Tanya. Think about how it would change your life. Think about how it would change your children's lives.'

She stood by the mantelpiece looking at a display cabinet inlaid with mother of pearl, or was it ivory? She couldn't tell but what did it matter. *Yes Mrs Vermallen, no Mrs Vermallen, three bags full Mrs Vermallen,* she thought, imagining servants and personal shoppers fawning over her. Houses would become fashion accessories, and her time would be spent tinkling with the trinkets inside. She glanced at a bust sculpture. *I'd move that for a start.* And considered the position of a Chinese screen, deciding it needed to go in a different room altogether.

She felt grudging admiration for the hand Olli had played, seeing it as akin to an absurd hike in the price of something, such as a bond or a house, for no obvious reason. After the initial shock, in creeps the gnawing thought that perhaps there is merit to the re-pricing.

But Tanya wasn't about to sacrifice the chance of true love. She wanted the electric effect, not a safe, sensible, strategic tie up.

Olli came to where she stood.

She shook her head, slowly. 'I'm sorry, Olli. I think you're decent, kind, a great boss, and clever, generous, and all that, but...' She let out a long sad sigh.

'Can't you see what a great start that is?' he said, a sprig of optimism in his voice.

She massaged her temples. 'Lay off, Olli, please. This is too much for me. I can't handle it. Look, I need to go, OK?' She went and got her bag, and slung it over her shoulder.

He came gingerly toward her, rubbing his chest as though he had indigestion. 'Hey, you're not going to resign on me, are you?'

'How can I? I've got kids to support.'

She saw hurt in his eyes.

'I'm sorry for how that sounded. I'm tired.'

'I'll call Geoffrey to take you home.'

'Thanks, but I'd prefer to walk for a bit. It's still early.'

He nodded. 'OK. I'll see you to the door.'

In the entrance hall, while Tanya waited for Olli to fetch her raincoat, an oil painting caught her eye, of an elephant and a scorpion.

'Do you like it?' he asked.

She nodded. 'I do actually, I love bright colours.'

'It's a particular favourite of mine, too.

He seemed overly pleased to her, as though her

approval was a sign of compatibility, and eagerly helped her on with her coat.

Keen to leave, she left it unbuttoned and tied the belt loose around her waist. 'Right, I shall see you on Monday.'

He opened the door, but not fully. 'My proposal still stands, Tanya, and I think you ought to give it very careful consideration.'

'Olli, don't do this to me,' she said with quiet frustration. 'It's not fair. I've told you how I feel. I don't want to offend you.'

'Hey, do I look offended?'

Although he managed a smile, he did, and she admired his bravery.

'I have thought about it and my answer is—'

'Maybe,' he cut in, 'let's keep it at maybe. I'm not asking you to give me an answer now. A decision of that magnitude needs a heck of a lot of thought.' He paused. 'You know, you may not have realized it, but you didn't say no earlier.'

She felt like screaming.

Talk about clutching at straws.

'You know how I feel. Let's leave it that,' she said, reluctant to leave on a sour note.

He smiled. 'Now you're thinking. That's all I'm asking you to do. Enjoy the rest of your week off.'

Enjoyable was the last word Tanya would have used to describe the following days. As far as thinking about Olli's proposal went, she didn't, for there was nothing to think about. The way she saw it, he had transferred his need onto her, and made his problem her problem. And she had to give it back.

How to do that without causing offence, however, reduced her to a bundle of nerves come Sunday night, with the shadows cast on her bedroom ceiling by a tree across the road scaring her, its sudden tussles with the wind making her jump.

Hurting Olli was the last thing she wanted to do, but she wasn't going to trade her happiness for his, however much money was on offer.

How, though, would he react once she cancelled all hope in his mind?

Not knowing made for a restless night's sleep.

He was, after all, a very rich and powerful guy, used to calling the shots.

She realised that yet again her job was at risk. But her soul was not for sale, to Olli or anyone else.

CHAPTER TWENTY SEVEN

'May I come in?' Tanya said, standing in the doorway of Olli's office, smart in a new single breasted lavender-blue suit, a treat to herself to celebrate solvency.

He stopped writing and looked up. 'Sure. It's good to see you. How are you?'

She walked confidently to his desk, smiling. 'Very well, thank you, couldn't be better, in fact.'

'Great. You look terrific.'

'I feel it.' She did, on account of something that had happened ninety or so minutes earlier.

He glanced at his computer. 'I see you're buying up a storm in Allied Capital.'

She rubbed her hands together. 'Yes. While I was away the price fell five points, which is even more than I'd hoped. The street seems to be suitably humbled, scared to ratchet up the price in case I become a seller again, which is exactly what we want.'

He grinned. 'There's nothing like deprivation to breed gratitude.'

'My sentiments entirely.'

He glimpsed at the chair the other side of his desk, but she remained standing. 'Thanks, but I've too many trades pending.'

He nodded. 'So, what's on your mind?'

'Well, I, er, I... erm...' Her lips started to quiver, her euphoria having suddenly disappeared. She rolled her eyes, and fanned her face with her hand. 'Um, what I,' she swallowed, and took a few deep breaths. 'Give me a second.'

'Sure, take your time,' Olli said, staring at her through highly amused eyes.

It's meant to be. You'll feel fine once you've said it.

She folded her arms to steady herself, and knew by how hot she felt that her face was bright red.

Wimp out now and he'll think you're pretty fucking sick, after waltzing in here with a smile on your face.

'I just wanted to say er... that um... we should try it out.' She gave a wave of her hand. 'Don't get the wrong idea. I'm not accepting your proposal or anything like that. I just think that unless we... you know.' She shrugged and opened her hands. 'I mean, we'll never know for sure it couldn't have worked, unless we do it.'

So much for getting it up and out.

Now she felt worse.

For what seemed like ages but was probably only a minute Olli fixated on his pen, holding it horizontally with both hands and twiddling it back and forth, and sliding it in and out between his thumb and forefinger.

And while she was waiting, it dawned on her what had happened.

How could I have been so stupid? If this turns out to be my nemesis, it will serve me right.

'Are you suggesting we make love?'

The intimate term made her feel sick. At the very best it would now be a detached fuck. But, like one of those toy dogs often seen on the back shelf of cars, she nodded with docility. 'And I wondered if you were free tonight,' she said, anxious to get it over with.

He snorted. 'Sure am now.'

'Your house? Eight o'clock?' she said.

'Sounds like a good plan to me.'

She rung her hands. 'Good, well that's settled then.'

He leaned back in his chair. 'Would you like to get a bite to eat first?'

She smiled. 'No thanks, I've got a lunch, and I'm on a diet. I tend not to have dinner anyway.' She broke eye contact, having just told three lies, the one about dieting the silliest, for she was very trim.

He laughed. 'OK. I'll grab something before you arrive.'

She peeked over her shoulder at the door. 'Right, well I guess I'd better go and check what's happening to the price of Allied Capital.'

'I guess you better had,' he said, grinning broadly.

She walked shakily back to her desk, sat down and stared vacantly at all the flashing lights.

I've just single-handedly shot myself in both fucking feet. How could I have been as dumb as to think Daphne could engineer a traffic jam? As if a dead person can fiddle with traffic cones, for Christ's sake.

Her dramatic change of heart had come about while she had waited for Ted, who had called to say that due to a traffic jam caused by road works he would be late. Minutes after his call while sat by her bedroom window staring up at a gloriously clear summer sky, stroking Daphne's shawl, she was struck, as if by a thunderbolt, with an urge to do something in Daphne's honour. And in that moment, the dots connected. Daphne had engineered the jam that had delayed Ted, and was willing her from beyond the grave to adopt a try-before-you-buy approach with Olli.

Now, however, she could see that her need to feel close to Daphne, as well as keep her job, had fed her imaginings, that feeling weak and vulnerable yet unable to face her fears, she had made sense out of nonsense.

As this sunk in, she also realised the colour of her new suit was similar to that of Daphne's shawl.

She recalled the first time she'd had consensual sex, and how she had got blind drunk beforehand, and knew she may well have to do the same tonight, if she was to make good on her promise. Her word being her bond, she wasn't going to renege.

A few drinks and you'll be fine. Just shut your eyes.

Jake sprang to mind, perhaps because she was wearing the same sheer nude lingerie as on the night she bedded him, and he had commented on its smoothness.

I'll email him tomorrow, confess my fib about my name, and ask him out on a date.

Whether she would was another matter, but she needed to think beyond the upcoming hours.

'How did the move go?'

Startled, she looked up to see Helen.

'Sorry, Tanya, I didn't mean to interrupt your train of thought.'

Tanya smiled. 'It's OK. The move went well, thanks. How are you getting on?'

'Great, but Lordy Lordy – this was one of Helen's favourite expressions – the man needs to learn how to relax. I've worked for obsessive types before but he takes the biscuit. He sends me emails at like three o'clock in the morning.'

Tanya laughed. 'That's Olli. He likes to keep his brain engaged.'

'Instead of his didgeridoo,' Helen said, referring to Nate.

Tanya's stomach turned over. Linking the uniquely Australian word to both Nate and Olli messed with her feelings and fantasies about Jake.

Not Helen's fault. Words mean different things to different people.

'Are you still involved in amateur dramatics?' she said, keen to change the subject.

'Yes, and we're putting on a production of The Sound of Music, and moi is playing the lead.' She fluttered her eyelashes, and laughed.

'Congratulations. When's the show?'

'It opens on the sixteenth of September, and thank the Lordy, as I've caboodles of rehearsing to do.'

This was nearly two months hence.

'Put me down for a ticket for the opening night.'

Helen's beautiful freckled face melted into an engaging smile. 'You can sit with my family, and you must join us for dinner afterwards. They'd all love to meet you.'

'Who's going from your family?'

Helen counted on her fingers as she spoke. 'There'll be my mum and dad, nana and granddad, two sisters and their hubby's, and my brother and his new girlfriend.'

In another life time, perhaps.

'How nice they will all be there supporting you.'

'They always come to my opening nights, even if I'm playing the part of a tree.' She looked at her watch. 'Lordy, Lordy, I'd better shuffle on. I don't want to upset the big boss.'

Tanya got through the day by focusing on work, Allied Capital in particular, and by the close of business she reckoned dealers had short-sold thirty million bonds to her, which she was certain they would struggle to lay their hands on. That meant they would be forced to buy bonds back from her, at a higher price.

The street is well and truly fucked.

421

Immediately realizing that within a few hours that would be her fate, she suddenly felt in need of a drink.

Half an hour later, she was sitting outside a wine bar, a glass of Sancerre in one hand, a cigarette in the other, reminding herself of three things. She had to feed her kids. Olli wouldn't be able to say she didn't it give a try. Daphne would be proud of her if she was alive.

Feeling as though she had bats never mind butterflies in her stomach, at five minutes to eight o'clock, she pressed Olli's doorbell.

Annie had obviously gone home for Olli answered, still in his work suit, holding his blackberry to his ear.

He smiled, silently ushered her in, took her hand and led her into the reception room, while uttering a series of 'Uh-huhs,' down the phone.

After motioning to the sofa table, which was graced with an open magnum of Cristal champagne, a fresh glass and Olli's near empty one, he went and stood by the window, looking outwards as he talked.

Tanya almost fell on the bottle in her haste to pour herself a drink and having done so, knocked back a big mouthful, before topping Olli's up and taking it to him. He winked appreciation but was too engrossed in conversation to look at her for more than a second, which came as a relief.

He appeared to be discussing the takeover of a mining company and was laying down the law as to how matters ought to proceed. But he remained polite, firm and challenging yet respectful, and while Tanya wasn't in awe of the power his nasal voice wielded, she was impressed with his manners.

If Bruce was in Olli's shoes, he'd be swearing and yelling by now.

Olli finished his phone call and strode toward her. 'I do apologize, Tanya, that was ungracious of me, but I had to take that call.'

'Don't worry. I know what it's like, remember. It sounds like an interesting deal. I hope you pull it off.'

'Why, thank you.' He gazed at her, and she sensed he was comparing her with Loretta, who apparently had no clue about business. 'May I sit next to you?'

She smiled nervously, and nodded.

He sat at a slight angle, and looked at her. 'How are you feeling?'

She bit her lip. 'If I'm honest, nervous.'

He patted her thigh. 'Hey, if you'd prefer just to talk, that's cool.'

'I'll be fine after a few drinks,' she said, and gulped the last of hers.

He immediately refilled her glass.

'Thanks.' She promptly downed another mouthful.

'When was the last time you made love?'

As if I'm going to tell him.

'With respect, Olli, your feelings are stronger than mine. I'm looking on this as sex, and while we're on the subject, there are a few things you should know. I always close my eyes, and I won't let a man bring me to climax. Please don't take it personally. It's just the way I am.'

He laughed. 'That's a challenge if ever I heard one.'

Me and my big mouth.

'It wasn't intended to be, seriously, so please don't look on it that way or you'll put us both under pressure. I only told you so that you don't get disappointed.'

'You could never disappoint me, Hon. Never.'

Maybe I should ask for a raise.

'Let's deal with the housekeeping,' she said. 'Personally I hate using what you call rubbers and I know I'm clean, but if you've any doubts about yourself, make sure you use one.'

And trust me, it will only be one.

After her night with Jake, she had got herself checked at a sexual health clinic.

'Worry not, Hon. I'm clean as they come.' He slipped his hand under her hair and began caressing the back of her neck.

She shuddered. 'My neck's sensitive,' she said, which conveniently was true.

'I doubt there's any part of you that isn't. You're a sensitive creature.'

She feigned a smile and concentrated on drinking.

His caress became a massage. 'Does that feel good?'

You can't deny him a response. You're either in or out.

'Mm, it feels nice.'

'You're real tight.'

'Another drink will solve that.' She leaned forward to get a top up but Olli took over, which she was glad about as it meant he stopped touching her.

He tapped his glass against hers and said 'Cheers' but she sensed he wanted to say something more meaningful, which made her feel guilty.

He edged closer to her. 'Would you like to listen to some music, Hon?'

'Actually, I'd prefer it if we just went to bed.'

Now feeling sufficiently drunk, she had no wish to prolong matters.

'Whatever you prefer is cool by me, Hon.'

She looked at the champagne. 'Can we take that with us?'

'We can do whatever you like.'

Traditionally styled with cream carpet and antique furniture, which Tanya assumed was Loretta's choice, Olli's bedroom was served by two en-suites.

He showed Tanya into hers, a spacious assault of white marble, contrasted with rich pink towels and a yucca plant.

'Annie keeps a good stock of everything. Look around. I'm sure you'll find whatever you need.'

'Thanks.'

He stared at her. 'May I watch you undress?'

She took a deep breath. 'If you want.'

At least he asked.

Champagne flute in hand, he sat on a wooden bench, next to a two-tiered square table with a pile of magazines on the lower section.

Don't go tripping on your knickers.

She diffidently removed her jacket, her only top piece aside from her bra, and put it on a hanger on the back of the door.

'May I unzip your skirt?'

'Why not,' she said, with cheerful awkwardness, 'it's got to come off.' She went to him.

He put his drink on the table. 'Turn around.'

'But the zip is at the side.'

He executed a half turn twist of her pencil skirt so it was at the back. 'I like lines to flow into each other.'

She turned around.

He unzipped her, and carefully brought her skirt down over her bottom and let it drop to the floor.

'Don't move, Hon.'

She did as she was told, and he gently pulled her thong past her knees so that it too dropped to the floor.

'Beautiful,' he said, and took hold of her with both hands, just below her hip bones, slipping his fingers under the loops of her suspender belt.

He kept her in that position for ages, a good eight to ten minutes in Tanya's estimation, and remained silent throughout. All she could feel was his breath in the crease of her bum and, after a subtle pull and a nudge of his thumbs to tilt her forward, on her pubes.

At first she studied the dice-sized tiles in the shower in front of her, wondering how the tiler had managed to cut them to fit so neatly around the jet sprays. But as time passed she came to admire the cleverness of what he was doing. Silence and uncertainty are a powerful combination, and she knew if it was Jake holding her, she would have got incredibly, rather than just ever so mildly, turned on.

He let go of her. 'Thank you, Hon. Now if you'll excuse me, I need to go and take a shower.'

She stepped outside her skirt and panties and picked them up, and turning to face Olli, noticed a hand mirror on his lap.

He smiled, put the mirror on the table, and rose from his chair. 'You have an amazing body.'

'Thanks.'

He stared at her breasts. 'Have you ever measured the depth of those things?'

She laughed. 'What, my boobs?'

He lowered the cups of her bra, and twiddled her nipples. 'These things.'

Blushing, she pulled the cups up. 'Do you mind?'

'Don't be shy, Hon. They're terrific. Hell, they could win competitions.'

She laughed to hide her embarrassment, picked up his drink and gave it to him. 'Why don't you go and take that shower?'

He sipped from his glass. 'Leave your stockings and suspenders on, Hon, OK?' he said, and left.

She locked the door after him, and stood buffing her shoulders to dispel her shivers, while cursing herself for not getting paralytic. Her embarrassment had proven very sobering.

I'm not having him scrutinising my bits. This will have to take place in the dark.

Eager to cover up before he reappeared she was bathed and in bed in about five minutes, and relieved to hear his shower still going strong.

Not wishing to think about what she was about to do, she filled her mind with pleasant thoughts and images. Such as the white leather designer bag and peep toe shoes she had her eye on. The smiley lady with jet black hair who made the best cheese and lettuce baguettes she had ever tasted. What colour she ought to paint her new shed, and where to go for her summer holiday. Nice thoughts and light thoughts only. Until Olli's bathroom door opened, when her ability to think at all ground to a halt.

He emerged wearing a green bath robe and a smile, wandered casually over to a tallboy to retrieve his drink, and placed it on his bedside table.

'Are you OK, Hon?'

Her whole body felt like a vibrator she was shaking so much, but she managed to say. 'Yes, thanks.'

He faced her and, smiling, took off his robe.

Oh. My. God.

The girth of his cock looked eye wateringly thick. And he was very hairy, a mass of ginger-blonde curls, and very freckly. But his torso was not half as wobbly as she had feared, more like that of a well padded teddy bear. Not that she was aroused, merely relieved. She had met a few tubby guys of average height with sex appeal, but Olli wasn't one of them. Granted he had a bit of a rocker look about him with his long hair, which she liked, but that was all, and it wasn't enough by far.

Starkers bar his watch, he glanced at her drink on her bedside cabinet. 'Hey, looks like you need a top up.' He breezily got the bottle from the tallboy, came to her bedside and filled up her glass, his cock dangling inches from her face.

She gulped, for not only did the tip look almost as wide as the base, but it was long.

That's where his extra inches went. No wonder he was looking at my arse. It would take a brave woman to accept that up her backside. He can't ever have had anal sex.

She wondered if he was expecting her to fondle it, kiss it even, but she could hardly bare such thoughts let alone act on them.

She thanked him for her drink.

'You're welcome,' he drawled.

Noticing a slight sway in his gait as he walked away, it crossed her mind he might be drunk, perhaps too drunk to perform, which is what she began to hope.

He stood his side of the bed feeling his nascent beard, and briefly returned to his bathroom, leaving the door open. Tanya watched as he put some cream on it.

An hour at most. Two hours, and I'll be home.

Finally, after shifting a few things around on his bedside cabinet, he took hold of the duvet.

Tanya immediately tightened her grip on her bit of it. 'Would you mind turning off your side light?' She had already turned hers off.

He sniffed and pinched his nose looking puzzled, but obliged. Moments later she heard a soft motorised sound, and the curtains retreated slightly, introducing a shaft of moonlight.

It's still better than the lights being on. Don't panic.

But as his heavy frame sunk onto the mattress, she did panic. In fact, she was seized by a raging panic.

I can't do it. It's no good, I just can't do it.

His natural scent was overpowering, the urge to leap out of the bed and run from the house enormous.

Calm down. You can do it. I can't. Yes, you can. No, I can't. Get a grip. You have to do it. You must. Close your eyes and breathe slowly. You've done it before for Christ's sake. You know the routine. Just do it.

To ease her anxiety she kept reminding herself that she was here by choice, that Olli was not forcing her, and that she was in control.

He sidled up to her and propped himself up on his elbow, the soft bristles of his emerging beard briefly touching her cheek, his hair her collar bone, as he manoeuvred into a comfortable position. Thankfully, his breath smelt sweet and pleasant.

He traced the contours of her face with his fingers and then buried them in her hair. 'You OK, Hon?' he whispered, massaging her scalp.

She uttered a squeaky, nerve-riddled, yes, but her body was dry and moist in all the wrong places, her chest tight, her limbs rigid.

It's no good. I can't.

'Olli, I'm really sorry, but I don't think I can go through with this, at least not tonight.'

Coward.

'Hey, you don't have to do anything you don't want to do, Hon,' he said soothingly.

'The problem is that I'm too tense.'

'Shush, that's not a problem. We can play a game where you try to remain tense, while I try to relax you.'

'Yes, but my body might not respond. It's like that sometimes. I don't want you toiling away to no avail.'

He stroked her forehead. 'Trust me, I'm not going to find this a labour. As a matter of fact, I'll enjoy you resisting. And if I get tired, I'll take a rest.'

'But I'm not sure I can do anything to you.'

'I'm not expecting anything. Tonight is all about you. I can take care of myself. You just lie back and allow your body to do whatever the hell it wants.'

Captain Altruistic, eh? Just let him get on with it, and get it over with.

She closed her eyes, and shut up.

He ran a finger up and down her breast bone. 'It's been too long, hasn't it, Hon?'

Nosey bugger. You're the third this year, and you won't be the last. Happy now?

'Mm,' she uttered.

He kissed the tip of her nose. 'I thought so.'

The prelude, light caresses of her neck, arms, and the folds of her armpits, did nothing to help her relax, and she was glad when he drew back the duvet.

All you have to do is lie here.

His breaths grew increasingly heavy as he studied her. 'Beautiful,' he kept saying, with big lustful sighs.

His friggin nickname should be spider eyes. Never again. I swear to God, I'll never do anything like this ever again.

His first port of call was her breasts which, after reverently feeling, as though inflated balloons that could pop, he came to treat like mounds of wet clay he was trying to re-sculpt, and, of course, ice creams. Friends to be reunited, too.

She cooed out of politeness but then appreciation, since what he was doing felt quite nice. It also meant his mouth wasn't on hers, which she was dreading but knew was unavoidable, especially when he began nibbling her neck.

As his tongue touched hers it took all she had to stop gagging, and much to her horror the urge didn't go away. To avoid that ultimate of all embarrassments, her face became one big fidget, with her showering his neck and his beard in dry kisses. That his beard was soft and not like a Brillo pad seemed fortuitous, but that he might know what she was up to made her feel awful.

Desperate for a way out of this mare's nest she began fantasising, about being used in all manner of grotesque ways by a gaggle of faceless men—and it worked. Now and again she was able to kiss him, and enjoy it, which perversely made what she was going through seem worthwhile, for it taught her two things of value: How to manufacture desire under stress, and that her frequent mental trips to Paradise Lust to achieve an orgasm were a blessing rather than a curse. The evening was not a total write-off.

Whilst they kissed, he mounted her, whereupon her fantasy promptly lost its potency. His cock was real, and she was too dry to take it.

Speak up. It will hurt. But what if he's not planning to penetrate me? I don't want him to think I don't think he knows what he's doing.

Now she was learning the pitfalls of shagging the boss, how her need to get things right, and to please, was distorting her reactions.

'Have you got any KY?'

'Shush,' he whispered. 'You're not getting anything yet.'

She felt stupid but then thought *Bloody cheek. Who the fuck does he think he is?*

He sat back on his knees and, using one hand to steer, the other to hold back the hood of her clitoris, began brushing the velvet-soft tip of his circumcised cock against it.

And as his raw egg-white like secretions soaked her bud, she felt a wave in the lower reaches of her abdomen as she too began to self-lubricate. But, almost as soon as she murmured pleasure, he ceased the tease and returned to his side-propped position.

Bastard. I was enjoying that.

The next thing she felt was him wanking against her thigh, with as much aplomb as a dog on heat. She found it crude and primitive, but for its resonance with her make-believe predators, exciting too.

Still on his side, he let go of his length and began fingering her pubic region. 'Is that a Hollywood, Hon?'

She gave a muted laugh. 'No, it's a Brazilian. A Hollywood is when they totally strip you.'

'That must be painful, no?'

'You get used to it.'

'How often do you get it done?'

'About once a month.'

'Well next time perhaps you'll allow me to shave you instead—Hollywood style.'

She felt a mix of embarrassment and shock, as well as anger at his presumptuousness of a next time.

'Thanks,' she said, struggling to sound calm, 'but I'm quite happy with my current method and style.'

'I'd use my shaving brush, Hon, and take real slow care lathering you up.'

She gulped. 'I'm sure you would,' she retorted, 'but it's not my scene.'

He waited for some seconds, and then brushed his lips over her nipples. They were taut and hard.

'Yeah, right,' he said, with a quack of a laugh.

Cringing with humiliation, she covered her eyes with her arm.

What the fuck is he playing at? How dare he trap and expose me. Just because I like the idea doesn't mean I like him. I've a good mind to go home. In fact, I will. He's breached too many boundaries with that little caper, and he's not getting away with it.

But what am I going to say?

She pictured his cock in her mind.

OK, let's be realistic. In the scheme of adult antics, his suggestion isn't that shocking. Tons of women get Hollywoods, and I'm sure tons of men shave their partners. He's only trying to find out what pleases me. If I storm out, he'll feel terrible. I've come this far, I might as well see it through.

He timidly touched her arm. 'I didn't mean to embarrass you, Hon.'

'You could have fooled me,' she grumped.

'I apologize. I can be such a klutz sometimes.'

She flipped onto her side, and grabbed her drink.

'I guess I'm in the dog-house now, aren't I?'

He's said sorry and admitted he's an idiot. What more can he do?

He kissed her cautiously on the shoulder, more of a peck than a kiss.

He's probably scared too.

She drained her glass, and rolled onto her back.

Come on, let's get on with it.

'Am I forgiven?'

'I'm still here, aren't I?'

'You're beautiful, you know that?' he crooned, 'inside and out. I promise I'll make it up to you.'

'Go on then.'

Suck me silly and fuck me senseless.

He got astride her and turned her lamp on. 'I only need it on for a second, Hon,' he said gently, 'while I remove your harness.' He began unfastening her suspenders.

She unhooked the back.

'Good girl,' he said, drawing the belt off her.

You pushover. You'll be licking his boots next.

They stared at each other, silently acknowledging the transfer of power that had taken place.

Hazily considering her behaviour, alcohol having taken its toll, she railed against her critic.

Someone has to lead, and someone has to be led. Besides, if he's doing all the work, he has a right to direct the proceedings. And I need a fuck.

He lightly slapped her thigh, and grinned. She poked her tongue out, and pointed toward the lamp.

'I will turn it off, Hon, but first I just want to check something out.' With that, he placed the raised circular section of one of her suspender strips, the bit over which the stocking goes, beside her nipple. 'Hell, your nips must be a couple of centimetres long.' He laughed. 'They're like a couple of earplugs.'

Earplugs? Hahahaha.

She burst out laughing. The analogy was so stupid, his delivery so disarming, it tickled her silly.

'Jesus, you could have thought of something a bit more glamorous.'

He looked perplexed. 'Like what, cigars?'

At this she shrieked.

He's right, he is a Klutz.

'Peanuts would have been better. At least they taste nice.'

'But they're not glamorous, Hon.'

She continued to giggle, until he began fondling her breasts while moving his length up and down her belly, when she became very quiet.

'Hon, may I steal one of your stockings?'

'I suppose so, but why?'

'Be a good girl, and you'll find out,' he said, and with uncharacteristic nimbleness bounded off the bed, and stood at the end of it.

She rolled each one toward her knees. 'Take them both or I'll feel odd.'

He removed them and hung them around his neck.

She looked at him expectantly, brow furrowed.

'Later, Hon.' Pulling her legs toward him, he then knelt on the floor.

She threw her arm back, grabbed a pillow and shoved it under the small of her back, her heart skipping at the sight of his head between her thighs. 'I hope you've cleaned your teeth,' she joked.

He glanced at her, pushed her knees up and gripped

her ankles. 'I won't tomorrow,' he said, and ran his tongue up her split.

She gasped and closed her eyes.

He was soon feasting on her, caring not a jot about the noise he was making, and she loved it. Think washing your hands in trifle, chewing a gobful of yoghurt, lapping and sucking at cream, eating soft, liberally buttered bread with your mouth open.

He thinks it's a piece of bubble gum.

She was referring to her labia, but not in a complaining way. Having it sucked and stretched to full hilt, and softly scratched by his beard, felt amazing and she kept rubbing her sticky, slippery folds hard against his face.

Spencer could never let himself go like this, not in a million years, she thought, groaning all the louder for having had that thought.

At last Olli was doing something very, very right.

His request for one of her stockings was also adding to her excitement because she was thinking of ways in which he might use it. It was the thrill of uncertainty again, the kick of not knowing what might happen. Or, as with her clitoris, which he was deliberately neglecting, when it might happen.

He kept her wanting a while, tonguing it sporadically and all too briefly, until she was in a state of considerable agitation, sighing with despair rather than delight. But she wasn't going to give him the satisfaction of begging, as that would show too much longing. As if he would oblige, anyway.

Eventually he tired of his game and prepared it for assault, easing away its protective shield with his fingers, at which point she lay dead still.

'Hon, this is a beautiful clitoris.'

Oh no, here we go. Police report coming up, she thought, close to bursting with frustration.

'It's like a pink diamond,' he added.

That he didn't say something ridiculous such as doorknob was something, but she felt intensely irritated by his inspection. As a consequence her brain shifted gear and she began deliberating whether or not to get some fish and chips on her way home.

Then all of a sudden he got down to business, and she felt a massive whoosh of ecstasy that made her body jolt and caused her to emit a deep grunt.

'Yes,' she kept uttering, ever more breathlessly, as he flicked, licked and drooled all over her pink diamond, at times suckling it so fervently she thought he was trying to uproot it.

Perhaps he wants to sell it to De Beers.

Astonished by his prowess, she mentally assigned another tick to the evening. But all good things come to an end, at least that's what she told herself when it all began to feel a little too nice.

'That's enough,' she panted, wriggling.

He looked up. 'Sorry, Hon. Would you like me to stop?'

Yes. No. Don't ask stupid questions.

She felt as clear as mud about what to do.

'No. I just needed a few seconds breather.'

She played this stop start game three more times, but the fourth time Olli ignored her. And pressed his hands firmly against her flesh, deftly kept her nub exposed with his fingers, and continued sucking.

She yelped and thrashed around, trying to wrestle free, but he wasn't letting her go anywhere.

No. Not here. Not with Olli, she thought, suddenly frightened, but it was too late. As she went to shout no and mean it, out came a continuous scream as she fell into that eye-rolling state of abandon, where her head spun dizzy, her flesh tingled, and her limbs jerked. And her insides became a medley of exquisite vibrations, as though warm water was gushing through her.

Afterwards, he came and sat on the bed beside her, and took her hand. 'How was that, Hon?'

She cocked a weary eyebrow at him and smiled. 'Not bad,' she said, very tongue in cheek.

Wearing a smug expression, he began penetrating her with his fingers and they both laughed at the squelching sounds it created. She felt as though she was sat in a puddle of cream.

'Are you ready for the next course?'

She rolled her eyes. 'What do you think?'

He let go of her hand. 'Get on all fours.'

She complied in a flash and peeked with pride at her swollen pussy, parting its glossy lips with her fingers to ensure clear access.

Standing at the foot of the bed, he began massaging and probing her anus with his thumb, while wanking off with his other hand.

Oh no. No, no, no, no, no, definitely not. I'd need the fire brigade to get the fucking thing out. It will be an emphatic no. Not even a topic for discussion.

When he stopped playing with himself, however, he didn't attempt anal sex but proceeded to push, what she quickly realised was her stocking, up inside her.

She swallowed her shock.

It's only a stocking, for Christ's sake, not a frying pan. Don't be a wuss.

He squeezed her bum cheeks when he was done, and mounted her doggie fashion. 'Does that feel good?'

She laughed. 'I would tell you if it didn't.'

As it happens it felt extremely good.

Leaving the stocking inside her, he pressed his cock against her split, and began pulling and pinching both her nipples, before abandoning one or the other in order to polish her diamond.

She moaned pleasure and moved her buttocks up and down.

'My Honey likes that, does she?'

She felt her heart go thud, instinctively averse to the possessive term, but not about to rain on her own parade continued to rub off on him. 'It feels good.'

'I know what you like, Hon. And what your cunt needs.'

She was both surprised and aroused by his use of the C word.

He stopped and climbed off her. 'Get on your back,' he said, smacking her arse.

She did so in a flash.

He then sat astride her and began retrieving her stocking, yanking it up through and tight to her split.

'Uh, that feels wonderful,' she said, wishing it was a mile long and contracting her muscles to heighten the sensation.

'Your cunt likes that, does it, Hon?'

She uttered a lingering 'Mm'.

He dangled her stocking by her nose and dropped it on her face. 'I wouldn't wear it home, Hon, unless you want every dog in the neighbourhood following you.'

He went down on her again, and having juiced her back up, mounted her, missionary position.

At last.

He guided her hand to his genitals, and rocked back and forth. 'Is that hard enough for you?'

She shivered in anticipation. His load felt luscious, his cock solid and smooth, the hairy flesh of his engorged balls tantalising tight. She ached to taste them, and suck his length, but resisted because it didn't seem the right thing to do. And because she was now desperate for the grand finale.

She pulled his cock toward her pussy.

'Are you sure you want me, Hon?'

Sure? Was he kidding? In that moment she had never felt surer of anything. 'Yes, yes.'

'Say it.'

'Fuck me.'

'No, Hon. Say: I want you to make love to me.'

Don't do this to me.

She flung her head from side to side as if saying no.

He waited patiently, the end of his warhead in firing position touching her entrance.

She dug her nails into his arse and tried to pull him into her, but he didn't budge.

Bastard.

'I want you,' she said faintly.

'Open your eyes, Tanya.' It was both a plea and an order, spoken with tenderness.

Thoughts swirled around in her head like leaves on a gusty autumn day, conflicting and unnerving thoughts.

He remained quiet, as she privately fought and felt her way to a decision.

She met his gaze, which she found emotionally painful, and swallowed hard. 'I want you to make love to me.'

He thrust into her with what felt like the force of a lion and the speed of a guillotine, and she was sure that were it not for her skin, her heart would be stuck to the ceiling.

Girth was definitely the new—everything!

Olli was soon fast asleep whistling like a north wind, making Tanya's exit relatively easy—until she opened the street door and set the burglar alarm off.

It freaked the fuck out of her, and her instinct was to leg it, which is precisely what she did, and when she stopped running she started laughing as she imagined what a shock it had to have been for Olli. But she reasoned it would have only been a few seconds before he realised what had happened. And seen the post-it she had left on his bedside table, on which she had scrawled *Thanks. See you tomorrow. X*

By the time she arrived home, however, she had long stopped laughing.

Now she felt sick to the pit of her stomach, and as though her life had taken a dreadful turn for the worst.

Far too fretful to sleep, she made a cup of coffee and sat by lamp light in her small lounge.

It wasn't that she felt cheap or promiscuous. She did, but that was irrelevant. What plagued her was what she had done to Olli.

The love she had seen in the soft lustre of his pale blue eyes, upon complying with his request to open hers, tore at her conscience. It was an almost sacred look of intense innocence, too pure to dishonour, which is partially why, despite misgivings, she had repeated his chosen words.

When you see something you shouldn't or don't want to, it's hard to forget it, and she felt she had come face to face with his courage, he, she was sure, with her self-serving cowardice.

Weak people say one thing yet do another, and that's what I've done. For all his power and wealth Olli is still a fragile human being, and I've knowingly played with his heart.

She picked at some frayed piping on the sofa arm.

He laid bare his soul in the name of love, while all I did was bare my flesh in the name of fear.

His encouragement was neither here nor there, for the way she saw it she was privy to her real feelings, and knew they were too shallow to justify intimacy.

How could I have done it, to him of all people? What sort of person am I?

Immoral sprang to mind, and she reflected on the word at length.

Morality is a matter of motive, and it's the quality of motive that defines character. And motive is a matter of choice. And I chose to sleep with Olli.

Suddenly, her mind became a battle field.

I'm to blame, I should have known better. No, you're not. It takes two. Yes, but I had the upper hand. I knew he cared about me more than I cared about him, so my downside was limited. Was it? Look at you now. But that's my fault. I took advantage. He's not an idiot. And you're not responsible for his feelings. Maybe not, but I still should have known better. Why? Because I should, because I'm a trader. Feelings are not bonds. You can't trade emotions. But before I jumped in the sack, I should have considered how I might feel afterwards.

She had put herself in a metaphorical box with immoral stamped all over it.

And there she stayed until she used her journal to rescue herself from torment, and began writing down the names of people she deemed moral and immoral.

This led to her creating a crude summary, lists of names of people she considered good, weak or bad, using arrows pointing left or right to indicate which way she felt the individual would veer if the chips were truly down. If typed it would have looked as follows.

GOOD	WEAK	BAD
Daphne	Barbara→	Him
Ted	Kay	Jim
Tanya?	Peter →	~~Peter~~
Alison	Bruce	Nate
Avril	Nina Stanzinger	Dale
David	Charlie Pedroy	
Freddie	Spencer	
Joe	~~Ludo Quagg~~	
Fiona		
Steve		
Ludo Quagg		
Olli		

By *Him* she meant her father.

In turning a blind eye to Tanya's suffering as a child, thereby, in Tanya's opinion, putting her own needs first, Barbara tended toward badness, hence the arrow. A good person would have found the courage to do the right thing. While Peter's treachery originally put him in the bad category, on reflection she didn't feel he belonged with those she regarded as real baddies.

443

She would have liked to have been able to put Spencer in her good column as a mark of progress, a sign she had moved on up after her divorce. But, believing Denton Fenshill's story about her and Steve Cranthorp made him an appalling judge of character, which she felt was driven by jealousy. A good person would not allow jealousy to blind them from the truth.

Ludo Quagg fared better as he was shamelessly transparent, a sign of integrity to her, and he had also apologised for rubbishing her, a sign of conscience.

Jim was just an out and out bully. Tanya didn't consider him as awful as her own dad, but he had hit Kay and Peter and more than once. And for not standing up to him Kay had to be classified as weak, despite her kind nature.

Although randomly drawn and inconsistently reasoned, the table did accurately reflect Tanya's feelings, and just looking at it made her feel better. That her *good* column was the longest was reassuring. The world was largely a good place.

Feeling calmer, her thoughts returned to Olli. What should she do? What could she do?

We all make mistakes, but it's how we deal with them that matters.

The only way to deal with her mistake, she decided, was to resign. That would show respect for Olli, and give her a way out of the mess she had created. She didn't feel she could face him every day knowing how much he cared, knowing she was the source of his pain.

As for what to say to him, ideas flowed freely for she had never liked working at Sky-Rise. Fear had driven her to push for the job, just as fear had driven her into Olli's bed. And it was time to face down her fears.

444

She barely thought about the financial sacrifice she would be making, because she was no longer in debt. She reckoned if she was careful she could manage for a year without a job and still employ Alison, which made her feel rich by comparison with the majority.

What had diminished in her life, she decided, was self-possession, the pride that comes from behaving with dignity and operating with honesty. It was time to regain control, to be true or at least truer to what she really felt come what may.

But am I being weak by resigning?

She wasn't sure but what did it matter? What mattered was that she was in a situation she couldn't handle, and had a right, a duty even, to change it.

That's what people do. That's why we have the luxury of choice.

CHAPTER TWENTY EIGHT

'You can't be serious,' Olli said.

'I am, and what happened last night has little to do with my decision.'

'Yeah, right.'

'I didn't say it had nothing to do with it. It did, but only in as much as it helped me to understand what's missing in my life. The thing is, Olli, I'm bored. I need excitement. I'm not cut out to be a portfolio manager. I'm a trader. I need to be back on a proper trading floor. It's in my bones and my blood. Sky-Rise is just too small and too quiet for me. I've got too much nervous energy to be happy sitting still and whispering.'

He shook his head. 'I don't buy what you're saying. If you want to scream and shout, join a dramatics society, like Helen, or a dance class. Or sign up at a gym, do some aerobics or a bit of kick-boxing. There are plenty of ways to get rid of nervous energy.'

'Number one, I don't have time for hobbies. Number two, I love the atmosphere of a big trading floor. Number three, I am not a nerd. I don't fit in here.'

'You mean you don't want to fit in here.'

Let him say what he wants. He's hurt.

'Is this your way of telling me you don't want us to make love anymore? Is that it, because if it is, that's cool by me? I can handle it.' He stood to take off his jacket and hung it askew over the back of his chair.

Yes, but what about me? I've not got a rubber heart, for fuck's sake.

'You're not listening, Olli. I slept with you because

446

I was looking for excitement, but I'm not leaving because of what we did. This is not about us, but about what I need as a human being to feel fulfilled.'

He looked at a globe to his right, a deep blue ball with colourful gemstone inlays, and with a sharp sweep of his hand spun it fast on its axle. 'You're not going to find fulfilment by running away.'

Don't admit to anything.

'I'm not running away.'

'In that case, why leave today? Why not stay until you've found another job. What's the rush?'

She wrung her hands. 'You ask a lot of questions.'

He gave a hollow laugh. 'I know. It started when I was about three years old. I used to drive my mom crazy, and do you know what she used to say to me?'

'What?'

'You sure ask a lot of questions, Olli.'

Tanya smiled.

He leaned forward, elbows on his desk and hands open. 'Sky-Rise is profitable and clean, Tanya. I see every transaction this firm does, and I can vouch for every one of my employees. Try finding that at a big firm. The banks can't be fixed. The system is beyond repair. They're all set to either shrink or go bust. But hey, if you want to join a Bear Stearns type outfit and see the stock price fall from a hundred and seventy bucks a share, to two, go right ahead.' He spun his globe again. 'Hell, you could make a ton of money here.'

'I appreciate all that, but it doesn't change my mind. I want money, but the job has to be right. Anyway, I could end up at a big hedge fund. I don't know yet. It depends what's out there. All I know is that I want and need a livelier environment.'

He ran his fingers through his hair and sighed. 'This is a knee jerk reaction, and whatever you may say, I still say you're running away.'

You've nothing to gain by explaining.

'With respect, Olli, the best authority on me, is me.'

His phone beeped, and he took the call on speaker phone. It was Helen, to remind him of his nine fifteen meeting in the City. 'Thanks,' he said, 'hold my calls,' and rang off.

Yet again he spun his globe. 'What the hell did I do to make you this scared?'

Don't rise to the bait.

'I'm not scared,' she said indignantly.

He didn't respond for some seconds, and rather than look at him, Tanya studied her nails, pushing back her cuticles with the side of her thumb.

'Let me tell you what I think.' He paused. 'I think you're scared of falling in love with me.'

She broke eye contact and resumed her manicure.

'It's obvious you really dig sex,' he continued, 'and it's pretty damn obvious you really dug sex with me. And now you're now running for the hills.'

He's taking this really badly.

'It's an interesting theory but, sadly, incorrect.'

'How do you know? You haven't even thought about it.'

Don't give him false hope.

'I don't need to. I know what I feel, Olli, and I can't think my way to feeling differently. If I said otherwise, I would be lying.'

He blew out his cheeks. 'You've got some *major* control issues with men.'

She swallowed her annoyance. 'I disagree, but even

if I did, so what? We've all got baggage. Everyone has a story to tell.'

'Why don't you tell me yours? You never know, you might just find it helpful.'

Tanya had never seen any upside in talking about the darkest part of her past, for fear if people knew she would be treated differently, which would reinforce her suffering. She'd be categorised as a type, placed in a societal box from which she couldn't escape. She liked to win on merit, and saw no advantage in being identified as a victim. She was long done feeling like one of those.

'Thanks, but I'd rather not,' she said, and stood up.

He emitted a cackle. 'I've just worked something out. A trade is like a scalp to you, isn't it?'

She nodded. 'Yes, but that's trading.'

'Ah, but most people trade for money, whereas you're in it for the kill, endlessly pursuing revenge like a squaw whose kids have been slaughtered.' He snorted. 'You ought to braid your hair, and wear a bandeau.'

She grimaced.

He feels you've scalped him.

'I apologize,' he said. 'That was rude of me.'

She shrugged. 'Perhaps you're right.'

Sighing, he picked up her letter of resignation. 'Why don't you hang on to this until you get a handle on what, if any, jobs are genuinely available?'

'That's a kind offer but I won't change my mind.'

He left the letter open on his desk, stood up and put on his jacket. 'I have to leave for my appointment, but I can think of a lot of firms that would benefit from your expertise. I'll make some calls.'

She raised her hand. 'Thanks, but I'd rather you

didn't. I appreciate the offer, but I'd prefer to stand on my own two feet, do things in the right way and in the right order. This is all about me, Olli, not you.'

He skewed his face, his expression one of doubt, put his blackberry in his pocket, and came and stood before her. 'Can we stay in touch?'

'Of course. When I'm settled, I'll give you a call, and we can have lunch.'

She wanted to suggest dinner so the lines would disappear from his forehead and the corners of his mouth would turn up, but knew it would be dishonest and self-serving. She looked into his sad eyes. 'Thank you for everything—including last night.'

He forced a smile, and went to take her hand but then thought better of it. 'Just remember that I'm on the end of a phone if you need anything.'

She resisted an urge to hug him. 'Thanks. I'll definitely call to arrange lunch once I've got a job.'

He opened the door. 'One last question, if I may.'

'Sure,' she said.

'Do you trust me?'

'Totally,' she said, without hesitation.

'Thank you.'

'But not to look after cufflinks,' she added, noticing one of his was about to fall out.

He held up his forearm, and she secured it.

He smiled. 'Thank you. I was a little tired this morning.'

She glanced at her watch. 'You have to get going.'

'I know,' he said, but he didn't move.

Their eyes met, and in his she couldn't see a trace of malice, just sadness.

'Well, I shall see you when I see you,' she said.

He gave a nod and waited for her to leave.

She hovered, her body veering toward the door while her feet stayed put.

Fuck it.

She grabbed his shoulders and kissed him on the cheek. 'Take care, OK?' she whispered.

As soon as she left the building, she burst into tears.

I will never hurt anyone like that ever again in my whole life. Not ever.

*

Jacob stroked his long beard, his lids half closed. 'What terms do you have in mind?'

'A partnership, but I can't afford to buy my way in, so I'm thinking a modest basic salary, and whatever else I'm due in salary and bonus being retained for however many years it takes to pay for my stake.'

He shook his head, his skull cap shimmering in a blade of sunshine peeping through the blinds. 'A senior trading position may be possible, but a partnership...' He shrugged and opened his hands. 'It's the details, Tanya. It isn't a simple process.'

It's my terms or no terms now.

'With respect, Jacob, I'm not here to discuss a job. I can get one of those this afternoon.'

Even if it's one clearing rubbish.

'KS and I have a long history,' she added, 'and I have an unblemished track record. I made money every year I was there. The loss incurred last year was, as you know, due entirely to corruption by Nate Walthak.'

He nodded. 'I will have a word with Bruce Ghoff. I cannot promise anything, but I will have a word.'

I'm not phoning him. This is his chance to prove himself, and make good on his promise.

Bruce's offer of help aside, she felt he ought to be begging for her services, but he was hanging on to his job by a thread, and her presence would be a daily reminder of his stupidity. Could he cope with that? Or would he validate his place on her list?

'Thank you very much, Jacob.'

She thought she saw the makings of a smile on his face, but it became a frown. 'Is it wise to leave a job before you have another one?'

Obviously not, in your opinion.

'Sometimes, Jacob, moves have to be made in the right order, like a game of chess.'

He gave a small nod, and put his hands together. 'Tell me, Tanya. If you had to make one change at KS, what would it be?'

Her instinct was to focus on KS' rulebook for employees, as it was a pet peeve, something she'd thought a lot about over the years.

'I'd tear up the handbook and start again, and aim for one a quarter of the size. A rule book is a blunt instrument, and KS' is way too big. I think people thrive best when you show faith in them, and set the bar high.' She paused. 'You can go on forever anticipating what a dishonest person might do, but that sort cock-a-snook at the law anyway, which means ninety nine percent of people get penalised for the one percent that won't even read a rule book. And KS' is embarrassing—a poor attempt to hijack common sense, and a brilliant attempt to scare people witless.'

'Interesting,' he said, his expression hard to read.

'There's also the cost to consider,' she said. 'KS is

in effect spending millions to lose millions: Paying consultants, lawyers and HR staff to create something that destroys morale and adversely affects productivity.'

Shut up. He gets the point.

She shrugged. 'In my experience, Jacob, when it comes to rules, less is more. But, treat people like infants and that's how they'll behave.'

He got up from his desk and came and shook her hand, which she took as a good sign. 'I will have a word with Bruce.'

'Thank you, Jacob. I'm much obliged.'

CHAPTER TWENTY NINE

Tanya watched on close circuit TV, from the ante room adjoining the stage of the auditorium, as clusters of animated faces, tongues wagging, most carrying notes and some kind of refreshment, arrived for the morning meeting. They knew something was up, as Bruce had asked all trading floor personnel to attend, and wagers were undoubtedly taking place as to precisely what.

She hadn't got the terms she wanted, but Jacob had promised her a partnership within two years, subject to performance. In the interim she would be head of debt trading. The sweetener was that Bruce willingly agreed to her request to report directly to Jacob.

It was standing room only with bodies lining the walls, and the air was thick with muffled disquiet, until Bruce took the lectern, when you could hear a pin drop.

He had told Tanya he was on a diet although he didn't look any thinner, but he did look happier, grateful no doubt that he still had a job. Jacob wasn't a fool. He knew that like Tanya Bruce's history with KS was valuable, and also that given his mistakes he had a lot to prove.

'Good morning,' he said. 'It's been a while since I've been able to stand here and deliver good news, but today,' he smiled, 'today is different. Today represents a major turning point in KS' fortunes. I am delighted to be able to tell you this firm still has the pulling power to attract top talent.' He paused. 'This past weekend our search for a head of debt trading came to an end, when we secured the services of a truly awesome individual.

I'm talking best of breed, a person with outstanding credentials, and an unrivalled commitment to fairness and transparency.'

Steady on, Bruce, they'll be expecting Warren bleeding Buffet.

She saw Freddie and Sam exchange looks of doubt and concern, and Fiona anxiously pulling at her fingers. Who was to be their new boss?

'Like me,' he continued, 'this individual knows that not only can KS rebuild its client-base, profitability and reputation, but that it will. And I am in no doubt that the skills and experience they will bring to bear, combined with their sense of ethics and engaging style, will expedite that process. I am, to borrow a British term, chuffed to bits by this appointment.' He paused. 'I guess now you're all wondering who it is? Well the individual wants to introduce themselves, and they're due here any minute now.' He looked at his watch, and stared at the main entrance, and all heads turned around to do the same, allowing Tanya to emerge – to add a fun element of surprise – from the door on the platform behind him, and quickly take her place at his side.

She coughed—a loud 'ahem'.

Heads instantly swivelled back to the lectern, and in a nanosecond there was jubilant uproar, as people took to their feet cheering, clapping, and whistling.

'Yes!' Freddie bellowed, leaping from his seat and punching the air, his copper hair bouncing as though a wig about to come off.

Catching Tanya's eye, Joe kissed his fingers and spread his arms. 'There is a God, after all,' he shouted.

She saw Andy embrace a tearful Fiona, and many other people give each other high fives, and back pats.

'Shinewater's bidding 83 for Allied Capital,' Rich hollered from the back of the hall. 'Can you get Sky-Rise to sell?'

'That means they're worth at least 90,' she replied with gusto.

Freddie rushed to shake Tanya's hand, and then Bruce's, congratulating them both. Others followed suit and the merry disarray continued as hope and relief saturated the atmosphere.

Tanya hugged a still weepy Fi, and then a fit, snappily dressed Joe.

'Great to see you back on form, Joe,' she said, adding, in a whisper, 'fuck the pair of them.' She of course meant Peter and Suzy who had just thrown a lavish engagement party.

'We wouldn't want to,' he said, chuckling.

'That's the spirit, Joe.' She paused. 'Are you looking this happy just on account of me, or?'

He winked, and it was clear to Tanya he had met someone. 'That's fantastic, Joe. I'm so happy for you.'

He thanked her and moved aside for Sam.

She shook his hand. 'It's great to see you, Sam.'

'And you. I always felt cheated I didn't get to work for you.'

He won't say that once I've asked him to volunteer for a pay cut. As he was on a guarantee, all she could do was ask, which she planned to do as soon as possible.

She laughed. 'Well, I always felt cheated I never got that trip to France in a microlight.'

'The offer's still open.'

'Thanks, I'll give it some thought.'

Feeling a nudge to her elbow she turned to see Spencer, holding a sheaf of papers near his face, looking shocked but pleased. 'Hello, Tanya, how wonderful to see you. Welcome back.'

'Thank you.' Her heart became a knot but she gave him a sparkling smile, and shook his hand firmly, before turning away.

She wished he had left while he had the chance, not relishing having to contend with his presence.

She returned to the lectern and waving her arms in the air cheerleader fashion, called for order. The room fell quiet.

'I know Bruce has a lot of business to get through, so I shan't hog the podium for long, but thank you all for that blooming marvellous welcome. To be among familiar faces again feels fantastic.' She heaved a satisfied sigh. 'Now I'm sure you're all dying to know why I've come back, and to be honest, so am I.'

Ripples of laughter.

'In short, I've returned because I believe in the inherent goodness and brainpower of this firm, and its potential to regain all the ground it has lost, and some. And strange as it may seem, because I actually missed you lot.' She shook her head. 'I know, I know. I'm seeing my psychiatrist next week.'

There was more laughter, which she let cease before continuing.

'On a serious note, whilst what has befallen KS is awful, I'm sure you will all agree it's nowhere near as awful as what befell those young girls. We can recover what we've lost, but they'll never be the same again.'

People nodded and sighed agreement.

Don't dwell on the negative.

She smiled. 'OK, back to business. In the first instance, I will be undertaking a comprehensive review of our trading operations, and I apologise in advance for the pest I will become as that review gets under way. I trust I can rely on your support and cooperation. For now, that's all I have to say about trading, at least securities trading, but I would like to touch on the trading of gossip, which I consider the single biggest threat to KS at this time.'

Adopting a pensive expression, she gripped the lectern. 'Gossip is a currency,' she paused for effect, 'and appearances, as we well know, can be extremely deceptive.' She waited for that to sink in too.

'The trial – she meant both Dale's and Nate's – will ensure we remain in the spotlight. So until it's over we must be ultra careful about the company we keep. Journalists are brilliant spies, and ace at protecting their sources, which means the onus is on us to distinguish between friend and foe. Chatting with anyone in the market poses a risk, and by anyone I mean clients too, since there are plenty of those who love to trade in dirt.'

Denton Fenshill sprang to mind and she glanced at Spencer, who stood, finger on his lip, eyes cast down.

Tossers, the pair of them.

She scanned the room. 'Just remember that behind every question is an agenda. Jokes about KS are another problem, in that how you react to them will speak volumes.' She gave a clap of her hands. 'OK, now for some good news. Never let it be said I do not come bearing gifts, gifts courtesy of Jacob Robensteyn that is. Jacob has graciously sanctioned a monthly dinner with a social emphasis, for about twenty people at a time.' She saw lots of bemused faces and laughed to herself. 'Don't worry,' she added. 'He has no interest in coming along to these soirées.'

There was much laughter.

'I'm sure he'll find the videos just as entertaining.'

More laughter.

'Bruce and I will be joint hosts of these evenings, and although we haven't yet agreed a format, we intend to make them fun. And needless to say, everyone who works on the trading floor qualifies as a guest—as long as they haven't quit.'

Too many people for her liking found her quip hilarious, especially Max, famous for his darting eyes and long-winded trades, whose laugh stood out.

If you don't want to be here, fuck off.

She felt outraged at the insults betrayed.

KS had already lost a lot of people but Bruce still reckoned about twenty percent of the firm's producers wanted out. With respect to those who had left, her view was good riddance. They were greedy and weak.

She waited for total quiet, reminding herself of the need to be diplomatic.

'I know some of you don't want to be here, and that's a shame, but while you are don't bite the hand that feeds you, because you'll only hurt yourself.' Her voice was even and firm. 'You know, when we say one thing but do another it can really mess up our mind. We're all walking contradictions, due to split loyalties and conflicting agendas, and we all, me included, sometimes fall into the trap of not practicing what we preach. But make no mistake. It is a trap.'

Trust me. I know what I'm talking about.

As she allowed time for her words to be digested, the mood turned solemn, but she didn't care. She had to be true to herself, and felt compelled to defend KS.

'I've chosen KS,' she continued, 'and I shall take

great pride in our ride back up the league tables, and in an ideal world I'd love each and every one of you to join me. I've got not a shred of doubt in my mind that KS will not just survive but thrive. But should any of you think otherwise, if you want to chat through your concerns, and hear my take on this firm in more detail, you know where to find me. I'll now hand over to Bruce.'

Bruce came and stood beside her. 'For the record, I second everything Tanya's just said,' he looked at her, his eyes full of painful contrition, 'every single word.' He then put his arm around her, and faced his troops.

There followed paced and poignant applause, and Tanya could tell from his tight grip of her shoulder that he was choked with emotion. She was too, and stood glorying in the warmth of hatchets buried and slates cleaned.

It felt good to be home.

Nearing six thirty that day, Spencer showed up at her grand corner office, with its double aspect view of the City and the River Thames. Bruce insisted she have it.

He knocked on her open door. 'Can I come in?'

She stood checking the contents of a filing cabinet, and glanced over her shoulder at him. 'Sure. I'll be with you in a second.'

He walked to within a few paces of her, and waited.

She selected the file she wanted, and turned to face him. 'What can I do for you?'

'I'd like to chat through my concerns, and hear your take on this firm in more detail.' His smile showed he was joking, his eyes that he remained desirous of her.

She laughed briefly, out of politeness.

'You're very articulate when you're angry,' he said.

'Thanks, but I'm not fussed what words I use, as long as I get my point across.'

He uttered a knowing 'Mm', no doubt recalling her last ones to him. 'It must feel very satisfying to know you were right all along about Nate.'

She shrugged. 'I can't say it does, given the nature of his crimes. I'm just relieved he's out of harm's way.' She paused. 'Now, what is it you want?'

He emitted a small cough. 'I've come to apologise for not replying to your email but I was away. And by the time I returned your Mr Vermallen was trying to take us over, so I felt it prudent to keep on the sidelines while all of that was going on.'

Wimp.

She smiled. 'No need to apologise, I wasn't expecting a reply. I just wanted to show my support.' He wouldn't have known otherwise from her message, but in truth she had got in touch because she felt randy.

'Thank you. It's nice to know I was on your mind. You've been on mine, too, and believe it or not, I was going to email you this week, to invite you to dinner.'

'No point now, we can talk whenever we want— unless you're still on your way to Piper Kline.'

She doubted he was but wanted reassurance KS was not at risk of losing him.

He shook his head. 'We couldn't agree terms, so I walked away. And despite what's happened I don't regret that, as they didn't handle matters very well.'

Who's he trying to kid?

'And you're not chatting with any other firms?'

'No. Like you, I think I'm rather wedded to this firm.'

She felt insulted by the comparison, but her duty to KS had to come first. 'I'm delighted to hear that. KS can ill afford to lose your services.'

Smiling, his shoulders went back and his hands went in his trouser pockets, tensing the cloth across his groin, and her eyes unconsciously fell to the outline of his cock.

'Can you?' he said.

He doesn't miss a trick. I walked right into that one.

She gave him an icy stare, a stare at great odds with how she felt. 'Yes! Now if you'll excuse me, I have heaps to do.' She went and sat at her desk, and opened her file.

'You said you would call, but you didn't,' he said.

She just shrugged, of the view that anything she said would be a hiding to nothing.

He pulled at the knot of his tie. 'Look, I'm sorry for what I said about your mother.'

And so you should be.

'Don't worry about it,' she said casually.

'Does that mean I'm forgiven?'

He couldn't even forgive me, for a two second kiss I didn't initiate.

'If you like,' she said.

'Mm, I can see you're still cross with me.'

'I'm not, but I don't appreciate you being glib. You make it sound as though all it takes to forgive is to utter three Hail Mary's or flick a switch, which is naive.'

'I see... So I'm not forgiven?'

Don't rise to the bait.

She smiled. 'Yes, you're forgiven.'

'Oh, Good, I'm glad that's settled. And since it is, perhaps now we can have dinner?'

I walked right into that one as well. Say yes to get rid of him. You do have to work with him.

'OK, but as friends and no more, and it will have to be towards the end of the month, because I'm booked solid for the next two weeks.'

Friends? Now you're kidding yourself.

He came and stood the other side of her desk. 'How about the twenty seventh?'

Her stomach turned over. He was talking August, but they first had sex on September the twenty seventh.

'I'm booked that night,' she lied, 'but I'll come up with a few dates and give you a call.'

'I shall make a point of being home all evening.'

She cocked an eyebrow. 'It won't be tonight. I'll get back to you sometime this week.'

'I was talking about the twenty seventh,' he said.

His aftershave was arousing nostalgia. 'I'll keep that in mind. Now please leave me in peace. I've got tons to do.'

'OK.' He paused. 'But does that mean you are free on the twenty seventh?'

'No, Spence. It means I'm tired.'

'Of course, I'm sorry. I'm being selfish.'

'For once I agree with you,' she said.

They both laughed.

He wished her a good evening and left, but remained on the trading floor, within her view, chatting with the smattering of people still around, females in particular. She felt that was deliberate and his way of tormenting her, and it pissed her off big time. She hated that she couldn't, as she had just pointed out in the context of forgiveness, simply flick a switch and turn off her feelings for him.

463

Chewing her lip, she kept a furtive eye on him as he chatted with a pretty Japanese analyst, and began to think about his frequent trips to Asia and the Far East.

He's probably got a girlfriend out there. He's too gorgeous not to get offers, and too insecure to turn them down.

If he did she felt it would account for his jealous streak, for it stood to reason to her that if he couldn't trust himself, he couldn't trust anyone else.

She reflected on the night of the Astrar Hoffman dinner, how excited he made her feel, how captivated she was by him.

A documentary she had watched on TV moons ago, not long after she got married, suddenly came to mind. It was about elephants in captivity, and seeing the poor creatures endlessly circle the same patch of ground, some having had their tusks removed, had made her cry. Now she realised her weeping had been for herself, that she had seen parallels between their hopeless, helpless lives, and hers, that she had felt like a caged animal with all its latent power trapped.

That was then. This is now. And now I'm on the brink of real power, of a freedom I've never known.

She made herself think of a diametric opposite to the elephants, and pictured in her mind a lion roaming the African savannah. It sent shivers up her spine.

Don't sabotage that dream. Don't let him fuck it up. Have dinner with him and you'll be risking everything, whereas just for a change he'll be risking nothing. As they say, 'first time shame on them, second time shame on you'. She drummed her fingers on her desk. *I've got to kill all hope stone dead. If I don't he'll keep chipping away, because he's got no downside.*

She called his mobile. 'Can you nip back to my office, for a quick word?'

He turned to look at her, and smiled. 'I think that could be arranged.'

As he made in her direction, she glanced at her watch, almost seven, and felt angry at the time she'd wasted on him.

He beamed as he entered.

'On second thoughts, I don't want to have dinner.'

'Why on earth not?'

'That's my business.'

He gave her a come-to-bed look. 'Are you scared of what might happen?'

Where do these guys get off?

'No, but I have no interest in discussing the past, which would be inevitable.'

'Was it so dreadful?' he teased.

Kill it. Now!

'Disappointing is the word I would use, *very* disappointing, in fact. And I'm done fraternising with people who consistently disappoint.'

He drew a sharp breath. 'Perhaps it's escaped your attention, but you are also eminently capable of disappointing.'

She leaned back in her chair and folded her arms. 'I know. I do it by design.'

He briefly held his temples with one hand, play acting in her view the hurt victim, and then he started nodding to himself. 'Is that what happened with Mr Vermallen?' he said, with a wry smile on his face. 'Did he disappoint you too? Or did you simply tire of him?'

He came to her desk and looked down his nose at her. 'You don't really expect me to believe you left

Sky-Rise simply because you missed KS, do you? You forget that I know you, Tanya.'

It was a piercing blow given the knocks, shocks and financial battering she'd taken, to say nothing of her termination. Winded and wounded, she sat breathing heavily, aware of his eyes on the swell of her breasts. And for a split second she was sorely tempted to tell him she had aborted his child, just to spite him.

But she was bigger than that, and her secret also gave her strength.

'I don't care what you believe, Spence. Your suspicious mind is your problem. You know, you really ought to get that sorted.' She paused. 'Now, if you'll excuse me, I want to get on.'

He gave her a disdainful look and left, and while it was a wrench for her to watch his virile frame disappear from view, she felt she had passed a test.

No pain, no gain. I'm not trading lust for love. One day I'll have both.

CHAPTER THIRTY

About to head out to lunch with Andy, Tanya quickly scrolled through the photos Helen had just emailed through, of her debut as Maria in The Sound of Music. Tanya didn't go, because she was too tired, and wanted time with her boys.

There were three of the whole cast, with a radiant and gorgeous Helen in the centre cradling a bouquet. And at least a dozen family shots taken after the show, each one captioned so Tanya knew who was who.

Never mind, she thought, feeling a twinge of envy. *We can't have it all.*

As Maria, Helen looked lovely but as herself she looked positively stunning: A carnation-pink strapless dress, her caramel hair drawn back on one side with a white flower, and her tiny waist emphasised by a wide white belt.

She came to a shot of Olli, smart in a tuxedo, cummerbund and bow-tie, sitting next to Helen at dinner, which she spent about two seconds looking at.

Ah, so Olli went. Good for him. He needs to get out more.

But a few photos on she came to a snap of him and Helen's father standing either side of Helen, and her reaction was visceral, disturbingly visceral.

He was staring directly at the camera, and seemingly therefore straight at her. And it was as though all the love she had seen in his eyes just before he entered her, was rushing into her all over again.

She poured herself some water from a jug on her

desk, a highball glassful, drank the lot straight down, and took some deep breaths.

I don't know what happened there, but Jesus. Phew! It must have been a trapped memory, or something.

Wheels of Fortune, known simply as Wheels was a hive of activity. The 'ch-ching' of its old fashioned till, used for tips, was going ten to the dozen, as trays bearing steak and kidney pudding, fish 'n chips, and toad in the hole, flashed by in the arms of mature waitresses with bright lips and back-combed hair.

A *spiffing old chap, just spiffing* brigade were at the bar pontificating in hullabaloo fashion: Up five decibels at fancy terms such as structured credit derivatives and reverse option hedges, down five for mundane topics. The Essex clusters were more subdued but it was early. *Wahays* and swoops at each other's privates usually came after a few pints.

Andy and Tanya clinked glasses.

'It's good to see this place doing so well,' she said.

'There's always a silver lining for some, Darlin',' he said, referring to the economic downturn.

Such as Helen. Was Olli touching her arm? What do you care if he was?

She smiled. 'Have you and Laura got matching jackets?'

Andy laughed. 'No, but where did that come from?'

'Take no notice,' she tapped her head. 'I'm just having an out-there moment.'

'You need some sleep.'

'I know, but it's finding the time. I put face cream on my toothbrush last night, I was so knackered. Not that I'm complaining with two million odd unemployed.

I've loads to be grateful for, my lovely bed for a start. That's one thing I've learned since renting. You can live in a box but still feel rich as long as you've got a decent bed.'

'I'm not sure Nate and Dale would agree.'

She laughed briefly, but then her expression became one of distaste. 'They'll go free after the trial, mark my word.'

Andy shook his head. 'No they won't.'

'You want to bet? The most serious charge they're now facing is unlawful sexual intercourse with a girl under the age of sixteen, for which the maximum prison sentence is a pathetic two years.'

'Is that all?'

'Yes, and come the trial they'll have been in custody ten months, so even if they're found guilty my bet is they'll walk free from court.'

Their food arrived, and Nate and Dale dominated their conversation.

Nate was off the hook for drugs trafficking because, contrary to sensationalist reports, the quantity of cocaine found was small. He had also escaped prosecution for brothel keeping, because the Norfolk property wasn't registered in his name.

As for people trafficking, an Albanian man had been charged with that offence, but not the slippery Nate. And there simply wasn't enough evidence to prove fraud in relation to the NCA trade. Taylor and Nate had stuck to their story – claimed a falling out had led to their using Denton Fenshill as middleman – and Hasseen was saying nowt, and staying put in Algeria.

Tanya often bristled with rage at the injustice of it all but knew she had done her best.

She paid the bill.

'One of the reasons I love this place,' she said, 'is that they don't employ young foreign women.'

'I know what you mean, Darlin, but we can't save the world, only ourselves.'

'Sounds like you're getting wise in your old age,' she joked.

'Don't get cheeky, just because you're the boss.'

When Tanya got back to her office, she immediately re-examined the photo of Olli and Helen to check for physical contact. But a wine glass obscured verification, so she used the zoom facility to magnify it, at one point to four hundred percent. Satisfied Olli's little finger was close, but not actually touching Helen's skin, she then pondered whether he was posturing toward her.

No. He always lists a tad to the right when he's sitting down.

On the other hand...

Jesus, what the fuck am I doing?

The words snoop and jealous leapt to mind, filling her with shame.

OK, that was snooping, but I'm not jealous. Curious yes, and probably surprised, but certainly not jealous.

But then she uttered a loud 'Huh'.

If he's with her, it's only on the rebound. It won't last. She knows sod all about finance and she'd drive him fucking bonkers with her singing. Don't be so sure. She's far from stupid, and she'd be a trophy on anyone's arm. Stranger things have happened. Another angry grunt passed her lips. *It's a dead cert the kids will be ginger, because they've got more or less identical colouring.*

The fact that she liked ginger hair eluded her.

Stop it, for God's sake. What's got into you?

Feeling ashamed, she told herself she would be pleased if Helen and Olli had found happiness together.

They are both lovely people. They deserve good things.

Suddenly noting the time and that she was due at a meeting with operational cost control, to argue for a reduction in overheads borne by her division, she forwarded Helen's email to her home computer, and signed off. And as she dashed through the trading floor, to the designated room, she kept scolding herself for wasting time.

A short time later, felt-pen in hand and about to write on a whiteboard, she came over clammy. 'I'm sorry, guys,' she said to her three male colleagues, 'but we're going to have to reschedule.' She held her stomach. 'I think I ate something at lunch that hasn't agreed with me.'

She went home and to bed, and although it was eighteen degrees Celsius, she kept her dressing gown on and put a blanket on top of the duvet. And bar trips to her miniature en-suite to throw up and for ablutions, she remained there until morning, most of the time awake.

Although she put her upset down to the salmon she had eaten for lunch, Olli and Helen remained on her mind, and countless times she imagined them walking up the aisle. Finally, she conceded that she was jealous, but for no other reason than that Helen had robbed her of an option.

Shivering, she tried to focus on work, and a meeting with one of KS' lending banks the next day, from whom she wanted more credit at better terms. But, her concentration kept lapsing, her mind bedevilled by the photo of Olli appearing to stare at her.

She had barely thought about him until today, and when she had her only emotion was guilt for not getting in touch. Now however she wondered whether she missed him, and realised that she did, because after all was said and done he had clearly been a force for good in her life.

His assertion – I realize I'm not what you want—right now, but I know I'm what you need – kept going round in her head, and made her think of Freddie and Fiona, who were now dating with her full blessing.

Is Fi ahead of the game? Or is she simply running scared?

She recalled something Jess Larance had said about forgetting being hard to do, and made her right. Out of sight, even out of mind, did not mean out of heart.

But do I care about Olli, or am I just jealous? And if I do care, how much do I care? And what, if anything, should I do about it?

She glanced at Daphne's shawl, and welled up.

Oh, Daphne, to have you to talk to.

She considered phoning Olli to fix lunch, but felt that would be wrong, because she would be operating with an ulterior motive and therefore using him.

Nor did it feel right to her to rush to find answers to her questions. Given that all her best laid plans had gone awry, and her haste to bed Spencer had cost her dearly, she was more reluctant these days to force life, more inclined to let it unfold.

A few weeks passed wherein she cogitated, ruminated and speculated, but to no avail. Conviction continued to elude her. Until, while browsing through one of Alison's magazines, she came across an article about food cravings, in which it was claimed people were chemically attracted to foods that proved bad for them. She found it a very interesting hypothesis, one that resonated deeply in the context of relationships.

Maybe that's why I gravitated toward Spencer; because he was bad for me. Hmmm. But why is it that we crave what's bad for us? There has to be a reason.

What popped into her head was *because we love what's bad for us, because we're gluttons for punishment; because we're addicted to bad love.*

But that seemed both crude and cruel, and illogical.

Life's about living, about staying alive, not trying to kill ourselves. It's got to be something logical and life enhancing. Maybe an imbalance of some kind trying to correct itself.

She couldn't sleep for trying to fathom what it could be, and during her mental meanderings recalled a slew of events from her childhood, the vast majority unpleasant. And it suddenly struck her that how Spencer had made her feel, which was for the most part anxious and unloved, was precisely how she had felt as a child.

That's it! I was drawn to Spencer because he evoked familiar feelings. Not good feelings, but familiar ones. And it was the same with Peter. I became addicted to bad love, because I grew up with it, and got used to it. It was all I knew. People stick to what they know.

She realised this line of reasoning had serious ramifications, because it logically followed that in order to feel the opposite of anxious and unloved, i.e. peaceful and loved, would feel unfamiliar.

Maybe Olli's unfamiliar, but good for me.

473

She went downstairs and made herself a cup of tea, and returned with it to her bedroom. Where she sat by an open window and smoked a cigarette—in the same spot she had been when her imaginings about Daphne had surfaced.

I realize I'm not what you want—right now, but I know I'm what you need.

OK, so he had agenda in saying that, but he's also perceptive and honest.

She laughed aloud imagining Spencer's face had she told him about Wagsy. Wimpy Mr Rivington would have been horrified and terrified, whereas Olli hadn't just joined her mission, but had taken over and led the way.

The thought that Helen might have his heart, suddenly made her feel sick.

'Olli.' His nasally voice now sounded like that of an angel's.

She grabbed her handset. 'Boo. Guess who this is?'

'Hey, Tanya! How are you?'

'Very well, thank you. I'm sorry I've not called before, but I've been snowed under.'

'Hey, I know the feeling. How's it all going?'

'In a word, great, but I shall tell you more when I see you. Have you got your diary to hand, so we can fix a date for that lunch?'

'Sure, but we're probably looking at mid October.'

'What about dinner,' she blurted.

'Dinner would be terrific, but I'm off to Chicago at the weekend to see my folks, and then I'm in the Middle East.' He paused. 'Would you mind phoning Helen? She knows my availability a lot better than I do.'

Her stomach sunk. 'Have you got any time before you leave for Chicago?'

It was already Wednesday.

He was quiet for a few moments. 'Are you in some kind of trouble?' He sounded concerned.

'No. I'd just like to see you.'

'Likewise, but my schedule is real tight. Look, have a word with Helen—'

'What are you doing tonight?'

'What's this about, Tanya? What's the rush?'

She took a deep breath. 'I've missed you.'

'Why, thank you. I've missed you too.'

Tell him how you feel. If you don't, he's not going to know.

She gave a small cough. 'The thing is, Olli, I realise I like you. I mean that I like you a bit more than like. And that I'd like to get to know you better.' Her heart was thumping. 'Is that something that still appeals? I understand if it isn't. If your life has moved on, I'll be thrilled for you, but if it hasn't, I just thought we could have dinner, or something.'

'Hey, are you asking me out on a date?'

'I suppose I am.'

'Suppose?'

'Yes. I am.'

There was a long silence.

Don't say another word.

Since her mouth felt bone dry, that wasn't hard.

'I'll be home by eight fifteen. Why don't you come on over?' His voice was gentle, and she sensed he was smiling.

'OK. I'll see you then.' She hung up, and sat at her desk in a daze, her body a bundle of tingles.

At seven fifteen she alighted from Ted's car at Sloane Square, and told him he could take the night and the following morning off, with pay.

'Thank you, my Lovely, that's very kind of you. My Eileen will be pleased not having to get up in the morning. Not that I can stop her, mind.'

His adoring wife always rose early to make him a packed lunch, and wave him off to work.

She smiled. 'That's love for you, Ted.'

'I know. She's a diamond is my Eileen. When I get home, I'll make her a nice cup of tea.' He glanced at his watch. 'Good, it's not half past seven yet. Coronation Street won't have started. I'll call her and tell her to record it, so we can watch it together.'

He drove off happy as a sand boy.

Bless him. Bless them. Bless love.

She made straight for a wine bar overlooking the square, and managed to nab the only free table outside. And in the glow of a pink grapefruit sky, she enjoyed a glass of Sancerre and a cigarette, while admiring the ability of cyclists to negotiate the often lunatic moves of drivers and pedestrians.

You wouldn't catch me cycling in London. Stop, start, twist, turn or die. Fuck that for a game of soldiers.

Jolted by a noise, she traced the cause to a traffic cone which she assumed either a bike or car must have clipped, because it was rocking to and fro in the kerb.

Daphne shot to mind. She laughed, dismissing it as coincidence, and checked her watch, only to discover to her surprise that it was five minutes past eight.

Where the time had gone, she didn't know. The last thing she remembered was staring at traffic and feeling relaxed, aware her critics were being quiet for a change.

I was obviously that chilled I tuned out. Amazing. But how come I re-engaged when I did? Don't start getting carried away about dead people. You only lost about twenty minutes. You just dozed for a bit, that's all.

She shuddered, suddenly feeling cold.

See, now you're scaring yourself. Get a move on, and get to Olli's.

A short cab ride later, and she was mounting the steps to his house.

He opened the door before she got to the top, and she felt a flood of affection on seeing him.

The cuffs of his shirt were folded back, his top button undone, and as she expected his shoes were off.

'Come on in,' he said, smiling.

He gave her a light embrace.

'It's good to see you,' she said.

'Why, thank you, and likewise.'

He hung up her coat, and they went into the lounge, where he poured her a glass of champagne.

As he gave it to her the golden curls on the back of his hand caught her eye, and her heart skipped a beat.

'Take a seat,' he said, motioning to the sofa. 'I'll sit opposite, so that I can look at you.'

She smiled, and sat down.

They talked for a bit about work. He had just bought into a company that mined titanium, a metal that costs a fortune to mine apparently. And when he had finished telling her about that, she broached the topic of her departure from Sky-Rise.

'I'm sorry for the abrupt way I left. I was scared and I did run. The sex freaked me, well not the sex as such, but when you told me to open my eyes.'

'Why?'

477

She shrugged. 'Not sure, too intimate, I think. I prefer to masquerade as a man when it comes to sex.'

He pulled a face. 'Hey, what is that supposed to mean? We're not all bad, as you well know, or we wouldn't be here having this conversation.'

'Sorry, that came out wrong. It's just that giving up control scares me.'

He stroked his thigh. 'You can't make love without surrendering, Tanya.'

She blushed, suddenly embarrassed. 'I know, but I wasn't ready to do that—but you made me. And it was too much too soon.'

He laughed. 'Personally, I thought it was perfect timing.'

She gave him a coy look.

'Hey, that reminds me. I still owe you a spank over my knee for setting off my alarm.'

Mm, yes, please.

She sank her jaw, and giggled. 'Sorry about that.'

'For future reference the code is one two one zero.'

'Ah, your birthday.'

I'll always remember the tenth of December.

'Hey, you remembered.' He spoke softly and looked surprised.

'How could I forget? It was a special night.'

He nodded slowly. 'It sure was.' He paused. 'What prompted your call?'

'Why, are you surprised I rang?'

He shook his head. 'No. I knew you'd be back, I just didn't know when.'

She baulked. 'What do you mean? How did you know?'

He ate an olive. 'Why wouldn't you be?'

'Hang on a minute.' She sat up straight. 'I'm not here for any reason to do with my house, or money, if that's what you're thinking. I've never been a kept woman, and I never ever want to be.'

There was a twinkle in his eye as he smiled. 'What's sniffy in rhyming slang?'

'Don't make fun of me. I'm being serious.'

Still smiling, he pinched his nose and sniffed. 'Hell, you wouldn't be sitting here, if I thought you were a gold digger. What I meant was that you need someone you can trust. That's the deal with you. You simply needed time to let your emotions percolate. But hey, I like it when you're sniffy. It's cool.' He ate another olive. 'I need to eat, Hon. Would you like to join me? There's a terrific Italian a few blocks from here.'

He's so friggin confident and so fucking annoyingly right.

'Yes, that would be lovely, but first I'd just like to make a few things clear, OK?'

He shrugged. 'If it makes you feel better, Hon, go right ahead.' He paused. 'You know, I like it when you're petulant. It's cool.'

She tutted and folded her arms.

He laughed. 'Is this our first argument?'

'I don't like you telling me what I need, OK? It makes me feel uncomfortable, and exposed.'

He sat forward. 'But Hon,' he said, his voice soft, 'you need to feel uncomfortable and exposed. It brings out the best in you.'

At that she burst out laughing. Whether he was just being a klutz, or deliberately winding her up, or trying to communicate something meaningful, she wasn't sure, but she found his clumsiness very funny.

'That's better, Hon.' He stood. 'Now come, let's go eat. I need food.'

With a resigned 'OK' she got up.

He came close and with both his hands pushed her hair off her face. 'You're beautiful, you know that?'

She tugged the lapel of his jacket. 'I don't like you thinking that you've won, either.'

'Hey, I don't always win, Tanya—but I sure want to win this one.'

She smiled, and kissed him. Passionately. And her heart melted as her loins moistened, and his cock stiffened. 'Let's go upstairs,' she mumbled breathlessly.

He drew back. 'Later, Hon, later. I need to eat.'

CHAPTER THIRTY ONE

Tanya parked in front of her lounge window, opened her car door as far as possible, until it met a low boundary wall, and eased her body out of the thin wedge.

Her house was quiet but not the garden and she followed the noise.

'Hello, my little rascals,' she said, proceeding down the centre path.

'Mummy!' Jamie and Harry cried.

'We painted the shed,' Jamie said proudly.

'I can see that, and what a brilliant job you've done. It's beautiful.' It was actually a brighter green than she expected, but she had bought the paint in a rush.

'Don't touch Mummy's clothes, OK?' Alison said in a raised voice.

'I painted that bit,' Jamie said, pointing to a section below the window, 'didn't I, Alison?'

Alison smiled. 'You certainly did, young man.'

'And, and, and I painted the door, Mummy,' Harry said.

'Yes, Harry has worked very hard too,' Alison said.

Alison's arms were full of paint splashes, and she even had a few on her face.

'Thank you, Alison. You must be exhausted.'

'I'm fine. We've all had a great time.'

Tanya looked at her boys, and grinned. 'Mummy's got a surprise as well.' She winked at Alison, who already knew what was coming, dipped into her bag and pulled out four pieces of paper. 'Guess what these are?' She waved them about, and paused to build momentum.

'These are tickets to... Disneyland in California! In two weeks time we shall all be getting on a *huge* aeroplane, and flying *all* the way to *America*, and we will all be staying there for *ten whole nights.*'

The boys squealed and jumped around.

'Well done, Alison, and thank you,' Tanya said, for Alison had done all the leg work, searched the internet and put together a holiday that didn't cost a fortune.

'Was the school OK about Jamie having time off?' Alison whispered.

Tanya had just been to see Jamie's teacher, to explain he was going to miss a week of school.

'Not really, but to be honest I don't care. The way I see it, if I don't spoil him, who will? He'll have enough to put up with when he grows up.'

Alison laughed.

'I've got a little surprise for you as well,' Tanya said. 'Olli's going to fly out to join us for my birthday, buy us dinner, and pay for us to stay at his hotel for that night. Not sure which hotel yet, but it's bound to be five star, because Olli does not like to rough it.'

Alison gasped. 'But do you really want me there? I honestly don't mind if—'

'Any more talk like that and you're going straight to bed, OK?'

Alison laughed.

'Now tell me what you think,' Tanya said. 'Should I introduce Olli to the boys beforehand, or wait until we're away?'

'Wait, as it will make the holiday and your birthday all the more special. You'll also be more relaxed, and I imagine Olli will too.'

'Good thinking, Batman.'

'It sounds like it's getting serious,' Alison said teasingly, her voice melodic, her pitch rising.

Tanya laughed. 'It's still early days, but I must admit we do get on.'

'I'll say you do,' Alison said. 'I've never seen you so happy. My mum and dad were saying the same—'

A ring on the doorbell interrupted Alison's flow.

'I'll get it,' Tanya said. 'You're covered in paint.'

The caller was Frank Parsons, Tanya's next door neighbour, a pensioner who seemed to live in baggy T-shirts, cropped trousers, and trainers.

He gave her a parcel. 'I took this in for you earlier, Ducks.'

It was for Alison, from Amazon.

'That's really kind of you, Frank, thanks.'

'You're welcome.' He bent down and plucked a dandelion, in its twilight phase of life, from a gap in the crazy paving, and gave it to her. 'Here you go, Ducks, make a wish.'

'Aw, bless you, Frank. Thank you.'

He smiled. 'See you later,' he said, and walked off.

For some seconds Tanya stood gazing at the blow ball, and then her eyes suddenly filled with tears. She glanced up at the sky and sniffed.

'This one's for you, Daphne. With all my love.'

She blew the seeds to the wind.